OUT OF THE PAST

"What a beautiful garden," the killer said, standing up and moving to the window, which was to the left and slightly behind the priest.

"We are proud of it," the priest said, picking up his pen. "And your name?" he asked.

"My name is Coogan. Does it sound familiar?"

"No, I'm sorry. Should it?"

"We knew one another well."

"Really, when? With age it's harder and harder to remember—"

"At Sacred Heart, you remember?"

With that Father Gordon quickly stood up, apprehension suddenly about his long narrow face.

"So you remember...I see you remember."

"No, I don't, I'm sorry. How did you find me?"

"It wasn't easy."

"I've changed. I don't do those things any longer. I was confused. I—"

"I have something for you," the man said.

"What's that?"

"This," he said, withdrawing the knife from his black bag. Before the priest could react, the man was on him....

PREDATORS & PRAYERS

PHILIP CARLO

LEISURE BOOKS NEW YORK CITY

This work is dedicated to all the victims
of sexual abuse at the hands of predator priests—
true wolves in sheep's clothing.

A LEISURE BOOK®

August 2005

Published by

Dorchester Publishing Co., Inc.
200 Madison Avenue
New York, NY 10016

ISBN 0-8439-5576-7

The name "Leisure Books" and the stylized "L" with design are trademarks of Dorchester Publishing Co., Inc.

Printed in the United States of America.

Visit us on the web at www.dorchesterpub.com.

ACKNOWLEDGMENTS

I am indebted to Don D'Auria for having the courage to publish this book. Special thanks to my agent, Matt Bialer, for always being there, for all his support, input and understanding. I also wish to thank his assistant Anna Bierhaus for her kind help, and my niece, Vanessa Mannanice, for her proofreading and editorial suggestions. And also a special thanks to Rosemary Serra for perfecting all the Italian used in this story. Many thanks to Paul Dinas for his input.

PREDATORS & PRAYERS

"Men never do evil so completely and cheerfully as when they do it from religious conviction."

—Pascal

I

PROBABLE CAUSE

ONE

The first murder occurred toward the end of June. For most of that month rain had fallen day and night. When it wasn't raining, the sky was low and mean and every shade of gray there was—drab olive and silvery gunpowder grays, sad ashen grays, the solemn hue of a cremated body. The temperatures throughout the entire month had been "unseasonably cold," as the weather people kept saying.

Then, on the morning of the killing, the sky abruptly cleared and the cold front that had been hanging about New York vanished. The sun returned and shined with a vengeance. The temperature by noon was 98 degrees, the real-feel temperature 103. Rubbery waves of heat rose from the streets and sidewalks. It was so hot people seemed to move in slow motion; no one was in a hurry to go anywhere, a rare thing for New Yorkers.

Saint Mary's Church was on West 39th Street, just off 9th Avenue, in the area of Manhattan known as Hell's Kitchen. The body was found by Maria Rodriguez, a short Mexican-American cleaning lady with long gray hair,

3

which she had tied back with a bright blue ribbon. There was no air-conditioning in the church, and the air was thick with the scent of burning candles and the lingering sweet-sour fragrance of frankincense from Sunday's mass.

Maria Rodriguez took her job seriously. A devout Catholic, she felt like she was cleaning God's house, and she scrubbed and mopped and polished as though He were watching her, carefully evaluating her work. The cleaner everything was, Maria was sure, the closer to God—and heaven—she would be.

Often, as she worked, Maria looked up at Jesus on the crucifix above the altar and dutifully made the sign of the cross, as she silently prayed to Him. It was so warm in the church, Maria could have sworn she saw Jesus sweating, but when she moved closer she realized it was only her imagination. Maria remembered well the time she had seen tears on the beautiful face of the statue of Mary, the mother of God. It had been in the Church of Guadalupe in her hometown of Matamoros, Mexico, when she was nine years old. Even now, some forty-two years later, Maria rapidly made the sign of the cross three times and kissed the extended fingers of her right hand as she thought about that fateful day.

The church was empty. It was too hot for anyone to come in and pray. The parish, Maria knew, was strapped for cash and the only time they had the air conditioner on these days was during Sunday mass, or for a special occasion, a wedding or a funeral mass. So few people came to the church to pray these days, regardless of the weather.

As Maria reached the confessional booth at the west end of the church, under a giant stained-glass mural depicting Jesus in the manger—the searing summer sun making the colors in the stained glass come alive on the floor of the church—she saw the shoes covered in hot pools of red, yellow and blue light. Large black oxford shoes protruding from under the red velvet curtain of the confessional. As Maria drew closer, her sweating face creasing with curiosity, she noticed the slowly moving puddle of something wet and glistening, a deep reddish-purple color. At first she thought the puddle was somehow being made by the stained glass, maybe even another miracle, she thought, but suddenly a peculiar odor came to her—the unmistakable smell of blood . . . of death. Cautious now, Maria moved closer, her heart beginning to race.

"Father?" she whispered, knowing that the side of the confessional where she saw the shoes was where the priests of Saint Mary's heard confessions, spoke in solemn tones, meted out justice.

Thinking maybe a priest had fallen and hurt himself, perhaps had a heart attack, Maria Rodriguez moved quickly now and pulled the worn curtain aside.

At first she could not quite discern exactly what she was seeing, but as her eyes adjusted to the mysterious dark inside the confessional, Maria screamed so loudly that the flames of the candles quivered with the high-pitched impact of the sound.

Still screaming, falling twice as she went, Maria ran from the church as if she'd seen Satan himself; the only witnesses to her fear were the statues of Jesus up on the cross and Mary and Joseph to the right and left of the altar.

The first police personnel to arrive were two female officers. They had just come on duty, were already covered in sweat, and in no mood to deal with the sight about to greet them . . . to haunt their sleep for weeks to come.

He was lying on his back. His throat had been cut from ear to ear, and there was something red and bloody—a piece of veiny meat—sticking out of his mouth, which now hung wide open. The taller of the two officers put her flashlight on him and for the first time they could see the intestines, a large blue-gray snakelike mass, on the floor just next to his body.

"My God," she exclaimed, backing up, pulling her partner with her.

Two

Captain Tony Flynn was a tall, high-cheekboned man with broad shoulders and the easy, fluid step of a professional athlete. He had receding salt-and-pepper hair and piercing blue-gray eyes that seemed to see right through most everything they came to rest on. Cop eyes. Flynn had just gone off duty and was leaving the Midtown North Precinct on West 54th Street, when he got the call that a murdered priest had been discovered at Saint Mary's. Flynn had worked a double shift, was bone tired, but without hesitation he slipped into his dark blue Ford and headed downtown, grateful for the car's air-conditioning. The press had already gotten wind of the murder and a half dozen reporters and as many cameramen greeted Flynn as he stepped from the cool comfort of the air-conditioned car. The heat slammed him in the face like a hot wet towel.

"Is it true a priest was murdered, Captain?" a reporter called to him.

"Is it true that he was mutilated?" another asked.

A calm, easygoing man, Flynn had a good relationship with the press, something he carefully nurtured over the years. He knew how vitally important the media had become in helping to crack cases, getting the word to the public, and he always went out of his way for reporters and news producers. "You guys," he said, "know more than me right now. Soon as I have a handle on what exactly happened here, I'll let you know." He smiled politely, nodded his head and walked around the reporters. He wore a short-sleeved white shirt and the dark blue tie with his initials on it that his daughter Jacky had given him for his birthday just the week before. Flynn had four daughters and they were all cops. Two detectives in the safe and robbery squad, one in the sex crimes unit, and the oldest, Robin, worked in the commissioner's office. He had heard rumors that Robin was having an affair with the commissioner, but Flynn had dismissed them as idle gossip by jealous people in the department who had nothing better to do with their time. There were, he knew, always rumors going around about women on the force, particularly the attractive ones, and each of Tony Flynn's daughters was attractive, which he had always viewed as both a blessing and a curse.

As Flynn began up the steps to Saint Mary's, he remembered when he was an altar boy in the Bronx, where he grew up—the smells of Sunday mass, the metallic ringing of the brass bells, the cardboard taste of the communion wafer, all coming to him at the same time. And with those also came memories of what had happened to him at the hands of that degenerate priest. Flynn had not thought of this for a long time, but now it all abruptly returned, flushed from the deep recesses of his mind. He had never told anyone about what had occurred in the room behind the altar where the priests and altar boys dressed for mass, sure no one would believe such a thing, least of all his mother—an obsessively devout Catholic who passionately believed in Jesus Christ, the Church and all its teachings. Flynn pushed these thoughts away and, his face a granite mask of stoic professionalism, he pulled open the heavy wooden door of the church and slowly went inside.

It had been many years since he had been inside a church—since his last daughter's wedding—and as he made his way to the confessional where the priest had been found, he felt an uncomfortable tightening in his gut. He did not like churches, their smells, the quivering candlelight, the solemn specter of the crucifixion and the ever-present stained-glass windows. Scratching his face, he silently walked up to the body, the fetid smell of death greeting him as he came closer to the corpse. The detectives who were already there moved out of his way. Tony Flynn was, they knew, one of the finest investigators the NYPD ever had, and he was respected and liked by all 1,257 detectives under his command. Flynn was the immediate boss of every detective who worked in Manhattan; he answered only to Chief of Detectives John Samuels. Flynn had offices in five different station houses and cots where he could sleep in each. He often worked in the field next to his men. He had been in numerous gun battles over the years, killed two men in fierce firefights, and had been shot twice himself, leaving him with a scar on his left cheek where a bullet grazed his face, and a cigarette-shaped scar where a bullet ripped through his left shoulder. He borrowed the flashlight of detective Sergeant Frank Salerno and shined it on the murdered priest, moving closer, careful about where he put his feet, bending down, his piercing blue-gray eyes slowly taking in and automatically analyzing, almost subconsciously, all the particulars of the crime before him.

"He's been castrated, Captain," Detective Salerno said.

"Can see that," Flynn observed.

For years Flynn had been thinking it was only a matter of time before some psycho started killing priests. There had been endless news reports of pedophile priests sexually abusing children all over the country, as if they had been given a license by God Himself to do what they pleased. Flynn wasn't at all surprised at the viciousness of the assault. He noted that the knife wound to the throat was a stab-slash cut. That the killer had driven the blade into one side of the neck and pulled it across the throat, neatly severing both the carotid arteries and windpipe at the same time, in one clean stroke. Flynn knew it was an efficient way to kill that was taught in the military and he was thinking the guy who did this had been, or still was, in military service; that he had some kind of martial arts training.

Standing upright, he told Salerno, a tall rail-thin man with aviator glasses covering perpetually suspicious eyes, to set up flood lights and have teams of detectives go over every inch of the church. To make sure that all the door handles of the church were dusted for prints. Maybe, he said, the killer hadn't worn gloves, had left a usable print somewhere convenient. He also said that he wanted to talk to all the priests who worked at the parish.

Knowing this murder would surely garner a lot of media attention, that it would be front page news, the lead-off story on the 6:00 news, Flynn ordered a command center vehicle brought over from the 40th Precinct. He turned away from the body and walked to the altar, his right knee and lower back hurting. He stared at Jesus on the cross, the little drops of hardened blood frozen on his eternally pained face. A disillusioned Catholic, Tony Flynn wondered how any God could allow the wholesale abuse of children entrusted to the Church.

You been sleeping, he thought, his eyes focused on Jesus's face, as he walked up onto the altar. He looked around this strange yet familiar place, sensing there was something important. Sure enough, he spotted blood on the east wall just next to the rear door, which led to the rectory at the back of the church. Moving closer, he saw that the words *HELL ON EARTH* had been drawn in blood. Sweat running down his face, Flynn took a long exasperated breath, knowing the press would have fun with this. He called Salerno over and both men stared at the bloody words.

Just then Monsignor O'Brian walked in the rear door. He was a small round man with a large round face and a bitter slit for a mouth. He had obviously just woken up. He seemed to waddle, penguin-like, as he walked toward Flynn and Salerno on the altar.

"What are you doing there?" he demanded. "You *cannot* be on the altar!"

"And who are you?" Flynn politely asked.

"I am Monsignor O'Brian."

"Well, Monsignor O'Brian, I'm Captain Tony Flynn. This is a murder scene, and we are investigating a murder that's—"

"Murder? Who—where?" the monsignor asked, genuine surprise suddenly about his pudgy face.

Flynn motioned for Monsignor O'Brian to follow him and led him to the body. When the monsignor realized what he was looking at, his eyes swelled out of his cherubic face and he raised his hand to his narrow mouth. He quickly made the sign of the cross and backed away, nearly falling into one of the pews. Flynn noticed the distinct smell of alcohol about him.

"You know who he is?" Flynn asked.

"Of course, yes, Father Sam Joseph, a very good man, a wonderful priest." Monsignor O'Brian began to cry, backing farther away, moving toward the altar, his face abruptly reddening as if he'd been slapped.

Flynn followed him. "I'm sorry," he said.

"Who would do such a thing?" the monsignor begged.

"We don't know just yet, but we plan to find out," Flynn said with a solemn confidence that seemed to reassure the monsignor.

A detective entering through the front door called to Flynn, "Captain, the Winnebago's here."

Knowing the Winnebago was air-conditioned, Flynn asked the monsignor to follow him outside so they could talk in comfort and privacy. The captain knew, too, that there was recording equipment in the police trailer, and he wanted to get a statement from O'Brian on tape.

Dutifully, the monsignor followed Flynn outside. A large contingent of reporters and cameramen had gathered around the yellow crime-scene tape that cordoned off the sidewalk in front of the church. Waves of shimmering heat rose from the street. There wasn't a cloud in the sky. The sun beat down with a vengeance, hard and white on the eyes. Flynn wished the rain would come back. He told Salerno to have men thoroughly search all the blocks around the church, the curbs, sidewalks, alleys, stoops, even the sewers, to see if they could find the murder weapon. He also instructed the sergeant to get a few teams to start questioning people who lived and worked on the block. Maybe someone had seen something suspicious. Flynn knew from many years of hard-earned experience that wearing down shoe leather and asking questions was how cases were solved.

Inside the green and white police Winnebago it was cool and comfortable. Flynn had Monsignor O'Brian sit at the table and poured him a glass of cold water.

"Monsignor, I'd like to get a statement from you," Flynn said.

"Of course."

"And I'd like to tape it."

"Why?"

"Just for the record."

"I see. I guess that's okay."

"Good," Flynn said, and before O'Brian could say anything more or think about it further, Flynn opened a locked drawer with a key on his keychain, withdrew a battered tape recorder and put it on the table. He pressed the Record button and sat down.

"First off, has Father Joseph had any kind of problems?" he asked.

"How do you mean?"

"Threats of any kind—any kind of problems at all."

The monsignor blinked several times, as if a dusty wind hit him in the face. He said that Father Joseph had no kind of threats or difficulties "that I know of." That he had been assigned to Saint Mary's from Saint Agnes, a parish in Rockville Centre, Long Island, about a year ago.

When Captain Flynn heard that his ears perked up, for he knew that the Rockville Centre parish had been plagued with scandal—thirty priests had been accused of abusing scores of children over a long period of time. The bishop running the archdiocese had worked under Cardinal Bernard Hound in Boston, who had been forced to resign in disgrace because of his inept handling—many would say criminal handling—of predator priests in Boston.

"I know what you're thinking," the monsignor said. "And yes, there were accusations against Father Joseph, but I believe they were totally unfounded and completely without merit."

"I see. Did Father Joseph live at Saint Mary's?"

"Yes, at the rectory in back of the church, up on the second floor."

"What kind of man was he?"

"A kind, very gentle fellow. One of the most selfless, giving people I've ever known."

At that moment there was heavy knocking on the door. Annoyed at the interruption, Flynn shut off the recorder and opened the door. A bald weasel-faced man covered in sweat stood there.

"I understand Monsignor O'Brian is here," he said, obviously out of breath, as if he'd been running, the strong sun causing him to squint.

"You are?" Flynn asked, already knowing the answer.

"John Mahoney. I'm the attorney representing Saint Mary's parish."

"Hello, John," O'Brian said, standing and offering Mahoney his thick hand, obviously pleased to see him. "You heard what happened, no doubt?"

"I did. The office received a call from Cardinal Edam. May I come in?"

"Please," Flynn graciously offered, annoyed by the lawyer's presence.

Mahoney walked up the three steps, wiping sweat from his brow with a faded plaid handkerchief. Flynn knew why he was here and where this was going, and he excused himself to use the john before Mahoney could say anything further. In the small bathroom, Flynn called Sergeant Salerno inside the church and told him to get warrants to search all of Saint Mary's premises, especially the second floor of the rectory. "I mean like ASAP. Tell them to put a super rush on them. There's a lawyer here," he whispered.

"I'm on it, Captain," Salerno said. Flynn and Salerno had worked together for eleven years and the two men seemed to talk in shorthand. Flynn threw some cold water on his face, flushed the bowl and went back outside. Mahoney and O'Brian were talking in serious, hushed tones. Mahoney said, "Captain, at this juncture I'm advising the monsignor not to talk with you any further."

"You are?" Flynn asked, acting surprised, though he knew this was coming. "Why's that?"

"We'd like to talk with him first back at our offices. Perhaps tomorrow you—"

"We're on the same team here, aren't we?" Flynn asked, his piercing gaze coming to rest on the monsignor.

"Yes, Captain, but there are certain sensitive elements at play that warrant our actions," Mahoney said.

"Such as?" Flynn asked.

"We'll be in a better position to discuss everything more comprehensively tomorrow. We'll be happy to meet with you in, say, the late afternoon, if that's okay with you."

"Sooner the better," Flynn said, and he began talking about the weather; that he'd been an altar boy at Saint Finbars in the Bronx, wanting to keep the monsignor in sight until they had the warrants in place. Flynn knew there might be evidence in the rectory that could help the investigation, but it might very well disappear because of Mahoney.

Flynn poured glasses of bottled water for them all and started talking about the stab-slash wound, explaining that it was a way to kill taught in the military. "You know," he said, "I was a Marine, fought in Korea, and that's where I saw that kind of wound for the first time." He went on to describe how the cut severed the arteries and the windpipe, and was always lethal.

Mahoney stopped him, saying he had to "get going." As he stood up and opened the door, the heat rushed in. The monsignor followed Mahoney down the stairs, Captain Flynn just behind him. When the press saw them, flashbulbs popped and video camera lights were turned on, as a cacophony of reporters' questions flew through the stifling heat. Sergeant Salerno came out of the church. He winked at Flynn. The two men met on the stairs to the church. Salerno said, "They are on the way. We got Judge Meyers to sign the warrants. They were e-mailed to Midtown North and Giordano's bringing them over right now."

"Way to go," Flynn said, as a black Plymouth—siren blaring, red light spinning—pulled up. Detective Frank Giordano hurried over to Flynn and Salerno with green papers in his hand. "Got here soon as I could, Captain," he said.

"Good work," Flynn said, turning to Salerno. "Pick three guys and we are going over Father Joseph's room in the rectory right now." Flynn walked back down the stairs to where Mahoney and the monsignor were standing. He handed the warrants to the lawyer. Mahoney glanced at them, his eyes narrowing. Not pleased, his face flushed with anger as he realized what Flynn had done. He looked up at Flynn. "Think you're cute, Captain—?"

"I think I'm running a murder investigation, counselor. We're going to search the rectory now." With that Flynn turned away from the lawyer, and he and Salerno and Giordano and three other detectives made their way to the rectory at the back of the church. It was in a three-story redbrick building in obvious disrepair. Its wooden window casings were rotting and flaking, the grounds covered with weeds. There was a four-foot cement statue of Jesus over the front door and pigeon droppings adorned its head.

As Flynn rang the bell, Monsignor O'Brian hurried up the stairs. He said, "I wish, Captain, you wouldn't just come barging into our homes like this. It's rude. It . . . we are not criminals. I want you to know I resent these tactics and plan to file formal complaints with your superiors, with the mayor and with the governor. The governor, you know, is a personal friend of mine."

"I'm just doing my job," Flynn said. "Nothing personal here."

"Your job does *not* include invading our privacy—disregarding the sanctity of our—"

"*I* determine what my job is, not you," Flynn said. The door was opened by a still shaken Maria Rodriguez. She was pale like chalk, crying and very upset. Flynn politely introduced himself and his detectives, and asked where Father Joseph's room was. Maria told him it was the first room on the left at the top of the stairs. Without further preamble, the stone-faced detectives all entered and went up the stairs, Flynn leading the way. The door was locked. Monsignor O'Brian said he didn't have a key. Flynn sent Sergeant Salerno to go see if they were on Father Joseph's body. As they waited, both the monsignor and the lawyer glared at Flynn. He glared right back, his gaze so intense they both looked away. Flynn sensed that the monsignor was trying to hide something, and that didn't sit well with him—and it was written all over Flynn's face plain as day. "How old was Father Joseph?" Flynn asked

"Fifty-six," the monsignor said. "He had a birthday just two days ago."

Salerno hustled back up the stairs, and he had a key ring in his hand. He used a silver Medeco key on the ring and opened the door. Father Joseph's room was neat and tidy, smelled of Old Spice aftershave. It consisted of a main room with a Pullman kitchen and old-fashioned bathroom with one of those tubs up on extended cast-iron legs. There was a large cross over the bed and portraits of the Virgin Mary on the wall between the two windows of the room, which afforded a nice view of the Hudson River, two blocks west of the rectory. There was a dresser and a desk, on which was a black Dell computer and a file box for computer disks, a small television and a VCR. There was also a pile of children's board games.

"Start looking, men," Flynn said. Each of the detectives, all hardened, experienced New York cops, began searching the place, looking in all the drawers, the closet, under the mattress. In a cardboard box in the closet one of the detectives found footballs, basketballs and soccer balls, catchers' mitts and half a dozen kites. Another cardboard box was filled with magazines of naked boys and half a dozen VHS tapes. Standing at the door, a very unhappy Mahoney looked on.

"Somehow these don't surprise me," Flynn told the monsignor, walking close to him, staring hard at him, his blue-gray eyes boring into the monsignor's face. Flynn remembered how the monsignor had just said that Father Joseph was such a nice fellow. A dedicated priest. Flynn was sure if he hadn't gotten the warrant, the box would have disappeared. The toys and athletic equipment, they all knew, enabled Joseph to get close to children.

Also in the box were news bulletins from NAMBLA— aka The North American Man Boy Love Association. Flynn knew the group openly advocated sex with children. The headline on one of the newsletters said: SEX AFTER 8 IS TOO LATE.

Captain Flynn booted up the computer and quickly found a huge trove of exceedingly hardcore pornographic photos of grown men having sex with pre-pubescent boys. The detectives silently gathered around the screen and, in quiet disgust, in angry unison, looked at the pitiful images. Flynn had a sudden bad taste in his mouth, and his icy gaze slowly moved to the monsignor. If looks could kill, the monsignor would have surely keeled over, dead.

"My Lord, I'm shocked," the monsignor proclaimed, rapidly blinking his eyes, as was his way.

"Yeah, me too," Captain Flynn said, wanting to put his foot up the monsignor's pompous ass.

THREE

Including Monsignor O'Brian, seven priests in all lived in the rectory. Flynn and his men searched each of their living quarters. In four of the seven residences, they found hardcore pornographic materials relating to children.

They did not find any child pornography in Monsignor O'Brian's apartment, though Flynn was certain O'Brian knew what was going on, had his stubby fingers deep into this filthy business. Without ceremony Flynn placed the four priests under arrest. When the press saw them being led from the rectory and put in squad cars, handcuffs on each of them, religious collars about their necks, they were in a fevered frenzy. Flynn wanted to give them a statement, show them some of the evidence right there on the street, but he knew if he did he'd be in hot water. So he kept his mouth shut and referred the reporters and always pushy news producers to the PD's public relations office.

Back inside the church, Flynn made sure the tech people thoroughly dusted all the doors, and photographs were taken of the body from numerous perspectives. By now, because of the stifling heat, the smell coming from Father Joseph was horrific, and flies gleefully fed on the dry, caked blood and food contents spilling from his severed intestines.

When Flynn was satisfied he had everything he wanted, that the crime scene had been worked properly, he gave Dr. Richard Russo, from the Medical Examiner's Office, permission to remove the body and take it to the city morgue over on 1st Avenue. Two morgue attendants, cracking jokes about the severed penis, picked up the body, still stiff with rigor mortis, and placed it in a black plastic body bag with the words CITY MORGUE on it in yellow block letters.

Clearly, Flynn knew, Father Joseph was a pedophile, a genuine wolf in sheep's clothing, but still someone had murdered him and Flynn was intent on finding out who, having a feeling in his gut that whoever murdered Joseph would soon kill again.

By now it was nearly 7:00 PM. Flynn went back to Midtown North and oversaw the arrests and booking of the four priests. The captain tried to talk to them, asked if any of them had seen anything suspicious, strangers hanging about the church, what part Monsignor O'Brian played in their illicit activities, but John Mahoney showed up, and he refused to let any of the priests say anything other than their names. Flynn walked to his office, a cluttered room at the back of the old precinct house, which was just down the block from the once famous Studio 54. He put on the air conditioner. He was soaking wet and he took off his shirt and used a wash cloth to rub himself down with cooling alcohol, then put on a fresh white cotton shirt and his tie. As he was knotting the tie, there was a gentle knock on the door. Standing there was Assistant District Attorney Carole Joyce Cunningham, a tall, square-shouldered woman with large dark brown eyes and a lion's mane of blond hair cascading to her shoulders. Cunningham was in charge of the sex crimes division at the DA's office at 100 Centre Street. She was, Flynn knew, a crack criminal attorney who rarely lost a case. She and Flynn had often worked together over the years and he was fond of her. She was a hardworking, dedicated woman with a great sense of humor, a difficult thing in their line of work. Carole was friends with Flynn's youngest daughter, Jacky. They lived in the same condominium complex on Hudson Street in Tribeca.

"Good to see you," he said. "Thanks for coming over." They kissed and hugged one another.

"Tell me what you've got," she said, sitting down, and Flynn ran down the case to her. Told her what he had seen and heard so far. She listened intently, not interrupting as he spoke. She thought of Flynn as one of the most competent detectives she had ever worked with, knew that he had finely tuned, excellent instincts and respected him. When Tony Flynn brought her a case it was complete. None of his cases were ever thrown out of court because of some procedural mishap. He showed her the evidence they had gathered at the rectory. She carefully scrutinized everything, her attractive, heart-shaped face turning hard and cold, her lips thinning against her large white teeth. Carole was a dedicated jogger. She ran a few miles every day before she went to work and she had healthy rose-colored cheeks, which paled noticeably as she looked at the photographs. She had been working in the sex crimes division now for nine years and had seen all kinds of brutal, horrific crimes perpetrated against women and children, but no matter how much she'd seen, how many sexual predators she put away, she still became outraged at the thought of adults sexually abusing children—stealing their innocence, their ability to trust.

When Flynn finished laying out the facts, they fast-forwarded through some of the VHS tapes found in the cardboard box in the murdered priest's closet. In them Father Joseph, in living color, was sexually abusing young boys. Carole wanted everything confiscated from the rectory brought down to her office.

"I'm going to present it all to a grand jury tomorrow and immediately get them indicted," she said. "I'll tell you right now, Tony, there will be no plea bargains for any of these cretins. I've been following most of the cases around the country involving the Church for years now, and I'm sick and tired of how they've been covering up and protecting these dirtbags. I know of one pedophile priest, Richard Shane, who'd been moved to twenty-seven different parishes over a twenty-two-year period. And in every parish he was abusing young boys. The last parish he was assigned to was in New Orleans, and he was working in a children's hospital—and even there, I mean with sick children, he was sexually abusing them."

"Hell of a thing," Flynn said in a small voice, imagining the infamy of what she had just described. Two jaded professionals, they stared at one another, a heavy silence hanging between them.

"What's your take on this murder?" she asked.

"Judging by the brutality and the fact that his penis had been shoved into his mouth, I'd say someone who'd been abused by a priest lost it and is looking for revenge. The priest was dragged into the confessional. There weren't any confessions today. What killed him was a stab-slash type wound in the neck. The perp pushed the point of the blade into the left side of his neck and drew it across his throat. I'm thinking someone with military training or know-how did it. After his throat was cut, he mutilated him."

"Anyone see anything?"

"A cleaning woman found the body and she said she saw a man with gray hair and a mustache leave the church when she entered, but there wasn't any blood on him and the M.E. says Father Joseph was dead a few hours before he was found."

"Tony, I want to hold a news conference and ask anyone who was abused by any of the priests in this parish—including Joseph—to come forward. We might very well turn up a lead on the killing, and I want to bring more than just the child porn to a grand jury. Under my watch, none of these men is going to get off lightly. I am going to make absolutely certain they are all put away for as long as possible."

"Great. I'm with you all the way. Whatever you need you just let me know."

"I already spoke to my boss and he gave me the green light for the press conference. I want to give the mug shots of the priests you arrested today to the media."

"Yeah, good idea. I'll get you copies right away. When do you want to do this?"

"I was thinking later today, but tomorrow might be better; gives us more time to put it together. Let's do it downtown. Say 11:00 AM. That okay with you?"

"I'll be there."

Her cell phone buzzed. She answered it, walking over to the windows, which overlooked yards, and spoke in hushed tones. Sergeant Frank Salerno stuck his head in the door. "Got something interesting, boss."

"Shoot."

"We ran Joseph's prints, and he's got a record. As a teen he was a Scout Master in Oregon, and he was arrested for molesting Cub Scouts while on outings in the woods. The mother of one of the victims found out and went to the police. Joseph was busted, pled guilty to second-degree rape and sodomy and endangering the welfare of a child. He did two years in a state prison. When he got out he went straight to a seminary in upstate New York and was ordained when he was twenty-four."

"So we've got to figure he's been abusing children within the Church for what, thirty-two years. Anything else?"

"No, just the one bust."

"Okay. How's the booking going?"

"It's all done. But that Mahoney lawyer's a pain in the ass, Captain. He gave me a hard time about keeping the priests away from other prisoners."

"And?"

"And they are all in the bull pen with everyone else. We don't have anywhere else to put them."

"I don't want them getting any kind of preferential treatment. When are they going downtown?"

"Seven tomorrow morning."

"Okay, keep me posted."

"Will do."

"Frank, make sure the press gets clear shots of them when they are put in the paddy wagon in the morning."

"Got ya."

Cunningham hung up. "My boss," she said, sitting down again, "is getting all kinds of phone calls about us treating the priests 'fairly.' Cardinal Edam himself phoned to complain about you and your 'sneaky tactics.' "

"He said that?"

"Yep."

"He's got balls to be calling me a sneak when all they've been doing is hiding and abetting, feeding and clothing busloads of child molesters."

"Tell me about it."

"I just heard that Joseph was arrested when he was nineteen for abusing Cub Scouts in Oregon. He copped a plea, did twenty-four months, then joined a seminary in upstate New York."

"He's had a lot of time to do a lot of damage."

"That's what I was thinking. Carole, what's your take on how so many priests came to be pedophiles?"

"I know exactly how it happened. In the mid-sixties and early seventies pedophiles realized that as priests they'd have direct access to trusting children and that if they were found out the Church would protect them; that the Church's only concern was with insulating itself and avoiding any kind of scandal. Not only that, but the Church paid them, clothed and fed them and put a roof over their heads. And worst of all, they did no check whatsoever on their backgrounds. Tony, we are talking here about dedicated, obsessed sexual predators—men whose whole lives revolve around the repeated molestation of children. These are not errant priests gone bad. Rogue priests. That's bullshit. These are individuals whose sunrise and sunset is sexual abuse, dominance and control.

23

Child molesters have always sought jobs where they ar
put into direct contact with children—Boy Scout leader:
day-care workers, school bus drivers, teachers, custodian
at schools . . . and priests. A priest is a larger-than-life fig
urehead, a representative of *God* Himself, and children ar
virtually helpless in their hands.

"I know of one priest, John Krol, who told his victim:
'If you want to get close to God, get close to me,' and wit
that he would proceed to molest them. And, as a matter c
course, they threatened their victims with hell and eterna
damnation if they told anyone . . .

"Tony, word travels fast in the pedophile communit
Molesters began becoming priests in droves, and that'
pretty much the sum of it. And of course as time went b
many of the predators moved up the hierarchy within th
Church, became archbishops, bishops and cardinals an
put in positions where they could actually make polic
decisions. They made sure if one of their own was foun
out they'd simply move him to another parish across th
country somewhere and hush the incident up; give mone
to the victims' families. They've paid out nearly a billio
dollars to keep quiet what was going on, always havin
the specter of God and hell over the family members c
the victims—parents and siblings, et cetera. Truth is, it'
kind of incomprehensible how they were able to get awa
with what they've been doing for so long. Far as I'm con
cerned, Tony, it's one of the darkest blemishes of ou
time—people in positions of trust like that doing thos
kinds of things to innocent children on such a large scale
Fucking reprehensible, pardon my language," she said.

"Well put. You do have a way with words, counselor."

"Nice of you to say, Captain."

The phone on Flynn's desk rang. It was Dr. Russo at th
Medical Examiner's office, telling Flynn he had begun th
autopsy of the murdered priest and that he had foun

"promising evidence" on the body. Flynn said he was on his way over to the morgue and hung up. Normally the captain would dispatch detectives to the morgue, but this was an important case and he planned to work it himself. He made plans to meet Cunningham at the District Attorney's office in the morning. Then he found Sergeant Salerno and the two of them headed over to the morgue. There wasn't too much traffic and they made it across town in fifteen minutes, parked in a spot reserved for official vehicles and headed into the morgue, located in the lower level of a squat blue brick building on 29th Street. Over the entrance was a sign that read: *Let conversation cease. Let laughter flee. This is the place where death delights to help the living.*

The New York Police Department had an office on the ground floor. It was always manned by two NYPD detectives who worked under Flynn and reported directly to him. It was these detectives who contacted family members of the dead brought to the morgue. They also gave facts of murders and suicides to the NYPD press office, which then released them to the media.

Grateful for the air-conditioning, Flynn and Salerno made their way to the NYPD annex. Surprised to see Captain Flynn there unannounced, the detectives on duty jumped up and stood at attention when he entered.

The walls, as always, were covered with grainy black-and-white Polaroids of dead people. Some were particularly gruesome—those who had been brutally beaten, pulled from the Hudson or East river. In the north corner of the office was a black spiral staircase that led to the lower level, where the actual autopsies were done and the cadaver rooms were located. Flynn and Salerno put on green surgical gowns and masks and went down the stairs, the rancid, sickening smell of human death coming up to greet them. The autopsy theater was in a long, sterile, all white room. There were eight autopsy stations, five of which were busy with ongoing autopsies. Flynn pushed open the swinging doors and entered. There were, as always, pennies that had fallen from the dead people's pockets on the floor. The room was lighted by long, powerful florescent tubes, which cast the room in brilliant white light, making the harsh black-and-white reality of death all the more visible. Flynn found Dr. Russo at station 2. Father Joseph was on the autopsy table, naked, his chest cavity pulled back, exposing his heart and lungs and other organs. The top of his skull had been sawed off and his brain was lying in the scale hanging next to the table. Over the years Flynn had seen thousands of bodies and he had stopped being affected by the sight long ago.

The doctor explained that the priest had put up a fight. He said that two of the knuckles on his right hand were recently broken, no doubt from punching his attacker. More importantly, Dr. Russo said, Father Joseph had scratched his assailant. The doctor showed them the cluster of flesh under the nails of his right hand.

Flynn knew this might prove to be very helpful because the killer's DNA could be extracted from the minute pieces of flesh under the priest's nails. The doctor now carefully used a manicurist's tool and scraped the flesh into a sanitized Petri dish, which he then placed in a plastic bag, numbered it and gave it to Flynn. The doctor said, "Tony, he was killed with a particularly sharp blade, I mean scalpel sharp, about six inches long, with a distinct curvature. You see here, where his throat was slit, it's an absolutely clean line, no serration at all. And here, where his stomach cavity was eviscerated, the cut is clean and very precise. I'd say someone with specific knowledge of human anatomy did this because he knew exactly where to make the incisions."

The captain stared long and hard at the destroyed priest, wondering if he was in hell—or heaven. Flynn thanked Dr. Russo and he and Salerno soon took their leave and went straight to the police pathology lab in the same building. Flynn asked the lab tech on duty, who was also an NYPD employee, to get a DNA work-up on the scrapings ASAP. It would take several days, he was told.

Soon the two detectives were on their way back to Midtown North. They were stopped by a large press contingent in front of the station house and Flynn told the reporters that there would be a press conference regarding the murder and priests' arrests at the DA's office in the morning. As Flynn went inside, Sergeant Salerno pulled aside a few reporters he knew and told them the time and place the priests would be put in the wagon to be taken downtown for arraignment.

FOUR

When Captain Flynn left the station house later that night, he drove downtown to meet his youngest daughter, Jacky, for dinner. He wasn't in the mood to talk with anyone. He was exhausted and the arthritis in his knee and hand was hurting him. Plus, he had a splitting headache that just wouldn't go away. All he wanted to do was climb in bed and get a good night's sleep, but Jacky had called and sounded distressed, so he had agreed to meet her at a small Italian restaurant on Greenwich Street of which they were both fond. Of all his four daughters, Jacky had always been the one with the most problems. He could never quite figure out why. She had been doted on by his wife and his older girls, but somehow she was always troubled, didn't do well in school—his three oldest were straight-A students—and had developed a serious drinking problem for a while, which ended when she agreed to go to the Betty Ford Clinic. Finished with the program, Jacky, like her three sisters before her, joined the police department. She did decoy plainclothes work right out of the academy, quickly made detective and asked to work in the sex crimes unit, where she'd been assigned for the last seven years. Flynn knew the work was hard and emotionally draining, but Jacky excelled in the unit, received numerous commendations and citations and made sergeant in a very short time.

He didn't find out that Jacky was gay until she finished the treatment at Betty Ford. One of the first things she did was sit him down, look him in the eyes and tell him that she was gay.

He was, at first, stunned and shocked, couldn't understand how a daughter of his could be "that way," but he learned to accept it; to live with it. All he wanted was for Jacky to be happy and if that's what made her happy so be it. But still, he hoped, deep inside, some day she might *change*, as he thought of it, find a nice man and settle down, maybe even have some children . . . .

Flynn had lost his wife, Jane, sixteen months earlier to stomach cancer. She'd had a protracted, heroic battle with the disease, but in the end the cancer ravaged her, seemed to eat her up from the inside out. When she passed on, she was little more than skin and bones, her hair all gone from the chemo, a mere shell of the healthy, vivacious woman she'd been. Tony had fallen in love with Jane the first time he'd seen her. He had been nineteen years old, she sixteen. She went riding past his house on a new Schwinn bike, and he was smitten. She had long black hair, luminous white skin and large pale blue eyes. She was the most beautiful girl he'd ever seen. He pursued her relentlessly and asked her to marry him when they were both still teens, and she said yes, though their families insisted they wait until she was twenty-one before they made such a long-term, serious commitment, which they did. Theirs turned out to be a wonderful union. Jane was the only woman Tony ever kissed and when she died a large piece of him died with her.

After Jane's passing, Tony Flynn immersed himself in his work, regularly did double shifts. It was the only way he was able to go on. If it wasn't for the work—and his daughters—he might very well have taken his own life, he was so distraught over his wife's loss. When he wasn't working, he was usually with one of his daughters, and all five of them met for dinner every Sunday no matter what. During all the years of his marriage, Tony never took his work home. He made sure when he shut off the car engine in front of the house, he stopped thinking about whatever case he'd been working on. His father, grandfather and great-grandfather had all been New York City detectives, and that had been one of the first things his dad had told him when he graduated the academy—*never bring your work home. Keep the garbage of the streets away from your family*—and they were words Flynn never forgot.

He found his daughter sitting at a rear table, her back against the wall, sipping an iced cappuccino. As he approached the table she stood up, hugged and kissed him. He ordered himself a gin martini. Jacky was nearly six feet tall and had his wife's sparkling pale blue eyes, thick raven-black hair, full heart-shaped lips, and a curvaceous figure. Jacky loved sports, tennis and golf, and went swimming in a pool in the neighborhood several times a week. She asked about the murder of the priest and he told her, briefly, about the case. She was, he could see, deeply troubled about something and when he asked her what it was she stared at the checkered tablecloth for the longest time, took a deep, pained breath and, in a small voice, told him that her unit had busted a brothel in Chinatown a few hours earlier called the Hell Fire Club.

"They supplied," she said, "women and girls, all freshly arrived from China, all brought over illegally, for kinky, sadistic sex. We've had them under surveillance for months. You remember that eleven-year-old Chinese girl we found in the river last week?"

"Of course, by the Manhattan Bridge."

"Well, these scumbags brought her over in December and she was murdered in a building they own on Mulberry Street just off Canal . . . during sex . . .

"We found films, I mean brutal, brutal S & M stuff where women and teenage girls were being tortured. Sickening. I'll tell you, Dad, I'm ready to throw the towel in," she said, her voice small and far away.

"Understandably. You bring down the principles?"

"Yes. A woman in her seventies who calls herself Sister Ping. She was promising the girls and women good jobs, and they ended up as virtual sex slaves."

"You have a solid case against her?"

"Very. We managed to bug the place two weeks ago and we've got her on tape actually selling the girls and arranging for more to be brought over. Not only her but all the people who worked for her. She was using the Golden Dragons as enforcers. She looks so innocent, you know, but she's as cold as stone and completely ruthless."

"Listen to me carefully, daughter: You managed to stop a human vampire here . . . think of all the women and girls you saved from her. When you put your head on your pillow tonight remember that. You and your team are putting a monster away where she can't hurt anyone else. Find solace and comfort in that," he said.

"I will . . . thank you, Dad," she said.

They ordered dinner and didn't talk shop any further, making plans to have a barbeque cookout on July 4th. Finished with their meal, he paid the check and walked her home. She seemed better now and she hadn't said a word about quitting the job. Deep inside he wished she did something else . . . that she wasn't subjected to the monstrous sex crimes people perpetrate on one another every minute of every day of every year. He even offered to help get her transferred to another unit, but she said no. He hugged and kissed her goodnight and watched her walk inside, admiring her statuesque beauty as she went, worried about her. He walked back to his car and began uptown, to his rent-controlled two-bedroom apartment at Riverside Drive and 101st Street, his mind reeling with the day's events, his bones aching, wishing Jane were there waiting for him with her kind ways, her all-knowing eyes. He missed her so much it stole his breath away.

FIVE

Father Paul De Mazio was a portly, red-faced priest with pure white hair. He was sixty-two years old, a kind, gentle man who looked like Santa Claus without the beard. He even wore granny glasses. Father De Mazio was assigned to the parish of Our Lady of Miracles Church at Riverside Drive and 125th Street. Every morning, before attending to his duties, he prayed fervently to Jesus Christ to help the Church through these terrible times; to give the holy father, Pope John in Rome, the strength, wisdom and courage to guide the Church to safe shores. Like most good Catholics, Father De Mazio was truly appalled by all the child molesters in the church, and by how cardinals, bishops and archbishops, the Church hierarchy, had handled "predator priests"—as he thought of them—when they were found out. Some mornings he couldn't even get out of bed he was so distraught and heartbroken at what was going on; how vast sums of money were going to the victims of abuse; how programs for the poor and needy, for orphaned children, for food kitchens throughout the country, were summarily being shut down without explanation or apology because of the child molesters who had infiltrated and defiled the Church—stealing it away from its original purpose.

This morning Father De Mazio had breakfast in the rectory after his prayers and made his way over to the church. There were leaks in the roof, the organ needed repair and tuning, stained-glass panels were missing and plaster on the walls was peeling and falling down. But there was no money to repair any of the church's many ailments, and Father De Mazio had taken to fixing what he could on his own. Good with his hands, he didn't at all mind doing little repairs around the church—after all, it was God's house, and he enjoyed doing what he could.

Today he was grouting some tiles he had replaced the day before on the wall behind an eight-foot statue of the Virgin Mary. He was just mixing the grout when the man silently entered through a side entrance of the church. He was a tall man with foreboding purpose in his step. He had a triangular face with high cheekbones, large dark eyes and thick, black hair down to his shoulders. Wearing all black, he carried a black shoulder bag, wore black sneakers. The priest didn't hear him approach.

Not able to find the priest he was looking for, the man in black silently made his way to Father De Mazio.

"Excuse me, Father," he said in a soft voice. "Can I please talk with you a minute? I need some help."

"Of course, my son," Father De Mazio said. He was in a hurry to get the grout on the wall because it dried quickly, but he would never turn away anyone asking for help. This man's whole life was about giving, assisting the needy. The priest put down the grout and spatula and approached the man.

"Yes, my son?" he asked. The man just stared at him, his dark eyes narrowing on Father De Mazio's benevolent face.

"I'm looking for Father Bernard. Doesn't he hear confessions today?" he said.

"Normally, yes, but Father Bernard had a stroke over the weekend. He's in the hospital."

"I'm sorry to hear that. Which hospital?"

"Harlem General."

The priest could readily see the disappointment on the man's face.

"Did you know Father Bernard?"

"Yes, many years ago, when I was a boy."

"I see," Father De Mazio said, knowing that Father Bernard had been accused of abusing children. He wondered if the man before him now was one of those children grown up.

"Are you troubled?" the priest asked. "Can I help you?"

"Yes, Father . . . very troubled," he said.

"Tell me how I can help, my son," Father De Mazio said, genuine concern creasing his sincere face, his wide brow.

"This is how," the man said. With lightning speed, he drew a curved blade out of the shoulder bag and slammed the shaft into Father De Mazio's gut. He pulled the blade up and to the left with terrific force, breaking ribs as he went.

Shocked, his eyes bulging, the hapless priest fell back, nearly knocking over the statue of the Virgin Mary. His intestines seemed to burst from his stomach cavity. It had happened so fast the priest had little time to react. His eyes were filled with shock and fear, for what he saw in the man's eyes was a terrible thing to behold—they were filled with a malevolence the priest had never seen before, so intense it didn't seem human. Surely this was an animal, a creature from hell, the priest thought. The man moved forward and struck the priest in the head with the handle of the knife and knocked him down, grabbed him by the hair and began to drag him toward the altar. Father De Mazio desperately tried to push his intestines back into his stomach, begging, "Why, why, why?"

Now the man grabbed the priest's left arm and dragged him up onto the altar. He bent down and drew the blade across the priest's throat in one swift movement. Gasping desperately, blood gushing from his severed arteries, Father De Mazio was soon unconscious. Dead. The man bent down and proceeded to mutilate him.

Then, using his pointer finger and the priest's blood, which was all over the floor, he drew the words *HELL ON EARTH* on the altar, turned and silently made his way back to the door he came in. He used a red bandana in his pocket to make sure he left no prints on the door handle. He then made certain he had no blood on him anywhere and in a few moments he was casually walking along Riverside Drive.

Just to the south of the church, an elderly Mexican man whose skin was wrinkled like a raisin was selling different-flavored snow cones. His name was Ramon. It was so hot, however, that the hard-earned block of ice he shaved for the sweet snow cones was melting quickly. When the man in black passed him, Ramon asked if he'd like to cool himself, but the man ignored him. "Snow cones, snow cones," Ramon called, thinking the guy was creepy.

The man in black took a right on 125th Street and

started toward Broadway, his step easy and unhurried. He soon disappeared into the humid darkness of the subway station at 125th Street, intent on drawing still more blood this day.

SIX

Tony Flynn was just reaching the District Attorney's office for the 11:00 AM press conference. He had 1010 WINS on the radio and was listening to the news, thinking about Jacky, worried for her. He wished, though he knew it wasn't going to happen, that she'd find herself a good man and settle down, maybe have a couple of kids. He had learned to accept that she was gay, but still he hoped that perhaps someday she'd *change*. He had spoken to several psychiatrists about Jacky and was told over and over that her homosexuality was something she could not control; that people's sexuality is predetermined by genetic propensity, things deep within recesses of the brain. Jane, his wife—as far as he knew—had never learned that Jacky was gay. Jacky had chosen not to tell her mother and made Tony promise he wouldn't tell her either. He never did.

As Tony pulled into the parking lot opposite the court building, he heard on the news that former governor of Oklahoma Frank Keating, who had been on the civilian council to monitor the Church's handling of the sex scandal it had become mired in, said that church officials were, "Acting like 'La Cosa Nostra' "; that they were stonewalling and hiding church records and were not coming forth with the names of the priests who had been accused of abuse. As Flynn listened to the news report, he agreed, thinking that indeed the Church had been acting exactly like a Mafia crime family trying to stay out of trouble, and he admired Governor Keating for saying so publicly.

He slipped out of his car and started toward 100 Centre Street, an austere brown granite building that housed the criminal and supreme courts of New York, the county jail, known as The Tombs, and the District Attorney's office. He walked to Jay Street where the entrance to the DA's office was located. News trucks lined both sides of the narrow street, their satellite dishes suspended above them on telescoping aluminum poles two stories high. Flynn showed his ID and took the elevator up to the seventh floor, pleased that Carole Cunningham was in charge of the case, knowing she would not cave in under pressure from anyone. Flynn was intent on seeing justice was done here; he believed in the system, knowing it wasn't perfect, but also knowing there was none better. He found Carole in her office. She didn't seem too happy. "They tried to shut me down," she said.

"Who?"

"My boss."

"Morganstein?"

"Himself."

"What happened?"

"He called me in this morning and asked me to cancel the press conference."

"Why?"

"He said it would unduly influence the jury pool."

"Bullshit."

"Tell me about it. I'm sure what happened was that he got a call from the governor."

"And what did you tell him?"

"I told him if he forced me to cancel the press conference, I'd hold my own press conference."

"Bravo."

"You ready?"

"Absolutely. You hear what Frank Keating said?"

"Yes. He's my hero," she said, grabbing the file she had on the case and the mug shots she had for the press. The two of them set out for the third floor where the media awaited them. The press room, at the end of a long wide corridor, was packed. Microphones had been set up at a beatup wooden podium with a dozen cameras pointed at it. When Flynn and Cunningham entered, everyone came to attention, automatically falling silent. Tall and straight and sure of herself, Cunningham walked to the podium and said, "I want to first thank you for coming. I will make a statement on behalf of the District Attorney's office, then Captain Flynn will tell you about the murder of Mr. Joseph yesterday and we'll both take your questions. For those of you who don't know Captain Flynn, he is in charge of the investigation of the murdered priest yesterday at the Saint Mary's Church on West 39th Street. However, before we address that, I want to ask for the public's help.

"In the course of executing a warrant yesterday at the Saint Mary's rectory, the police searched the residences of the seven priests who lived there, and they found child pornography in Mr. Joseph's room, as well as in the rooms of four other priests." She stopped here to give time for her words to sink in, then gave out blown-up mug shots of the four priests who were in possession of the porn, as well as a photograph of Father Joseph.

Pleased, Flynn watched her work, her every move. She had, it was obvious, the New York press in the palm of her hand, no easy task. Sunlight streaming in through the over-sized windows came to rest on her blond hair and made it seem like luminous threads of gold. "Please," she said, looking directly at the cameras, holding up several mug shots, "if anyone out there was accosted by any of these individuals, come forth. Contact the District Attorney's office. We need your help. I promise, if you wish, anything you tell us will remain absolutely confidential.

"As to the murder of Mr. Joseph, Captain Flynn will address that," she said and stepped away from the podium. Flynn had, over the years, held hundreds of press conferences and he was relaxed and natural as the blind eyes of the cameras turned to him. In plain, simple language he told the media about the murder, leaving out the more graphic details. He then asked anyone with information about the crime to call the 800 number the NYPD had set up. Finished with his statement of facts, the captain answered reporters' questions for fifteen minutes, thanked everyone for coming and promised to keep the media informed about the progress of the investigation.

Just as the press conference was ending, as Flynn and Cunningham were walking back to the elevators, they got word of the murder of Father Paul De Mazio at Our Lady of Miracles Church. When Flynn heard that the priest's throat had been slashed and that he too had been castrated, he knew for certain it was the same man. He was not surprised there had been another killing.

Flynn and Cunningham quickly left the building, jumped in his car and sped uptown. He put on the siren, took the Westside Highway. There was little traffic. Cunningham used her cell phone to call her office and ask that a warrant be drawn up immediately to search the church and all its premises, including the rectory. She didn't have any preconceived notion that priests at the Our Lady of Miracles parish had any kind of pornography, but she wasn't about to give anyone the opportunity to get rid of any illicit materials. Flynn, in turn, used his cell phone to call Sergeant Salerno. He ordered him to hustle up to the church, seal it, call for the tech people to come do their thing.

As they proceeded uptown, the Hudson River was on their left and the sun glistened off it brilliantly. Both Flynn and Cunningham put on sunglasses. Flynn was an excellent driver and he expertly weaved in and out of traffic until they reached the 106th Street exit. He got off the highway and headed north on Riverside Drive, parked on the wide sidewalk out front and he and Cunningham stepped from the car and headed inside. They were met by the uniformed cops who had first responded to the call.

"The priest," one of them explained to Flynn, "had been found by another priest, who immediately called 911. Me and my partner rolled on it, took one look and called it in."

"You didn't go up on the altar, touch anything?"

"No, sir."

"Good job," Flynn said, turning to Cunningham. "You sure you want to see this—it's going to be gruesome."

"Yes, I want to see," she said. "I'm a professional, Captain."

Flynn took off his shades, and he and Cunningham slowly began down the center aisle, careful about where they stepped. Father De Mazio was as the killer had left him, a ghastly sight in a church, a solemn place of worship. Flynn heard Cunningham draw a deep breath. The altar, he noticed, was on a slightly raised platform. Shadows made by quivering candles skulked along the walls like they knew dark secrets they were not about to share. Tony moved to the edge of the altar and let his eyes scrutinize the crime scene, then turned to Cunningham. She had paled noticeably, but didn't look away, was hard-jawed and steely eyed.

She had seen many photographs of bodies over the years, but seeing one up close and personal like this in a church was another thing entirely, the smell of the body coming to them in the still, hot air. There was, Flynn noted, a large pool of blood around the priest. The killer had stepped in it and left a distant footprint. "Bingo," he said, pointing out the print. He said it would be best for the crime scene personnel to work the altar before they went any closer to the body. They carefully retraced their steps. As they reached the entrance, Sergeant Salerno arrived with four teams of experienced detectives. Flynn told them what he'd seen and said he wanted the tech people to thoroughly work the altar area before any of them even went near the body. "Meanwhile I want all you guys to hit the sidewalks and question neighborhood people. We are expecting warrants from downtown. Let me know when they arrive." He turned to the uniformed cops who'd first gotten the call. "Where's the priest who found the body?" he demanded.

"In the rectory."

"Show me the way," Flynn said.

He and Cunningham followed the cops around the corner, to a honey-colored three-story building with a crucifix over the front door and stained-glass windows. He told the uniformed cops to make sure no one left the building unless he gave the green light. He and Cunningham made their way up the six worn steps. He knocked. The door was quickly opened by a tall, blond priest.

"I'm Captain Flynn," he said, showing his gold badge. "This is Assistant District Attorney Cunningham. We understand the priest who found—"

"Yes, he's here, please come in," he said, then turned and led Flynn and Cunningham to a living room at the back of the building where a distraught priest sat, crying into his cupped hands.

In a gentle voice Flynn introduced himself and Cunningham. The priest's name, he learned, was George Korman. "Please," Flynn said. "Tell me what you saw." He pulled up a chair facing the priest.

"Father De Mazio," he said between sobs, "received a call from his brother John, and I went to find him in the church. He had been doing some repairs on tiles, and there he was on the altar—like that—butchered . . . . Who would do such a despicable thing? Do you think it's the same man who murdered Father Joseph at Saint Mary's?"

"Most likely," Flynn said.

"Father De Mazio was such a good man . . . such a good man," he kept repeating, as if talking to himself out loud. In despair the priest shook his head from side to side, his face breaking into an anguished mask of uncontrollable grief.

Flynn waited for him to compose himself. Standing, he turned his attention to the blond priest. "Can you please tell me who is in charge of this parish."

"Bishop Arnold, but he's away just now, visiting his sister in New Jersey."

"I see—we'd like to search Father De Mazio's quarters . . . would that be okay?"

"I don't see why not," the priest said, but Flynn saw a sudden uneasiness in his eyes.

"Can you show us where it is?" Flynn asked.

"Certainly. Upstairs, this way," he said. As they started up the steps, the doorbell rang. The blond priest went to answer it, and there stood a detective who worked for the DA's office, holding the warrants Cunningham had requested in his hand. Grateful, Cunningham thanked him, checked the warrants and without a word put them in her purse. They continued upstairs. Father De Mazio's room was austere. There was a statue of the Virgin Mary, a white seven-day candle, a bed—that was it. There was no illicit material of any kind. Flynn used his cell phone and told

Salerno to bring up a few more men so the rest of the priests' quarters could be properly searched. The doorbell rang again and they heard the front door open. In moments John Mahoney came up the stairs, his face stiff and angry, covered with sweat. Flynn wasn't surprised to see the lawyer. He said hello and introduced Cunningham.

Mahoney said, "I came over as soon as I heard. I saw your news conference, counselor. You managed to pollute the jury pool beyond repair. We plan to ask for a change of venue."

"Sorry you feel that way," she said. "Did you see the materials we confiscated?"

"I did. Seems to me you should be more concerned about the *murdered* priests, counselor."

"We are very concerned about them, but, apparently, unlike you, we are also concerned with the abused children."

"Yes, and meanwhile another priest has been *killed*. I'm not at all surprised with all the bad press the church has been getting. The media is *obviously* intent on making a bad situation worse . . . Catholic-bashing, and you aren't helping."

"You've got balls to stand there and say that with a straight face," Flynn said. "With the help of lawyers like you the Church has been doing nothing but playing games. That's the problem. Not the media. Or anyone else."

"What are you doing to catch this madman?" Mahoney demanded, obviously wanting to change the subject.

"Everything we can," Flynn said. "We were just about to search the priest's quarters. You have a problem with that?"

"You have a warrant?"

"We do," Cunningham said and stuck the warrants in his face. He grabbed them and began reading. They left him standing there and, with the help of Salerno and three other detectives, they continued their search.

They found nothing that shouldn't be there, until they reached Bishop Arnold's quarters. They were much more luxurious than the others. There was a thirty-six-inch Sony Trinatron television, an expensive stereo and DVD player, a very well appointed kitchen, an elaborate wine collection, a box of Cuban cigars, a marble bathroom and even a pink Jacuzzi tub. With John Mahoney looking on, Cunningham booted up his computer and within minutes she found files filled with pornography involving pubescent boys and girls. Now quiet like a dusty wooden Indian in front of a cigar store, Mahoney stared at the images, glistening beads of sweat running down his ferret-like face.

"What do you say to this garbage, counselor?" Cunningham asked, her fierce brown eyes narrowing on him. He didn't answer her. She asked one of the detectives to disconnect the computer so she could take it downtown, turned to the blond priest and asked how Bishop Arnold could be contacted. He gave her his cell number. After conferring with Flynn they decided to call the bishop. He answered on the third ring. She introduced herself and told him what happened.

"My God, my God," was all he could say, and explained that he was on the Jersey Turnpike on his way back to New York; that he'd be there in about one hour, traffic permitting. Cunningham said she'd wait for him, hung up. Mahoney had asked to speak with him, but she ignored him.

"You do anything to cause him to flee, you will be arrested on the spot for obstruction, you understand?" she demanded.

"I've been a lawyer for twenty years—of course I understand," he said.

Condescending scumbag, she thought. Mahoney saw the

resolve and anger in her eyes and said nothing more, walking off to stay out of her way. He knew he was standing on thin ice now and wasn't about to piss her off any more than she already was, though he planned to do what he could to get her off the case.

Flynn and his men searched the basement of the building and didn't find any illegal materials. By now the police technicians, photographers and latent print people had finished with the crime scene, and they all left the rectory and began back toward the church. It was ninety-eight degrees with seventy-five percent humidity, not a cloud in the sky. Just the act of walking on the steaming sidewalk was arduous.

The press had, of course, gotten word of this murder, and there was a mob of media people up and down Riverside Drive, standing in the fierce sun like they had no sense. Flynn assigned a detective to watch the rectory, told him to make sure nothing was removed, and to let him know as soon as Bishop Arnold arrived. Flynn asked Mahoney if he'd like to see the body. The lawyer declined. The captain and Cunningham left him standing on the shadeless church steps and went inside.

The footprint on the altar had been taken off the floor with special lifting tape by police technician Josephine Peters. She was waiting for Flynn near the altar. As Flynn and Cunningham approached, she said, "Captain, I got a very good lift. It's a Reebok sneaker, size eleven and a half, relatively new."

"Okay, we've got his foot size," Flynn said. "That's a good beginning. Log it in, Josephine, make copies of it ASAP, and make sure nothing happens to it."

"Yes, sir."

Flynn, closely followed by Cunningham, approached the body. The priest's blood had coagulated and looked like melted chocolate. Flynn got down low and carefully looked at the way his throat had been cut. The wound, he said, was identical to the one on Joseph.

Flynn had called the Medical Examiner's office and asked Dr. Richard Russo to come over. The doctor now entered the front door, walked to the altar and he, too, studied the body. "If the same hand didn't do that," he said, pointing to the priest's neck, "I'm a monkey's uncle."

"I was just thinking that," Flynn said.

The doctor first checked the priest's fingernails. There was, he noted, no sign of any fight, nothing but a little plaster under the priest's nails. He noted the multiple stab wounds on the priest's chest, counted six of them. Flynn and Cunningham stood silently and let the doctor work.

"What killed him," he said, standing and facing them, "is the wound to his throat. The rest of the wounds, though potentially lethal, were done after he was dead. Tony, you are looking for a particularly strong man who obviously hates priests. I say he's strong because he actually broke ribs with the upward stroke of the blade when he eviscerated him."

"I'm going to call the Feds down at Quantico; maybe they can point us in a direction," Flynn said.

"I was just going to suggest that," Cunningham said. "You know he won't stop until he's brought down. Anything on the DNA work up, doctor?"

"Maybe tomorrow."

They all knew that if, in fact, the killer's DNA was on file they would have his identity and, hopefully soon have him. Flynn's cell phone sounded. It was the detective Flynn had left guarding the rectory, Bobby Roe. "Captain, I think we might have a witness," he said.

"Yeah, who?"

"I've got an old Spanish guy out here who says he thinks he saw the killer."

"Great, bring him in," Flynn ordered.

Soon the front door opened and there stood Ramon, the snow-cone maker, outlined by the fierce summer sun. Flynn and Cunningham went to meet him. He was a small, frightened man and was clearly not comfortable talking to the police. As Flynn drew closer he could readily see the apprehension on the man's wrinkled face. Right off Flynn knew that he was probably here illegally, but still he had come forth. Flynn greeted him with a warm smile and firm handshake. Ramon said he could not speak English well. Flynn called for Detective Alvarez to come translate, offered Ramon a seat in one of the rear pews and they all sat down, facing each other.

With Detective Alvarez's assistance, Ramon said, "I am a very poor man. To earn a little something to eat I sell the snow cones. I made the wagon myself with things I find that people throw away. They throw away so much here in New York. I sell my snow cones on Riverside Drive and 126th Street. Today, maybe eleven o'clock, eleven-fifteen, I see a man walk from the side of the church. I am always looking for customers and so I watch who walks on the sidewalk. As he came closer to me, I asked him if he'd like a cooling snow cone, and he just ignored me. Like I wasn't there. Right away I could see, I mean in his eyes, you know, that there was something . . . something odd about him—like he was angry . . . very angry. I look in his eyes for a second and they are dark and dead like the eyes of a shark. I swear, that's what I think to myself, you know— that he has eyes like the shark, black and cold like marble. As a young boy I live in the Yucatan and many times I see the sharks and he had those eyes."

"Can you describe him?" Flynn asked.

"*Sí*, tall like you, but thin. He has the black hair and the thin pale face with the big bones here," he said, indicating the cheekbones. "And he wore all black. That was another reason I noticed him, you know. I mean that he was wearing black on a day so hot.

"And so my ice melts and I go back to the place where I sleep, in this little room in the basement of a building on 124th Street. I clean the building and they let me stay there. I'm so tired because of the heat and I take a siesta and when I wake up and come outside, I hear about the priest, you know, what happened," he said, twice making the sign of the cross.

"Do you think you can work with a police artist to help make a sketch of this man you saw?" Flynn asked.

"*Sí, Capitano.* I am old, but my eyes and my senses are good. I want to help. I must help."

"Thank you," Flynn said, and immediately arranged for a Spanish-speaking police artist to come work with Ramon to create a composite of this man with the shark eyes. Flynn then explained to Ramon, Alvarez still translating, that the police were not interested in whether or not he was in New York legally; that because of his help and the fact that he had the courage to come forward he, Flynn, would make sure Ramon secured a green card. That put a big smile on Ramon's face.

The front door opened and in walked Bishop Arnold, a large heavy man with hanging jowls and drooping eyes; he kind of looked like an aged basset hound.

Flynn politely introduced himself and Cunningham and proceeded to give Arnold his Miranda rights and put him under arrest.

Stunned, Bishop Arnold demanded an explanation. Flynn said, "We secured a warrant to search the rectory and found your collection of child pornography."

"Oh, that," he said. "I can explain that, I was doing research on the subject to better be able to assist priests who sinned and—"

"Tell it to the judge." Flynn stopped him and ordered the bishop to be booked.

Sergeant Salerno led him away, Arnold angrily protesting, telling Flynn he should be searching for the priest's murderer, "not arresting me, you fool," he said.

SEVEN

Police artist Susan Rodriguez was a short, determined woman with observant dark blue eyes. She had a pleasant disposition and was easy to talk to. Coincidentally, she only lived six blocks from Our Lady of Miracles, and two years earlier had been married at the church by Father De Mazio. She had heard about his murder on NY 1, and was devastated, crying, demanding of God to know why such a good man had been murdered.

It was her day off, but when she received a call to go over to the church and work with a witness, Susan wiped away her tears, grabbed her sketching pad and pencils and was out the door in three minutes flat.

By the time she reached the church, Father De Mazio had been taken to the morgue for autopsy. Fluent in Spanish, Susan was introduced to Ramon by Detective Alvarez. Ramon had seen the stiff body of the priest placed in the morgue body bag and carried from the church. Very traumatized by such a sight, his hands were trembling and the color had completely drained from his face. For him, a priest was a holy entity, a trusted confidant of God, someone with a direct connection to Jesus Christ himself, and to murder a priest was a terrible thing. An unspeakable crime. Surely anyone capable of such a thing was sent by Satan, Ramon was convinced, and would later explain.

Looking Ramon directly in the eyes, Susan calmed him with a soothing voice and immediately began to talk to him about the man in black he'd seen leaving the church. Ramon would be, she immediately realized, a good subject to work with because he was a people person; he paid attention to the world around him and who was moving in it.

Susan created the sketch by starting with the shape of the face, then the hair, particular details of the eyes, ears, nose and mouth, the set of the eyebrows. She worked slowly and patiently, repeatedly showing Ramon the sketch, erasing and correcting the drawing until he said he was pleased. "That is the *hombre* I see," he proclaimed with confidence.

Susan was looking at a high-cheekboned, triangular-shaped face with full lips, severe eyes, a broad forehead. He kind of looked, she thought, like a fusion of the actors Antonio Banderas and Benicio Del Toro. Finished, Susan brought the drawing to Captain Flynn, who was still overseeing the questioning of neighborhood people, shopkeepers, teenagers playing games in the street, people sitting on their stoops. Susan told the captain that Ramon was easy to work with, that he was an excellent witness. "I'd bet this is a very good likeness of the man who left the church," she said, holding up her sketch for Flynn to see.

He took a long, slow look at the drawing. "Mean-looking bastard," he said, and thanked Susan for coming right over on her day off. She told him what a "wonderful priest" Father De Mazio was. The captain promised to do all he could to catch his killer. He asked her to log in the drawing with the NYPD and to get copies of it to his office ASAP. She promised he'd have them within hours and hurried off, intent upon her mission, deeply saddened by the murder of Father De Mazio.

Over and over again, Tony Flynn heard from neighborhood people what a nice guy, a caring, giving man, Father De Mazio was.

Tired and hot, Flynn was pissed off. He viewed the whole island of Manhattan as his beat—as indeed it was—and someone had decided to kill and butcher at will, as he pleased, on Tony Flynn's watch, and Flynn was intent upon stopping him. He was planning to put together a lean, mean task force of seasoned New York detectives he personally knew to track down the killer and bring him to the bar, or put him in a grave. Flynn was just about to call his boss, Chief of Detectives John Samuels, and ask for permission to form the task force, thinking about the detectives he'd choose, when his cell phone buzzed—it was Chief Samuels calling him. He said that he wanted Flynn to meet him at the commissioner's office at One Police Plaza in an hour. Flynn said he'd be there, and he and Cunningham soon left the parish of Our Lady of Miracles, fourteen detectives still knocking on doors, looking for clues—for anyone who might have seen something more.

Captain Flynn got on the Westside Highway and headed downtown, pleased that they had a witness. He had worked numerous serial murder cases over the years, including the notorious Son of Sam case. Flynn knew that in serial murder cases witnesses were rare because the killer picked the time and place and didn't strike unless he felt safe, unobserved. Though there had only been two murders so far, Flynn was sure there would be more—that the killer of the priests had a burning hatred that could only be satiated by blood.

"My boss wants to see me right away," he said to Cunningham.

"Yeah, mine too. He just called me. You think the snow-cone man really saw him?"

50

"I do. The guy came walking from the side of the church just at the right time, and he's wearing all black. I think . . . I'm thinking that may play into it."

"How so?"

"His writing the words 'hell on earth' at both crime scenes might indicate that he's a Satan freak, and those people often dress in black. That Night Stalker serial killer in L.A. a few years ago, as an example, was a Satanist and he always wore black."

"Interesting. . . . Seems this priest was a really good egg."

"Yeah, all I kept hearing was what a great guy he was—caring, giving, do anything he could to help anyone who came to him. That's another reason why it is such a crying shame how the Church has been doing the two-step and not coming clean. I mean they themselves have tarnished, maybe beyond repair, all the good priests—the ones who really care, the ones who genuinely want to help . . . it's criminal. I'm planning to have the drawing distributed to the media and posted all over the neighborhood of Our Lady of Miracles and the church on 39th Street where Joseph was murdered. A lot of breaking a case like this is about working with the public, getting tips. Somewhere people know who this dude is, and we've got to find them and hear what they have to say."

"My office has been inundated with calls from citizens saying they were abused by the priests we arrested at Saint Mary's. And by Father Joseph. I'm meeting with twenty-nine of them tomorrow morning."

"Somehow that doesn't surprise me. You know, I'm thinking the killer might very well come forward. That he just might want to talk to you if he were abused by one of these men. Maybe even Joseph himself. I don't think it's an accident that Joseph was killed first."

"I'll keep my eyes open for him. If he looks anything like the sketch he shouldn't be hard to spot."

"You know, maybe for that reason we should hold off giving the sketch to the media. If this is him, he might very well get in the wind when he sees it."

"Yes, you have a point."

"We'll hold it a few days, see what happens. I'm hoping we get his DNA tomorrow. That'd be a lucky break. If he's on file, we'll have him."

"I've got my fingers crossed," she said, turning and looking at Flynn as he drove, admiring his strong jawline, handsome profile, long straight nose, the scar on his face just below his cheekbone.

"If you don't mind my asking, Tony, how'd you get that scar on your cheek?"

"I don't mind. A bad guy holding up liquor stores in Brooklyn shot at me at point-blank range. I turned away just in the nick of time, but the bullet grazed my face. I was very lucky. Another inch or so and I wouldn't be here . . . it was a .45 loaded with hollow-tip rounds. It happened so long ago, I kind of forget it's there," he said, rubbing the scar, remembering the searing pain of the wound, the deafening explosion right in his face. "I was thinking of having a plastic surgeon fix it but decided against it," he said.

"It's . . . well you know, it's kind of—sexy," she said. "In a rugged way."

"Really?"

"Yes."

"Hmm. Who knew. I saw Jacky last night. We had dinner at The Tuscan Inn. She told me about the bust her unit made."

"Unbelievable, what monsters—they were selling and renting women and girls to sexual sadists from all over the world. We confiscated their computer, and they had customers from everywhere—Germany, Japan, Denmark. Very rich individuals. My unit is prosecuting this Sister Ping. She's a seventy-two-year-old woman, looks like someone's grandmother, but a real black widow spider. Eyes like two pieces of coal. . . . Jacky tell you about the Chinese guy in the elevator?"

"No, what Chinese guy, what elevator?"

She didn't answer him. He repeated the question.

She said, "As we were going down in the elevator after the arraignment, just as the elevator doors were closing, this Chinese dude appeared out of nowhere and . . . and he threatened Jacky—"

"How? What'd he say?" Flynn asked, turning toward her.

"He looked at her, pointed at her and said: 'Start looking over your shoulder, bitch.'"

"Really? She didn't tell me."

"She probably just forgot."

"You don't forget something like that. These Chinese gangs are ruthless, kill a cop in a second. Most of them are illegal immigrants brought over by the gang heads and they have a completely different mindset. Life for them is very cheap—meaningless."

"She probably just didn't want to worry you."

"You said that some gang members had been arrested, too. Where are they now?"

"Rikers, but I understand they've made bail."

"I need to know who the boss is—and where he lives."

"His name is Harry Yu. I've got his address at the office, I'll call you with it."

"Good, thank you."

"Tony, don't go doing anything to create problems for yourself."

"You don't have to concern yourself with anything like that," he said, and used his cell phone and called Detective Rocco Genovese, a very good friend of his. He got him on the line and made plans to meet up with him at One Police Plaza.

"Please, Tony, don't tell Jacky I mentioned this. I wouldn't want her to think I'm telling you things out of turn."

"Of course, but thanks for mentioning it," he said. He soon dropped her off at her office, tried to reach Jacky on her cell phone but couldn't get through. He made his way downtown to the NYPD main headquarters, which was just next to the famous Brooklyn Bridge, parked in the underground lot and took the elevator up to the top floor, where the commissioner's office was located. Now not only concerned with the murder of the priests and the inevitable political fallout, Flynn was thinking about his daughter Jacky, wondering why she had not mentioned this threat. When he reached the sixth floor, he used his cell phone to try Jacky again, but his boss, Chief Samuels, was just down the hall sitting in a blue plastic chair outside the commissioner's office. Talking on his cell phone, Samuels waved Flynn over. Flynn pocketed his phone and made his way to the chief.

Chief Samuels was an introspective man with a bald head, broad shoulders and narrow, suspicious eyes. He had come up through the ranks and was a demanding chief who responded to headlines and news stories. He knew well how important the crime drop in New York was, how it made the city much safer, a good place to live, to start a new business, to bring up children; how it had brought in many millions in tourist dollars. He and his detectives had, in fact, a lot to do with the drop in crime, and he was very proud of it and not shy about saying so.

As Flynn reached him, Samuels closed his cell phone, stood up and gave Tony a big bear hug. The two men were close. They had graduated in the same class out of the police academy and saw each other socially. Both men loved to fish. Chief Samuels had a forty-one-foot Bertram deep-sea fishing boat, and they went fishing every other weekend during the summer months, weather permitting.

"Sit down, Tony, sit down," the chief said. "Please run everything you have by me."

Flynn told him all that had happened. These two men knew one another so well they also spoke in a kind of shorthand, and it didn't take long for Flynn to lay out the case, its facts, what he saw, and what he thought. "If we are lucky," Flynn said, "and the perp's DNA is on file we'll have him. If not, we at least have a good sketch of him—a snow-cone guy with good eyes saw him leaving Our Lady of Miracles Church."

"What about the priests with the porn—damn disgrace that is; makes me ashamed to be a Catholic, you know. Men in a position of trust like that doing those kinds of things . . . an abomination."

"Carole Cunningham is prosecuting them."

"Well, that's good. She's as tough as rusted nails and an excellent lawyer. Needless to say, I'm getting calls from everyone—the mayor, the governor, the head of every Catholic organization. By the way, this lawyer for the Church, Mahoney, he called to complain about you."

"First-grade asshole."

"I know who he is. He's a member of my golf club—an arrogant stiff. Tony, far as I'm concerned, you do what has to be done, you hear?"

"I hear."

"I'll back you to the wall. Don't pull any punches here."

"Thanks, John, I appreciate you saying that. I want to put together a task force, maybe twelve hand-picked guys, that okay?"

"Absolutely."

"And I want to hold off on giving the drawing we have to the press. There's a possibility that the perp may very well come forward now. Present himself as a victim, and we wouldn't want to do anything to cause him to book."

"I agree."

"Okay."

The door to the commissioner's office opened and his secretary said they could go in. As they entered the office, the commissioner was talking on the phone, sitting behind a giant desk, which was in front of oversized bullet-proof windows that afforded a sweeping view of the East River and Brooklyn Bridge. Next to the windows was a large graph showing how many murders there had been in America's largest cities—Washington, D.C., was first, New York last.

A tall, gangly, sour-faced man with longish gray hair combed straight back, Commissioner Louis Peters was originally from Boston and spoke with a Boston accent. He had beady blue eyes, an upturned nose and narrow lips, carried a huge silver .45 auto with a mother-of-pearl handle in a fancy black leather holster on his hip. Unlike Flynn and Samuels, who were at heart cops, Peters was a politician, a manipulator of people, an adept administrator who had the sensibility and soul of the head of a successful bottom-line corporation. His heroes were corporate geniuses, Henry Ford, Jack Welsh and Bill Gates. They were the men he looked up to, looked to emulate. He had only recently been given the job of commissioner—eleven months ago—had been stolen away from the Boston Police Department by the New York mayor with the promise of more money and the prestige of running the NYPD, the largest police force in the world. However, the rank and file of the PD didn't like him. Not only was he an outsider, but he wasn't one of *them*. He had publicly condemned several shootings that the police had been involved in, and he had aggressively sided against the police unions when they were negotiating their new contract.

Peters stood and shook hands with Samuels and Flynn and offered them seats in front of his desk. He didn't offer them anything to drink, a cold beverage, some coffee.

"I want to first thank you both for coming on such short notice," he began. "I called you in because of the murders of the two priests. And because of the press conference this morning at the District Attorney's office.

"As I'm sure you both know, all the New York newspapers have front-page stories about these murders. My phones have not stopped ringing because of them. The governor, the mayor, Cardinal Edam and the Catholic League have all called. Gentlemen, we need these murders solved quickly. Catholic priests being butchered, castrated and eviscerated in churches is a very dark stain on our city. I wanted to see you both to let you know how politically sensitive these murders are. The people at the Catholic League are up in arms. They are saying that the press conference this morning seemed a lot more concerned about priests having pornography in their possession than catching the killer . . . and I agree."

Flynn could see where this was going, and he didn't like it. He moved uncomfortably in his chair, stared at a white sailboat in the river behind the commissioner, thinking that a man who has an oversized desk and gun usually has a small penis.

"Yes, of course," the commissioner added in his clipped Boston accent, looking at the chief, "the priests having pornography is a crime, but I'm thinking the message we want to send out is not about that. Frankly, I don't believe that issue should have even been brought up at the press conference to begin with. My concern is with catching the killer—"

"If I may interrupt you, sir," Flynn said.

"Yes?" he asked, not liking the interruption, but knowing that Captain Tony Flynn was a legend in the department, highly respected, a first-rate investigator. A man you wanted on your side.

"First off, Chief Samuels here had nothing to do with the press conference. ADA Cunningham asked me to attend it and so I went."

"I see."

"Commissioner, with all due respect, if what you are telling us is to whitewash the fact that these priests are child molesters, that we should look the other way about that, I'll give you my badge right now. During my watch, they're not going to get any kind of pass."

A sudden, heavy silence filled the space between the three men. The commissioner's face reddened slightly, his cheeks taking on a distinct strawberry hue. He was not accustomed to being spoken to like that. He glared at Flynn and Flynn glared right back. Tony had, the commissioner could readily see, the quiet resolve of a man who knew he was right and was gladly willing to do battle to prove it. Truth was, Tony often thought about retiring, getting a plum job in the private sector, doing some traveling, maybe buying a fishing boat and hiring himself out down in the Keys somewhere. Though he loved police work— bringing down bad guys, keeping the streets safe, predators behind bars—there was no way he was going to allow some politically motivated bureaucrat to dictate how to do his job. Flynn knew only too well that Peters had been running the Boston PD as the Catholic Church was openly protecting molesters, circumventing justice, and there was just no way that he would allow that to happen in New York on his beat.

Peters smiled, said, "I admire you, Captain Flynn. I've read your file. You are one of the most respected men on the force, most decorated, and I wouldn't want to see you leave the department. You are a great asset to any police department. I agree with you. Fact is, I'm not asking you to give anyone 'a pass.' What I'm saying is that we should first concern ourselves with catching this madman, this cold-blooded killer . . . don't you agree?"

"We'll get him. We have a witness, a good sketch of him, and we will have his DNA tomorrow and if it's on file, we'll have him. But, as well as bringing him down, I want to make sure these predator priests, any predator priests, are treated like the lowlife, bottom-feeding dirtbags they are. And I need to know you feel the same way."

"Of course I do. I have five children and seven grand-children of my own. Your sentiments are my sentiments, Captain."

"Good to hear."

"Tell me how you might have his DNA."

"Joseph, the priest murdered at Saint Mary's over on 39th Street, he scratched him and there were particles of flesh under his nails."

"Excellent. First good news I've heard today. Look, Captain, you work this as you see fit. Just please let us know about any more press conferences before you have them, and please understand that I am behind you one hundred percent here. Use all the men you need. Don't worry about overtime. I was talking to the mayor as you arrived and the city is willing to post a $25,000 reward, and Cardinal Edam is offering an additional $25,000 to sweeten the pie."

"That'll definitely help," Flynn said.

"This sketch you talked about—you do plan to give it to the media, let them know we have a suspect; that we know what the killer looks like."

"Not just yet. We are thinking the killer might very well come forward—present himself as a victim, so just now we don't want him to know we've made him."

"Hmm, yes, of course—good thinking. I hope we are in sync now," Peters said, offering Flynn his bony hand. Tony took it and shook it, looking the commissioner straight in his blue eyes, not liking what he saw. This was, Flynn was sure, not a man to be trusted.

"Please, then, keep me abreast of the investigation," the commissioner asked.

"Yes, sir," Flynn said, and soon the meeting ended.

"You've got balls," Chief Samuels said in the elevator on the way down.

"Nice of you to say, John," Flynn said.

Downstairs the two men parted and Flynn tried to reach his daughter Robin. She was, he was told, at the mayor's office.

EIGHT

Lt. Detective Rocco Genovese was a bull of a man with a barrel chest, thick forearms and shoulders so wide he had difficulty fitting through most doorways. His hands were ham-hock sized, his fingers like thick sausages, his legs like two tree trunks. He had a full head of black hair, the dark skin of Southern Italians, a jutting square jaw, a broken nose, and large dark eyes under long lashes. Rocco Genovese didn't smile often, but when he did he revealed large white teeth. He never smoked, never drank alcohol, and was the head coach for the Police Athletic League Boxing Team.

In his early twenties, Rocco himself had been a professional fighter, but in his seventh fight he killed a man in the ring, quit the fight business and soon joined the NYPD. Like Flynn, Rocco came from a distinguished line of police officers—his father and grandfather had been New York City detectives, were there during the worst times of New York City's rough-and-tumble, violent history.

Rocco's father was the first cousin of the infamous Vito Genovese, the head of the Genovese crime family. When Tony Flynn left One Police Plaza that day, he found Rocco waiting for him outside. The two men were close, had been best man at one another's weddings, were the godfathers to each other's children. They knew each other from grade school in the Bronx, having lived next to each other on Arthur Avenue. *If*, Flynn had often said, *I had to be in a foxhole, I'd want to be in it with Rocco Genovese.* They shook hands and embraced.

"What's up?" Rocco asked, concern arching his thick brows. Briefly, Tony ran down all he had on the murder of the two priests. Rocco listened attentively; he was a devout Catholic, still went to church every Sunday, and was sick and tired of the scandals the Church had gotten itself into. Rocco had, for the last year, stopped giving any money when the basket was passed around at the end of the mass. He would not allow his hard-earned dollars to be used by the Church to pay off victims of child molesters, who, he believed, should never have been allowed to become priests to begin with. Rocco said, "I'll bet my house the perp was a victim of abuse by priests."

"Yeah, of course—I'm thinking the same thing, kind of

stands to reason," Tony said. "Either he was a victim or close to someone who was. But the reason I called you Roc is because of Jacky." Rocco was Jacky's godfather.

"What's wrong? Something happen?"

"No, but I hear she was threatened by one of the Golden Dragons. They were doing the strong arm work for this fancy S & M sex ring in Chinatown—"

"Yeah, I heard about the bust. Was being run by a little old lady. You know who made this threat?"

"I do. That's why I called."

"Let's go explain the facts of life to him," Rocco said. They took his car, which was double-parked out front, and drove to the 21st Precinct on nearby Hudson Street. Using the name Carole Cunningham had given him, Harry Yu, they checked the information about all the Chinese gangs in Chinatown in the Hudson Street precinct computer and were able to get Yu's mug shot and address, 13 Mott Street. They made their way over to Mott Street and found the building, a dilapidated four-story tenement. They parked on Canal, walked back to the building and began ringing each of the four bells, none of which had any names on them. The door was soon opened by an elderly Asian woman, fear in her eyes. Tony showed his badge and politely asked where Harry Yu lived. She pointed to the top floor. They made their way slowly up the stairs. The hall reeked with the smell of cigar tobacco and marijuana. Tony knocked on the door. After a time an irritated voice asked who it was. "A friend. Sister Ping sent me," Tony said.

Momentarily, the door was opened by Harry Yu himself, a tall, skinny Asian with long, stick-straight black hair. All he had on were skimpy leopard-skin briefs. His neck was crowded with gold chains, his two front teeth were gold and he had an elaborate gold and red tattoo of a dragon all over his bony chest. His eyes got wide at the sight of Rocco Genovese. He was a scary sight. "Sister Ping not send you," Harry Yu said, closing the door.

Rocco stopped him. "That's the truth. Can we come in?" Tony asked, pushing past him without waiting for an answer.

There were two naked Chinese women sitting on a brown velvet couch in the living room. They made no effort to cover themselves at the unexpected sight of Tony and Rocco Genovese. On a fancy black marble table in front of them, there was a glistening mound of pearly white powder—high-grade cocaine—and an elaborate freebase pipe. A porno movie involving bestiality played on a gigantic plasma screen. Chinese rap music came from large speakers. Rocco did not like rap music, and Chinese rap music was just about unbearable.

"What you want?" Yu demanded.

"To talk," Tony said. He took Yu's skinny arm and led him into the kitchen, which was at the end of a long narrow hall. They passed a bathroom with an open door. Two more naked women inside the bathroom were in flagrante delicto.

In the kitchen there was a large box of baking soda and the paraphernalia for making freebase. Tony said, "You must be a real stud, having four ladies at once."

"What you want?" Yu again demanded, his face bunched into an angry snarl.

Tony said, "Listen to me very carefully. My name is Flynn. I'm a captain in the police department, see," he said and showed Yu his shiny gold badge. "I understand one of your people threatened my daughter—"

"Who you daughter?"

"The detective who busted Sister Ping—you know, with the long black hair—people say she looks just like me."

With that, Yu's face changed. Now he knew exactly why these two grim-faced detectives were there.

"I came to tell you, Harry, that if you or any of your people does *anything* to harm my daughter, I will personally find you, put a serious hurt on you and dump you in the river. You understand me?"

Yu just nodded his head, but didn't answer. Rocco reached out and wrapped his giant hand around Yu's neck and effortlessly lifted him off the ground, as if he were a mere rag doll, and suddenly Rocco's gun was in his other hand and he pushed it into Yu's mouth, knocking out his gold teeth.

Slowly, Rocco pulled the hammer of the gun back—*click*.

"You understand?" Rocco demanded, his Bronx-accented voice seeming like a growl coming from a predatory carnivore, his black eyes boring into Yu's panic-stricken face.

"I understand, I understand," Yu mumbled, his eyes bulging out of his narrow, pale face. Rocco dropped him and put his piece away. Without another word the two detectives turned and left.

NINE

Since he was a boy, he had fantasized about killing priests, men with clerical collars, a cross swinging on a chain about their necks. Even as a child, he had hated crosses—what they represented, the people who wore them, the repression they represented.

All the years he had been hospitalized, he carefully planned what he was doing now. Before he was finished, all the world would know about him; how he went after the *real* sinners. How he killed the pope. He didn't particularly care whether he lived or died. What he cared about was revenge; destroying those responsible for what had been done to him; for what had been done to the legions of children all over the country at the hands of priests. Men disguised as messengers of God, disciples of good, who were in truth deviant predators.

He had studied, over many years, everything the Catholic Church had done during the Inquisition and the Crusades; how they tortured, raped and murdered in the name of God. *The lying hypocritical bastards!* he thought, as he stepped off the train at Canal Street, went upstairs and made his way north to the Church of Saint Joseph of the Holy Family on Mulberry Street. Built in 1829, it was one of the first Catholic churches in New York. He had methodically plotted what he would do today; he knew exactly how many priests lived in the rectory and that they would be gathered there now for lunch. He knew that the pastor who ran the foster home where he was put as a boy was now stationed at the Church of Saint Joseph. He had waited many years for what he was about to do today. His intention was to shake the Church's very foundations. To terrorize not only its priests, but its bishops, archbishops and cardinals, to the core of their corrupt souls.

The hatred he carried in his heart seeped into his blood. He walked straight to the rectory in the rear of the church. It was pleasantly shaded by tall elm and maple trees in which sparrows chirped. He rang the bell. A pale gray-haired priest soon answered the door. This was the man he was looking for. This was the man who had helped rip away his soul.

"Yes?" the priest asked. Just the sound of his voice caused hot blood to actually redden the killer's face.

"Father," he said, his voice pleasant and friendly, belying the venomous anger he felt, "my fiancée and I would like to get married here next month, and I would like to make the arrangements. My fiancée is in California right now, but we were hoping we could maybe reserve a date, find out how much it would cost and all."

"Are you both Catholics?" the priest asked.

"Oh yes, devout Catholics, Father," he said.

"Come in," the priest offered, having no idea about the monster that lurked behind the handsome face in front of him now. The priest had just been listening to the news and was very upset over Father De Mazio's murder. He had known Father De Mazio well. This priest's name was Peter Gordon. He was tall and thin and walked with a slight limp. He led the man in black to a rear office. The smell of cooking food permeated the air. The office was simple: a large portrait of the pope, a desk, two chairs. Oversized bay windows offered a view of the church's rear yard, where the priests of the parish grew vegetables—tomatoes and cucumbers, zucchini and squash, and they had a huge, prodigious fig tree, planted in the 1920s, that produced huge amounts of calamati figs every year.

"We were just about to sit down to lunch," Father Gordon said. "But I can go over the basics with you now and reserve a date. When did you have in mind?"

"The third Saturday of August, if possible, Father," he said in a pleasant voice.

"Let me check the book," Gordon said, and withdrew a large black appointment book from the top drawer, opened it and looked for the third Saturday in August.

"Yes, that day is available. We can offer you two times, mid-morning and in the afternoon."

"We were thinking about the afternoon."

"Fine, say three o'clock?"

"Perfect."

"The cost will be five hundred dollars, plus extras if you want an organist, music, flowers, et cetera."

"Okay, good. When my fiancée comes back she'll make all those choices."

"Yes, as it should be. Women have strong feelings about such things."

"What a beautiful garden," the killer said, standing up and moving to the window, which was to the left and slightly behind the priest.

"We are proud of it," the priest said, picking up his pen. "And your name?" he asked.

"My name is Coogan."

"And your fiancée?"

"Loretta. Does my name sound familiar?"

"No, I'm sorry. Should it?"

"We knew one another well."

"Really, when? With age it's harder and harder to remember—"

"At Sacred Heart, you remember?"

With that Father Gordon quickly stood up, apprehension suddenly about his long narrow face.

"So you remember . . . I see you remember."

"No, I don't, I'm sorry. How did you find me?"

"It wasn't easy."

"I've changed. I don't do those things any longer. I was confused. I—"

"I have something for you," the man said.

"What's that?"

"This," he said, withdrawing the knife from his black bag. Before the priest could react, the man was on him, covered his mouth with his left hand, pulled back the priest's head and in one swift movement drew the razor-sharp blade across the priest's exposed throat, severing the arteries and windpipe. Blood gushed forth in a pulsating torrent. The priest tried to scream out for help, but his vocal cords were robbed of the breath needed to make sound. The killer brought him to the ground and went to work on him.

Finished, he stood and calmly went looking for the other priests in the rectory. He found one in the kitchen, killed him, found another upstairs in deep prayer and killed him, too. He didn't know if either of these priests were abusers, but that didn't matter. They were, in his mind, an intricate part of the Catholic Church and therefore as guilty as any of the molesters, he thought.

Satisfied, he took a quick shower, carefully washing off the blood he'd gotten on himself. He then calmly put on a change of clothes he had in his bag, made sure to wipe away any fingerprints he might have left in the bathroom and soon left by the rear door. He was in the rectory twenty-three minutes.

Pleased, his plan taking life, dimension and form, he casually walked away from the church, looking forward to his trip. Now they would fear him; now they knew that they had to answer for their sins; now they knew that the systemic raping of thousands of innocents, the lies, their diabolical covering up, their arrogant condescension, would have to be paid for . . . with pain, with fear—with blood.

No priest, no bishop, no cardinal, would be safe. Soon he would leave for Rome, intent upon bringing justice to the very heart of the Catholic Church—to the Vatican. He knew the pope would soon be presiding over a televised Congress of Cardinals from all over the globe, to discuss church policy for the coming year, and he planned to be there and kill the pope in front of the whole world, including the men who were directly responsible for the rampant aiding and abetting of predator priests. He had been planning this and saving for it for a long time now. All was ready, everything in place. He had his ticket, passport, Father Joseph's identification, even an apartment near the Villa Borghese. After he was done, there would be, he was sure, books and films about him, how he made the Church pay for its criminal hypocrisy, and he was pleased. A slight smile played on his full lips as he moved farther away from the Church of Saint Joseph of the Holy Family, thinking about the pope . . . killing him—the slight smile turning to a severe line filled with malice.

TEN

When Tony Flynn arrived at his office in Midtown North that day he found a pile of messages on his desk. The first one he returned was to Carole Cunningham. She told him her boss had reamed her out for what she said at the news conference. That the DA's office was besieged with phone calls, telegrams, letters and e-mails from angry Catholics from all over the country about her remarks. For her "Catholic-bashing," and her "backward priorities." And yet two hundred people so far had phoned to say that they had been victims of sexual abuse at the hands of Catholic priests. Many of these individuals, she said, were coming to the office to give statements—details of what had happened to them.

"But, Tony," she said, "the Supreme Court ruling today crippled us. Did you hear that they just decided that state statutes doing away with time limits regarding sex crimes were illegal? Worst ruling the court ever made far as I'm concerned. Over eight hundred sexual predators will be going free, including many priests convicted of molesting children. And Austin Johnson's walking. Remember that sadistic monster?"

"Who can forget him."

"And the six-year limitation for sex crimes is back in play, which closes the door on ever prosecuting any of these cases. But the priests who abused within the limits, I plan to have arrested immediately; you with me on this—will you back me?"

"To the wall."

"Great, thank you. Having you around makes me feel a hell of a lot better. How'd your meeting go?"

"As well as can be expected."

"I hope I didn't create any kind of heat for you."

"You didn't, don't concern yourself."

"I have that address you wanted."

"That's all right, I won't be needing it."

"Okay," she said, sounding a bit confused.

"Word has already been passed," he explained.

"I see," she said. "Tony, please let me know soon as you find out about the DNA."

"Should know soon. And you let me know how you make out with the victims. Whatever you need, you have—I'm here."

"You're the best. Thank you."

"No, thank you, counselor," he said. The thought of inviting her to dinner briefly crossed his mind, but he didn't ask her. When he hung up he sat there a few minutes thinking about Carole Cunningham. She was, he thought, a hell of a woman, had brains, street smarts, balls, a well-defined sense of fair play, of what was right and wrong, and she was willing to gladly put herself on the line for her beliefs. He wondered if she had a boyfriend. He knew she wasn't married. Any guy, he decided, who hooked up with her was a lucky man.

As he was looking at his messages, his daughter Jacky returned his call. After asking if she felt better—which she said she did—he said: "I understand you were threatened at the courthouse yesterday."

"It was nothing, don't concern yourself—"

"Jacky, something like that should always be taken seriously—particularly when it comes from one of the Chinese gangs. You know how ruthless they can be."

"Of course."

"*Anything* like that ever goes down, I want you to tell me! As well as being your father, I'm your boss—and I'm telling you this as your boss, as an order—you understand?"

"I understand," she said in a small voice, knowing he was right, wondering how the hell he found out so fast. They talked about their planned July 4th get-together and soon hung up. Flynn was about to make himself an iced coffee when he was told that a lawyer from Boston, Bob Shine, who represented Voice of the Faithful—a group of Catholics who banned together to fight the intransigence of the church in Boston—was calling for him. Flynn sat back down and picked up the phone. "Captain Flynn here," he said.

"Thank you for taking my call, Captain. I saw you at the news conference yesterday on CNN. I wanted to call and say thank you for telling it like it is. As well as representing Voice of the Faithful, I represent quite a few victims of abuse by priests. If there is anything I can help you with, please feel free to let me know. The Catholic Church is a very powerful entity with deep pockets and I'm thinking you might very well need some outside assistance."

"Thanks for the offer," Flynn said. "I appreciate it. It's all kinds of mind boggling—how they were able to get away with all this for so long."

"Problem was, still is, the Church hierarchy took the position that they would do anything to avoid scandal and just kept moving pedophile priests from one parish to another, all over the country, and of course, they kept abusing kids. Bernard Hound alone was directly responsible for over two hundred predator priests being allowed to stay in the ministry and not reporting any of the abuse claims to authorities. What he did do was send priests, who were in fact attorneys, to the homes of victims to talk their parents out of pressing any criminal charges, and paid them off. We finally got Hound out of office, but the damage he's done is irreversible—and runs very deep. Many of the victims, in fact all of them, were severely scarred psychologically by what happened, have marital problems, drug and alcohol issues, and every one of them is undergoing therapy. Far as I'm concerned Hound is one of them, I mean a molester, but at this juncture that's just my opinion. In any event, I'm coming to New York next Thursday and was wondering if we can meet."

"Yes, I'd like that," Flynn said, knowing this lawyer had a treasure trove of first-hand information that could help him in many ways, on numerous levels.

"If possible, I'd like to take you to lunch," the lawyer offered.

"That would be nice," Flynn said, and they made plans to meet at The Tavern on the Green in Central Park at 1:30 Thursday.

When Flynn hung up, he again stood to make himself coffee, but Sergeant Salerno burst into the office, wide-eyed and all excited, and said "Captain, we just got word that three priests were murdered at the Church of Saint Joseph at Mulberry and Prince. All of them had their throats cut."

"Three?" Flynn asked, incredulous.

"Three!"

"Let's go," the captain said, no longer tired, adrenaline kicking in, and he was up and out of the office. He and Salerno jumped into a black Ford, turned on the siren and sped downtown. As Salerno drove, Flynn made calls, ordered the crime scene sealed, demanded that no one, not even cops, be allowed in the rectory; ordered tech people to the scene, and a mobile command center to be parked in front. He then called Carole Cunningham, got her on the line and made plans to meet her at the crime scene. He also called his boss and left a message on his cell phone.

Somehow, this didn't surprise Flynn—the fact that multiple priests had been killed, he would later say. He knew that the killer of the first two priests had a searing hatred inside him, but what did surprise him and caught him off guard, was that he struck twice in one day, only hours apart.

When they arrived at the Church of Saint Joseph of the Holy Family, hundreds of neighborhood people and a crowd of reporters had already gathered at the crime scene tape.

Flynn listened to the uniformed cops tell how they had responded to a 911 call. The gardener for the grounds, they explained, entered the rectory through a rear door and found a priest in the kitchen. They then carefully searched the house, thinking the perp might still be on the premises, they explained, and found the other murdered priests.

"Captain," the older of the two said. "He didn't just kill them, he cut them up in pieces, and he castrated them. I never saw anything like this, and I've been on the job twenty years . . . a massacre, a fucking massacre, sir. It looks more like a wild animal did it than a human being. When we realized what we had, we backtracked out, called it in and sealed the scene."

"You did everything right," Flynn said. He took a long deep breath, smelling death in the air and turned to Salerno. "Let's you and I first take a look-see, then we'll bring in the tech people. Come on."

He turned and, careful about where they put their feet, the two hardened, seasoned homicide men slowly made their way around to the back of the rectory and found the rear door wide open. A gray fist of gnats hovered at the threshold. There was no blood on any of the four steps that led directly into the kitchen, a large country-type affair with a well-worn butcher-block table, all manner of worn pots and pans hanging from hooks, food still cooking on the stove, herbs growing in small pots lining the windowsills. They found the first priest on the kitchen floor, his stomach cut open, his organs all over the floor, his heart sitting right on the butcher-block table. The smell was horrific; a heavy odor of blood and human waste wrapped itself around them. Bottleneck flies fed on him. Flynn moved closer, took a long look at how the priest's throat had been cut . . .

"Definitely him," he said. "The wound's identical."

"We've got a real monster here, Captain."

They next found Gordon. He had been even more mutilated, they noted. Flynn saw the appointment book still open on the desk, covered with thick, drying blood. They checked the rest of the ground level of the house, found nothing more, moved upstairs where they discovered the other priest, so mutilated he didn't quite resemble a human being any longer.

"To do this, the killer had to be covered with blood," Flynn said. "Let's look in the bathroom." They walked down the hall and found the bathroom. It was obvious someone had recently showered, and when they looked closer they discerned pinkish drops of water about the tub. They both knew it was blood.

"So he took a shower and no doubt brought a change of clothes," Flynn noted. "An *organized killer*, as they call them down at Quantico."

"You call the Feds yet, Captain?"

"I was just going to when you came into my office. We have to prepare our people for this. Frank, I want no one in here but those who are absolutely necessary, clear?"

"Clear."

"All kind of brass are going to show up to put their two cents in and get their pictures taken, and I want all of them kept out. Except Chief Samuels. Anybody breaks your balls let me know."

"Will do."

"I want this whole place worked over thoroughly. Pick three teams of our guys to look over the techs' shoulders. Let's get to work," Flynn said. They slowly made their way back downstairs, not touching anything, Flynn imagining the killer moving about the house, going about his grisly tasks. Flynn had seen thousands of murder victims over the years. People who had been shot and stabbed and run over, drowned, beaten to death, blown up, hung, poisoned, but he'd never seen the concentrated savagery that had been perpetrated on these priests.

Thankful to be back outside breathing fresh air, Flynn quickly put together the teams of technicians that would work the crime scene, personnel from the Medical Examiner's office and the homicide detectives who would actually work the rectory. They were to look for clues, carefully search all the priests' residences, computers, closets. He gathered them all under the dappled shade of a giant maple tree in the south corner of the rear yard, just next to the fig tree. Already, news helicopters were buzzing overhead. Flynn looked up and there were reporters and cameramen lined along the roofs of buildings across the street from the rectory. Knowing cameramen with long-distance lenses might get shots of some of the bodies through the windows, he ordered Salerno to have uniformed people go up on the roofs and clear the press and onlookers. The last thing he wanted to see was a photograph of one of the dead priests on the front page of a newspaper. *The Post* or *The National Enquirer*, he knew, would pay well for such a shot.

"Okay, listen up, people," Flynn said. "I want to prepare you for what's inside. Three priests have been murdered and mutilated, eviscerated and castrated. I'm telling you now if anyone here has a weak stomach, don't go inside. We'll find someone else to do the job. I won't hold it against you. . . . Anyone want out?" Each of them stayed put, sixteen people in all. As Flynn spoke Dr. Richard Russo from the Medical Examiner's office arrived with Carole Cunningham. They entered the grounds and cautiously made their way to where Flynn and the others had gathered. Flynn greeted them, then continued: "Needless to say, these murders are going to be front-page news all over the world, and it's up to us, the NYPD, to break this case . . . to stop this man.

"I'm telling you all right now that this case absolutely has top priority. It comes before all things you might have been working on. Any of you need anything, let me know. Don't concern yourselves with overtime. The commissioner has authorized all the overtime pay necessary to get the job done. And done properly. From here on in I want all of you, the people here, to stay on this case. Make certain that no one from your respective units responds to any of these crimes. I am forming a task force to deal with this and you all are part of it as of right now. You will report to me directly. In that the first killing happened at Saint Mary's, we're going to call ourselves 'The Saint Mary's Task Force.' Most important, people: I don't want any of you talking to reporters under any circumstances. All information regarding this case will be issued to the press via me and proper channels. This is very important; if I find out any one of you is leaking to the media you are off the case, and I'll personally make

sure departmental charges are brought against you." He
let his words sink in, then continued, "I want to introduce
you all to ADA Carole Cunningham and Dr. Richard
Russo´from the Medical Examiner's office. ADA Cunningham will be prosecuting the case. Okay, let's do it,"
he said.

They all silently made their way inside the rectory,
Flynn leading the way, telling each technician what he
wanted done. These were all hard-nosed, steely-eyed professionals, but none of them was quite prepared for the
carnage that greeted them. Before anything, Flynn had
each body and the place where it had been found photographed from numerous angles and videotaped. Carole
helped direct the video technicians because it would be
she using these ghastly images in court, in front of a jury,
when they caught the killer. When both she and Flynn
were satisfied that they had all they wanted on film, the
fingerprint people began doing their job.

The killer again left a footprint in blood in several of the
rooms and Flynn made sure they were properly lifted,
knowing that these prints would indisputably put the
killer at the scene. The footprints were identical to the
print found on the altar at Our Lady of Miracles Church.
Silently, they each went about their assigned tasks. The
rectory was not air conditioned and the temperature was
in the mid-nineties. Sweat covered all of their faces, stained
their shirts and blouses, and the smell was horrific.

Chief Medical Examiner Russo carefully viewed each of
the bodies: the wounds to their throats, the cuts that severed limbs, eviscerated the bodies. When he was done, he
called Flynn over to the priest found in the kitchen. "Captain, for sure the same man who killed the two priests uptown killed these men. The cuts to their throats, this
stab-slash wound, are virtually the same," he confirmed
and soon went upstairs to examine the priest killed there.

Flynn went back outside and designated six teams of detectives to question neighborhood people.

"If anyone saw anything, I want you to locate them and find out exactly what they saw. Don't be shy," he told them.

Chief Samuels arrived. Tony took him inside and walked him through the crime scene and they went back outside. Chief Samuels, pale, obviously upset, said, "I don't have to tell you the field day the media's going to have with this. Tony, spare no expense here, use all the people you need—this madman's got to be stopped and stopped quickly! What do you think he used to cut them up like that?"

"Dr. Russo says a meat cleaver and a sharp, curved blade."

"Never saw anything like that . . . not even in 'Nam. Looked like some kind of berserk animal did it. Not a human being."

"I'm thinking we might very well be looking for someone recently released from a mental institution," Flynn said. "He's obviously not playing with a full deck."

"I'm getting too old for this," Samuels said. "Between me and you Tony, I'm thinking of retiring. I . . . I've been having dizzy spells. After a time police work in this city—I guess any big city, can be a very unhealthy thing, you know."

"John, don't go anywhere until this case is resolved. Promise me that. I need you."

"I'm with you on this one."

"Good to hear. I hate to think of who the general would replace you with. He doesn't know diddly-squat about what real police work is."

"I'm seeing this through."

"Captain!" one of the detectives called from the rear doorway. Her name was Barbara Green. She was a short, red-faced woman who wore thick glasses, and was one of the best criminalists the NYPD ever had, Flynn knew.

"Don't let me hold you, go ahead," the Chief said. "I'm going to phone the commissioner and tell him what we've got here."

Flynn walked up the stairs to the kitchen.

"What's up, Barbara?" he asked.

"The perp definitely showered when he was finished with the murders. I opened the shower drain and found some fresh strands of long thick black hair that doesn't match any of the victims here. I already compared them," she said, holding up a cigarette pack–sized Ziploc plastic bag with several long strands of black hair inside.

"I'd say," she said, "he's got hair down to his shoulders."

"The witness we found uptown said he had long black hair."

"Well, here it is," she said, handing it to the captain. He took a long careful look at the hairs, wondering where the head that belonged to these hairs was right now. And what was going on inside that head to make him capable of doing such barbarous things.

II

DRAGON SEED

ELEVEN

Later that same day the killer took an Alitalia flight to Milan, Italy. He had never been on a plane before and it was an unsettling experience for him. Flying on a Jumbo 747, he had a window seat and he marveled at how the huge craft lumbered out to the takeoff runway, going faster and faster and was suddenly in the air, directly over the Great Jamaica Bay. The sun was melting into the horizon and set the bay on fire, as the huge craft sharply banked east, toward Europe.

The plane was full and there were a number of priests on the New York to Milan flight. He bristled at the sight of these men.

Several times he was even tempted to go over to one of the priests and ask how he could be a member of a Church that allowed the sexual abuse of children, but he controlled himself, sat patiently reading the book on Rome he had bought just last week. He loved books. He loved to read. They had been his salvation. He never had intimate relationships with people. He had intimate relationships with books.

All the years he'd been in Creedmoore State Hospital for the criminally insane, he had fantasized about this trip, going to Rome and taking revenge for all those who had been violated by *real wolves in sheep's clothing*, as he thought of them.

For him this trip was a dream come true, and he often put down his book and reviewed in his mind what he would do and how he would do it. How he would dress, present himself. How he would get the pope's security to allow him to get close enough to the pope to use his knife. It was made of cinicum plastic, which was harder than steel, scalpel sharp, and could not be detected by metal detectors. He had stowed it in his luggage and would use it on the pope, watch him fall to the floor, blood gushing from his severed arteries.

Soon the stewardess served dinner. He had chicken and a half bottle of white wine. He normally didn't drink alcohol, but the smiling stewardess with the pretty Italian eyes said it was free and so he took it.

Often, he wondered about his own origins; he never knew either of his parents, their names, what they looked like, where they came from. He had been brought up in homes for orphaned children run by the Catholic Church, and the priests would never answer his questions about who his parents were, where he came from. How he got there. The name of the institute where he had been kept the longest was the Sacred Heart of Jesus Home for Boys in upstate New York, where Fathers Joseph, Bernard and Gordon had all once worked.

When he was twelve, he managed to sneak into the records office. He wanted so very badly to find out who his parents were, where his mother lived, sure that if they knew what was being done to him—how he was forced to commit sex acts on the priests who worked at the home, and many priests who just came to the home because they had access to the many boys who had no one to complain to, turn to, ask for help—his parents would rescue him, go to the police . . . tell someone.

For the longest time, he thought what he was experiencing at Sacred Heart was normal. That all children in all places were forced to do such things, but after a while he realized that he was a prisoner in a place controlled by sadistic sexual degenerates, and for hours every day he prayed to Jesus and Mary that the abuse would stop; that he would be taken away from the home. But his prayers were never answered and he came to believe that there was no God, no Mary, no heaven. No hell. That all those things had been made up by evil men in the Church so they could control and manipulate the masses to do as they said, the way they said it, when they said it. *Don't eat meat on Friday; don't curse; don't lie; don't steal; don't masturbate.* Yet the priests were beasts who only wanted one thing—sex from the children in their charge, he came to realize.

Sitting on the plane on this night, he remembered the time he snuck into the records office and a priest found him looking through the files. He was taken to the basement where he was tied to a beam in the ceiling, regularly used for such things. He was whipped, then sodomized by two priests, one after the other, until he bled, all the while the priests threatening him with God, with damnation, for *his sins*, for his disobedience . . . further fueling the seeds of insanity, which had already been planted inside his head.

They left him in the basement tied to the beam the whole night. No food. No water. And all during that time he planned and plotted to kill the priests who had raped him, and when he was big and strong enough that's exactly what he did. To gain his tormentors' trust, to be able to get them to relax their guards, he became like them, an abuser. He did all he was told with alacrity and enthusiasm, even abusing, as he was ordered, boys when they were first brought to the home, teaching them what was expected of them, having sex with them as the priests and men in civilian clothes filmed them.

These films, he later found out, were sold to pedophiles all around the world for profit, in Amsterdam and Hamburg, New York and San Francisco, he knew. When his abusers believed he was truly one of them, he struck.

As a bald priest in a seat three rows in front of him stood to use the restroom at the rear of the plane, he snapped out of his reverie. The sight of the priest's clerical collar caused hot blood to flush his cheeks. Oh, how he was tempted to follow the priest to the john and choke the life out of him; but he'd wait. He'd be patient and cunning, not rash and foolhardy. He had made that mistake once before and had been put away for twenty-one years because of it. That would not happen again.

After the stewardess served dinner, they showed *Finding Nemo*, and he enjoyed watching it on the little screen built into his seat.

After the film, they turned down the overhead lights and people began to dose. He didn't think he could sleep. His mind kept going back to the murders he had committed and he was pleased, knowing that his revenge had begun; that his carefully thought out plans had finally taken form. Though, he knew, it was just the beginning, that before he was done the world would know him as the one who had the courage to strike back at the corrupt Church.

While he was at Creedmoore, he read every book he could get his hands on about serial killers, had studied their successes and failures, and he was now putting to use the lessons he garnered from studying killers, even the texts written by former and present FBI agents out of the Behavioral Science Unit at Quantico, Virginia.

He soon fell asleep and dreamed about his tortured childhood. He often had the same dream and in it his tormentors burned in hell . . . their screams a beautiful chorus.

When he woke up, dawn was just breaking. The captain announced that they would soon be landing, said the temperature in Milan was eighty-seven degrees Farenheit, the skies clear. The stewardesses served breakfast—coffee, fruit and cereal—and he very much enjoyed being given food by smiling, pleasant people who wanted nothing in return, a rare experience for him.

Most of the priests on the flight now stood up to freshen themselves in the lavatory, passing him as they went.

To keep from thinking about them, he looked out the window, excited about being in a new place, far away from the nightmare that his life had been. He smiled. Something he did not often do. He was, in fact, a particularly good-looking man with naturally oversized lips, high, well-formed cheekbones, large almond-shaped eyes, a triangular-shaped face framed by long straight black hair. Often, he knew, women stared at him, their eyes slowly following him. As a boy he had been a particularly beautiful child, hence the reason he had been so obsessively put upon, in such demand, by the deviant predators that had always surrounded him.

He never had a girlfriend. All things related to love, affection, compassion, sex, were foreign and obscene to him. His sexuality was a confused cacophony of morbidity, sadism and anger. He was certain his childhood had much to do with the way he was, but he often wondered if, perhaps, there was something in his makeup, his genes, that made him the way he was.

At Creedmoore State Hospital he had seen many psychiatrists over the years, but had never truly opened up to them, told them what he'd been through, saw, was made to do. All he was concerned with was making the doctors believe he was cured, that he was fit to be back in society; and therefore he kept his mouth shut and told the psychiatrists what they wanted to hear, and in the end it worked because they pronounced him *cured* and set him free. That was two years, nearly to the day, before he killed Father Joseph at Saint Mary's Church on 39th Street.

The huge plane slowly rolled to the left and approached the landing strip. The landing made him nervous and he tightened his seatbelt, grabbed the seat arms and held them tight. He had read somewhere that the most dangerous time of airplane flights was when the plane took off and landed—and in the back of his mind somewhere he was thinking that *maybe* God would punish him. Force the plane to crash because of what he did. Because of what he planned to do. But the plane landed so smoothly he didn't even realize it had touched down until people applauded the fine landing and he looked out the window. The sun shone. The Italian sky was cloudless and very blue. They were twenty minutes early. As the 747 taxied to the Alitalia terminal, he gathered his things, anxious and in a hurry to get to Rome. Waiting his turn to disembark, he thought about the pope, his plan to get close to him—the lesson he would teach all the corrupt power-hungry perverts who had taken charge of the Catholic Church.

He soon disembarked and walked to the processing area, where he showed his passport, which he had acquired with stolen identification, and he was allowed to enter Italy. He walked down a flight of stairs to the area where the luggage carousels were located. Here he had to stand right next to priests waiting for their luggage. The little hairs on the nape of his muscular neck stood on edge. But he didn't say anything. He kept a calm demeanor, and he was proud of himself—the control he was able to wield over his emotions. A bona fide schizophrenic, it was not easy for him to marshal his emotions, to keep his feelings in check.

His luggage was one of the first pieces down. He grabbed it and made his way outside without being stopped or challenged. Though he had slept only a few hours, he was not tired at all.

Outside, it was warm, but the air was crisp and clean and there was a nice breeze. He walked to the domestic terminal, bought a ticket on an Alpi Eagle flight to Rome for 76 euros, found the gate and soon boarded the plane.

He figured that by flying to Rome via Milan he would avoid the eventual police scrutiny of all recently arrived males in Rome from New York, if he managed to get away after killing the pope. He knew exactly where the pope would soon be and he had detailed maps, blueprints and diagrams of all the Vatican's buildings; its underground catacombs and grounds, to aid in his escape.

The flight from Milan to Rome was only fifty minutes. When he disembarked, he was able to walk outside without showing his passport. There was a taxi strike and he had to take a bus to Rome proper. He marveled at the landscape, the gentle, rolling hills, the pastel-colored houses, the tall elegant cypress trees.

An attractive woman took the seat next to him. She was tall with auburn hair and green eyes. She tried to strike up a conversation with him, but he wasn't interested in talking with anyone, though he was taken by her beauty. She said her name was Diane. That she was an American writer working on a novel that took place in Rome. He wanted to tell her how he loved to read, how reading had helped him escape his confinement, how he learned about the world through books; but he said nothing of all this, and she fell silent.

As the bus drew closer to Rome, the Colosseum suddenly loomed large and real and he stared at it in absolute wonder. He had always been fascinated by ancient Rome, the Colosseum, the incredible violence, bloodletting and sexual sadism that went on inside its four-story, 157-foot walls. He imagined gladiators fighting to the death, men and women being fed to wild carnivores, tigers and lions and bears, the extreme debauchery, all things that excited him and stirred his imagination—and aroused him sexually. He sometimes had hallucinations, which to him were as real and tangible as his right hand.

He had read that beautiful women and girls— disgraced vestal virgins and females taken from conquered lands—were bound to thick wooden posts in the center of the Colosseum and that the scent of female bulls in heat was wiped on their sex and that male bulls would become aroused and have intercourse with the bound women, actually killing the women as they did so—all the while the crowds screaming lustfully, cheering on the sight. He also read that up to five hundred prostitutes were always waiting under the Colosseum to have sex with the Romans who became aroused by all the violence, the bloodlust that he believed was a much-denied, inherent part of human nature; the Romans of old, he also believed, knew how to live, were honest and not ashamed of their own sexuality. Until, of course, the hateful you-must-do-as-I-say Christians came along, and the Emperor Flavius Valerius Constantinus, known as Constantine the Great, put an end to the gladiatorial contests and the operatic violence.

He stared, transfixed, at the honey-colored Colosseum, his mind playing over things he read about what had occurred in the Colosseum, seeing the images before his eyes until it disappeared out of sight. It would be one of the first places he visited, he resolved.

The bus dropped him off at Via Crescenzio, a wide thoroughfare which ran directly to Vatican City. It was much warmer in Rome than Milan, nearly one hundred degrees, and the fierce Roman sun blazed in a cloudless sky. He walked to the apartment he rented on the northeast side of the Villa Borghese, on Via Corelli, in a four-story limestone, nothing fancy. He knew that once it all began, the police would be checking hotels and pensions for men recently arrived from New York, and it would be just a matter of time before he was found out. He had, therefore, devised a simple though clever scheme in which he rented the apartment over the Internet through a real estate outfit based in Venice. He had presented himself as a Canadian citizen, paid for the apartment for one month with a one-month deposit—1600 euros—using Wells Fargo money orders. He had the keys sent to a P.O. Box in Montreal, then had them mailed to him in New York.

The apartment was on the top floor, in the back of the building. It had a small terrace, a kitchen and bath. It was clean and bright and would serve him well, he was sure.

He carefully unpacked his things. The knife he would use to cut the pope's throat was undisturbed. Highly illegal because it was made out of plastic harder than steel, he had bought it online from an underground chat room set up by a German paramilitary group known as The Red Way. The identification he had taken from Father Joseph—his photo replacing Joseph's—was also undisturbed in a secret compartment he had carefully cut into the suitcase. He would use the identification to gain unencumbered access to the Vatican. Pleased, he got down on the floor and did one hundred push-ups, then one hundred sit-ups. All the years he'd been in Creedmoore State Hospital he had done thousands of push-ups and sit-ups every week. He knew he would have to be physically strong to do what he planned, and now his body was lean and muscular. He showered and went looking for the disguise he would use.

He found exactly what he wanted in one of the many shops that catered to church personnel in the area of the Vatican. He purchased two priest's outfits—one white, one black—skirts, summer blouses and two stiff, white clerical collars. Carrying his purchases, he walked slowly to St. Peter's Square and marveled at its size, splendor and grandeur. He stood there for the longest time just staring at the magnificent square and St. Peter's Basilica, watching thousands of sweating tourists from all over the globe who came to visit and be inspired by the most famous Catholic church in all the world. He found a place in the shade and studied through cold, dark, hate-filled eyes the Vatican—the place, he knew, that was truly responsible for everything, all his problems; for the unspeakable things that had been done to him. There were posted signs around the square announcing in seven languages the Congress of Cardinals the pope would be addressing.

He took a long deep breath and walked south along Via Gregorio toward the main entrance of Vatican City. He soon realized that the whole of Vatican City was surrounded by seventeen-foot-high brick walls, that there were security cameras mounted in strategic places along the unwelcoming walls every fifty feet. At the main entrance to the Vatican he stopped. Armed guards carrying machine guns were checking identification as people—priests and nuns and workmen who were employed in the Vatican—drove and walked onto the grounds. He didn't want to be conspicuous so he crossed the street and entered a trattoria, ordered an espresso and took a seat facing the Vatican entrance. He solemnly sat there studying how thorough the guards were, looking for weaknesses.

Pleased, he immediately realized that there was a constant flow of priests in and out of the Vatican and that their identification was only quickly looked at, and many times no one checked ID at all, which some priests wore around their white-collared necks in see-through wallets. After an hour, he left the restaurant and continued south and walked around all of Vatican City.

It was, he quickly realized, an impregnable fortress built to keep out hostile, invading forces and assassins. There was a half-mile-long line of tourists waiting to get into the famous Sistine Chapel. He wanted very much to see the chapel, but would not stand on any line. He boldly made his way to the front of the queue and walked right in, nobody challenging him as he went. He paid €15 and walked in, admiring the statues, paintings and marble works he passed. He stopped at a window that afforded a good view of the Vatican grounds. He could see the pope's residence and the building where the pope would soon be addressing the cardinals, the St. Augustus auditorium. Workmen were carrying chairs inside the building. He knew if he could get onto the Vatican grounds, he'd have no problem entering the hall and getting next to the pope. He knew, too, that the pope, when he was up to it, gave a mass every Wednesday at 5:00 AM, and that he had weekly audiences with the public. He walked on with the tourists and soon found himself in the Sistine Chapel, amazed and in awe at the brilliant work of Michelangelo. Another man who had been victimized by the church . . . and had himself been an abuser . . .

He knew through his many years of studying the Catholic Church that Michelangelo was a dedicated pedophile; that he lusted after young boys and that he had been arrested and jailed in Florence several times for having sex with minors, all of which Pope Julius II used to get Michelangelo to make the superhuman effort to do the chapel ceiling. Michelangelo's own guilt and the diaboli-

cal machinations of Pope Julius II, he knew, drove
Michelangelo to create one of the most extraordinary
works of art in the sordid history of mankind. He had begun the ceiling in 1508 and finished it, for the most part,
in 1512, leaving him with severe arthritis in his right
hand, neck and spine. When Michelangelo died, his hand
was little more than a twisted claw because of his work on
the chapel ceiling.

Standing among the gawking tourists and looking up at
the glorious magnificence of the chapel—its brilliant
depth, the incredible colors, the very real emotion on the
faces—he felt strangely moved, thinking maybe a supernatural entity had assisted Michelangelo, for it truly
seemed like some kind of miraculous force had been at
work here.

When he looked back down and began to leave the
chapel, he saw the red-headed woman who had sat next to
him on the bus from Rome, the writer. She spotted him,
smiled and waved; he smiled, nodded curtly, turned and
left the chapel.

As he made his way to the exit, he passed windows
that opened onto the inner sanctum of the Vatican; its
lush, impeccably well-manicured grounds, the three
domes of St. Peter's Basilica. It all looked more like the
home of a very wealthy aristocrat, a king, than a place of
spiritual pursuits, the heart of the most popular religion
of all time.

He soon left the Vatican, and went and bought a plastic
wallet, then returned to his rented apartment and tried on
the priest's outfits and collars. They fit him perfectly. Hesitantly, he looked at himself in the mirror and was
shocked to see his face above the stiff white collar he hated
so much, but it would serve him well today, he knew. He
put on the white cassack, carefully combed his hair, stud-

ied a blueprint of the building where the pope would be speaking, again practiced walking with his shoulders rounded, retrieved his knife and Father Joseph's doctored identification. He also took with him several hundred euro notes and maps of the Vatican grounds, then went back out and returned to the Vatican. As he drew near the front gate, he put Joseph's ID in the plastic wallet attached to a thin chain around his neck and boldly walked to the Vatican entrance. The guards saw him coming and he smiled pleasantly, humbly bowing his head somewhat. They waved him in without questioning him. He was not nervous at all. He was on a righteous mission he was intent upon completing. He walked straight to the Saint Augustus auditorium, a two-story dome-shaped structure. The pope, he knew, would just be arriving. There were more steely-eyed guards at the entrance, but they too waved him in. Inside, he found the door that led directly to the basement. He walked two hundred feet, went up a flight of stone steps, opened another door and he was at the back of the stage on which the pope was now talking, greeting the cardinals. He moved to the left side and could suddenly see the pope. He was sitting in a special wheelchair at the edge of the stage, addressing the cardinals in a weak though firm voice, animatedly moving his hands as he spoke. The pope's aides were standing to the left and right of him. He was a mere twenty feet away from the pope now. All was working perfectly. His heart raced as he stared at the pope—hatred filling his eyes, turning his face to a rigid mask of chiseled stone. He knew he had to move swiftly and decisively, have the knife already in his hand when he made his attack.

Staring at the place on the pope's neck where he would stab him, he reached for the blade and slowly drew it out.

No one noticed him. All eyes were on the pope. His body was like a coiled spring now, as lethal as a cocked pistol with a hair trigger. He waited for the right moment. Sweat covering the wide expanse of his high brow slowly ran down his face.

TWELVE

In New York, foreboding, lead-gray clouds had gathered in the skies. The temperature suddenly dropped. Strong winds off the rivers blew the stifling heat up and away. People could breathe now, move with some bounce in their step. With the sudden change in temperature, lightning tore open the darkening skies and thunder boomed over the Church of Saint Joseph of the Holy Family as if giant cannons had been discharged. Soon a heavy rain fell, further cooling the steaming streets and sidewalks.

Tony Flynn was thankful for the rain, the pleasant breeze and cooler weather. It made being in the rectory somewhat more tolerable. Because there had been three murders at one time in one location it took many hours for the crime scene to be properly worked.

When Flynn's detectives searched the priests' living quarters, they didn't find any kind of contraband. However, when they searched Monsignor Dreyfus's apartment, they did find personal ads and newsletters from NAMBLA, and pornographic images of young boys on his computer and on disks he had locked in his desk. Some of these images, Flynn quickly realized, were of priests who had been murdered there that day. When the monsignor arrived at the parish, Tony Flynn himself cuffed him and read him his rights.

And when neighborhood people saw the monsignor, a heavyset, supercilious individual with several chins, handcuffed and taken away in a police car, they booed him and threw eggs and tomatoes at him.

Apparently, Flynn soon found out, the monsignor had been accused of molesting neighborhood boys whose families had accepted money and expensive gifts not to bring police charges against him.

When Flynn's detectives finished working the crime scene, Flynn allowed personnel from the morgue to remove the bodies for autopsy. He ordered the whole of the church grounds sealed and posted uniformed cops to make sure no reporters entered the crime scene.

ADA Carole Cunningham had never left the scene. Flynn said it wasn't necessary for her to be there; that he would keep her abreast of all that happened, but she said she wanted to see and know everything with her own eyes. He admired her dedication and professionalism.

With curious, observant eyes Carole took in all that was done; how Tony Flynn didn't miss anything. Watching him work, she thought, was like taking a course in how to properly work a crime scene.

When they were finally ready to leave, Flynn offered to drive Carole home. She lived in the same building as his daughter Jacky, on Hudson Street. She said yes and they left together. In the car on the way to her place, she asked him if he'd like a nightcap.

"Excellent idea," he said.

"Have you eaten?"

"Truth is I didn't have time."

"Want to grab a bite, too? I know a nice little place that's open all night."

"Sure, I'd like that," he said, remembering that all he'd eaten the whole day was a piece of pizza on the run.

They didn't talk much about the murders now, the arrest of Monsignor Dreyfus, though Flynn did tell her he was attending the priests' autopsies in the morning. She said she'd like to come, if he didn't mind.

"I don't mind, no," he said. "But are you sure you want to see them . . . they can be very, you know, unsettling."

"Truth is I've always wanted to see one but never really had the chance."

"Sure. I'll bring you in."

The name of the restaurant was Chez Louise. It was a quaint French bistro on Hudson Street, a block south of Carole's place. It was surprisingly crowded given the hour, but Carole said the food was good and reasonably priced; that a lot of people ate there after partying at one of the many clubs in the area.

Tony was used to eating dinner at all hours because of the midnight-to-eight shift he had often worked over the years. They found an empty booth that was comfortable and roomy. Tony ordered a dry gin martini, she a vodka martini. There was soft classical music coming from speakers above their table. The drinks were served. They touched glasses.

"To catching him," Carole said.

"Yeah, to catching him," Tony said and downed half his drink, enjoying the slow gin warmth as the alcohol hit his stomach and began to spread through his system. They ordered dinner, he filet of sole, she a mushroom omelet. "You mind talking shop?" he asked.

"Not at all."

"It's ironic because for the longest time I've been thinking sooner or later someone was going to start killing priests like this. I had a dream about it just a few weeks ago."

"There have been some isolated killings across the country. A man was convicted of killing a priest in

Rockville Center just last month. But nothing like this . . . on this scale, with this kind of savagery."

"I'm calling the FBI in the morning. At this point we have enough to get a good profile on him."

"What about the composite drawing?"

"I'm thinking . . . I'm thinking in lieu of what happened today we better get it out there. What are your thoughts?"

"I think he's on a mission to kill priests and won't stop until he's dead or in jail; and yes, I agree with you, at this point the sooner we give it to the press the better."

"I'll have our P.R. department distribute it in the morning. The reward money is up to fifty large now and that'll help for sure. I'm still hoping we have his DNA on file."

"I'll bet you my condo we are looking for someone who was severely abused by a priest as a child."

"No doubt," he said, and ordered himself another drink. She took a glass of chardonnay. Their dinner was served. "I've been wondering how a sharp lawyer like you ended up in the DA's office?" he asked.

"Ever since I was a child I wanted to . . . this might sound a bit over-used, but I wanted to help. To make the world a safer place; and working as a prosecutor, putting my trial talents to that use seemed to be the best way to do that. True, the money's not good, but Tony, you have no idea the satisfaction I get by putting away a sexual predator where they can't hurt anyone anymore. As you well know, there are real monsters out there, twisted cunning individuals who know how to work the system; who know how not to leave clues and evidence. I prosecuted one rapist who approached all his victims—teenage girls—from behind. In twenty-seven attacks, not one victim ever saw his face. We finally got a look at him because of a security camera in a laundry room. The day the jury brought back a guilty verdict, I felt ten feet tall, knowing that sadistic creep would never hurt another girl. . . .

And you, Tony, how'd you end up in law enforcement, if you don't mind my asking?"

"I was born to be a cop. My father, his father and his father were all cops. It's in our genes. Ever since I was a kid I wanted to put away bad guys, and like you, I find the work satisfying. I mean it's not about a paycheck for me. It's always been something more. We, the police, are the first and last lines of defense against anarchy. We are what keeps the wheels of a civilized society moving smoothly. Far as I'm concerned, I've got the best job in the world."

"You still feel like that even on a day like this?"

"More so at a time like this, because something like this brings home in living color how bad it can be—the kind of cold-blooded killers moving around freely. Today it's someone killing priests; tomorrow it'll be someone killing old ladies; and next week it can be someone torturing and killing children.

"We live in an exceedingly dangerous, inequitable world and unless the bad guys are kept in check, and at bay, which is all we could ever really hope for, it won't be safe to leave your own home. It's not just New York. It's the same in any big city anywhere in the world. I've been meaning to ask you, where are you from?"

"Born and raised in San Francisco, the North Beach section."

"Great city."

"I love it, miss it very much."

"How'd you end up in New York?"

"I applied to Columbia Law School and they accepted me on a full scholarship."

"How come?"

"My grades—I had a 4.0. And I graduated Columbia first in my class, applied to the District Attorney's office and they accepted me right off the bat."

"First in your class at Columbia, I'm impressed. I'm

sure you could have gone to work in any of the major law firms."

"Fact is I received offers from quite a few of the top firms around the country."

"You have brothers, sisters?"

"I'm an only child," she said, and Tony saw a sudden sadness come into her eyes.

A naturally inquisitive man, he said, "What kind of childhood did you have, if you don't mind my asking?"

"Not good," she said . . . and nothing more.

"How so?" he pressed, hoping he wasn't being rude, making her uncomfortable. He didn't want to do that.

"I lost my father when I was six in a car accident and my mother re-married two years later, and the man she married was a creep . . . a manipulative, abusive alcoholic. I left home soon as I could. He was, in fact, one of the reasons I came to school out east. . . . Truth is he was *the* reason," she added, became tight-lipped, her deep brown eyes seeming to ice over.

This was a subject Carole rarely spoke of or thought about. A long time ago she had repressed what had happened, filing it deep into her subconscious somewhere. But as she sat there now, on this night in that place, images, sights, sounds and even odors, crept back to her, unsettling her. She moved uncomfortably in her seat, finished her wine and asked for another. Flynn ordered a martini. He sensed she wanted to talk, though wouldn't unless he encouraged her, let her know he genuinely wanted to hear; that he cared.

"How was he abusive?" he asked. "I hope I'm not being nosey."

"You aren't being nosey," she said. "He was a traveling salesman and whenever he came back from a trip he'd have great gifts for me—fancy dolls and clothes, shoes, all kinds of things. At first I thought he was the nicest person in the world, you know, and I was just nuts about him. When I used to see him coming up the walk, I'd jump around like an excited puppy. After he gave me my gifts he would always ask for a kiss, and one day when I went to kiss him on the cheek he kissed me with . . . he really kissed me. As if I were a grown woman, his wife, you know. My mother wasn't home. She had a part-time job in a bank on Columbus Avenue and I didn't know what to do . . . how to react, and so I . . . I kind of kissed him back. And the next thing I knew he was . . . this is very hard for me. It's something I never really told anyone, except my mother later on and she didn't believe me. He convinced me that he loved me and what he was doing should be our 'golden secret' and until I was . . . I was fourteen years old he was sexually abusing me. My mother wouldn't believe her precious husband would do such a thing. I started running away, and in the end I went and lived with my grandmother, my father's mother—the sweetest, most giving person I've ever known, and because of her, her love, her understanding, her encouragement, I managed to get past what happened and find a life for myself. I guess, in the end, that's why I became such a good student: I buried myself in schoolwork, studying, reading books, and stayed away from boys."

Tony took a long deep breath and, in turn, told her how he had been abused by a priest in the Bronx where he was an altar boy, surprising himself that he was telling another person about the incident that had happened so long ago. A lifetime ago. He hadn't even told his wife, he was so uncomfortable about what had occurred.

"And that," he said, "was, what, forty-eight years ago. I always thought he was just a sick creep but realized, more or less only recently that there are a lot of priests out there doing such things. It's a hell of a thing, destroying a wide-eyed kid's trust like that, their relationship with God, with the Church, with spirituality. After that I wouldn't even go into a church anymore. Even when I was married and my girls were baptized, I only entered the church reluctantly. To this day, I don't like being in one." He finished his drink and ordered still another. She reached over and took his hand. Their eyes locked. They slowly moved toward one another and they kissed, there in the booth like that, like two teenagers. Tony had never kissed a woman other than his wife, Jane. Kissing Carole Cunningham there in public was, for him, a strange, unusual thing, though he enjoyed it very much. He soon called for the check. She insisted on paying it. He walked her home. Knowing Jacky lived in Carole's building, he would not kiss her goodnight, though he wanted to. She seemed to understand, to read his mind.

"Would you like to come up for a drink?" she asked, her sultry eyes steady, warm, inviting.

"Yes, very much," he said, and he followed her inside, in the elevator and up to the top floor, concerned he'd run into his daughter, but the elevator opened directly into Carole's loft, and before he knew it she kissed him so deeply it felt like the big toes in his shoes curled. "I've been wanting to do that for the longest time," she whispered.

"Yes, so have I," he said.

THIRTEEN

It was as though the hand of God reached down to save the pope that day, for just as he was about to strike, to run onto the stage and plunge his knife into the pope's neck, the pope suddenly keeled over and hit the floor with a meaty thump. Panic-stricken, nearby cardinals, Vatican guards, the pope's aides and secretaries all ran to his assistance at once.

The killer moved forward, intent upon using the sudden confusion to his advantage, but in seconds the prostrate pope was surrounded by a wall of concerned people. Still he tried to get close enough to the pope to use his blade, but that proved to be impossible.

Knowing he only had one chance, he decided to wait, to bide his time, to strike at the right moment, and this definitely wasn't it. He knew now he could readily get into the Vatican, near the pope, and he slowly backed away, quickly making his way down the stone steps, and was soon outside, walking toward the front gate, the plaintive wails of sirens filling the air.

FOURTEEN

When Tony Flynn woke up, he was in Carole Cunningham's bed. Naked, she silently lay next to him, her breath coming slow and steady. The pale gray light of dawn shyly entered the bedroom windows. Tony picked up his head and studied her beautiful form, her narrow waist, full breasts. He smiled, pleased that such a fine looking woman would want him. The taste and smell of her still about him, he quietly slipped out of the bed. He was tempted to stay there, but he had much to do and the prospect of running into his daughter unsettled him. He quickly dressed and left Carole a note saying that he would call her later in the day.

Outside it was hot and humid, and just the two block walk to his car caused sweat to cover his high brow. Exhausted, Tony knew he had to get some more sleep before he could tackle the day, and he started to his place on the

Westside Highway, parked in the garage and went up to his apartment, his muscles and bones aching. He hadn't had a good night's sleep in five days straight. Thinking about the killer, wondering what he was doing, thinking, planning . . . where he would strike next, he remembered the ghastly sight of the murdered priests at Saint Joseph's, horrific images of murdered priests passing before his eyes.

As Tony was parking his car, he got a call on his cell phone. There had been a murder in Central Park. A female jogger had been found left in the woods on the uptown side of the park. Flynn drove over to the crime scene near the Harlem Meer and walked to where the woman had been discovered. She had apparently been dragged into the woods as she was jogging early that morning. Her torn jogging outfit was lying on the ground. Her naked body had been left in a narrow stream that ran through this part of the sprawling park. She had obviously been raped. Large clumps of her hair had been torn from her head, and her assailant had tied her legs into an obscene position. Lt. Mike Kostas out of the 24th Precinct was working the murder. He told Flynn that a bird watcher taking pictures of a hawk in a tree had found the woman; that she had managed a shoe store on East 46th Street, lived alone on West 89th Street. The victim was the same age as Jacky. Not tired anymore, Tony made sure the crime scene was worked properly, gave a statement to the press, discussed the case with Lt. Kostas, and drove back to his place to shower, change and get back to work. There was no way he could sleep now. He had some toast and coffee, swallowed two aspirins, took a cold shower, thinking about the jogger's family—how her mother and father would be devastated by the news; how he would feel if that had happened to one of his own daughters. He was glad that all his girls were cops, carried guns and knew how to use them.

FIFTEEN

Smiling pleasantly, he passed the Vatican guards, took a right on Via Gregorio and watched an ambulance come barreling down the street and turn onto the Vatican grounds. He waited. The ambulance soon came speeding out of the entrance, siren blaring, took a right and sped off. He noted that the ambulance came from Mother Cabrini hospital on Via Leonardo Da Vinci. He smiled— glad he hadn't made a move on the pope inside the auditorium. He hailed a cab and had it take him to the hospital. Wearing the cassock he had no trouble entering the facility. The pope, he soon found out, had a stroke and was on the third floor. Thinking he could get close to him here in the hospital, he entered the elevator and went up to the third floor. The pope was in a corner room at the end of the hall. Five Vatican guards were stationed outside his room, number 313. There was no way, he quickly realized, he would be able to get past the guards. Silently cursing, he went back downstairs, planning to return to the hospital, thinking about a way he could get past the guards. It would be no easy task.

He began back to his apartment, his mind playing over what happened. As he walked he kept seeing priests moving about Rome's streets, and the sight of them, their collars, the crosses around their necks, brought his mind back to the Sacred Heart Home for Boys, and distorted kinetic images, like a silent movie, of what had been done to him moved inside the diseased swamp that was his head. He tried to force the images away but he could not, and he became more and more incensed as he passed priests, arrogantly strutting about as if they were better than everyone else. His hands began to tremble with rage.

Inside the rented apartment, he took off the priest's skirt and got under an ice-cold shower. In the past when he showered like that, with cold water beating down on his head, the memories of his youth that plagued him diminished, but now the cold water didn't help. He stepped from the shower and, still wet, did push-ups until his triceps and pectoral muscles burned. He dressed in black, took his knife and went back out and began to explore the city, knowing if he were to succeed he had to know Rome better. Using a map, he began to navigate its streets, avenues and piazzas. He made his way to the beautiful Trevi Fountain, where people were throwing coins into the waters, where lovers kissed and made vows of fidelity to one another. As dusk came on, the restaurants began to fill. Eating in Rome was a serious business and he marveled at the magnificence of the food he saw being served, displayed on long tables. He next walked to the huge Piazza Navona, filled with glorious fountains spewing tall plumes of water. People gathered around the fountains to cool themselves, and sat in outdoor cafes lining the piazza.

Everywhere he looked he saw priests, many of whom, he realized, were walking with family members who had come to Rome to visit them. What struck him most about these priests was how insolently they strutted about, as if their lives had more meaning—significance—than those around them, and the sight of so many priests again began to incense him. He wondered which of them were molesters.

He left Piazza Navona because there were too many priests there and went straight to the Colosseum. He slowly walked all around this silent place of death, a giant mausoleum filled with the legions of ghosts of those who perished inside. He was sure that in another life, another time, he had known this place, imagining the gladiatorial contests, the smell of food and blood, the animals' roars, the screams of pain and screams of delight. He wanted very much to enter the Colosseum, but it was closed tight. Feral cats seemed to be guarding it. The cats, sensing there was something terribly wrong with him, his mind, hurried away as he came close, talking to himself out loud now. He made his way to Via Nazionale and went to the central train station, passing still more priests and nuns.

Most everywhere he went he saw people getting around on bicycles and he decided he, too, would get a bike; that it would be a fast, easy way to move about Rome and would make his mission all that much easier. There was a small bike shop near his apartment and he bought himself an inexpensive black bike, a lock and chain, then got on the bike and made his way back toward the Vatican.

As he moved along the cobblestone streets, he wanted to pull out his knife and ram it into the neck of priests he saw, but he controlled himself; he would pick, like all disciplined predators, the time and place to strike. But the need to hurt a priest grew and grew more still—like lava coming from a volcano. It soon became a burning sensation—a raging inferno inside his being over which he had, in reality, little control.

He stopped at Via Scossa, an empty, twisting street near the Vatican. It was late afternoon, nearly one hundred degrees, the time of day when Italians took their siestas and the narrow street was deserted. He wasn't there three minutes when a heavyset priest walked by. He could clearly smell wine on the priest as he passed him. He followed him, drawing his knife as he came up behind him, and when he was sure the coast was clear, he violently grabbed the priest by the hair. But the priest was wearing a wig, and it came off right in his hand. Quick and catlike, the priest turned and struck him in the face.

"Vai via, ladro!" *Get away, thief,* the priest demanded.

But he attacked the priest with an animal-like ferocity, plunging the blade deep into his stomach and pulling it up. The priest fell back and hit the ground hard. He bent down and slashed his throat. Blood exploded from the horrific wound. In shock, his eyes swelling, the priest feebly grabbed and tried to close the wound in his neck. "Perchè, perchè?" *Why?* his eyes begged. The killer quickly mutilated him, spit on him and left him lying there like that, his blood slowly moving across the smooth well-worn cobblestone street.

He mounted his bike and moved back toward the Vatican. He stared at the magnificent square with its one hundred forty-seven stately statues, turned and returned to his rented flat, knowing that soon all hell would break loose; that everyone in the Church would soon know about his omnipotent power; that the time to answer for their crimes had come; that they would not be safe anywhere.

He washed the priest's blood from his clothes, laid down, soon fell asleep and dreamed about the Sacred Heart Home for Boys, not hearing the screaming hee-haw sounds of sirens hurrying to the murder scene from many directions at once.

SIXTEEN

Chief Inspector Nino Maranzano was the first high-ranking police official to see the murdered priest. The body had been discovered by a couple on their way home from lunch; the police were summoned and Maranzano was called at his home. A burly, wide-shouldered Neapolitan who had many run-ins with *the Camorra,* Naples's version of the Mafia, Maranzano was a no-nonsense cop. He was happily married with one child. His nickname was "the bulldog," for Maranzano was a tireless, stubborn investigator and didn't let go once he got his teeth into something.

A highly religious man, Maranzano loved the Catholic Church and believed that the pope was the closest mortal to God on the face of the earth. He also believed in hell and heaven, the Ten Commandments and most all of the dictates of the Catholic Church. The scandals the Church had become mired in in the United States had nothing to do with Italy, a country with one of the largest Catholic populations in the world.

When Maranzano pulled up to the crime scene and got out of his black Fiat, he was appalled at the sight of the mutilated priest lying there like a discarded piece of meat outside a Neapolitan butcher shop in broad daylight. The priest's eyes were wide open and he stared at the Roman sky as if he were still asking *why.*

Chief Inspector Maranzano made the sign of the cross several times and said a silent Hail Mary. All of the many policemen in their well-fitting, stylish uniforms stood and stared in silent anger and disbelief at this barbarous murder of a holy man, as they collectively thought of him.

Maranzano bent down and studied the wounds. It was obvious the priest had died because of his cut throat, that the mutilation had been done after he was dead out of sheer cruelty.

Slowly standing, Chief Inspector Maranzano made a solemn oath to Jesus Christ, his jaw muscles bulging, to find the man who had done this—hoping the murderer would give him cause to kill him; to put a bullet in his head. Life in prison for such an individual was too good.

In all the twenty-one years Maranzano had been a policeman, he never worked on a case involving a murdered priest. And standing there and studying the body, he knew there would be a lot of pressure to solve this case—and to solve it quickly. He knew, too, that a message would soon be forthcoming from the Vatican and from the president of the country to find the killer.

Already, news crews were gathering to document and report, in solemn, dramatic tones and gestures, as was the Italian way.

Priests from the Vatican now came hurrying down the street to give their murdered colleague his last rites. Normally Maranzano would not let anyone near a murder scene, but he knew he could not turn away the priests, five of them intent upon their mission. They formed a tight circle around their fallen comrade and proceeded to pray. All the police personnel stood at solemn attention while the prayers were being said, offered to heaven, including Inspector Nino Maranzano.

When the priests were done, Maranzano ordered the criminalists to work the crime scene, and he ordered a growing number of Roman detectives to search the surrounding streets, question people who lived in the area, to have the sewers and roofs searched for the murder weapon, knowing if they located the knife they would be a step closer to finding the killer.

In the last light of the day, Maranzano could see how horrific the wound to the throat truly was. So deep, the priest's head had nearly been severed. Like Captain Flynn in New York, Maranzano immediately knew that such a wound was an assassin's. That men who worked as commandos for the government and men who worked for the Mafia were taught to kill in such a way.

Now, for the first time, Maranzano learned the identity of the priest, who was, he was told, a bishop from Milano,

Giovanni Boldera, a much-loved, much-respected man of God who tirelessly worked to help the poor.

Shaking his head in disgust, Maranzano ordered the bishop's body to be taken to the morgue for an autopsy.

SEVENTEEN

As Tony Flynn stepped from a cold shower, vigorously wiping himself with a rough terrycloth towel, he first heard about the murdered bishop in Rome from CNN. Reporter Ann Fitzgerald was in Rome, on Via della Conciliazione, reporting how a bishop had been "murdered and mutilated near the Vatican," which immediately caught Tony's attention. When he heard that the bishop's throat had also been cut, he stopped dressing, stood still and listened to the report as they showed a shot of the bishop's body being placed in a morgue wagon and Chief Inspector Nino Maranzano giving terse orders to detectives, his hands gesturing angrily. They cut to a commercial break. Flynn finished dressing and hurried out of the house, wondering if the killer had left New York and traveled to Rome, or if this was a copycat killing, which he knew frequently occurred in well-publicized serial murder cases.

Flynn's first instinct was that someone else with a grudge against priests in Rome had done this crime, inspired maybe by the New York killings. Then again, he was thinking, the killer might very well have traveled to Rome because Rome—the Vatican—was the very center of the Catholic Church, its life-blood, its heart and soul. It was obvious the killer had a deep-rooted, venomous hatred for the Church and what better place to express such hatred than in Rome. If, Flynn knew, getting into his car and heading downtown, the killer had traveled to Rome there would be a record of his trip, which could very well help crack the case.

As Flynn made his way to the Midtown North Precinct, his cell phone sounded. It was his boss, Chief Samuels, telling him about the murder in Rome. Flynn said he had already heard about it and that he planned to call Rome as soon as he got to his desk. He also said he wanted permission to release the composite sketch to the media and give it to police jurisdictions all over the East Coast. Samuels said he thought that was a good idea and gave him the green light. He asked about the murdered woman in Central Park. Tony told him about the brutality of the attack, how the victim had been bound by cord, that detectives were canvassing the park and buildings on Central Park North, looking for someone who may have seen something. "Keep me posted," Samuels said.

"Will do," Flynn said.

As soon as Tony hung up, his phone sounded again and this time it was Carole Cunningham. She too wanted to tell him about the murder of a bishop in Rome. He told her that he'd seen the report on CNN and planned to contact the Rome authorities right away. Because of a meeting at her office, she said, she would not be able to go with him to the morgue. They made plans to talk later in the day, neither of them even mentioning what had happened between them; it didn't, in the light of day, seem appropriate given all the circumstances. Though after he hung up, he wished he had said something.

When Flynn arrived at Midtown North, he was stopped by a group of reporters who had taken up station in front of the precinct. They would be there, Flynn knew, until the case was solved or something more spectacular occurred. They also mentioned the Rome killing and wanted to know if there were any links to the New York murders.

"That's something we are looking into right now," Flynn said, excused himself and made for his desk up on the second floor. On his way to his desk he asked Sergeant Salerno to come into his office. Salerno said that the task force had taken over a room in the basement of the building and had set it up to work the case exclusively.

Flynn said, "Make sure they have everything they need and make certain none of them talk to any reporters. Frank, we have to reach out to the guys in Rome working the murder of the bishop. I'm thinking the cases may very well be linked; what's your take?"

"If they are, Captain, that means our guy had to just leave for Rome. That he killed the priests downtown and took off. Seems like a long shot. I think what we have here is a copycat killing. A lot of people have hard-ons for priests and the Church these days, you know."

"Frank, call Rome and get the guy in charge of the case on the horn, a Chief Inspector Maranzano. I want to talk to him ASAP, find out exactly what they have."

"Will do. If he doesn't speak English I can translate for you, Captain."

"I didn't know you spoke Italian."

"Fluently."

"Excellent. I want to get over to the morgue soon as I make a few calls."

"Okay, Captain," Salerno said and hurried to his desk in the squad room and placed a call to Rome, as Flynn phoned the Behavioral Science Unit of the FBI at Quantico, Virginia, and left a message for agent Sam Henderson. On the verge of retiring, Henderson was one of the originators of the unit and knew more about serial killers than most any man alive. He had personally interviewed seventy incarcerated serial murderers, Flynn knew, wrote four books about serial killers, and he had helped crack serial murder cases all over the world. Flynn had first met him when he took a course given by Henderson on serial killers fifteen years ago at Quantico. The two immediately had hit it off, as professionals in law enforcement often do, and had become tight over the years.

Flynn knew the DNA results would not be ready for hours, but still he phoned the lab and left a message. Just as he hung up, his daughter Jacky called to tell him about the murdered bishop in Rome. He said he already knew and they made plans to go out to his daughter Julie's house for Fourth of July. He didn't want to go to any kind of party just now, but it was a family tradition and he wasn't about to disappoint his daughters.

Salerno buzzed him to say that he had Chief Inspector Maranzano on the line, that the Chief spoke English. Flynn picked up the phone and politely thanked Maranzano for taking his call. "Chief, the reason I phoned is because we've had a series of knife-murders of Catholic priests here in New York over the last several days—five priests in all, and I understand that a bishop was murdered in Rome; that he'd been castrated and eviscerated and his throat had been cut. I was wondering if that's true?"

"Yes, Captain, most definitely—I saw the body myself. The fact is I just returned from the morgue. What killed him was the wound to his throat—a very lethal cut, an assassin's way of killing."

"A stab-slash wound?"

"Exactly."

"That's how the priests here were killed. The thing of it is we just had three killings in a church rectory downtown, and if it's the same man, he had to leave later that day for Rome."

"Captain, this was a very bestial, sadistic killing; he castrated the priest after he was dead—"

"Same thing happened here," Flynn said, getting a feeling in his gut that the killer he was hunting had gone to Rome.

Maranzano said, "If it is the same man, his name will be on airline manifests somewhere. Do you have any suspects yet, perhaps a name, Captain?"

"No, but we do have a sketch of him. If you like I can e-mail it to you right now."

"Please, I'd appreciate that, thank you."

"And we will have his DNA later today. The first priest he killed scratched him and there were skin and specs of blood under the priest's nails. If we have his DNA on file we'll soon have his identity."

"Interesting, Captain. You see the killer apparently spit on the bishop—and our criminalists found saliva on his forehead. We are analyzing it right now to see if it's the bishop's or the killer's, and if it is the killer's and matches what you have, we'll know for sure whether it is the same man."

"As you may know, Chief Inspector, we have had a large problem with predator priests in the Catholic Church. And I'm thinking what we might have here is a former victim looking for revenge."

"I've heard about the problem; fortunately, we do not have infamy here."

"I'm thinking if it is the same guy, he may have gone to Rome because the Vatican is there."

"Yes, of course. Can you also send me morgue shots of the priests—especially the wound to the throat. I'd like to compare it to the wound Bishop Boldera suffered."

"Yes, of course. Chief Inspector, if it is the same man, he will kill again and soon. It might be a good idea to stake out the Vatican; he very well might be hanging around it."

"Yes, *si, naturalmente*," Maranzano said. "When will you have the DNA?"

"Should be later today and you'll have it soon as we do."

"Thank you. I very much appreciate your assistance. As you may realize the murder of a priest, a bishop, here in Roma, in Italia, is a very grave crime with serious repercussions. This murder is a top priority. The prime minister and an emissary from the pope himself have already called and asked me to spare no resource, no expense in catching this *monstro*. Captain, I will look forward to getting the sketch you spoke of, and the DNA. Please, feel free to call me anytime. And, if you are ever in Roma, you must let me know. I should be honored to show you around, take you for a nice meal."

"Thank you, I certainly will," Flynn said. They exchanged e-mail addresses and soon hung up and Flynn just sat there thinking this out, feeling more and more convinced that the priest killer had gone to Rome. Sergeant Salerno knocked on his open door. Flynn summarized his conversation with Maranzano and told Salerno to e-mail the composite sketch to Rome as soon as it was released to the press in New York.

The phone interrupted them. It was Special Agent Sam Henderson returning his call. After the two friends asked after each other and their families, Henderson said, "I knew I'd be hearing from you, Tony."

"Fact is I meant to call sooner, but I've been jammed and wanted to have as much as possible to give you. I'd like to send you everything we have at this point and hopefully you can help us."

"You think the same guy killed all the priests—how many so far?"

"Five. I do. He killed them all with a stab-slash wound to the throat, very precise and exact; and each of them were eviscerated and castrated."

"The genitals taken away?"

"Actually, no. He left them there, but he threw the severed penis of one of the priests at the statue of Christ on the cross behind the altar."

"Interesting. Before I say anything about what I'm thinking, I'd like to review the whole file."

"We'll send you everything today."

"Make sure to include all the crime scene and morgue shots."

"I'm on my way now to the morgue to view the autopsies of the three priests he killed yesterday and I'll upload the photographs to you. We also have a composite of him. A vendor saw him leaving the church on Riverside Drive. I'll send that, too. I should mention, Sam, that he wrote the words *HELL ON EARTH*, in blood at two different scenes."

"Send me photos of them, too. You know he's going to keep killing priests until he's caught or killed."

"Sam, we are thinking he *might* have even gone to Rome—"

"The killing of the bishop near the Vatican?"

"Exactly, I just got off the horn with the Chief Inspector working the case and the wounds sound identical. Is such a thing possible, Sam . . . I mean a serial killer traveling like that? So far?"

"Most definitely. I know of numerous cases in which killers traveled great distances . . . from state to state, even to other countries. Serial killers are all about staying free to be able to keep doing their thing. This concept about them leaving clues, subconsciously or otherwise to get caught is a bunch of bull. So, yes, he could very well have gone to Rome, particularly if he has a thing, which he clearly does, against the Catholic Church and its priests. But like I said, Tony, I want to examine the whole file and all the photographs you have, then I'll work up a profile for you."

"That's what I was hoping. How long do you think that'll take, Sam?"

"Twenty-four hours, more or less, once I see everything."

"Great, thank you, Sam."

"Anytime, pal."

Tony hung up and felt better, knowing Sam Henderson was in his corner. He and Salerno next went down to the basement where the task force had set up shop. Phones had been installed to field calls about the case, follow up leads and statements from the public, and to take information from victims of abuse by priests. A large map of New York hung on the wall, as well as crime scene photographs and a large blow up of the composite. Someone had written in magic marker on the composite *wanted dead or alive*. Large red pins were stuck into the map where there had been murders. Tony called for the attention of the fourteen detectives working the case.

"Listen up. Our guy may have gone to Rome to kill priests there," he said.

"Good riddance," one of the detectives observed.

"As I'm sure you all know a bishop was murdered a block from the Vatican. And his wounds are identical to the wounds of the priests killed here. At this juncture we are only thinking it may be him, but if it comes to pass that we are sure he iced the bishop, we are going to start working airline manifests. If he did leave for Rome he had to have gone yesterday and that'll narrow down the possibilities.

"Between us in this room, I think it is him. That he went to Rome because the Vatican is there. We'll know for sure soon enough because the guy who killed the bishop apparently spit on him and so they'll also be able to do a DNA workup. Meanwhile, I want you all to work the case as if he is still here. We'll be releasing the composite soon and hopefully someone who knows him will contact us."

Another of the detectives told Flynn that she'd been getting calls from people who said they had been abused by one of the murdered priests. Flynn told her to refer all such calls to Cunningham at the DA's office, and he and Salerno soon left the station house and again traveled crosstown to the New York City morgue.

Reporters had staked out the morgue, hoping to get some kind of scoop, but again Flynn politely referred them to the NYPD Public Relations office and went inside and downstairs to the autopsy room. The three priests who had been killed at the Church of Saint Joseph of the Holy Family were in different stages of being autopsied. Dr. Russo was overseeing the autopsies. He told Flynn that the killer had "unusual strength"; that he actually severed the top of the spinal columns of two of the priests and broke numerous ribs when he cut their throats and eviscerated them.

"Captain," he said, "I've been in this business for twenty-two years and I've never seen such brute animalistic force. He also broke the wrists of one of them when he grabbed him. We are talking here, Tony, about an individual with incredible power. I'm telling you now if you corner him be prepared to kill him because you wouldn't want to fight with this guy." He showed Flynn and Salerno where the knife had severed the spines and actually broke through ribs.

Flynn knew that insane individuals, psychotic people were indeed capable of superhuman feats of strength. Over the years he had dealt with such people. Indeed he'd nearly been beaten to death by a guy who escaped Bellevue's psych ward in 1992, and standing there, studying the priests' severed ribs, Tony remembered the awesome strength of the man—how he'd thrown him about like a rag doll; that it took six bullets to bring him down. He was one of the two men Flynn was forced to kill in the line of duty.

Russo gave the captain a disk containing the autopsy photographs of the priests and the autopsy reports, each of which said the cause of death had been a "severed carotid artery and windpipe."

Flynn thanked Dr. Russo for the expedited autopsy reports and he and Salerno headed over to the lab, where they were greeted by Ng, a small pensive man who ran the NYPD crime lab. He told them that they had finished the DNA workup on the materials found under Joseph's nails and that they were in the process of comparing the breakdown to those that were on file. He gave a copy of the genetic code they had to Flynn.

"When will we know?" Flynn asked.

"Couple of hours," Ng said. "We've given this absolute number one priority, Captain. I'll call you soon as I know."

Flynn thanked him and he and Salerno left the morgue, the rancid, bad-meat stink of the corpses staying with them. They got back in the car and headed downtown on the FDR Drive for the press conference at One Police Plaza about the case. There was little traffic. The fierce sun beat down relentlessly, forcing them both to put on shades, each of them silently hoping that the killer's DNA was on file, though knowing that the only way it could be in the NYPD data bank was if the man they were looking for had been arrested for a sex crime.

New York legislators and Governor Pataki had been trying to pass laws forcing all people who were arrested to give DNA—as they were compelled to give fingerprints, but that hadn't come to pass yet and was, in fact, a serious impediment for cops working the front lines, trying to solve cases, put away rapists, child molesters and sexual carnivores.

They rode downtown in contemplative silence, each of them remembering the murdered priests on the autopsy stations, their rumpled black clothes and shiny gold crucifixes on an aluminum table next to them, illuminated by the harsh white overhead lighting. The press conference was being held in a large auditorium on the ground floor of police headquarters. The air-conditioning system was on the blink and the room was packed with overheated reporters, producers, cameramen—the cameras' bright lights adding to the stifling heat.

Chief Samuels, Carole Cunningham, the mayor, the commissioner, representatives of the Catholic League, John Mahoney, the Church's lawyer, and most of the hierarchy of the New York Police Department were there.

The police brass were, for the most part, all good, Irish-Catholics who were outraged at the killing of their priests and it showed on their angry faces—their tight lips, hard jaw lines, cold blue cop eyes. Flynn's daughter Robin was also there. He hugged and kissed her hello. She was a tall dark-haired woman who was a mirror image of his wife. He also nodded and said hello to Carole, who returned his greeting. An easel covered by a black cloth stood to the left of the stage.

The mayor strode to the podium, crowded with microphones, his long horse-shaped face appropriately stern, and told the assembled press how outraged he was at the killing of religious people dedicated to good, and promised every resource was being utilized in the hunt for "this madman." He told them, too, about the special task force of hand-picked detectives, and introduced Commissioner Peters, who parroted the mayor's sentiments, adding:

"Through the tireless diligence of the task force detectives working the case, under Captain Flynn's able direction, a witness has been found who helped create a composite of the killer," he said, angrily pointing at the easel, as Robin Flynn dramatically pulled away the black velvet cloth that had been covering Rodriguez's charcoal sketch, blown up now to an impressive three feet by four feet. Flashbulbs popped. Cameramen zoomed in on the sketch, as it was instantly relayed to live news shows around the country, indeed the world, for Fox, CNN and BBC news crews were there.

"This," the commissioner said, "is the man we believe responsible for the murders of Catholic priests here in New York over the last several days.

"Please, anyone with any information about this man, his name, where he lives, works, contact us at the 800 number you see on your screens. There is a fifty thousand-dollar reward being offered for information leading to his arrest and conviction. Thank you. I'd like to now introduce Captain Flynn. He will answer any questions you may have."

Reluctantly the commissioner stepped aside—this was a man who loved the attention of the press—and Flynn took position behind the podium, flanked by the mayor and commissioner, with Carole Cunningham behind him. He told the press in a cold and clinical voice the facts of the three priests murdered at the Church of Saint Joseph of the Holy Family, and said the police believed that the man in the sketch had done all five killings.

When he said he would take questions, the first, asked by a *New York Times* reporter, was whether the police believed the murder of the bishop in Rome was in any way linked to the New York killings. Flynn said that possibility was being looked into, and nothing more. The second question asked was whether the police believed the sex scandals of the Church had anything to do with the killings. Flynn said that was "a possibility we are study-ing."

The press conference soon ended and within minutes calls began pouring into the special 800 number, which connected directly to the task force in the basement of the Midtown North Precinct.

Mahoney, the lawyer, approached Flynn and said, "I want to apologize, Captain Flynn. We got off on the wrong foot. I realize you are doing your best in a very dif-ficult situation. I want to thank you, personally and on be-half of Cardinal Edam, for all you've done." He reached out his long bony hand and the two men shook.

"I appreciate your coming over," Flynn said, though he was thinking the only reason he had come over and apolo-gized was because he—and the Church—had tried to get Flynn thrown off the case without success. Flynn knew Mahoney was all about playing hardball, that he and his firm had been ruthlessly unsympathetic and exploitative of people who had been victimized by predator priests.

Mahoney asked, "Captain, do you think the killing in Rome has anything to do with the murders here in New York?"

"Counselor, the truth is I do believe they are related; that perhaps the same man, or men, are responsible."

"Men, you think more than one man is involved?"

"It's a possibility we are looking into . . . you know, counselor," Flynn added, "you've been publicly defend-ing the Church . . . have appeared at their news confer-ences, in court on their behalf, and you *might* very well be in danger—"

"How do you mean?" Mahoney interrupted. "Danger?"

"I mean someone has a serious hard-on for the Church and you've been publicly defending them. That person's anger, counselor, could very well be turned against you, move in your direction. You follow my drift?"

"Yes, of course. You have a point."

"I'd suggest you look into hiring a bodyguard," Flynn said.

"How about police protection?" Mahoney asked.

"I'll talk to my boss, but because there hasn't been any kind of actual threats against you, I doubt if that's possible. We are already stretched thin, you know, with budget cuts and all."

"I see," Mahoney said, his eyes moving about the room like two nervous fish.

Flynn excused himself and walked over to Carole, who was talking with a few reporters, telling them how many calls the District Attorney's office was receiving from victims, particularly in Brooklyn, where Cardinal Daily—another protégé of Bernard Hound's—was in charge. Daily, like Hound, was under a lot of pressure to resign as a direct result of his insolent way of dealing with victims. Flynn's cell phone beeped. It was Dr. Ng calling to say that there was no match to any of the DNA they had on file. Disappointed, Flynn thanked the doctor for calling and hung up. His daughter Robin waved good-bye and left with the commissioner. Carole excused herself and came over to him.

"You think it's him in Rome?" she asked.

"At this point we aren't sure, but it could very well be because the wounds are identical. I spoke with the Chief Inspector in charge of the case and I just got off the phone with the lab. His DNA doesn't match any we have on file."

"Bummer. It was too good to be true. I wanted to tell you that we found out Father Joseph was at one time the head of the New York chapter of NAMBLA, and he worked at a home for boys in upstate New York. There were charges that he abused children at the home, but nothing ever came of them."

"How a man like that could even become a priest is amazing."

"My office is getting a lot of pressure from the Catholic League. They've orchestrated a letter-writing campaign and we are getting mail from all over the country about our "Catholic-bashing.' "

Tony saw Chief of Detectives Samuels wave him over. He excused himself to Carole. She said she had to get back to her office, that she had still more appointments with victims who were coming in to give statements, possible evidence in the charges being brought against the priests who had child pornography in their rooms, on their computers. Flynn, staring at the delicate pearl of sweat which had beaded above her full upper lip, made plans to speak with her at the end of the day. He winked at her. They shook hands, smiled discreetly and off she went. Flynn approached his boss. The chief said, "Tony I received a call from the pope's representative in Rome. He gave me this long speech about how our priorities are backwards and that we seem more concerned with, and this is a quote: 'a few errant priests' indiscretions, than catching the killer.' The pope himself, he said, has grave concerns about our 'attitudes.' "

"What'd you tell him?"

"I wanted to tell him to take a long walk on a short pier, but I told him that we are doing everything humanly possible to catch the killer. He asked me to make sure there weren't any more public statements about what was or wasn't found in the priests' residences and I told him we are not in the position where we can give any of these priests any kind of preferential treatment. That's what he was asking for—nerve, huh?"

"Big time."

"Anyway, Tony, just please be careful about what you say publicly, okay?"

" 'K, boss," Flynn said and asked for permission to send the composite and the DNA breakdown to the Rome police. Samuels gave him the go ahead and soon left the press conference, saying the room was so hot you could bake bread in it.

Back outside, as Flynn and Salerno were returning to their car, the captain received a call on his cell phone from the task force, informing him that one of the priests who had been arrested had been badly beaten up in the van on the way to Rikers Island, and that the Church's lawyers were demanding that all the priests be placed in P.C., protective custody. Flynn rang off and told Salerno what happened.

"Even in jail," Salerno said, "where you've got all kinds of low lifes, these guys have something to worry about. Seems the bad guys have more sense than the law, you know."

"Yeah, seems that way," Flynn agreed and they got back in their car, thankful for its air-conditioning and headed uptown, the city's black tar streets and sidewalks so hot you could feel the heat right through the soles of your shoes.

EIGHTEEN

In Rome the temperature that day hit 40.2 Celsius, 104.4 Fahrenheit. It was so hot that people left their homes, offices and shops only when they absolutely had to. Stray animals all over Rome were dying of heat prostration. All the glorious fountains of Rome had red-faced sweating people gathered around them, seeking some small relief from the stifling heat.

It was, the weather experts said, the hottest summer in Rome since 1908, when they first began to keep records. It

hadn't rained anywhere in Europe for ninety-one day
and throughout all of Italy, indeed all of Europe, crop
were being destroyed by the unrelenting heat. Fires, fec
by dry, brittle foliage, raged in Italy, Spain, Germany, Por
tugal and France, even England and Switzerland, and
people were dropping dead from the heat, being burn
alive in fast-moving forest fires.

Not knowing that a composite of him had been released
to the media, he left his apartment and slowly pedaled hi
bike toward the Vatican. As he drew closer to the Vatican
he immediately noticed that there were many more police
about now, sitting in cars, walking the streets, stationed on
corners, gathering in any available pools of shade they
could find. Perhaps, because of the furnace-like heat, dis
tracted by it, none of the *polizia* or *carabinieri* took note o
the handsome dark-haired man on a bike. He made hi
way back to the hospital and learned that the pope had
been moved to Vatican City, was convalescing there
Mulling over this news, planning again to try to get at the
pope inside the Vatican, he headed back toward the Pi
azza Navona. Because of the heat, there were not so many
tourists there but still some diehard groups from the
States, China and Japan were following weary tour guides
carrying limp flags on the end of long poles.

He headed over to the Colosseum, thinking that be
cause of the heat there would be fewer tourists, as indeed
there were. He was able to chain his bike just outside the
entrance gate, paid the €10 admission fee and suddenly
found himself inside the infamous arena. It was as long
as a football field, its honey-colored walls and columns
witness to one of the most bloody, sadistic spectacles in
the history of mankind. A thing that was particularly ap
pealing to him given his twisted, obsessive inclinations
toward violence. He slowly walked to a quiet corner on

the shaded side of the Colosseum, closed his eyes and just stood there, as overheated tour groups followed Colosseum guides who told of the violence, the stench of the bodies, the exposed entrails, the strong odors of the food given to the crowds for free by the Roman government; how the dead were taken from the *porta della Morte* at the north end of the Colosseum, how men with masked faces carrying torches would put flame to those thought dead to make sure they were not feigning death to save themselves. These were all things he found exciting and interesting, imagining the violence, the slashing swords, horrific wounds, free-flowing blood, pointed arrows finding their targets with a meaty thud, the great emperors looking on. He heard, as when you put a seashell to your ear you experience the sea, the roar of the bloodthirsty crowds, the screams of hapless victims, the bellowing roars of the lions and he could clearly see in his mind's eye—brought on, no doubt, by his psychosis— the sexual debauchery, the prostitutes under the Colosseum giving relief to the bloodlust brought on by the violence, serving both men and women right there out in the open.

When he opened his eyes, she was standing some ten feet in front of him, looking at him, the redheaded woman, the writer he'd met on the bus and saw at the Sistine Chapel.

"Hello," she hesitantly said, an equally hesitant smile on her face, obviously knowing he had not been too friendly, or interested.

Outlined by the magnificent backdrop of the Colosseum, its tawny earth colors, she seemed very beautiful with her green eyes, red hair, oval-shaped face.

"Hello," he said, coming out of his reverie. "We keep running into one another."

"Yes, I hope I didn't disturb you . . . you seemed so engrossed."

"No, you didn't disturb me," he lied. "I'm just very taken and amazed by this place. It's like all my life I've been hearing about it, reading about it and here it is . . . bigger than life itself. It's kind of like seeing something you'd dreamed about suddenly real."

"Yes, I know exactly what you mean. I'm using it in my story."

"How do you mean?"

"I'm writing a historical novel that takes place during the reign of Julius Caesar, specifically about Marc Anthony, his childhood and his relationship with Caesar and Cleopatra."

"Sounds very interesting. You have a title yet?"

"Not really."

"This your first book?"

"Actually, my third."

"I love to read," he said, a sudden sadness coming to his face, she noted. This was an observant woman.

"Yes, me, too," she said.

"So you came to Rome just to do research?" he asked.

"Kind of. This is actually my second trip to Italy for the book. I like to know as much about the truth of a thing before I start to write. It really helps when you sit down with a blank piece of paper in front of you."

"Have you started writing it yet?"

"No, still doing research. But I will soon."

"Here in Rome?"

"Down South. I rented a place in Amalfi and I'm planning to write it there. I wasn't prepared for this heat, though."

"Tell me about it. Just unbelievable. How long does it take to write a book?" he asked, kind of fascinated, for he had always coveted books, the magic of the written word; how they had transported him all over the world, back in time, into the future.

"For me, the first draft takes three, four months, then another couple of months to polish it, strengthen the dialogue, define and develop the characters, get everything right."

"How fascinating. I thought writing a book takes, you know, years."

"When I start to put the story down on paper, I pretty much write all day seven days a week, but the research part does take a lot more time, for me anyway. I've been investigating this story for, what, over a year now. Are you in Rome on vacation?" she asked, her green eyes curious and intelligent, engaging.

"I am. Since I was a kid I've always been fascinated by all things related to Rome. I think . . . I'm sure, I had another life here; I mean *here* in the Colosseum."

"As a gladiator?" she asked, a slight smile playing on her heart-shaped lips.

"I'm not sure really," he said with grave sincerity.

"You believe in reincarnation?"

"Just look at children who are prodigies, can brilliantly play instruments at very early ages," he said, his eyes moving off her to the stately columns of the Colosseum behind her, more interested in them than her, it seemed. Though he found her very beautiful, could sense that she was interested in getting to know him, none of that appealed to him. He was in Rome on a mission he was intent upon fulfilling. Sensing that she was distracting him, she said she had an appointment with a professor at the University of Rome and had to go, though she offered him her card, which had her cell phone number and a San Francisco address on it. Her name, he noticed, was Diane Pane.

He told her his name was Frank Lewis. She smiled and walked off. He admired her long muscular legs and full figure, small waist, large hips, as she went.

He slowly and contemplatively walked around the entire Colosseum, as excited clouds of sparrows noisily moved about overhead. A Colosseum employee announced in five languages that the Colosseum would soon be closing; that everyone had to leave.

Reluctantly, he started toward the exit, planning to return many times before he left Rome; before he finished his mission.

He found his bike where he left it, unlocked the chain and went west on Via dei Fori Imperiali. He hadn't gone a hundred feet when he spotted a large news kiosk. He slowed and stopped, thinking he might be able to buy an English newspaper, wanting to read about the blood he'd drawn, the havoc he caused back in New York. Dismounting the bike, moving slow and catlike as was his way, he was shocked to see the composite sketch by Susan Rodriguez on the front page of a dozen different Italian newspapers, big and bold and there for the world to see. Feeling like he'd been slapped hard by a thick callused hand, he got back on his bike and quickly pedaled away, his mind reeling with what he'd seen, wondering how the hell the police had gotten a description of him, but then he remembered the snow-cone man outside Our Lady of Miracles Church on Riverside Drive.

He knew that unless he changed his appearance quickly, he'd be apprehended, or killed. The murder of a bishop in Rome was a reprehensible crime, and he knew the Italian police might very well kill him rather than arrest him and let the case move through the courts. He spotted a pharmacy on Via del Corso, locked up his bike, went inside and bought an electric hair cutter and a weak pair of distance glasses, paranoid that people would recognize him in the shop.

In a hurry now, he pedaled back to the rented apartment and without hesitation, covered in sweat, he cut off all his long black hair, then shaved his head clean, put on the glasses. With the glasses and bald head he looked completely different and he was pleased. He took a cold shower and put on the priest's outfit he bought, hanging the large crucifix around his white-collared neck.

Smiling, he slowly walked about the room, bending over slightly, perfecting his priestly persona. If he were to gain access to the Vatican's inner sanctum, get near the pope, he truly had to appear like a priest as he approached the entrance on Via Porta Angelica.

Sure the authorities would not suspect that he would kill again so soon, he went back out carrying Father Joseph's ID and his knife. It was dark now and with the coming of night the temperature had gone down somewhat and a breeze came from the east. He mounted his bike and pedaled right back toward Vatican City, intent upon getting inside. The bike, he thought, was the perfect prop. He entered the Villa Borghese and made his way through the majestic park, passing numerous statues of lions and famous Romans, young couples walking hand-in-hand looking for discreet spots to show their hot-blooded affection. In the sprawling park it was cooler and the breeze rustled the tall, sensuous cypress trees that filled the park. As he passed the zoo its resident male lion let out a mighty roar, which echoed and rumbled across the wide expanse of the park. He soon left the park and continued west, passing many policemen as he went. They waved and nodded respectfully to him, convinced he was a priest. Some of the police officers were actually carrying his composite, but he appeared nothing like the sketch now.

However, when he reached the Vatican entrance on Via Porta Angelica, there were now a dozen police cars neatly lined up and as many police carefully scrutinizing the ID of anyone wishing to enter the inner sanctum of the "Holy City," as Italians—these police—thought of it. It was, for them, the deeply rooted foundation of their religious beliefs, and they would protect it to the death.

He immediately turned away, instinctively knowing he could not pass a thorough identity check, caught off guard by the overwhelming police response to what he'd done. He slowly pedaled around all of Vatican City, looking for a place he could enter, scale the walls, but it was impregnable—and there were security cameras everywhere.

Angry and frustrated, emotions he never dealt well with, he made his way west . . . a new plan forming in his warped mind.

As he passed the Vittoria Bridge spanning the twisting, slow-moving Tiber River, he spotted him—a lone priest casually walking away from the Vatican, starting to cross the bridge. He began to follow him, planning his attack as he silently drew closer and closer to the priest, as he made his way onto Via Garibaldi, a narrow street lighted by a lone lamppost down the block, lined on both sides with ancient two-story earth-colored buildings.

This was a Franciscan monk, Father Marco Juliano, in Rome to beg the Vatican for money to help feed orphaned Albanian children. A truly pious man intensely devoted to helping the downtrodden, he was sixty-seven years old, had worked in Africa, the slums of Rio de Janeiro, and most recently in Bosnia. He had taken a vow of poverty and had one pair of sandals, two sets of robes, a couple of pairs of underwear, simple toiletries, and those were all his worldly possessions. In the winter he refused even to wear socks. He reasoned that if Christ could suffer on the cross, die for our sins, the least he could do is swear off materialistic possessions.

The killer knew none of this and wouldn't have cared one way or another. In his mind this Franciscan monk was a bona fide member of a corrupt criminal enterprise, a soldier in an army of out-of-control, power-hungry deviants, who were manipulating good, God-fearing people for their own benefit, pleasure, comfort and greed.

Aware of the murder of Bishop Boldera, sensing someone coming up behind him, Father Juliano turned, and was greeted by the image of a smiling priest on a bike coming toward him, certainly no one to fear. He didn't see the knife in his hand.

"Excuse me, Father," the killer said, getting off the bike. "I'm lost—can you please direct me to Via Nazionale?"

"Certainly," Father Juliano answered, but before he could continue, the smiling priest plunged his knife into the left side of his chest with the speed and accuracy of a rattlesnake, directly into his heart. He pulled the blade out. The priest fell to the pavement, blood gushing from his chest. The last image Marco Juliano's eyes registered was the killer kneeling over him, his face now a twisted mask of hatred, bringing the razor-sharp, blood-covered blade to his throat. *Forgive him, Holy Father*, was his last thought before his life was stolen away from him, and the mutilation began.

Then, quickly, the killer mounted his bike and nonchalantly pedaled away, intent upon drawing still more blood . . . out of control. Believing that he would not be able to get near the pope now, he hunted priests all over Rome that night, and before he was done, he killed two more—one near the train station on Via Magenta; another just off Via del Corso, near the Pantheon a little before midnight. He nearly got a third close to the Trevi Fountain, but a police car coming around the corner from Via

Panettera stopped him. The intense heat had kept many people who would have surely been on the streets, crowding the piazzas, promenading, inside and he went about his bloody tasks without any witnesses but the priests he killed, he thought.

Satisfied, covered in sweat, blood on his black cassock, he pedaled back to the apartment on Via Corelli, forming a new plan that involved the writer Diane Pane. He had sensed a certain vulnerability about her, which he felt sure he could exploit to his advantage. He knew if he stayed in Rome now it would only be a matter of time before he was stopped and brought down before his mission was truly completed. He planned to leave the timeless city, let things cool off, then return to kill the pope, or at the very least some of the cardinals who lived in Vatican City. And, if possible, he would go back to New York, the last place the police would be looking for him and continue his work.

Pleased now, he was sure all those in the Church would know that they were in grave danger; that they were paying for their dirty perversions; that *God* was not protecting them the way he had not protected him when he was a young boy.

NINETEEN

Chief Inspector Nino Maranzano was in the middle of a four-course late night dinner with his wife, Lina, in a small restaurant on Via Margutta, celebrating their twentieth anniversary. Wanting this time to be alone with his wife, Maranzano shut off his cell phone—a thing he rarely did—intent upon enjoying a romantic dinner with Lina, undisturbed. But the front door suddenly burst open and three of his detectives rushed in, politely excused themselves and told Maranzano about the murdered priests. Apologizing to his lovely wife, an architect who looked much like the Italian actress Claudia Cardinale, with her high cheekbones and large round eyes, he was forced to leave her even before the bottle of Dom Perignon in a frosted ice bucket on a stand next to their table had been opened. Accustomed to such interruptions, Lina said she understood, that he should go, but he saw in her dark eyes annoyance that even tonight he was being taken away from her, hurrying off because of his job.

Lina had known when she married him that he was a policeman in a city rife with crime, but over the years she had tired of his hurrying off during important moments . . . when they were having their first and only child, on holidays—New Year's, Christmas—times when she needed him, during intimate conversations, even when they were in the middle of lovemaking, and a distance of sorts had developed in their once near perfect union.

Lina had met Nino fresh out of college. He was a captain then, the most handsome man she'd ever seen, who already had a reputation as a fearless crime fighter, a hard-knuckled intellectual who stood up to the infamous Camorra of Napoli, who had killed Mafia hit men in shootouts. Stories had been written about him in *Panorama*, *L'Espresso*, *Corriere Della Sera*, and *La Repubblica*. They had both fallen in love at first sight and were married sixty-three days after they first met.

Now, he hugged her and kissed her and told her he loved her very much. "Più della mia vita," more than life itself, he said. "I'll be back as soon as humanly possible," he promised, and hurried toward the ornate wooden doors of the restaurant. The waiters and the owner of the restaurant bowed as he went, for Nino Maranzano was a true man of respect, a crime-fighting celebrity with fierce dark eyes and a beautiful wife, who he was now leaving alone with their second course: hand-rolled black linguine and grilled lobster in silky olive oil from Tuscany, adorned with lemon zest, finely chopped parsley and exquisite black truffle from Piemonte.

As he sped to Via Garibaldi in his Fiat, Maranzano received the full details of the murdered priests—each had his throat cut, had been mutilated. And he was sure that a bold, cunning predator the likes of which he'd never known was stalking Rome, defying the police, him personally, and all that was good and right and correct with society—including God Himself.

This killer, he was thinking, was on *una missione* and would have to be hunted down like any wild animal, like an out-of-control jungle cat that had gotten the taste of human blood.

Maranzano carefully scrutinized each of the bodies, the crime scenes. He quickly had the bodies placed in body bags and sent to the morgue on Via Giovanna, knowing the Italian press, indeed the world press, would have a field day with these murders; that it would be on the minds and lips of every Italian in the country, in the north and south, for Italians, he knew, held the Catholic Church in high esteem and reverence.

In all his colorful career, Nino Maranzano had never faced the public scandal, the inevitable outrage, that these murders would surely beget. He ordered every available policeman in Rome to question people on the blocks and in the neighborhoods where the murders had occurred. No one, he was told as dawn was shyly showing itself, skulking into Rome's ancient avenues, streets and piazzas as quietly as a passing cloud, had seen the killer. The fierce Roman sun returned. By 8:00 that morning it was already 99 degrees with 70 percent humidity, and no hint of even a breeze.

Maranzano heard several reports, however, of a bald priest on a bicycle hurrying away from murder scenes. At first no one had connected him with the killings, for many priests used bikes to get around Rome. But as Maranzano made his way back to his office, at nearly 9:00 AM, he began to wonder about this priest on a bike.

He called a meeting of all of Rome's senior detectives, twenty-two serious-faced men and women and explained his theory. He said, "I'm thinking the killer has cleverly disguised himself as a priest. If I were him and my mission were to kill priests—as his clearly is—there would be no better disguise than to become a priest—the object of his hunt, his obsession. I can guarantee that our people and the *carabinieri* saw him pedaling about Roma last night and even politely greeted him.

"People, we are hunting a very cunning individual obsessed with murdering our priests. I'm thinking he is the same man who killed the priests in New York. The coincidences are too great for it not to be him. I want all of you to start visiting hotels and pensions. He has to be staying somewhere in Roma, and I want him found! Also, I want the names of all men traveling alone recently arrived in Roma from New York." He now held up the composite sketch Tony Flynn had sent him.

"Based on the assumption that we are looking for this man, he has cut off his long hair and is now bald, and he has a bicycle—a bicycle that he had to buy somewhere in Roma. I very much doubt that he brought a bike from New York, but if he did there will be a record of it on airline manifests. My instincts tell me he bought the bike in Roma, and I want you to question the sales people in all the bicycle shops in Roma and find out if anyone fitting this man's description purchased a bike," he said, angrily holding up the composite. "And, too, he had to buy a priest's cassock; question the people in the shops who sell such clothing, starting with those closest to the Vatican. I want no stone unturned. He's out there, probably within walking distance, and I want him *found!*" he shouted, his black Neapolitan eyes blazing, his strong jaw set into a severe line.

He added, "I tell you all now, if, when you find him, he gives you the slightest cause, take him down. A man like this does not deserve to breathe the same air as decent people. We must send a message that anyone who does such things in Italia will meet a quick and final justice," he said and finally told them to go find him and soon returned to his office.

There were numerous messages for him from the Vatican, the courts and the prime minister's office. Before he returned any of those calls, he phoned his wife. The answering machine picked up and he listened to his own deep voice asking to leave a message.

TWENTY

Carole Cunningham phoned Captain Flynn to tell him that one of the priests, John Sulivan, who had been arrested at Saint Mary's Church on 39th Street—where the first priest, Father Joseph, had been killed—had agreed to testify at a grand jury against Monsignor O'Brian, the man in charge of the Saint Mary's parish.

Excited by this willing, articulate witness, she said, "We had him brought down from the Tombs earlier and he hasn't stopped talking. He's giving us facts, places, names and dates—the whole enchilada. His testimony is going to finally expose how the Church hierarchy here in the States not only knew about the predator priests, but that they themselves are an intricate part of the apparatus they carefully created—like busy spiders weaving webs to abuse children.

"Tony, he's saying that children in the Church's control were and still are being used in child pornography, which he says he actually helped make and which they were selling to pedophile groups around the world. We finally have a priest who was on the inside willing to tell the truth about what's really been going on. He says that more than half of all Catholic priests are homosexual, and once pedophiles learned they would be protected, fed and clothed and given the best free legal council— and unencumbered access to trusting children—they joined the Church en masse and became part of an underground society whose sole purpose was and is systematic abuse."

"Where is he now?" Flynn asked.

"We ordered in some Chinese food for him and he's having dinner. I swear I want to punch his face, but I've been all smiles; not easy, I can tell you. We are putting him into the witness protection program. Everything he's said has been videotaped and recorded. Truth is he is an excellent witness, candid and sincere and looks you right in the eye as he talks. When he's finished eating we are going to begin again and not stop until he's told everything he knows. Tony, he says that Rome, the Vatican, knew *all* about everything but just turned a blind eye; didn't give a damn about the victims. Far as I'm concerned, we're going to indict anyone who had information about what was happening and did nothing—including cardinals and the pope himself if necessary," she said with steely conviction.

141

"Let's meet later. When you're finished, buzz me and I'll come down. Maybe we can grab a bite."

"I'd like that," she said, and they soon hung up.

Thinking over what he just heard, Flynn went back to work helping to field the hundreds of calls pouring into the task force. At 10:00 Cunningham phoned to tell him she was finished. He left the war room at Midtown North and drove down to her place. She played for him some of what John Sulivan said. As well as providing detailed times and places, he had given a long list of priests who he said were a part of the "brotherhood," as he called it, all of whom would be, Cunningham and Flynn agreed, arrested over the next few days by both detectives from the District Attorney's office and detectives working out of the task force.

It was now that Cunningham received a call from a colleague at work who said that she had just heard the news that John Krol—one of the most infamous of all the predator priests, a bug-faced man whose skin was lined like a wrinkled paper bag—had been brutally beaten to death in a Boston prison by a fellow inmate. When Carole hung up, she told Flynn the news. "I'm not surprised," he said.

"I'm going to use this incident as leverage to get other priests to testify against one another. This is a war and we are going to win it."

"Good idea," Flynn said, admiring Carole's mind—her tenacity, how she'd use anything she could to get the job done. They ordered pizza and salads, had dinner, hugged and kissed and Flynn went back to the war room to help designate detectives to arrest priests named by John Sullivan, and to thoroughly canvass the parishes where there had been murders, follow up on the many leads pouring into the police hotline.

Near 4:00 AM Flynn first learned that two more priests had been killed in Rome; that they each had been murdered in the identical fashion as the first—and the ones in New York. He hurried upstairs to his office, carrying his fifth cup of coffee in as many hours and put a call in to Chief Inspector Maranzano in Rome. The Chief Inspector confirmed that indeed two more priests had been killed. He said, his voice grave and filled with quiet rage, "Captain, I'm convinced the man you are looking for is here. I've ordered my people to begin working the airline manifests, to look for a single man from New York traveling alone.

"We received reports," he went on, "of a bald-headed priest on a bicycle leaving the area of two of the murders. I'm thinking that he's cut off his hair and is disguising himself as a priest."

That, Flynn thought, fit well into his hypothesis that the killer had indeed gone to Rome for revenge against the Church . . . that he was intent upon terrorizing priests and the Church hierarchy itself. Maranzano continued: "The wounds are so identical to the wounds in the autopsy photos you were kind enough to provide, it is a certainty the same hand is responsible. I've also ordered my people to question shop owners who sell priest clothing and those who sell bicycles."

Flynn wanted to say that he was doing the right thing, but did not want to seem as if he were talking down to the chief inspector. He was, Flynn was thinking, an extremely able investigator who knew well the nuts and bolts of real police work.

There was a soft knock on the chief inspector's door. A young aide stood there. Maranzano asked Flynn to hold on. He turned his attention to the aide and wanted to know what was so important that he interrupted his conversation, his dark eyes boring into the aide's young face.

"Sir, we just received the results of the DNA comparison from the lab—"

"Ahh, very good, bring it in," Maranzano ordered, quickly opening the sealed packet and scanning the report, which, on the second line, stated that the DNA samples from New York definitely matched the DNA taken from Bishop Giovanni Boldera.

Maranzano said, "Captain, I was just handed the DNA comparison results, and they confirm what we've suspected. Your killer definitely came to Roma."

Though Flynn had suspected all along that his quarry had gone to Rome—and was somewhat relieved to have it confirmed—he was still taken aback by the fact that the killer had traveled halfway around the world for the express purpose of killing human beings. This added a deeper, diabolical dimension to the investigation, to what was driving the killer.

Flynn finished his coffee and sat back, taking a long deep breath, the multiple ramifications of this reality quickly running through his mind. Chief Inspector Maranzano continued, "Captain, I think it's best for now that neither the press nor the Church find this out."

"Of course, I agree," Flynn said, knowing, however, that he could not keep it from his boss, and consequently the commissioner.

Maranzano went on, "The press knowing about this will only impede our investigation, and make this more of a media circus than it already is . . . if that is possible," he added. "Captain, I would suggest that you start reviewing all the videotape of the passengers who boarded flights to Roma from the New York area."

"Since 9/11 all the airlines are videotaping everyone going through security and he'll definitely be on tape and we'll find him," Flynn said, his mind already working on the intricate details of how to do this without tipping the media—and the Church. "We'll get on it as soon as possible," he said. "With the help of the composite we should be able to make him immediately."

"Excellent. Captain, I want to assure you that no resource will be spared in the apprehension of this man. These murders are outraging all of Italy. The prime minister called me about them, as well as an emissary from the pope himself.

"Captain, I saw myself the bodies of his victims and it is clear that he eviscerated and castrated them after they were dead, or very close to death, out of sheer cruelty."

"And revenge, Chief Inspector. As I've told you, we have a serious problem here with predator priests, and we believe this man, as a boy, had been severely abused by a priest, or priests.

"Some of the priests housed in the rectories where the murders occurred actually had child pornography in their rooms, and one of these individuals has agreed to tell us all he knows. The numbers of molesters in the church, and the extent to which their influence reaches, is mind boggling. Please don't misunderstand, Chief Inspector, I'm not defending in any way what this man has done, I'm just trying to give you a handle on what might be driving him. The priest I'm telling you about says that individuals in the Vatican—bishops and cardinals—not only knew about what was going on, but helped cover it up; and therefore enabled the molesters."

"Captain, I am a devout Catholic and words cannot express how outraged and disappointed this scandal, what the Church has allowed to happen, makes me. It would, like you say, seem logical that a severely abused boy could very well grow into a full-fledged psychopath, as this man clearly is. Captain, I want you to know that I will assist you in all your investigations into the criminal activities of these child predators who have found their way into *my* Church," he emphasized, venom dripping from his words.

"I appreciate that, Chief Inspector," Flynn said.

"I believe you have the death penalty in New York, correct?"

"We do."

"Regardless, Captain, of why this man is doing what he is doing, he would be an excellent candidate for the death sentence . . . don't you agree?"

"Most definitely," Flynn said, it obvious to him that the Chief Inspector wanted the perp dead. But Flynn knew New York's death sentence—put into law by Governor George Pataki in 1999—was, in reality, a death sentence without teeth, for none of the six men given the death penalty to date had been executed. Five of them had killed cops, one of whom was a dear friend of Tony Flynn's.

He said, "This brings up a question I've been meaning to ask you, Chief Inspector. When you do apprehend him, do you think the Italian judiciary will allow him to be extradited back, to New York?"

"This will have to be answered by the public prosecutor and the courts. As I'm sure you know, Italy and the States have an extradition treaty for murder."

"Yes, I do know," Flynn said, remembering well when in 2001, he traveled to Milan to bring back a fugitive who had killed his own wife and two children and fled to Europe, and was apprehended in Cortina, Italy.

Flynn and Maranzano made plans to speak later in the day and after Flynn hung up he sat there mulling over whether he should wake up Carole Cunningham and his boss, to give them this news, but decided it could wait a few hours, until 8:30 or so. Instead, he went back downstairs to tell the task force detectives on duty, people he knew well and trusted implicitly, that he had reason to believe their target went to Rome. He designated detectives to start contacting airline security so they could view all video of male passengers boarding the flights to Rome on

Tuesday evening, certain that the killer had gone to Rome that day.

However, they soon found out there were many more airlines that flew from Kennedy and Newark airports to Rome than they first had thought, for most all the major airlines had indirect flights, which, of course made the task of checking the surveillance videos that much more difficult. Altogether eleven airlines flew, with stop-overs in other countries, to Rome from the East Coast.

Knowing the coming day would be a busy one, Flynn went back upstairs and lay down on the folding cot he had set up in his office for a catnap. Flynn had, over many years of practice, perfected the art of catnaps, for his work often involved demanding twenty-four hour shifts. He set his portable Braun alarm to wake him in two hours, at 6:00 AM; it would be, he knew, noon in Rome, and the last thought he had before slipping off to a fleeting though restful sleep was where the killer was in Rome; if he was seeing the sights, the Colosseum, the Vatican, the Circus Maximus.

TWENTY-ONE

The name of the bookshop was Rinascita. It was on the very fashionable Via Veneto, which was lined with four-star restaurants that had fancy glass-enclosed air-conditioned cafes and elegant clothing shops representing all the famous Italian designers—Armani, Missoni, Versace, Ferre, Krizia, Fendi, Gucci and Moschino. The bookstore was just down the tree-lined block, a hundred steps or so, from the heavily guarded American Embassy.

Diane Pane, a little after noon that sweltering July day,

entered the bookstore. She was looking for more books about the feud between the peoples of Calabria and Sicily, for her novel involved the famous bad blood between these two stoic peoples who lived only five kilometers apart. Both groups were Italian, but had disliked and feuded with one another since the beginning of time. Their bad blood, she knew, first began over the fishing rights in the bountiful Tyrrhenian Sea, which separated the two peoples, and escalated to violence, the regular drawing of blood, clandestine attacks on one another's homes and villages. Diane, dressed in comfortable sandals, khaki shorts and a halter top, was adding to the tall pile of books she already had on the history of the two lands, on ancient Rome, Julius Caesar, Marc Anthony and Cleopatra.

While researching her stories, Diane pretty much stopped paying attention to the world around her. She totally immersed herself in the elements, characters, locales, histories and times her stories played out in. She believed one of the keys to the commercial success of her novels was her research and it was something she enjoyed doing immensely. She now spotted a hard-to-find book about Julius Caesar written by the Roman scholar Cicero—translated into English—and she quickly grabbed the book and opened it, pleased by this rare find.

Once a devoted professor of literature at Berkeley, Diane had walked away from teaching after the death of her husband and began writing professionally seven years ago come January. She was lucky early on, for she found a well-connected, enthusiastic San Francisco agent, Loretta Brown, who encouraged and prodded Diane, and she immediately sold her first book—a love story that played out before, during and after the great San Francisco earthquake of April 18, 1906.

The book, *That Fateful Day*, became a best seller and was

optioned for a film while still in galley form.

Diane's husband—a man she loved very much—also a professor at Berkeley, died after a long, painful bout with brain cancer. Diane had done everything she could for him—slept in his hospital room with him, spoon fed him, held his hand, read Greek mythology to him—a subject he loved—and was there the night he passed on. She watched him take his last breath, closed his still open eyes.

Diane was devastated by her husband's death. She began eating like there was no tomorrow, drinking excessively, cried herself to sleep every night for weeks after he passed on. So taken by her loss, she even thought about suicide. But above all, Diane Pane was a fighter. An only child with an abusive, alcoholic mother, Diane had left home at eighteen, worked two jobs and put herself through college with the help of scholarships. Three months to the day after her husband's death, Diane resolved to get on with her life, and wrote a proposal for her first book, which secured her the agent and a lucrative book deal with a New York publisher.

Soon after Diane signed a book contract, she began jogging every day and for several months researched the San Francisco earthquake, the reality of the devastation it caused, the many lives it destroyed, and carefully studied hundreds of black and white photographs. She soon lost all the weight she had put on and, for the most part, didn't think of anything but her book, and because of it she was able to finally put the loss of her husband behind her.

Diane had had a few relationships since her husband's demise, one of which was with the editor of her last book, but they all proved to cause more problems than they were worth—a distraction—and Diane had pretty much resolved to dwell alone in the world of books.

At forty-four, Diane never looked so good, had earned a

lot of money, could go where she wanted, when she wanted, how she wanted; she was, for the most part, content.

Though deep inside, Diane still yearned for love and, often, when she wrote love scenes, she became so aroused that she felt compelled to pleasure herself. A thing she was becoming somewhat tired of.

Now, in the bookstore on the Via Veneto in Rome, her cell phone buzzed. Annoyed by its disturbance she handed the book to the clerk, said she wanted it, to please hold it, and quickly made her way outside to answer the phone. Diane hated people who chatted on cell phones in loud voices like there was no one in the world but them. Stepping back into the Roman heat, she said, "Hello."

"Diane Pane?" he asked.

"Yes?"

"It's me, Frank Lewis . . . I hope I'm not calling at a bad time."

"Not at all," she said, surprised he was phoning at all.

"Diane, I want to apologize for being so standoffish; it's just that I was really taken by the Colosseum—"

"Oh, that's okay, not to worry, no need to apologize, I understand," she said.

"I didn't mean to be rude—"

"You weren't, don't concern yourself," she said, curious about the sudden interest, her perfectly arched brows coming together, seeming to make two question marks, as they did when Diane was puzzled.

"Anyway, I'm calling because I'm leaving Rome—it's just *too* hot here—and I was going to go down South. I understand it's cooler and I'm thinking it would be nice to be near the ocean. Diane, I was wondering if you'd like some company on the drive down? When did you say you were leaving?"

This all caught Diane off guard. She had been planning

this trip for months, had her rented BMW already waiting in the garage of her hotel down the block, two boxes of books on the backseat, her luggage and personal effects filling the trunk, and her plans did not include traveling with anyone else. But as she remembered him—his outrageously handsome face, sincere dark eyes, shy, respectful ways, she warmed to the idea. She said, "I was planning to leave tonight, when it got cooler and there'd be less traffic. Do you have a destination?"

"I've heard Positano is breathtakingly beautiful and I've arranged to stay at a hotel up on the cliffs."

"Yes, it is lovely," she said, knowing it was, this time of year, overflowing with rich tourists showing off their riches, very difficult to get around, its beaches ridiculously crowded, but she said none of this to him, not wanting to put a damper on his plans.

"Perfect," he said. "If you like, I'd be happy to share the driving, and pay for the gas."

"That won't be necessary," she said, smiling to herself. "Sure, you're welcome to come," she said before she realized it, the words seeming to come out of their own volition. "I can drop you in Positano on my way to Amalfi," she added, not wanting to seem like she had any kind of designs—that she was pleased he called. "I have to drive right through Positano to get to Amalfi—"

"Great. If you like, I can come and meet you later."

"Okay, sure," she said. "Meet me in front of my hotel, The Pantheon on Via Veneto, just near the Villa Borghese . . . say 8:30—that good?"

"Perfect—just perfect," he said, a rare smile coming to his handsome face, knowing he could reach the hotel by walking through the shadows of the sprawling park.

"Okay, then, I'll see you later," he said, obviously pleased. "Ciao," he added, and disconnected.

Hmmm, she thought, gladly walking back into the air-conditioned shop, promising herself that if he proved to be difficult in any way, a distraction, she'd get rid of him pronto. She felt no kind of threat from him, was not concerned about traveling alone with him at all.

Back in the bookstore, she bought the book by Cicero, three other books about ancient Rome, some maps of Southern Italy, paid for them and walked to The American Café on the corner of Via Veneto and Via del Corso, took a seat in the air-conditioned café, ordered an iced macchiato and thought about her traveling companion, liking the fact that he had not immediately come on to her. That indeed he had been "standoffish," didn't come over to her in the Sistine Chapel, was shy and introspective when she'd first met him on the bus from the airport to Rome; she was pleased that he'd phoned, thinking he *might* even be more than a traveling companion. Maybe he was gay, she thought, let down by that prospect, knowing that there was a large gay community in Positano.

Maybe that was why he was so reserved. I'll soon find out, she mused, opened her book about Julius Caesar and began to read the preface, immediately drawn into it, forgetting him, her mind going back to her story.

TWENTY-TWO

Chief Inspector Maranzano was just leaving his boss's office, where he'd been thoroughly grilled by ten different ministers in the Rome Department of Justice, all Catholics, all outraged that an American serial killer had the temerity to come to Rome for the express purpose of killing priests, disciples of God, respected members of their religion. The men they confessed their sins to; the men who married them, baptized their children, prayed over their bodies when their end finally came. They were so angry that they shouted and cursed and demanded, in no uncertain terms, that Maranzano find the killer and make sure that he didn't see the inside of a courtroom.

They wanted, they said, his body to be riddled with bullets and for the Chief Inspector to make sure it was shown on the Italian news, for like that, they said, the Italian people would find solace, some relief for the heated-anger and public outrage the priest killings had caused.

Sweating, knowing his career rode on the successful outcome of this case, Maranzano left the meeting and oversaw the deployment of hundreds of *polizia* and *carabinieri* all over Rome, and using the composite sketch it didn't take long to find the shop where the killer had bought the priest cassock. In fact, the shop keeper still had the 50-euro note the killer had used to pay for the outfit, which was immediately checked for prints, put under a special purple light, but there were no discernable prints on the bill, which the police would keep, they told the shopkeeper, for evidence.

They also discovered the bicycle shop on Via Salaria where the killer had bought the bike he used, an inexpensive Botecchia model that cost 112 euros. The shop owner, a young muscular man who for the last four years had raced in the Tour de France, also told the tight-lipped, angry-eyed Italian detectives who quickly filled up his shop, that the killer was polite, spoke little Italian, and had paid for the bike in cash, which he had already deposited in the bank, he said.

"But," he added, "I've seen him pass the shop twice with the bike and so I think he lives nearby."

When Chief Inspector Maranzano heard this, he flooded the entire neighborhood where the bike shop was with two hundred fifty-seven police personnel, set up a command center and had his people knock on every door, question every person in the street, question all the shop owners, looking for the killer.

A S.W.A.T. team of heavily armed sharpshooters was brought in, and they patiently waited in the black and red van for the killer to be found, knowing that he must die, knowing, too, that the death must appear as if he had wielded a weapon. Already an undocumented .22 pistol was given to them, which they were to put in the killer's hand when he was dead . . . on the way to hell where he would burn forever, they were sure.

Chief Inspector Maranzano kept trying to reach his wife but there was no answer at their home, or her cell phone, which she always had with her, never shut off. It was often the only way he was able to locate her when he was in the field. *Strange*, he thought.

The killer had just stepped from the shower and was toweling himself off, looking forward to meeting Diane Pane, proud of his perfect pitch to her, the inflection in his voice, how he so sincerely said her name—*Diane*, when he absently looked out a window which faced Via Corelli and he was stunned to see *polizia* and *carabinieri* up and down the block.

They hadn't yet, he knew, found out exactly where he lived, but they obviously knew he was staying in the neighborhood, and it wouldn't be long before they came banging on his door. In a hurry he dressed, put his few things in a leather shoulder bag and bolted from the apartment, up the stairs and onto the roof.

TWENTY-THREE

That morning Tony Flynn first phoned his boss, Chief Samuels, and told him that their quarry was definitely in Rome; that his DNA was matched with the killer of the priests in Rome. There was a long, pensive silence.

"Glad to be rid of the scumbag," Samuels said, as he cleared his throat.

He continued, "Tony, I think maybe you and one or two of your people should go to Rome and see if maybe you could help them out. I know the public here, the mayor and governor and the Church will all demand that he be brought back, and maybe you could start the wheels moving in the right direction."

"Sure, I'd like to go, John," Flynn said, hoping he'd be asked to go to Rome, knowing it was, from a political point of view, the prudent thing to do.

Sitting in his kitchen in his home in Pearl River, a plate of ham and eggs in front of him, Chief Samuels imagined the news footage of the killer, in chains, being led off the plane that brought him back.

"I'll take it up with the commissioner right away," he said. "And get back to you ASAP."

"Fine," Flynn said, hung up and phoned Carole Cunningham.

"Hope I didn't wake you," he said.

"I've been up for hours, couldn't sleep, was watching the news—"

"He's definitely in Rome. He's been positively IDed via the DNA."

"Really," she said, kind of incredulous. "You sure?"

"The DNA has been definitely matched."

"Hmm," she said. "At least he's out of our hair," knowing she'd now be able to focus more of her energy on prosecuting the priests who had been arrested in the last few days, and the priests, cardinals and bishops that John Sullivan had named, getting more of them to talk, to turn on one another. That was the key, she knew. She was relatively certain none of the higher-ups, the bishops or cardinals, would prefer jail over cooperating with her, the District Attorney's office, knowing that jails were a notoriously dangerous place for child molesters—thinking about Krol's death just the day before. She had learned that the man who killed him was a neo-Nazi who carefully planned the murder for over a month, facts she planned to use to turn other rogue priests because all jails had a large population of skin heads and neo-Nazis, only too happy to do in a child molester guised as a priest. *Ironic*, she thought, that a neo-Nazi killer would end up helping her, a prosecutor, get leverage in going after one of society's most heinous criminals.

Flynn said, "I'd like you to check into the extradition treaty we have with Italy and let me know your thoughts. If it's possible we want him back here to put him on trial."

"Of course. I'll do it right away and I'll call some friends I have in the Southern District and get back to you."

"Great, thanks, we'll talk later then," he said, got up to shower and head out to Kennedy airport with a dozen task force detectives to start looking at video tapes of passengers getting on planes bound for Rome, a daunting task he wasn't looking forward to, but something that had to be done, even if the killer was in Rome. Flynn knew that if they could locate actual video of the killer it would make the Roman cops' job, and by extension his job, that much easier.

He took a quick shower and shave in the captain's bathroom—letting ice-cold water run over his head and body for a few moments—changed his clothes, and was about to go downstairs to designate his people for the trip out to the airports and to put together a comprehensive list of priests named by John Sullivan to be arrested in the New York, tri-state area. Salerno buzzed him, said, "Captain, I've got a guy on the line who swears he knows who the killer is. Says he was a patient of his a few years back at Creedmoore State. He was in South America and returned just last night, saw the composite on the morning news and called. Captain, he says he was hospitalized for killing a priest when he was twelve years old." That caused red lights to spin in Tony's head, a chill to run up his spine.

"What's his name?" he asked.

"Dr. Charles Hartock, on line four."

Immediately, Flynn picked up line four.

"Hello, Dr. Hartock," he said, hoping this was the break he was looking for.

TWENTY-FOUR

All the buildings on Via Corelli were three and four stories tall, shaded by elm, maple and cypress trees of equal heights. He was able to easily pass from one building's roof to the next, always stepping gingerly with his rubber-soled shoes; he didn't want to alert any of the people in the top-floor apartments—many of whom knew about the hunt for the priest killer—that someone was on the roof.

From the roofs he had a bird's-eye view of the police activity on Via Corelli and the surrounding streets. His luck was still apparently holding out, for none of the police, believing the element of surprise was theirs, had yet come up to the roofs, though there was a circling police helicopter and he had to duck behind a standing wall or parapet frequently to avoid detection. He had no idea how they knew he was staying on the block, but that didn't matter. All that mattered now was meeting Diane Pane and getting out of Rome. Hiding in shadows, he peered down at the police hurrying back and forth on the block, waiting for the right moment to flee.

TWENTY-FIVE

Dr. Charles Hartock was a bear of a man with a well-trimmed gray beard, dark inquisitive eyes, broad shoulders, a barrel chest. He looked, Flynn thought when he first met him, more like a professional wrestler than one of the foremost psychiatrists in the United States, whose expertise was the specific psychoses suffered by children who had been the victims of prolonged abuse. Dr. Hartock had written numerous papers on the subject, three books, which were in fact case studies of different patients under his care, and lectured around the world. He'd been in São Paulo, Brazil, for the past five weeks interviewing convicted murderers for a planned book on the correlations between abused children and violent criminal behavior. He had found that 87 percent of the convicted murderers in the infamous Solori prison had early histories involving physical, mental or sexual abuse, some of a nature so reprehensible that even he, a man in the field for twenty years, had a hard time comprehending how adults could be so barbarous to the smallest, most vulnerable members of society. He had, to date, interviewed convicted murderers in

The Netherlands, India and the United States—at Starke Prison in Florida and Angola State in Louisiana. Hartock still had an office in Creedmoore State Hospital, and an office at East 99th Street and Park Avenue, on the ground floor of the co-op building in which he lived. These days he didn't see that many patients—only special cases when he was called on by a colleague to help evaluate and suggest treatments. He was devoting most of his professional time to writing, to putting down on paper all he had personally seen and learned over twenty years of careful, clinical observation, wanting to share his wealth of knowledge with others in his field. His books and papers were, for the most part, written for professionals, not the public at large, but still his books sold very well, and were translated into thirteen languages.

When, earlier, Flynn had heard what Hartock had to say, he asked if it would be possible to speak with him in person. Hartock readily agreed, and Flynn and Salerno jumped in a black Plymouth and sped uptown, hoping Dr. Hartock was the break they'd been looking for. They double-parked in front of Hartock's office, stepped from the car, quickly approached Dr. Hartock's brass-handled door and rang the bell.

Hartock himself opened the door. "Please come in," he said, shaking both the detectives' hands with a mighty grip. He led them to his office, which had barred windows facing 99th Street, a pleasant tree-lined block. The walls of Hartock's office were crowded with diplomas, degrees, proclamations, awards and black-and-white photographs of children he had worked with over the years. A large air conditioner in the westernmost window quietly hummed, making the room cool and comfortable.

"Please, gentleman, have a seat," Hartock offered, gesturing with a large right hand toward two leather chairs in front of his mahogany desk.

"Can I offer you something cold to drink?" he asked.

"Nothing, thank you," Flynn said, Salerno shaking his head no.

"I appreciate you seeing us right away," Flynn said.

"Least I could do," Hartock said. "Like I told you, Captain, I was in Brazil and arrived home just last night, saw the story on NY1, the sketch and called. I'm sure it's him. His name is Frank Coogan—but that's what *they* named him."

"Who are they?" Flynn asked. "Mind if we take notes, Doctor?"

"Not at all; it's a long, involved story with many facets."

"We have all the time you need," Flynn said.

Salerno took a worn reporter's notebook out of his right rear pocket, a black felt pen from his shirt pocket. "Please," he said.

"I first met Frank," Hartock said, "when he was sent to Creedmoore after killing a priest at the Sacred Heart of Jesus Home for Boys in upstate New York. The murder occurred when he was twelve, but by the time he made his way through the system he was six months into his fourteenth year, a very troubled boy. Based on the notes in his file at Sacred Heart, he'd been left on the steps of a church in Spanish Harlem. He'd been battered over a period of time, had signs of severe physical abuse, serious head and brain trauma, broken limbs and black eyes. His age was approximated at twenty to twenty-four months. He spent the next several months at the Harlem Hospital and was finally placed in the Catholic charities foster care program. He was, in fact, adopted several times, but was returned by his adoptive parents. A particularly beautiful child, most every couple interested in adopting a boy wanted him, but quickly brought him back—"

"Why?" Flynn asked, curious.

"In a word—aggression. He attacked children already in the homes, threw an infant girl down a flight of stairs, tried to stab one of his foster mothers with a kitchen knife; and he set fires. He was designated as incorrigible and sent to Sacred Heart."

"How old was he then?" Flynn asked.

"Seven. Like I said, Frank was a very attractive little boy and I fear that, in the end, played strongly into the tragedy his life became. You see—and this we only discovered many years later—priests who worked at the home were predators and they freely and regularly abused the multitude of boys under their care. Prepubescent children without family or guardians who had, naturally, no one to turn to for help. Would you like to see a picture of Frank?"

"Yes, please," Flynn said, excited at the prospect of an actual photograph of the man he'd been hunting, who was front-page news on all three of the major New York newspapers. Dr. Hartock stood and lumbered over to the west wall and removed a black-and-white glossy in a silver frame off the wall, handed it to Flynn. "This is Frank at seven . . . when he first arrived at Sacred Heart. I have no idea who took it. I found it in his file." Flynn took the frame, put on his glasses and together he and Salerno studied it. The photograph was of a dark haired boy with huge walnut-shaped eyes, a small upturned nose, full heart-shaped lips, broad cheekbones, a lion's mane of black hair recklessly cascading down to his shoulders. He was so attractive, his features so refined and delicate, for a moment Flynn thought he was a girl.

There was, Flynn could see, a distinct sadness in the boy's eyes, and, too, a strange distant element, like the seed of insanity had already been planted but not yet taken bloom. They reminded him of the eyes he'd seen in caged animals at the zoo left in small spaces for too long.

Staring at the photograph, Flynn wondered how this innocent, adorable child could turn into a serial killer, a dedicated predator of men. That question ringing in his head, in his eyes, about his face, he looked to Dr. Hartock for the answer.

TWENTY-SIX

Inspector Nino Maranzano was sitting in the mobile police center on Via Pietro when the walkie talkie on the foldable table in front of him crackled and came to life: "Chief Inspector, we located him!" came the excited voice in a rush of words. "He took an apartment on the top floor of number 17 on Via Corelli. We found the bike in the first-floor foyer; an elderly woman in the building just IDed him. She said when she first saw him he had long hair, but now it's gone."

"Don't move. I'll be right there!" Maranzano commanded, leaping from the vehicle and sprinting full out to Via Corelli, a block away, and on to number 17. The S.W.A.T. team, masked and dressed all in black, their sleek, blue-black weapons cocked and ready, joined him. Maranzano ordered both sides of the block closed off, and coordinated teams of people up to the roofs and without further hesitation he ordered the S.W.A.T. team into action. Moving as one, in a straight line, as if a giant insect about to strike, they hurried inside the building and quietly hustled on the balls of their feet to the top floor, each absolutely intent upon taking out *l'assassino del prete*—the priest killer, as they had collectively taken to calling him. One of them carried the .22 they were going to plant on his lifeless body. At the door marked number 5, three men took up positions on the right, two on the left, and the sixth man, a particularly large, powerful man, using a custom-constructed battering ram that weighed sixty kilos, charged the door, easily smashed it open, sending its lock flying, as the other five simultaneously ran inside, ready to kill, eyes wide, followed by Maranzano. Covered in sweat, adrenaline coursing through all of their veins, they discovered the apartment was empty, though they quickly realized that he'd just showered, the tub and floor still wet. Maranzano ordered all personnel to close in on the buildings surrounding Via Corelli, to keep a sharp eye on anyone entering the Villa Borghese, just down the block. Maranzano knew the park was the perfect place for the killer to flee, and he ordered *carabinieri* and *polizia* to saturate the park, for *carabinieri* on horseback to patrol the northeast side of the park, and he ordered blood hounds to be brought to the apartment, *immediatamente*. He also ordered a team of criminalists in to dust for fingerprints, to look for clues.

His heart racing, sweat covering his face, stinging his eyes, he watched from a roof down the block as the S.W.A.T. team gathered in front of the building from which he had just fled, wondering how the hell they had found him so quickly. He saw Inspector Maranzano come running down the street, knew instinctively that he was heading the hunt for him. He could readily see that this was a powerful, dangerous man—a potent adversary who would never stop chasing him. Now in front of the building, he watched Maranzano give orders to the black-clad S.W.A.T. team, and all of them rush into the building. Sure they would soon be searching the roofs, he now opened the trap door of the building he was on and made his way down the marble stairs, as Maranzano and the S.W.A.T. people hurried up the stairs of number 17.

When he reached the ground floor, he peered out the front door and saw teams of *polizia* gathering in groups, entering buildings, loading weapons. Taking a long deep breath, he bent himself over and moved down the two stairs to the sidewalk as if he were a cripple, hunched back, infirm, turned left and began to feebly hobble toward the park. Nearly bent in half, he looked like a walking question mark, a trick he'd learned from another patient at Creedmoore State Hospital for the criminally insane.

He had never thought of himself as insane. He was sure the rest of the world was at odds with itself . . . was insane.

He hadn't gone ten paces when a sergeant in the *carabinieri* spotted him, but so convincing was his act that the sergeant didn't think of challenging him, and he made it across the street and was just about to enter the park when someone called out: "Attenzione . . . fermati!" *Attention, stop.* But he kept moving, as the commands to stop became louder and more demanding, grew frantic. Just inside the park, he dropped the infirm act and took off like a deer. Shots rang out, echoing off buildings lining the park. Bullets zipped past him, hit nearby trees, tore up the dirt at his feet.

As a mob of police chased the killer, Maranzano heard about the man running into the park, that shots had been fired, the report of which he could hear coming through the open window of the apartment. He and the S.W.A.T. team ran down the stairs and headed for the park.

Sure they had him, Maranzano ordered all the park's exits sealed, the dogs brought over, helicopters to use their flood lights to illuminate the park. Quickly the dogs arrived, two large blood hounds with tired, watery eyes and comically floppy ears hanging nearly to the ground. They picked up the scent right off and began after him, baying as they went, anxiously pulling their handler. Maranzano followed close behind, barking orders into his walkie-talkie, which was in his left hand, his 9mm custom-cut Barretta in his right hand. Helicopters roared overhead, their giant flood lights eerily illuminating the park. Tall thin shadows danced frantically. Sirens screamed as police vehicles converged, racing toward the park, which quickly became saturated with anxious *carabinieri* and *polizia*.

Never having smoked, a naturally endowed superb athlete, the killer ran west with disarming speed, toward the Via Veneto exit of the park, staying in thick foliage, using darkened nature paths and the natural camouflage offered by the sprawling park, the screams of the sirens ringing in his ears, the roar of the helicopters overhead, the howls of the blood hounds behind him. As he went he saw two excited *carabinieri* on huge chestnut-colored horses moving in the direction from which he had come, one of the horses looking in his direction, as if the horse knew he was there, what he'd done, that he was being hunted.

Running, he made for the Via Veneto; the lions in the nearby zoo, disturbed by all the noise, the kinetic hub-bub, the spinning red lights, let out powerful roars. He passed the statues of four majestic lionesses in a row in front of a whispering fountain. They reminded him of the Colosseum, and he was angry that he had to leave Rome so quickly, but he had caused, he knew, real fear to live in the cold hearts of the *perverse criminals* in the Vatican, as he thought of them. And he planned to return to Rome so he could continue his work . . . kill the pope.

Thirsty, he knelt and drank from the fountain the lions guarded. The water was cold and sweet. Night had completely cloaked the park by now and in his black clothes he was just about invisible, as he continued on, carrying his shoulder bag, calming himself, wiping sweat from his face and bald head. Near the Via Veneto exit he hid behind a thick cluster of hedges, which had been dried to a bright yellow color by three months of draught. He didn't want to be late to meet Diane. His best hope of getting away now, he knew, was her.

Waiting for the right moment, he calmed himself further, watching speeding police vehicles with screaming sirens move back and forth, and again he heard the male lion in the nearby zoo let out a mighty roar.

Sitting there, waiting, he began to fantasize about the Colosseum, hearing the cheers, the howls and growls of the bloodthirsty crowds. He often saw images before his eyes, as when you dream—but he was wide awake; he was hallucinating, a direct by-product of the damage that had been done to his brain.

TWENTY-SEVEN

Dr. Hartock said, "When I first began work with Frank, he refused to even talk with me—to say anything at all about why he killed the priest; about what had been done to him. During our sessions, he'd just sit and stare at me, all clammed up, his eyes defiant.

"He believed, initially, that I was part of the system that had brutalized him, and he viewed me as just another tentacle of the monster that had made his life a living nightmare. It took me nearly a year to get him to talk about what happened at Sacred Heart, to gain his trust. Ultimately I did it with books."

"Books?" Flynn asked.

"I had a copy of *Huckleberry Finn* on my desk and he kept staring at it. I gave it to him, and he read it in two days. Actually he devoured it. When he returned to my office with the book and I asked him if he liked it, I saw him smile for the first time in a year of trying to get him to open up, and I gave him another book, Melville's *Moby Dick*, and the same thing happened, and so we began discussing the books I gave him—Jack London's *White Fang, Call of the Wild*, Hemingway's *The Old Man and the Sea*— which he was comfortable talking about. In fact he talked about them with great enthusiasm. He loved to read. I kept giving him books and he just ate them up. They, the books, I came to realize, were the only true link to the outside world he ever had. I should mention that he was fascinated by ancient Rome and really enjoyed reading about it. He used to say that he was sure he had a life in Rome . . . as a gladiator in the Colosseum. And like that, after nearly another year of us talking about books, writers, writing, ancient Rome, he slowly began telling me about himself; about what had been done to him; about how he'd been abused by a cadre of priests and men in civilian clothes who regularly came to the home for sex. I'll tell you, gentlemen, my jaw fell open and I sat there appalled at what Frank explained happened to him, and many other boys at Sacred Heart.

"I naturally contacted the authorities, and there was an investigation, but the Church managed to convince the authorities that Frank was insane and all he said was a figment of his warped imagination; the deranged ranting of a problem child making up stories. This was all before the truth about the serial predators which had infiltrated the Church came out. Made public as it is now. And nobody would believe the boy."

"But *you* believed him?" Flynn asked.

"Absolutely. You see I had to pull it all out of him. He didn't tell me anything without patient coaxing.

"Gentlemen, Frank was severely sexually abused pretty much from the first day he arrived at Sacred Heart. The home—as we all know now because of the scandal the

Catholic Church has become embroiled in, and hundreds of depositions from people who were abused at the home—was run by a group of dedicated degenerates and sadistic pedophiles whose only concern, indeed obsession, was the abuse of the children in their care.

"This was, for me, one of the saddest stories I've heard in twenty years of studying abused children. I wrote a paper on the case, but the Church heard about it, sued me and in the end I wasn't able to even publish it."

"If possible, I'd like to read it," Flynn said.

"Certainly," Hartock said, walked to one of the six tall gray file cabinets on the east wall of the office, slid open a bottom drawer and drew out a thick file, opened it and handed Flynn the paper he'd written about Frank Coogan. It was entitled: *The Sinners at Sacred Heart*.

Flynn thanked him, scanned the pages, said he'd return it. The doctor told him he was welcome to keep it; that he had other copies.

Sitting back down, Dr. Hartock went on: "I worked with Frank for nearly all the years he was hospitalized. I was one of the four physicians who signed his release papers. I felt he had made a miraculous recovery, that he managed to get his years at Sacred Heart behind him with all the therapy—one on one and in groups—that he'd undergone. But apparently he didn't. Frank fooled all of us."

"Apparently," Flynn agreed, seeing and feeling this case now from a different perspective, thinking that the Church had, in a very real sense, created the monster Frank Coogan had become.

"I should mention," Dr. Hartock said, "that the first priest murdered, I believe on Monday at the Saint Mary's Church on the West Side, Father Joseph, he worked at the Sacred Heart of Jesus Home for Boys; and he was one of Frank's abusers."

"Really," Flynn said, somehow not surprised to hear this, the bizarre puzzle that had been before him suddenly coming together.

"When was Frank released from Creedmoore?" Flynn asked.

"He was first let out of the hospital two years ago, had a nine-month mandatory stay at a halfway house, did well, and was released to live wherever he wished, but he was still reporting to the hospital."

"Did he work?" Flynn asked.

"Most definitely. Frank is a computer whiz. He secured a very good position at Microware, created software for them. He just loved computers. Their precision, their exactness, their indifferent perfection. 'Computers,' he often said, 'don't lie.'"

Flynn asked, "Do you know, Doctor, if there are any recent photographs of Frank? I mean as an adult." He had no idea about what was happening in Rome; how Inspector Maranzano was swiftly closing in on *l'assassino del prete*.

TWENTY-EIGHT

The blood hounds getting closer, he could clearly hear the angry voices of the men in the S.W.A.T. team and Maranzano issuing orders, as they followed the baying hounds, who knew their quarry was nearby and bayed incessantly.

Knowing he had to move soon or he'd surely be captured, killed, he heard the screeching of tires, a loud crash, stood and looked toward the Via Veneto. A *carabinieri* vehicle with its distinct black and red markings, speeding along the Via de Porta, had crashed into an old Fiat being driven by an elderly nun, whose head had struck the windshield hard, shattering it. Unconscious, covered in blood, the nun was slumped motionless behind the wheel, her mouth hanging open, most all her teeth knocked out because of the crash. The *carabinieri* ran to her aid and in that moment, he stood and quickly left the sanctuary of the park, crossed the street without being stopped, as all the *carabinieri* struggled to get the nun out of the smashed Fiat.

Calmly, now, he made his way straight toward the Hotel Pantheon, a mere 150 feet from the park. Just as he reached the four-star hotel, he saw Diane walking out of the lobby carrying plastic bags filled with the books she'd bought earlier in the day. She spotted him, smiled and waved, having no idea about the raging psychopath that lurked behind his large half-moon smile; that the wailing of police sirens all over Rome was because of him.

"Hope I didn't keep you waiting," he said, gently shaking her hand, slowing his heart, presenting a calm façade.

"Not at all. I checked out earlier in the day. I just went inside to get some things I left with the concierge. The car's here. Just down the block," she said, and led him to a green BMW 525. "That all the luggage you have?" she asked, pointing to his shoulder bag, as they walked.

"I overnighted my luggage to the hotel before I spoke to you," he said, in a big hurry to get into the car, though careful about seeming anxious in any way.

"I see," she said. "All ready?"

"Absolutely," he said. "If I knew it was going to be this hot in Rome I swear I wouldn't have come," he added, wiping sweat from his brow, offering to carry her bag of books, which she let him do.

"Same here. I would have left weeks ago if it weren't for my work," she said.

"I really appreciate you letting me come with you like this, Diane," he said, making a point of opening the door for her, hearing the baying blood hounds as they drew closer and closer.

A gentleman, she thought, *a rare bird these days*. "I'll be happy to drive," he said. "If you like."

"No, that's okay. I like to drive," she said, getting in the car, reaching over and opening the door for him, arranging herself comfortably. Within minutes they were on the no-speed-limit Autostrada heading south at 90, away from Nino Maranzano, the blood hounds, the legions of angry *carabinieri* and *polizia* tearing up the Villa Borghese.

There was little traffic. They seemed to fly. Diane asked if he'd mind a little music, he said no, and she put a Bhudda Bar disc into the car's CD player. The relaxing, ethereal music filled the cool interior of the leather-smelling car.

"Nice music," he said.

"Glad you like it. So, Frank, please tell me about yourself," she said. One of Diane's *gifts*, as she thought about it, was getting people to open up; to talk about themselves.

"Not so much to tell," he said, intent upon making her like him, feel comfortable with him, want him around. Though he'd told her he had arranged to stay at a hotel in Positano, he knew he couldn't stay in any hotel; that he'd be recognized, the police summoned. His plan was to stay in the house Diane rented—by force if necessary—but he was hoping she invited him. He knew that would be preferable from numerous points of view, least of which was that he wanted to make Diane Pane his ally, not his prisoner.

TWENTY-NINE

"I've not seen any photographs of him as an adult," Dr. Hartock said. "Truth is, he hated cameras because he'd been forced to have pictures taken as he was abused. There could be, however, some photos of him as an adult at the hospital, or maybe where he worked."

"Do you know where he lived?" Flynn asked.

"Yes, he'd been staying in a state-subsidized transient hotel over on West 92nd Street and Broadway—The Greystone."

"If you would, Doctor, please tell us about the priest he killed as a boy; how did he do it? And what about the murder caused him to be sent to a psychiatric hospital, not a prison?"

"The priest's name was John Atkins. He was, according to what Frank eventually told me, a bona fide sadist and had caused the boy great pain over a period of years during sex acts—"

"What kind of pain?" Flynn asked, curious, leaning forward, not liking any of this.

"Seemed Atkins had a penchant for binding his victims, whipping them and forcing them to sodomize him with their penises and various objects. As all sadists, he became sexually aroused by inflicting pain, by terrorizing his victims, and he terrorized Frank many times over. He even took boys from the home to underground S & M clubs here in Manhattan—in the meat district—and forced them to commit all kinds of perversions. Unspeakable things. He was, apparently, particularly fond of Frank and often forced him to have sex. Frank, as you might imagine, grew to hate this man and he managed to steal a carving knife away from the kitchen where he worked cleaning dishes. He stole into Atkins's room in the middle of the night by climbing up a tree and going into an open window.

"Frank first cut Atkins's throat, then proceeded to mutilate his body. He cut off his head and took the severed head outside and stuck it on a post at the front gate and ran away. The police arrested him two days later, after he stole an apple pie from a farmer's windowsill some ten miles from Sacred Heart, and, deemed insane, he was sent to Creedmoore where I first encountered him."

"Was he hallucinating? Did he hear voices?" Flynn asked.

"In fact, yes. I diagnosed him as a severe schizophrenic psychopath with sadistic tendencies, filled with unbridled hatred.

"When I first heard about the priests' murders, I didn't initially think of Frank—not until I saw the composite sketch; then of course I knew . . . I knew it was him. When I realized it was him, I had to sit down; took the wind right out of me, you know," he said and Flynn could see that Dr. Hartock felt guilt about signing Frank Coogan's release papers, though he didn't say anything along those lines.

Flynn now explained that they had DNA proof that Coogan had gone to Rome; that he had killed and mutilated the three priests there.

"I'm not surprised he went to Rome," the doctor said. "I know he always felt the Vatican, their policies and dictates, were responsible for the predators infiltrating the Church. Especially the pope."

"You think he traveled under his own name?" Flynn asked.

"That's a hard question to answer. As I told you, Frank is a genuine computer whiz, and I would expect if he had a mind to he could have readily secured a false identity by hacking into various government offices and agencies."

"That's what I was just thinking," Flynn said, taking a long, deep breath, moving uncomfortably in his seat, wanting to get to the hospital, the place where Coogan had lived, worked, hoping he could find a current photograph of him, thinking about his trip to Rome, that he would take Rocco Genovese with him and leave Salerno in New York to oversee the task force, the arrests of the people named by John Sullivan, make sure his orders were followed.

THIRTY

•

When Maranzano and the S.W.A.T. team reached the Via Veneto exit of the Villa Borghese, they were soaking wet. Huffing and puffing, the two blood hounds were more excited than ever, knowingly sniffing the 99-degree air, the still warm sidewalk with their huge shiny noses. When Maranzano saw the accident, the unconscious nun being put into an ambulance, he immediately knew the priest killer had gotten out of the park using the distraction of the accident, and he angrily ordered the army of police under his command to start searching the surrounding streets and buildings, shops, cafés, rooftops, alleys and cellars.

Pulling their handler along the Via Veneto, passing the expensive boutiques, baying and barking as they went, the dogs headed straight to the Hotel Pantheon, seemed interested in it, raised their massive heads and howled, then headed off down the block, where they came to a sudden stop, their eyes becoming confused. Their trainer told Maranzano that the dogs had "lost the scent."

The first thing Maranzano did was show the revised composite sketch—he'd had an Italian police artist redo the sketch from New York without hair—to hotel employees, the people at the front desk of The Pantheon, and none of them had seen such a man, they said. But still, Maranzano had the hotel thoroughly searched, brought the overheated hounds to every floor—nothing. Tired, the hounds laid down in front of the hotel and refused to track, knowing their quarry had vanished.

Through most all this, Maranzano kept trying to reach his wife without success. He now ordered the altered sketch to be posted all over the neighborhood and he had police vehicles with loud speakers cruise the streets and avenues, circle the piazzas, telling people to be on the lookout for *l'assassino del prete*.

As the Roman police continued to search for the killer, Maranzano got into his car and hurried to his home— which his wife had designed—situated on a gently sloping hill on the outskirts of Rome, a white villa with a sweeping view of the ancient city. She was not there. He found a note from her on the kitchen table saying that she was leaving him, that their relationship had soured, that she was sick and tired of his running out on her whenever he pleased.

Stunned, Maranzano stared at the note, her neat handwriting, wondering where Lina had gone . . . if there was another man.

Feeling as though he'd been hit over the head with a club, he called her sister—no answer; he called her friends, her mother in Tuscany, their son on vacation in Mykonos, Greece, and no one knew where she was.

Knowing he had to get back to work, suddenly feeling tired, beat up, older, Maranzano sped back to the Via

Veneto and continued to oversee the hunt for *l'assassino del prete*, wondering where Lina was; why she hadn't told him how unhappy she was; why he hadn't noticed. He prided himself on being an observant man, on picking up all the idiosyncrasies of people, body language, facial gestures, yet he hadn't detected anything amiss with his own wife—his beloved Lina. He wanted to slug himself in the face.

THIRTY-ONE

"I was born," he told Diane, "in the New York area."

"Where, exactly?" she asked, switching lanes on the fast-moving Autostrada, rapidly leaving Rome farther and farther behind.

"Truth is, I'm not sure," he said, and went on to describe being brought up in foster care, different homes, leaving out the abuse, Creedmoore Hospital, his animus for the Catholic Church, its priests, bishops, cardinals. Hated images of things that had been done to him flooded his head.

"So you never knew your parents?" Diane asked, bringing him back to the interior of the car.

"No, but I was adopted by a very nice couple and it was they who turned me on to books," he lied, wanting to talk about books, not himself—a subject he was particularly uncomfortable with.

An unusually perceptive woman, Diane sensed his discomfort. "What kind of work do you do?" she asked.

"I design software. And I do websites for people. In fact a San Francisco-based company recently made me a nice offer and I've been seriously thinking of moving out to San Francisco when I get back to the States. I'm kind of tired of New York. It's a nice place to visit, but not live—too crowded, too impersonal . . . too noisy."

"San Francisco is a great town," she said. "I love it. The pace of life, the bay, North Beach, Chinatown . . . the Golden Gate, the endless skies, the hills. I have a house on Edith—a dead-end street on a hill just above North Beach."

"How nice. Born and raised there?"

"Yes, in San Francisco. In the Marina district," she said, wanting to tell him that all of the Marina district had been built on landfill from the 1906 quake, but not mentioning it; how as a child she used to fantasize all the time that bodies were down there; that the ghosts of those killed in the quake would rise from the ground to haunt the people who lived there . . .

He said, "I'm so curious, if you don't mind, how did you become a professional writer?"

"To make a long story short, I've always loved books, became a literature professor at Berkeley, the man I was married to died, I quit teaching and began writing, was lucky, found a good agent, secured a publishing deal right off the bat and I've been writing ever since."

"How long?"

"More or less seven years, but it seems like I've been doing it all my life," she said and they drove on in silence, listening to the calming Buddha Bar CD.

"Again, if you don't mind my asking," he said, "how did your husband die? I hope I'm not being too nosey. Forgive me if I am."

"Cancer," she said, and nothing more.

"I'm sorry," he said.

Now it was Diane who wanted to change the subject. "What's your favorite book?" she asked, believing you could learn a lot about a person by what they read, the authors they liked.

"I have a lot of favorite books, but . . . *One Hundred Years of Solitude* is up there."

"I know it well—taught a class on it, Gabriel Garcia Marquez. Have you read his short stories?"

"All of them."

"What other authors do you like?" she asked, warmed by the fact that he liked one of her favorite books of all time.

"I've got eclectic taste. There's a lot of them."

"Who, like who?"

"Hmm . . . well in no particular order of preference: Jack London, Yukio Mishima, Capote, Hemingway, Anais Nin, Guy de Maupassant, Chandler, Hammett, James Cain . . . let me see, of course the late great Shakespeare, Dante, Hugo, Schiller, Scott, Crane and most all the Russians— Dostoevsky and Chekhov, Tolstoy and Gogol . . . also, I like Pearl S. Buck a lot—"

"Love her," Diane interrupted. "*The Good Earth* and *Dragon Seed* are two of my favorite books—have you read *Dragon Seed*?"

"Yes, of course—very moving, way ahead of its time."

"Not many people know about that book; how did you come across it?"

"I was so taken by *The Good Earth* that I went and found everything she'd written and discovered *Dragon Seed*," he said, remembering well the fiery anger he had felt in his gut when he first read this book, one of those Dr. Hartock had secured for him, the story of a poor Chinese family caught up in the invasion of China by the Japanese. How a boy in this family was repeatedly raped by a group of drunken Japanese soldiers and grew into a fierce partisan fighter, a general who fought relentlessly to help rid his beloved country of the hated, sadistic Japanese. For the first time, there in the car, he realized that was exactly what happened to him; that he too would not rest until he made the Church pay for what was done to him. No matter what, he resolved as they sped south, he'd kill the pope—the man he held responsible for the *dragon seed* that had been placed inside him.

And if he couldn't get to the pope he'd seek out, find and murder the cardinals who made up The Congregation for the Doctrine of the Faith. Even more so than the pope, he knew, these cardinals were directly responsible for the Church becoming a safe haven for molesters; a playground for pedophiles.

THIRTY-TWO

When Captain Flynn and Frank Salerno left Dr. Hartock's office, they first went to the Greystone, a somewhat seedy, transient hotel just off Broadway. As Salerno drove, Flynn made phone calls—spoke to the detectives he'd sent out to the airports and learned that the MTA and airport security were cooperating fully. They were scrutinizing video tape of passengers going through security, boarding planes to Rome, directly or indirectly. Flynn was hoping they might soon have a photograph of Coogan, but having video tape of him would be better still. He next called Carole Cunningham and briefly told her about Dr. Hartock, what he had told him about Frank Coogan.

Pleased they now had a name and history, the identity of the killer, Carole was not at all surprised to learn that the perp had been abused by priests over a long period of time. She was, however, surprised to learn that he had killed a priest as a boy, that he'd spent twenty-one years in an insane asylum . . . that he was placed in a release program two years earlier. Flynn asked her to make certain none of what he told her went public until the NYPD was ready to release the information. She promised she'd stay mum and told him five of the priests John Sullivan named had been arrested, that none of them had yet talked, though the murder of John Krol had scared them all and made them "much more apt to open up," she said.

Flynn, like Cunningham—and most professionals in law enforcement—hadn't lost any sleep over Krol's murder. Cunningham had read that morning a *Times* editorial vehemently condemning a prison system that would allow a homophobic skinhead in the protective custody unit—a clear danger to a convicted child molester. But they said nothing about Krol's many victims.

She told Flynn that she was convening a grand jury and presenting evidence against the priests who had possession of child pornography, and was going to use John Sullivan to help get indictments. She was hoping, she said, to get Bishop Arnold and Monsignor Dreyfus to turn state's evidence, absolutely certain that they knew much about the inner workings of the Church. They made plans to meet that night.

Flynn next called Chief Samuels and ran down to him what he had learned, and explained that they were on their way to the hotel where Coogan had lived to see what they could learn there, hopefully find some usable evidence, a photograph of him. Pleased that the killer's identity had been found out, the chief congratulated Flynn and told him to keep him posted. He said he was going to call the commissioner. Flynn would have preferred if the commissioner, for now, was kept out of the loop, but he had no say in that, he knew, and there would be hell to pay if such information was not passed along forthwith.

Just as Flynn hung up, as they turned uptown on Central Park West, he received a call from Sam Henderson at the FBI's Behavioral Science Unit. He said he had "an early rudimentary profile" on the killer. Flynn asked Hen-

GET UP TO
4 FREE BOOKS!

You can have the best fiction delivered to your door for less than what you'd pay in a bookstore or online—only $4.25 a book! Sign up for our book clubs today, and we'll send you **FREE* BOOKS** just for trying it out...with no obligation to buy, ever!

LEISURE HORROR BOOK CLUB

With more award-winning horror authors than any other publisher, it's easy to see why CNN.com says "Leisure Books has been leading the way in paperback horror novels." Your shipments will include authors such as RICHARD LAYMON, DOUGLAS CLEGG, JACK KETCHUM, MARY ANN MITCHELL, and many more.

LEISURE THRILLER BOOK CLUB

If you love fast-paced page-turners, you won't want to miss any of the books in Leisure's thriller line. Filled with gripping tension and edge-of-your-seat excitement, these titles feature everything from psychological suspense to legal thrillers to police procedurals and more!

As a book club member you also receive the following special benefits:

- **30% OFF all orders through our website & telecenter!**
- **Exclusive access to special discounts!**
- **Convenient home delivery and 10 days to return any books you don't want to keep.**

There is no minimum number of books to buy, and you may cancel membership at any time. See back to sign up!

*Please include $2.00 for shipping and handling.

YES! ☐

Sign me up for the Leisure Horror Book Club and send my TWO FREE BOOKS! If I choose to stay in the club, I will pay only $8.50* each month, a savings of $5.48!

YES! ☐

Sign me up for the Leisure Thriller Book Club and send my TWO FREE BOOKS! If I choose to stay in the club, I will pay only $8.50* each month, a savings of $5.48!

NAME: _____

ADDRESS: _____

_____

TELEPHONE: _____

E-MAIL: _____

☐ **I WANT TO PAY BY CREDIT CARD.**

☐ VISA   ☐ MasterCard   ☐ DISCOVER

ACCOUNT #: _____

EXPIRATION DATE: _____

SIGNATURE: _____

Send this card along with $2.00 shipping & handling for each club you wish to join, to:

Horror/Thriller Book Clubs
20 Academy Street
Norwalk, CT 06850-4032

Or fax (must include credit card information!) to: 610.995.9274. You can also sign up online at www.dorchesterpub.com.

*Plus $2.00 for shipping. Offer open to residents of the U.S. and Canada only. Canadian residents please call 1.800.481.9191 for pricing information.

If under 18, a parent or guardian must sign. Terms, prices and conditions subject to change. Subscription subject to acceptance. Dorchester Publishing reserves the right to reject any order or cancel any subscription.

JOIN NOW!

derson to run it down to him, saying nothing about the fact that they had just learned the killer's identity, curious to see if the profile was accurate.

Henderson said, "He's between thirty and forty, white, as you know, perhaps however a light-skinned Latino, in very good physical condition. He works with computers—perhaps as an occupation—definitely a victim of abuse by priests over an extended period of time. And he has a deep, seething hatred for the Catholic Church. As a boy he had regular, very intense fantasies of harming priests, in fact he very well may have attacked a priest, even set fire to one or more churches."

Amazed, Flynn listened. "He is extremely driven, won't stop assaulting priests until he's either captured or killed. I believe he did go to Rome and did kill the priests there. And that he *often* thinks about killing the pope, who he holds directly responsible for the abuse in the Church, and more importantly, his own abuse.

"Tony, this is a particularly cunning psychopath who will do anything to fulfill his *mission*, as he sees it. This would include changing his appearance, disguising himself, using civilians. Clearly, he views the murders as his destiny. A destiny he must fulfill. The murders make him feel whole and complete and remove the stigma of being an abused child. Abused by people who represented themselves as close to God, an omnipotent power. I should mention that we are talking here about an unusually handsome man, endowed with naturally attractive features who, as a boy, was extremely good looking. Might very well have looked more like a pretty girl than a boy. Tony, to a pedophile he was, in a word, irresistible."

Stunned by the uncanny accuracy of Henderson's profile, Flynn briefly ran down what Dr. Hartock had just told him and Salerno, none of which surprised Sam Henderson. Henderson said he'd proof and formalize the profile and e-mail it to the task force through official channels. Flynn thanked him several times over, explained that he was going to Italy to help with the investigation there; start the wheels of extraditing Coogan back to New York— if he was taken alive. "Which doesn't seem likely," he said.

They parked in front of the Greystone Hotel, quickly found the manager, a short round man of Indian descent wearing a baggy white shirt to his knees and a gold embroidered vest. He had huge round eyes, smelled of curry, Salerno noted. His name, he said, was Habib. He explained that Frank Coogan lived at the hotel for nearly a year. He said: "He was a gentleman, always polite, never made noise, never complained. In fact," he said, "I very much enjoyed having him in the building. He did the website for the hotel and upgraded our computer, very good with computers; he used to talk to it, funny, huh?"

"Yeah, funny," Flynn said.

"Is he in some kind of trouble?" the manager asked.

"No trouble. Did he perhaps leave any of his possessions here?" Flynn said.

"Yes. In fact he still has his room. He said he was visiting relatives in Europe and that he'd be back in a month, more or less."

"Can we see it?" Flynn asked.

"Certainly, sir," Habib said, grabbed a large set of keys from a drawer in his office and they followed him into the elevator, up to the top floor, down a corridor that had seen better days, lighted by dim bulbs, the smell of cigarette smoke in the air. Habib stopped at a corner apartment, number 1313. Inside, it was all neat and tidy—a sunny studio with a Pullman kitchen, bathroom, two windows that faced west. From the window you could see the Hudson River at the end of West 92nd Street through the thick foliage of the many trees that lined the block. There was a bed, a TV on a wooden crate and boxes of books, no photographs immediately visible. Knowing that evidence could very well be found in the room, secreted in the books, on the computer, Flynn called task force headquarters and ordered several teams of criminalists to go over the apartment with a fine-tooth comb, turned to the manager and said, "This is a crime scene now—"

"Crime, what crime?" he asked, his eyes widening.

"And we must seal the apartment."

"Sir, Mr. Coogan won't like this."

"It doesn't matter what Mr. Coogan likes," Flynn said. "He is a fugitive from justice."

"Oh my goodness, a fugitive from justice. What did he do—is he a terrorist?"

"I'm sorry but I'm not at liberty to discuss the case. You'll find out soon enough. When we finish here, probably by midnight tonight, we'll be on our way and you can have the place back, but until then only police personnel are allowed in, you understand?"

"Yes, thank you, sir," Habib said, as he quickly backed out of the apartment on nervous, fast-moving feet.

Flynn's cell phone sounded. It was Chief Samuels. He said he had spoken to the commissioner and that he had in turn spoken to the mayor, who had spoken with the governor and Cardinal Edam, and they were all demanding that the NYPD hold a news conference to announce that they had discovered the identity of the priest killer, which the governor, mayor, and cardinal were all eager to attend. Flynn knew he had no say in this, but he would have preferred to get more things in place before there were public announcements about Frank Coogan, least of which was a photo or videotape of him to show at the press conference, give to the media, a bone they would relish and gnaw on ad nauseam. The press conference would be, the chief said, at 6:00 PM, in time for the evening news.

Knowing well-publicized murders were a political thing, Flynn wasn't surprised that they all wanted a press conference. He said he'd be there. Salerno used crime scene tape he had in the car to seal off the apartment, both of them commenting on its number, 1313. Three teams of criminalists soon arrived and began to carefully print and scrutinize the apartment, looking in every book, with the help of two teams of experienced detectives Flynn assigned to the task.

They found numerous books on martial arts, one in particular of interest—a dog-eared Chinese text book with simple drawings on how to kill with a knife—where to insert the blade, where to cut for maximum effect. They also noted that Coogan had a lot of books on ancient Rome, not surprising considering what Hartock had told them.

As the apartment was searched, Flynn and Salerno left and sped to Creedmoore State Hospital in Queens, an austere redbrick building on eleven acres of wooded land, all the windows barred, security like that of a maximum-security prison. This was the place where the State of New York kept its criminally insane, the most dangerous people in any society.

Dr. Hartock had called ahead, and they were expecting the police. The doctor in charge, Alex Lawson, however, said they could not see Frank Coogan's file without a court order. He was a tall, effeminate man with long pink hands, clearly out to protect the hospital and his own interests, Flynn knew, for he was one of the doctors who signed Frank Coogan's release papers.

"I understand," Flynn said, smiled and called Carole Cunningham and asked her to find a judge to sign a warrant ASAP, gave her a few of the particulars as to why they wanted the warrant, and asked her to have it faxed to the hospital. Flynn purposely did this in front of Dr. Lawson.

The doctor said, "Captain, I don't mean to make things more difficult for you than I'm sure they already are. It's just that I have a mandated protocol I must follow."

"I understand," Flynn said, "not to worry." He was as pleasant as he could be, not wanting to antagonize Lawson, knowing he could be of assistance.

"Are you sure that Frank is responsible for the murders?" the doctor asked.

"Sure as rain," Flynn said. "His DNA was found at one of the murders."

"If I may ask, in what form?"

"Skin and blood matter under the nails of a priest who tried to fight him off."

"I see," the doctor said.

Flynn continued, "And he's been linked, via DNA, with the murdered priests in Rome, too."

"When Dr. Hartock called me and told me that Frank was responsible for the killings, I nearly dropped the phone. . . . Frank, you see, was one of our prize patients. He gave us all . . . hope, you see."

"How so?" Flynn asked.

"As I believe you know, Frank had a tragic childhood, was severely battered as an infant, had serious head trauma and brain damage, and then ended up at Sacred Heart, which proved to be nothing more than a place where children were regularly and repeatedly abused. The priest he murdered . . . well it was a very brutal, sadistic killing involving mutilation and decapitation, and when Frank was brought to us he was a *very* troubled boy, to say the least. None of us expected the full recovery he eventually exhibited, and we were all very pleased.

"Frank was a pleasure to be around; always a gentleman. As you may know, he loved books, was extremely well read and he . . . well he made us here at the hospital feel there was hope. Hope for him and hope for our other patients.

"Unfortunately, Frank is only one of many people who end up here because of severe abuse as children—physical, mental and sexual—and combinations of all three, and for us Frank was like a ray of sunshine in a world of darkness, mental illness and instability. I'm really quite shocked that he . . . that he committed these murders. He was one of the few patients who was released from the hospital that I, that we all felt had made it, had come back from the other side, had a real chance at a productive, meaningful life. And now . . . now this," he said, sadly shaking his head, genuinely distressed, it seemed, over what had happened. "He fooled us all," he said.

"Apparently," Flynn said.

The warrant arrived at Dr. Lawson's fax machine. He briefly scanned it and opened a thick file already on his desk with his long pink hands. He said, "If you like I can make a copy of everything in his file."

"Thank you. That would be helpful," Flynn said. "What we really need, doctor, is a current picture of him. Might there be one in his file?"

"Of course," Lawson said. "It's mandatory that all patients who are released from the institution be fingerprinted and photographed." He looked through the file. "But, well . . . there's no photograph here," he said, again going through the whole file. "Nor are the fingerprints here."

"Did Coogan have access to the files?" Salerno asked, his cynical cop eyes regarding the doctor.

"No . . . not as such, but he did update my computer several times—a genius with computers, you know—and he was alone in my office, which is where his file is kept," he said, the realization that Coogan had taken his photograph and prints slowly spreading on his face.

"He stole the photograph," he said, through suddenly tight lips.

"All the time I thought he was being helpful, but he was stealing from me; planning these killings," he said, shaking his head. "Son of a bitch," he said.

"Yeah, son of a bitch," Flynn said. His cell phone buzzed. It was Chief Inspector Maranzano calling from Rome. Flynn went out in the hall to take the call.

THIRTY-THREE

A woman with a mission, Carole Cunningham strode into the grand jury room, her head high, shoulders back, carrying a rust-colored file six inches thick. She wore a simple gray suit, her blond hair pulled back tight, no makeup on her face whatsoever.

The grand jury consisted of twenty-three citizens drawn from a jury pool of several hundred prospective jurors on the second floor. Having no idea about the case that was going to be presented to them, the grand jury was made up of men and women of many different ethnicities, young and old, professional and blue-collar workers, conservative and liberal—a fair representation of New York's citizenry. It was a large room with high ceilings, oversized windows, through which streamed brilliant shafts of the fierce summer sun, particles of dust drifting in the golden light. The room was, thankfully, well air-conditioned and comfortable.

Carole, speaking in a pleasant businesslike tone, introduced herself, briefly explained the function of the grand jury, their importance in a society ruled by laws, and warned the jurors that what was going to be presented to them involved the sexual abuse of children; Catholic priests who were charged with the "possession of child pornography, conspiracy to sexually abuse children, with endangering the welfare of children, and with abetting those that would abuse children."

She asked, based on those initial facts, a stenographer documenting her every word, if any of the twenty-three jurors wished to be excused. To raise their hands if they did. None of them indicated they wanted to leave, and obviously what Carole had said caught their attention, for they were all now listening to her attentively, the bored expressions about their faces gone. Wanting to make sure they all understood exactly what was about to occur, Carole clarified: "Ladies and gentlemen, I warn you now that what you're about to hear and the images you will see are very graphic, sexually explicit images involving minors and adults. If any of you wish to leave, please do so now," and, again, they all stayed put.

Carole thanked them, and proceeded to call Father John Sullivan to the witness box. Wearing his white collar, Sullivan was sworn in and, using him as a kind of road map into the netherworld she was taking the grand jury, Carole succinctly laid out the facts, the case against the various priests, as Sullivan explained and clarified with all his firsthand information, insights, observations and personal experiences. The jurors' curiosity quickly turned to anger and indignation, and many of them were shaking their heads in disgust, in dismay.

Speaking in a sincere voice, looking directly at the jurors as he spoke, Sullivan told them how he had joined the Church in his late twenties because he learned, from a pedophile he'd met on a sex junket to Thailand, that if he joined the Catholic Church he'd have free access to all the children he wanted; that the Church would protect him if he was found out; how much of the Church hierarchy was made up of men like him.

"I mean people," he said, "who lust after children. They call themselves 'the brotherhood'." He explained further how in the seminar he attended in upstate New York, he immediately met men who, like him, "joined the Church for one reason and that was that they'd have access to all the children they wanted," he said.

He told how the Church used its considerable power and resources to hush up the families of any children who complained to parish leaders, but most often the threat of God and hell was enough to scare children into cooperative silence, he said.

"My favorite way of seducing," he explained matter-of-factly, "was to tell the children that they would go to heaven if they willingly did what I wanted, and they did."

He said, too, that he had been moved to seventeen parishes, all over the country, when his behavior became "problematic."

"Did any of your superiors report you to the police?" Cunningham asked in a booming voice.

"No, absolutely not. Never. We were all about protecting one another and using the resources of different parishes to give money to parents when and if they found out."

"Money that had been donated by the faithful?" she asked. "Money that was supposed to go to the needy?"

"Yes," he said. "Exactly."

Knowing that getting indictments against all the priests—Bishop Arnold, Monsignors O'Brian and Dreyfus—was the first step in her planned attack against those in the Church who were both directly and indirectly responsible for the exploitation, Carole showed no emotion. She led Sullivan where she wanted to, presenting the facts in a cold, professional manner, though her normally warm brown eyes had turned cold, as she showed the grand jury images found in the priests' rooms and on their computers. And by 3:00 that afternoon, the grand jury gladly indicted all the priests who had been arrested and Monsignors O'Brian, Dreyfus and Bishop Arnold—the individuals she was the most interested in at this juncture.

That done, Cunningham did not dismiss the grand jury. She told them more arrests were imminent; that she would be asking them to hand down still more indictments.

The indictments in hand, Carole returned to her office, sat at her desk and personally called each of the lawyers representing the priests who had been arrested, told them that their clients had been indicted and made arrangements to send them each copies of the indictments. She then called John Mahoney, the attorney who represented Monsignors O'Brian and Dreyfus and let him know that they had both been indicted. The last attorney she contacted was Bishop Arnold's. He, more than any of the others, Cunningham wanted to turn into a state witness, for she was sure he had a wealth of information she could use to indict others in positions of authority—*the decision makers*, as she thought of them, within the Church.

"Please," Cunningham told Arnold's attorney, "let your client know if he cooperates with us, I can guarantee him immunity . . . and if he gives us enough to make substantive arrests, no jail time at all."

Carole hated the idea of Bishop Arnold not doing time, walking away from his crimes, but she was willing to do it to get others in positions of power. If the Feds, she reasoned, could use Sammy Gravano—a man who admitted killing seventeen people—to get John Gotti, she could use Bishop Arnold, or anyone else, to nail the people really behind the epidemic of abuse within the Church.

She believed men in the Vatican itself were as responsible for the abuse as the priests who turned the Church into their own personal harems of trusting children. She knew the murder of John Krol would weigh heavily on Monsignors O'Brian and Dreyfus, and Bishop Arnold; that the prospect of going to jail was now, for them, terrifying . . . hell on earth.

Her trap set, Carole Cunningham sat back and waited for her phone to ring.

THIRTY-FOUR

Standing in front of the Pantheon Hotel on Via Veneto, Chief Inspector Nino Maranzano was fit to be tied. Somehow the priest killer had slipped through his grip, gotten away—out maneuvered him. As he stared at the two overheated basset hounds, he knew that he had to have gotten into some kind of vehicle. He ordered all the taxi dispatches and taxi drivers in the area questioned. He also sent people to question the bus drivers whose routes took them through the neighborhood. For sure, if the killer was on foot the hounds would still be tracking him. Maranzano even checked to see if any cars had been stolen in the area, and none had, as of yet, been reported. He went back into the air-conditioned command vehicle, had an espresso and again tried to reach his wife, his brow creased with a combination of worry, curiosity and anger.

How, he wondered, could Lina be so indifferent to him. She knew he'd be worried, that because he was a policeman, intimately knew the brutality men were capable of, he'd be more than concerned. What, he wondered, had he done to make her so mean to him? Surely, he thought, there was another man—that he'd been blind to his own wife's true nature . . .

On a wall of the command vehicle, there was the revised sketch of the killer and as Maranzano stared at it he remembered how he, the killer, had left the mutilated priests on the streets, there for all to see and know—his streets, in his city, the place he was responsible for keeping safe. His mind drawn back to the hunt, Maranzano thought of Captain Tony Flynn, wondered if maybe Flynn had learned something more that might help him. He picked up his cell phone and called Flynn in New York.

THIRTY-FIVE

Diane Pane was, Frank Coogan thought, a very nice woman. He had never had a relationship with a woman, had never even kissed a woman and yet for the first time in his life he was thinking of that—of being *intimate* with Diane Pane.

They were now approaching the infamous port city of Naples, its millions of lights shimmering in the near distance off to the left, the nearly full moon glistening on the wide expanse of the great bay of Naples.

"You hungry?" Diane asked. "Naples is just ahead and they've got the best pizza in the world."

"I'm not that hungry, but sure, if you want to stop that'd be great," he said, and she pulled off the Autostrada and drove toward the port, took a left at a sign that said *Centro*.

"You know Naples?" he asked.

"I was in the early stages of researching a story about the *Camorra* and was here a week some years back."

"What's the *Camorra*?"

"It's the Neapolitan version of the Mafia," she said. "Very secretive, very violent, and never really written about."

"And you wrote a book about them?"

"No, I ended up passing on it in fact because I couldn't get anyone to tell me the truth. But I spent time here and discovered the pizza," she said. "I don't have many weaknesses," she explained, "but pizza is definitely one of them, and you can't find better pizza anywhere."

"Why's it so good?" he asked, amused.

"The secret is wood-heated ovens, the sauce—and of course the buffalo mozzarella . . . it's incredibly fresh, like made the same day. I know a great place just ahead," she said, and soon parked the car in a small piazza lined with yellowed palm trees, more victims of the draught. A man immediately appeared out of the shadows, wanting money for them to park.

Speaking fluent Italian, Diane gave him a few euros and promised to give him a tip if he kept an eye on the car. He said he would and went back to watching a soccer game in a battered little glass booth on a tiny black and white television, and she led the way to a trattoria-pizzeria with a brick oven in the front window filled with glowing red-hot ambers.

Diane wanted to sit outside where they could see the car. "Naples is a place where you must keep your eyes open," she said. He immediately noticed a television near the ceiling and he made sure Diane sat with her back to it. She ordered them each a margarita pizza, his with mushrooms, hers with artichoke hearts and extra basil.

"I never met anyone like you. You have such an interesting life," he said.

"Nice of you to say," she said, admiring his perfect features, full lips, huge almond-shaped eyes, deep and full of secret intensities, thinking not many men look good without hair, but he looked even better. For some inexplicable reason Diane felt drawn to him, unusual for her to warm so quickly to a man—any man, and she was sure it had to do with his being so standoffish . . . so hard to approach. She was glad he called.

Again, wondering if he was gay, she said, "You have a girlfriend back in New York, Frank?"

"No," he said. "I was seeing someone, but it didn't work out," not wanting to tell her that he never even had kissed a girl, that he was a virgin.

Though, suddenly, sitting there at this quiet restaurant in Naples, memories of what had been done to him flooded his mind and he felt the sinewy muscles of his body tighten.

Diane saw the color actually drain from his face, his eyes harden, become distant. Thinking he was upset because she asked if he had a girlfriend, reminded him of some deep hurt, she regretted the question.

"I'm sorry," she said. "I was nosey, I—"

"Nothing to be sorry about," he said, forcing the images away. Their pizza was served, the crust slightly burnt, smelling so good it made his mouth water. Suddenly hungry, he cut himself a piece and bit into it—and it was, like she said, the best pizza he'd ever had.

"Delicious," he said, wiping the sweet-tasting marinara sauce from his lips. Looking up, he saw on the television screen the New York composite of him with long hair, then the revised composite with short hair.

Nearly choking on the pizza, he wondered how they so quickly found out that he changed his appearance, stunned at the accuracy of the sketch. They then showed a shot of Maranzano being interviewed in front of the mobile command center right there on Via Veneto, his jaw set into a concrete-hard line, his eyes seeming to bore into the camera. No one in the restaurant was paying attention to the broadcast, heard the announcer say the Church was offering an €100,000 reward for information leading to the killer's arrest; that the pope himself made a personal plea for help in apprehending him.

Not wanting to make Diane uncomfortable in any way, knowing he needed her help, her hospitality, to stay at her place, he smiled and told her how much he liked the pizza, and asked her questions about her book, which she happily answered, pleased at his interest, pleased that he loved books. They finished their pizza—he insisted on paying, and headed back to the car. The sour-faced man in the booth immediately appeared, as if by magic, telling Diane he *"Non ho mai smesso di guardare la macchina,"* *Didn't take his eyes off the car.* She thanked him, tipped him and they were soon back in the BMW heading south.

He asked Diane about the place she was staying, how she found it, how big it was, how much it cost to rent, hoping she'd get the hint that he'd like to stay there, and, apparently, she did, for she said: "So, Frank, do you have friends in Positano?"

"No, actually I don't."

"Why did you choose to stay there?"

"No reason in particular—I heard it was very nice, near the ocean and that's all. I love to swim, the freedom of being in the water, and I don't get many opportunities to swim in New York."

"I see," she said, thinking about inviting him to stay at the house she rented, a spacious three-bedroom, two-bath duplex, and there'd be, she knew, plenty of room for him; but she didn't want to seem pushy, like she had any kind of designs on him.

Sensing her thoughts, he said, "I heard that Amalfi is really nice too?"

"Oh, it is," she said and went on to list, as they passed

Mount Vesuvius on their left, the virtues of Amalfi—the sweeping views of the Tyrrhenian Sea, the quaint earth-colored houses, the relaxed pace of life, the great food, the lovely piazzas, the famous Amalfi hospitality, and before she knew it she said: "Frank, if you like, you are welcome to stay in the house I rented. It's huge with three bedrooms and there's plenty of room for you."

"Oh, that is so nice of you, Diane, but I wouldn't want to impose, get in your way. I know you are going to be working and all, I—"

"You won't get in my way," she said. "There are all kinds of decks and terraces where I can do my work and it's a big place, actually a villa with a large garden and a pool. If you like, you'd be welcome," she said.

"Gee . . . well, yes, sure I'd like to; a pool, too, great! Thank you so much, Diane," he said. "That's very nice of you." He smiled in the dark interior of the fast-moving car, glad he didn't have to force his way into the house, very aware of his knife, still strapped to his leg, believing that sooner or later he would have to use it; that it was just a matter of time, given all the press about him, before Diane realized who he was, what he'd done, and hurried to the authorities. He wouldn't let that happen, he vowed. He had a plan and he wasn't going to let anyone or anything get in his way. She was, he forced himself to remember, only a means to an end.

THIRTY-SIX

His name was Giuseppe Pisano. He was a short powerful man with bad teeth and hands as strong as iron vices. For the most part Giuseppe Pisano was mad at the world and most all the people in it—the young and old and everyone in between. Giuseppe had one pleasure in life and it was soccer—actually it was, with him, a burning soulful passion that bordered on obsession: He often fantasized about killing referees who ruled against his beloved team—Squada del Napoli, the team of Naples—and maiming, in cunning diabolical ways, star players of opposing teams. He had a huge portrait of Armando Maradona, the Argentine soccer superstar who led Squada del Napoli to victory in the 1994 World Cup, the best day in Giuseppe Pisano's sixty-six years of life. Maradona had left the Naples team for greener pastures, but Giuseppe Pisano felt certain he would return one day soon, and Giuseppe even lit candles in the Saint Gennaro Church and prayed for that fateful day.

Giuseppe's mother's brother was a *capitano*—captain— in one of the four ruling Camorra families that controlled Naples and the surrounding provinces, the greater area of Italy known as Campania. It was because of Giuseppe's uncle that he was given the job of parking attendant in the busy Piazza Luigi. It was easy work and he was always able to pocket some money meant for the city coffers and, too, he was often tipped, for everyone knew that Giuseppe was *connected*, a man you wanted as a friend, not someone to be angry at you.

When, that night, Giuseppe returned to his little booth, after being tipped by Diane Pane, he kept thinking that the man she was with looked familiar, but he couldn't place where he knew him from. Probably, he decided, he had him as a customer before. The soccer game over now, Giuseppe changed channels on his little black-and-white television to watch the news, angry that he didn't have a color TV to enjoy his beloved soccer games, and there was the story about the hunt in Rome for *l'assassino del prete*.

A particularly religious Neapolitan, Giuseppe silently cursed the man who could kill priests like that—cut them up like animals and leave them on the streets. "An infamy," he said out loud, twice making the sign of the cross. On the news report they showed the slain priests being placed in the morgue wagon; they showed the house where the killer had stayed; they showed, too, the Villa Borghese—the place the killer had fled when the police closed in on him—and they again showed the sound bites Chief Inspector Maranzano had given to the press. Giuseppe Pisano knew who Maranzano was, knew that he had shot to death members of a rival Camorra family. And then they aired the composite sketch of the killer—and Giuseppe's eyes bulged from his bald head, as he slowly stood and brought the palm of his right hand to his forehead, exclaiming, "Mamma mia, mamma mia, that's him—that's where I saw that face."

Then the news announcer read the plea from Papa—the pope, to help find and stop the killer, and lastly the news announcer, an attractive blond woman named Lilli Gruber, who said the police were offering a €100,000 reward for information leading to the arrest of *l'assassino del prete*.

Normally, Giuseppe Pisano would be hard-pressed to call the police. He came from a close-knit society in which the police were viewed as the enemy. But any reservations he had about dealing with the police now were quickly dispelled by the €100,000 reward and the fact that the man he saw, he was sure, had killed priests . . . *an infamy*, he repeated in the dusty solitude of his little booth. He pulled a battered red cell phone out of a back pocket, started to dial and stopped.

Maybe, he thought, he should first tell his uncle, but he immediately thought better of that. His uncle would, he was sure, take all the money for himself, saying if it wasn't for the good job he provided Giuseppe he would have never even seen the man.

"Vaffanculo," fuck him in the ass, he murmured and called the police in Roma and demanded to speak, in his rough Neapolitan accent, to Chief Inspector Maranzano, imagining the giant color TV he would soon own, clothes, jewelry, maybe, even . . . a woman.

THIRTY-SEVEN

At Creedmore Hospital, Captain Tony Flynn walked into an empty visiting room at the end of the hall so he could take Maranzano's call in private.

After initial greetings, Maranzano told Flynn how they located the flat in which the killer had been staying; that he had fled just before they broke down the door; and he told about the hot pursuit through the Villa Borghese.

"But, in the end," he said, "he got away. I'm thinking he commandeered a car somehow and managed to slip past my people."

Pleased to hear that Maranzano smoked out Coogan, Flynn told him about the call from Dr. Hartock and briefly ran down what they had learned about Coogan's history;

how he murdered a priest when he was twelve years old. He explained that he was now in the hospital where Coogan had actually been kept, talking to another of the doctors who had treated him, signed his release papers, trying to locate a current photograph of him.

Flynn said, "It seems before he was released he stole photographs of himself taken when he was let out two years ago from his file."

"But how did they allow a crazy man like this out of the hospital?" Maranzano demanded, angered by the knowledge that hospital officials in New York were responsible for all his problems here in Rome.

"Yeah, well, that's the million-dollar question. They screwed up big time," Flynn said, and promised as soon as they located a photograph of Coogan, or video of him as he passed through security at the airport, he would make sure to send it to Maranzano straight away.

Flynn also told him that he'd been asked by his boss to go to Rome, to see how he could help. Flynn said nothing more about extraditing Coogan back to New York.

Maranzano didn't think he needed any help from a New York captain of detectives, but he had taken a liking to Flynn, knew that Flynn really had no say in the matter, and said he, Maranzano, would personally pick him up at the airport. "When do you plan to come?" he asked.

"Tomorrow sometime. I'll call and let you know soon as I have the details," Flynn said. Maranzano was just about to ask if he knew what hotel he'd be staying at, if he was coming alone, when one of his men frantically gestured that there was a very important call for him. Thinking something had happened to his wife, Maranzano told Flynn he had a call he must take. That he'd get back to him.

"What's happened?" Maranzano demanded, sure there was bad news about Lina, an accident, something terrible.

"A man in Napoli, a parking attendant, says he saw him. He was with a woman. They had pizza in a place in the Piazza Lucia."

"Pizza?" Maranzano said, grabbing the phone. "Pronto," he said.

"Chief Inspector Maranzano?" Giuseppe Pisano asked.

"Si."

"I saw him; he was with a *bella* American woman who spoke Italian. She was driving a BMW," he said in a thick Neapolitan accent.

Originally from Napoli, Nino Maranzano immediately slipped into dialect and asked Giuseppe Pisano why he was so sure it was him.

"Because," he said with absolute certainty. "I see him on the television. They park the car, had the pizza and come back, and I stand one meter away from him. I look him right in the face. I swear on the grave of my parents it is him."

"When did you see them?" Maranzano asked.

"They left five minutes ago."

Maranzano quickly calculated the time it would take to drive to Napoli from Roma and it fit perfectly. Wanting to see how observant Giuseppe was, Maranzano asked him the color of the car.

"Dark green—a 525 with a tan inside," he said.

"What did the woman look like?"

"Pretty. Blue eyes, dark hair. Big tits. Nice *culo*."

"And what was she wearing?"

"Shorts and a yellow shirt. Like a man's undershirt, typical American."

"Why do you say she's American?"

"The accent, and the way she sticks her tits out when she walks."

"And him—what was he wearing?"

"All black," Pisano said with certainty, and Maranzano knew it was him.

Maranzano took his cell phone number and told him to stay put, that he was on the way—

"The reward, Chief Inspector; you catch him, it is mine, no?"

"Yes, of course. I will personally make sure. You have my word," Maranzano said. "I'll be there soon. I'll take a helicopter—"

"Please, Chief Inspector, let me meet you somewhere. This is nobody else's business, *capito*?"

Maranzano knew about his concern, that he had a *padrone*, and this *padrone* would, inevitably, demand all the money.

"This is our secret," Maranzano said. "You have my word of honor."

"I await you," Giuseppe Pisano said, pleased Maranzano was a fellow Neapolitan, thinking he would surely get to meet the pope; that the pope himself would bless him, Giuseppe Pisano.

Within minutes Maranzano and three of his best men were speeding to a police heliport just outside of Rome.

Again, he tried to reach his wife without success, more and more concerned that something happened to her. He wondered if somehow the priest killer knew about Lina and had hurt her. As they reached the heliport Maranzano reluctantly called a friend of his at *polizia* central and reported his wife missing, asked that an all points be put out for her and her white Jaguar. He truly didn't want to do this, knew it would get the rumor mill working overtime:

Maranzano's wife left him; Maranzano can't control his own woman; Maranzano's wife ran off with a traveling salesman . . . an Albanian waiter. But none of all that mattered to him now. What mattered was finding Lina.

. . . And putting an end, once and for all, to this Frank Coogan, a madman who never should have been allowed out of the hospital in the first place. *As great as America is, Americans do stupid things,* he was thinking as the blue and white police helicopter lifted and roared off in a southerly direction.

THIRTY-EIGHT

Unaware of the law enforcement firestorm building up just behind her, Diane Pane guided the sleek BMW along the sensuous twists and turns of the famous Amalfi Drive. A thin two-way highway cut into solid rock cliffs that dramatically rose ten and twelve stories above the Tyrrhenian Sea, on which now the low full moon hung, the color of fresh butter, glistening.

If, Diane well knew, she told one of her friends back in San Francisco that she had invited a man she just met to stay at her place they would have looked at her like she was nuts. However, sitting there, Diane felt an unusual level of comfort with her passenger, listening to him tell her about different books he liked. Over the years Diane had learned to trust her instincts and her instincts now told her that she had nothing to worry about concerning the man sitting next to her; that it was she, not he, who initiated contact with him, who invited him to stay, who walked up to him in the Colosseum. She liked the free-

dom of making decisions based on her own mind, free
will, life experiences, rather than what was supposed to
be right or wrong, proper or not, according to society's
dictates, rules and regulations.

No man, she thought, who looked like him would have
to force himself on a woman, and she liked his shyness;
and she admired the minute attention he paid to details in
the books he'd read, not popular best selling tomes but
important, meaningful books, the French, Russian and
American classics, and obscure South American and Mexican authors few Americans even heard about; how he
could recite passages and sentences from most every book
he liked, having no idea that while he was locked up in an
asylum for the criminally insane, he had all the time in
the world to carefully read, contemplate and remember
everything he'd read.

When they finally reached Positano, Diane slowed,
stopped and they got out of the car at a lookout and admired the small town, built into jagged cliffs along the
ocean. But it was very crowded with cars and buses and
people, she quickly pointed out, and they returned to the
BMW and drove on to Amalfi. He said his luggage would
not arrive in Positano until the next day. Like Positano, she
explained, Amalfi was constructed into the face of a
mountain that grew straight out of the sea, but Amalfi, she
said, was much wider—not as closed in as Positano and
not as steep.

She said, "And here in Amalfi the houses aren't right on
top of one another and they are all these lovely pastel colors, and you don't have planeloads of rich tourists acting
rich, you know. Amalfi is much more laid back, not filled
with tourists. I love it here. San Francisco and Amalfi are
my two favorite places."

"You like living by the sea?"

"Very much, great to help get the creative juices going."

"You ever have writer's block?"

"No, never. Guess I'm lucky. But then again I do a lot of research before I pick up a pen and that helps . . . I mean I know the characters I'm writing about, and I know exactly where they are, what they see, what they feel, their conflicts and obstacles. That all helps a lot."

"Do you have an outline?"

"In my head only, but it's more like a general idea. I like to try and make the story, the characters, tell and feel what happens on their own."

"I'd very much like to write a memoir. I've been thinking about it for years," he said, unwanted black-and-white images coming to him, circling in his mind like a carousel in a Bosch painting.

"Then do it," she said. "You should do it; set a goal for yourself, like a certain amount of pages each day—a number of words, and stick to it."

"Jack London used to write 1,500 words a day no matter where he was."

"Yes, like that. The key is to stick to a comfortable regimen. That helps a lot. The house is just a little farther . . . there," she said, pointing off to the right, turning up a road that serpentined to a honey-colored villa perched on a cliff a kilometer out of town. On the left there was a large garden filled with fruit trees and on the right was the pool area. The rear of the home faced the moonlit sea. The house was completely surrounded by a tall white metal fence. There was a sign on the fence that said, *Attenti al cane, beware of dog*.

The house was designed and built by the famous Italian architect Mario Presoni for a very wealthy Milan industrialist, who'd been killed in a car crash three years earlier. A real estate speculator bought it and rented it out by the week, month or year. It had appeared in many design magazines, and on the covers of *House and Garden* and *Architectural Digest*.

Diane used the remote that had been sent to her in Rome and a panel of the fence slid open. She drove into a curved driveway, stopping in the two-car garage.

"It is magnificent," he said. "I never saw such a nice house; how'd you find it?"

"Through some friends in San Francisco," she said, and together they inspected the villa, which was called Casa Bella Luna. Diane had seen numerous photographs of the place online and in magazines, but even she wasn't prepared for how lovely it was, well planned with a huge kitchen that had windows facing the ocean, a glass-enclosed dining room, everything white with gorgeous marble and tile trim; the amazing fully tiled bathrooms with glass ceilings and the enormity of each of the bedrooms with floor-to-ceiling windows and hand-painted terracotta-tiled decks outside each room.

He helped Diane bring all her things in from the car. She directed him to the bedroom at the east end of the house, while she took the one at the west end. She plugged in her laptop wanting to check her e-mails, but the phone line of the house wasn't working. She was exhausted from her long day in Rome, its unrelenting heat and near 100 percent humidity, the drive to Amalfi. She told him that she was tired and going to retire; that she wanted to get up early to jog and get some work done. He, too, said he was "really tired," and that he was also going to bed.

Diane locked her bedroom door, showered and slid into bed with the book she'd bought earlier about Julius Caesar by Cicero. Diane always read before she went to sleep, a habit left over from when she was a child. Lying there, however, she kept thinking about him . . . intimate, personal thoughts she would rather not have, hoping it wasn't a mistake to invite him to stay, knowing he could very well distract her from her work—the book she'd been researching and thinking about now for over a year. She heard him get up and move about the house.

Knowing how lucky he'd been, he, too, could not sleep. Truth was, he always had a hard time sleeping when there was a full moon. Often, he thought, laughing, it was because he was a bona fide lunatic, a man whose jumbled brain circuits were affected by the gravitational pull of the moon.

Marveling at the beauty of the house, he walked onto the huge veranda outside the living room, sat in a comfortable white lounge chair and gazed at the moon reflecting off a calm sea, the scent of lemon, orange and peach trees all coming to him at once.

Sitting there, he thought about Diane; how special she was, how fortunate he was to meet her, and he hoped nothing happened to put him in the position where he would have to do something unpleasant to her. The thought of hurting her made him uncomfortable. She had been nothing but kind to him and he didn't want to become the thing he hated. Killing priests, the pope, for him, was easy; fact was, he enjoyed it and looked forward to sending more of them to hell where they belonged, making the Church realize that there would be consequences for their despicable actions. Hurting Diane, however, was another thing entirely.

Even priests who weren't abusers, he felt, were equally responsible, for they had to know what was going on and chose to keep silent, to protect the Church, its reputation, not the innocents put in their care. If a person had knowledge of someone's plan to commit a murder and they did nothing, they were, in the eyes of the law, equally responsible and could be arrested and put on trial for murder. *Accessory, they call it,* he thought.

He again began to think about writing an honest memoir of what had happened to him, leaving nothing out, how he had the dragon seed planted in his psyche, his soul. He wondered if he could call his book *Dragon Seed*. It seemed, he was thinking, a very good title.

"Can't sleep?" Diane asked, silently walking onto the veranda in bare feet.

"No . . . I thought I'd enjoy the view. Just amazing. I've never seen anything like it. This place . . . Diane, this place is magical," he said, looking up at her, his dark eyes filled with the brilliant light of the Italian full moon behind her. "Diane, I hope you don't mind my saying this, but you look so very beautiful in the moonlight."

"No . . . I don't mind," she said in a soft voice, smiling, wanting to tell him how lovely he looked in the soft unobtrusive light, but she hesitated. She didn't want to give him the wrong message, begin something she might regret too soon.

"Don't look so bad yourself," she said.

The doorbell rang, startling both of them; he bolted up as if he'd been shocked.

"Who could that be?" he asked, actually demanded.

"I don't know . . . I'll see," she said, getting up and moving toward the front door.

He quickly walked to the edge of the veranda and looked down. The sea was twelve stories below. Gentle waves illuminated by the moon caressed the base of the cliffs. If they had somehow found him, if that was the police at the door, he'd jump and take his chances. He would never allow them to put him away again. Listening, intently, he waited. If he had to jump, he'd have to run hard and leap to get as far away from the cliffs as possible. The cliffs rose at a soft angle and if he went straight down he'd surely be smashed on the jagged rocks. Calculating how far he'd have to go to miss hitting the rocks, he waited, preparing himself to run and jump.

THIRTY-NINE

Giuseppe Pisano rode his battered Viper motorbike, frequently looking over his shoulder as he went to his clandestine meeting with Chief Inspector Maranzano near the port, on Via Colombo. Fearful that his uncle listened in on his telephone calls, and wanting to be sure no one saw him talking with the police—a dangerous enterprise in Napoli—he had asked Maranzano to meet him at the port, a place where he knew few, if any, people would be moving about.

Riding motorbikes since he was a teenager, Giuseppe Pisano handled the Viper as if it were a natural extension of his body, turned effortlessly, weaved in and out of traffic with the nimble certainty of a jack rabbit.

The first thing he'd buy, he decided, was a car. Nothing too fancy. But something that could take him anywhere he wanted to go no matter what the weather, even if it was raining—a car he could be proud of. People would see him drive by and say there goes Giuseppe Pisano in his new car. He would, he resolved, also buy himself a new suit right away so when he met the pope he'd look like a man of substance, a trusted confidant of the Church . . . the man who was responsible for the capture of *l'assassino del prete, the scum*, he thought, spitting as he turned on Via Colombo.

Nino Maranzano watched Giuseppe riding toward him.

Giuseppe immediately recognized Maranzano from seeing him on television, in newspapers. He was, Pisano was thinking, a fierce-looking man, no one to fool with, with his iron jaw and serious coal black eyes. Eyes that looked, Pisano thought as he stepped off his motorbike and approached Maranzano, like two bullet holes.

"It is such a pleasure to meet you, Chief Inspector," Pisano said, respectfully shaking Maranzano's hand, bowing his head.

"The pleasure is mine," Maranzano said, thinking Pisano looked like a weasel. Maranzano took out an original rendition of the sketch the Italian police artists had done and slowly held it up for Pisano to see. "Is this the man you saw?" he asked in a friendly tone.

"Si," Pisano said, "that's him."

"You are sure."

"Absolutely, Chief Inspector. I am terrible with remembering names, you know, but I *never* forget a face."

"If you are making this up because you are after the money, you will be a very sorry man."

"I'd never do such a thing—I love the Church; this man is a low-life scumbag; he should be hung by his balls."

Maranzano gave Pisano a long hard look. He saw no deceit in his face, about his eyes. He believed, Maranzano was sure, what he was saying. Maranzano said he wanted Pisano to show him this pizza place, bundled him into an unmarked police car with dark windows and they sped off to the Piazza Lucia, followed by three more unmarked police vehicles, Pisano complaining that he didn't want to be seen, that he didn't want to get out of the car.

"Don't worry," Maranzano said. "You are my friend. I won't let anything happen to you. I promise."

"*Grazie,*" Pisano said, as the police car sped on to the restaurant. When they arrived, the owner of the place, a tall sleepy-eyed man whose face was spotted with flour, was just locking the front door. Pisano histrionically pointed out the table where the couple had been sitting. When the owner saw the famous Nino Maranzano step from the police car, heading straight toward him, his eyes grew wide with surprise—and fear.

"You know who I am?" Maranzano asked.

"Of course, Chief Inspector, but I've done nothing wrong, I—"

"We are not interested in you. There was a man and woman here earlier, a little while ago. They sat there," he said, pointing at the table as though his finger was the barrel of a gun.

"Yes, I remember them. An American woman who spoke good Italian."

"Has anyone else sat there since then?"

"No. They came late."

"Where did the man sit?"

"With his back to the street, there," he said, pointing to the suddenly important cane chair.

"We must go over that table," Maranzano said, signaling to the criminalists in the SUV behind his vehicle. Two fast-moving, no-nonsense men jumped out of the SUV carrying black suitcases. Wearing tight rubber gloves they set up their equipment around the table, then proceeded to carefully dust every square inch of the table and the chair where Frank had sat. Maranzano had brought copies of Frank's prints that had been lifted from the apartment, and from the bike he used when he killed the priests.

Before Maranzano began an all-out manhunt for the killer in the south, away from Rome, he wanted to be absolutely sure the man Pisano had seen was the priest killer. As the criminalists searched for viable prints, with the help of a blue light and ninhydrin powder, Maranzano questioned the owner. "Did you see his face?" he asked

"Si. I waited on them, Chief Inspector."

Maranzano held up the composite sketch for him to see. "This him?" he asked.

"Si, it is him. I don't look so long at him, you know, but si, it looks like him; he was a good-looking man, I remember that."

"Did the woman seem stressed at all . . . like she was there against her will?"

"No, not in the least. She was smiling and happy—a real pizza aficionado. She's been in the shop before, she told me. Said we make the best pizza she ever had."

"Did he talk?"

"No."

"Did you hear him speak Italian?"

"No, Chief Inspector."

One of the criminalists called Maranzano. As he approached the table the criminalist said, "For sure, it's him. We have a perfect match with the index and the pinky finger here," pointing to the prints. Maranzano looked through the thick magnifying glass the criminalist held above the prints for him to see, and even he could readily discern that the prints were identical to those lifted from the apartment in Rome.

"And so he comes to Napoli," Maranzano said, walked outside and began making hurried phone calls. He first ordered the task force to Naples, then contacted the minister of justice and told him they tracked the killer to Naples and that he was setting up a command center there.

Everyone in law enforcement in Italy was outraged at the killing of priests, took the murders quite personally and worked as though someone in their own family had been killed, cut up and left to die in the street, and everything Maranzano asked for he received in triple-time.

FORTY

Cardinal Edam, the governor, mayor, the police commissioner, much of the police brass, Chief of Detectives Samuels, Carole Cunningham and Tony Flynn attended the press conference at One Police Plaza that day.

This time there were even more reporters than before. The international press had become hugely interested in the story and there were news crews from all over—South America, Mexico, Italy, the Philippines, the Middle East . . . even China and Russia, both of whom were intent upon showing how decadent and lawless the United States truly was.

The sexual mutilating and killing of Catholic priests in New York and Rome—on top of the scalding sex scandals the Church had become embroiled in—was big news. It had all the sensational elements the modern day press had become so obsessed with.

Today, thankfully, the air conditioner was working. The mayor and the police commissioner, never ones to miss a photo op, stepped forward. The mayor cleared his throat to get everyone's attention, said he had good news, and told the press they knew the killer's identity. Then the police commissioner dramatically took the podium, waited for the press to become quiet, turning left and right so the cameras would get shots of his profile.

"Because of the relentless, excellent police work done by our people we have a suspect in the murders of the priests," he announced, waited a few seconds more, giving the cameras his left profile, the side, he believed, that looked best. He then introduced Captain Flynn, who explained how the police received the suspect's name, Frank Coogan, and briefly told the press about Coogan's history, emphasizing how he'd been abused as a boy at the Sacred Heart Home for Boys—to the obvious dismay of Cardinal Edam—how he murdered a priest when he was twelve; how he'd been in a state hospital until two years ago; that he'd been linked to the murders via DNA. Flynn then took a few questions and, in a hurry, he left the podium to head for Kennedy Airport for an 8:00 PM flight to Rome. Reporters tried to talk to him but he referred them to Commissioner Peters. His daughter Robin arrived and Tony walked over to her. "Bummer you won't be with us for the fourth, Dad. The kids were looking forward to it," she said.

"I don't want to go to Rome, believe me; I have to go."

"I know. You just be real careful, Dad, please. Promise me you will," she said in a low voice only he could hear.

"I promise I'll be careful," he said, smiling.

"I love you a lot," she said, hugging him long and hard. "We'll miss you."

"We'll do it when I get back."

"Okay, we'll do it when you get back—safe traveling," she said, and they hugged again.

"You see Jacky?" he asked.

"No, she said she'd be here."

"Tell her I'll call her."

"Will do."

Before he left, Commissioner Peters cornered Flynn and profusely congratulated him on "cracking the case so quickly," and told him to make sure he received plenty of news coverage in Rome, making certain the press got shots of him talking with Flynn.

He said, "We want the world to know how dedicated and professional our department is; that we'll go to the very ends of the earth, if necessary, to make certain justice is served. Tony, I'm going to recommend you for promotion regardless of how this works out."

"Thank you, sir," Flynn said, but the truth was that he didn't want to be promoted; he enjoyed working in the field next to his men. The last thing he wanted was to become an administrator—another bureaucrat.

"Keep me posted," the commissioner said.

"I will, sir," Flynn told him, in a hurry to leave, which he promptly did, Carole Cunningham following close behind.

At this point Carole had read Frank Coogan's medical file, and was not all that surprised that a severely abused child had grown into a killer. She had expected something like that all along. What did surprise her, however, was how cunning and driven Coogan was—that he traveled so far for the purpose of killing men in the clergy.

Carole wanted to go to Rome with Flynn, she even discussed it with her boss, but she had a sitting grand jury, more evidence to present them and more indictments coming down.

As she had hoped, Bishop Arnold's indictment was apparently having the effect she wanted, for his attorney had called and said they wished to cut a deal. Hurrying, Flynn and Cunningham made for the elevators.

Rocco Genovese was going to Rome with Flynn; he was, Flynn knew, the perfect man to accompany him, spoke fluent Italian, was fearless and loyal and an excellent investigator.

As they made their way down to the parking lot, Carole briefly ran down to Flynn how Arnold was agreeing to talk.

She said, "Tony, this could very well lead to Rome, to the Vatican."

"I'd be surprised if it didn't," he said, as they stepped into the elevator.

"I'm meeting with Arnold's lawyers in an hour."

"What about O'Brian and Dreyfus?"

"Nothing so far."

"I'll call you soon as I land to see how it went. You need anything, contact Salerno. He's in charge of the task force while I'm away."

"Will do. When will you be landing?"

"Ten tomorrow morning."

"I'll look forward to speaking with you then."

"It'll be in the middle of the night here."

"That's okay, I haven't been sleeping much anyway. As far as the extradition agreement we have with Italy, there is definitely one for murder, but the fact that we have the death sentence here in New York could become a sticky issue. We might very well have to promise not to seek the death penalty to get Coogan back. But, Tony, I'm thinking we may not even be able to try him in a criminal court because of his mental illness; he had serious brain damage as a child."

"I've been thinking about that."

"I've got to tell you I cried when I read his file, one of the saddest stories I ever heard. To be so young and so helpless and so put upon and controlled by a bunch of perverts with a crucifix in one hand and their dicks in the other. It makes my blood boil, you know."

"Yeah, mine too," Flynn said, as they reached the lower level of the garage and she silently walked him to his car. Wanting to kiss him goodbye, she made sure no one was watching and, as they reached his car and he turned to her, she took him in her arms and passionately kissed him.

"Please be careful," she said. "And please make sure to call, okay?"

"Okay."

"I'll miss you."

"And I you."

He smiled, took her in his arms and in them she felt safe; felt like nothing could harm her. Feeling all fuzzy inside, she was surprised at how quickly she had become attached to Tony Flynn. She looked him in his incredibly blue eyes, kissed him again, turned and walked away. He watched as she went, her tall, well-proportioned body, her sure athletic gait, her great legs. At the elevator she turned and waved, threw him a kiss, which he promptly returned, slid into his black Ford and went to pick up Rocco Genovese at the Hudson Street precinct. Tony was taking one suitcase and it was in the backseat. As he exited the garage, he began calling his other daughters to let them know that he wouldn't be able to make their July 4th party, the first one he'd be missing in years. He wasn't able to reach Jacky, though. Just as he took a left onto Canal, his cell phone buzzed. It was one of his detectives at Kennedy Airport phoning to tell him that they found video of Frank Coogan getting on an Alitalia flight to Milan. Pleased by this, knowing the video of Coogan would be an essential tool, Flynn asked if it was usable.

"That's the thing, Captain, he was wearing a baseball cap with the brim pulled down and we only got half his face. He's traveling under the name of Frank Richardson."

"Well, get it to the lab right away and have them enhance it as best they can. And tell Salerno to make sure to send it to Chief Inspector Maranzano in Rome."

"Will do, Captain."

Flynn called his boss to tell him that they had video of Coogan, and that he had ordered it enhanced and released to the press and given to the Italian authorities.

"Excellent," Samuels said.

Flynn reached the precinct. Rocco was standing out front with a black suitcase. When he saw Flynn he smiled and waved, then slid into the car.

"All set?" Flynn asked.

"Fuckin' A," Rocco said, and off they went.

As Flynn and Genovese made their way out to Kennedy Airport, a cable repairman was climbing up a scuttle ladder to the roof of 136 West 117th Street. He was overweight and had some difficulty fitting in the small space to the roof.

Sweating, he struggled and pulled himself up. The roof was so hot you could fry eggs on it, he would later tell his wife. Even before he reached the roof, he heard the crows cawing. He didn't like crows, and he didn't like going up to roofs during the summer months—especially in this area, but he had no say in the matter. Standing upright now, wiping sweat from his brow, he spotted the crows, a half dozen of the large black birds perched on top of a parapet wall, making a lot of noise. He went looking for the main connection box to the building, the racket the crows were making distracting him. Since he was a boy he had an aversion to crows, their jet-black eyes, their pointed peaks . . . their insistent cawing on weekend mornings when he was trying to get a little extra sleep.

As he walked, a strange odor came to him—the scent of something dead. Probably an animal, a rat or squirrel the crows had brought up to the roof, he thought. As he stepped over a waist-high parapet wall, he first spotted her, a naked female with her legs tied open and clumps of hair torn from her head. A container of milk and a loaf of bread lay on the scalding roof next to the body. The crows had fed on the bread and picked out both her eyes. His eyes swelling out of his face, he moaned, turned and ran back to the narrow scuttle ladder, in such a hurry he fell and broke his ankle.

One of the first detectives to respond to the call that day was Tony Flynn's daughter Jacky.

FORTY-ONE

Every muscle coiled, his incredibly strong body tense, about to explode, Frank Coogan waited. Keeping a good ten feet away from the edge of the veranda in case he had to run and jump, he listened for the sound of the *polizia*, hurried steps, men's voices, the loading of weapons, remembering the determination of the *carabinieri* in Rome, remembering Nino Maranzano running down the block.

For the first few months of Frank's stay at Creedmore, he was so violent he had to be kept in restraints, as the priests sometimes kept him in restraints when they abused him. Now, standing there as tense as a coiled spring, his heart racing, he remembered the hospital—its smells, the shrieks and screams of other patients, seeing it all so clearly . . . passing like a black-and-white slow-motion film before his eyes. He would never go back, allow himself to be put in restraints again. He'd die first.

"*Grazi,*" he heard Diane say, and she soon came back with a big smile on her face. "It was the house caretaker and his wife. They said they saw the lights on and wanted to know if I needed anything, something to eat."

"Do they live on the grounds?" he asked, his muscles relaxing, his heart rate slowing.

"Just down the road. I understand she's a fantastic cook. You like Italian food?"

"My favorite."

"Mine too. Eating here, in Italy, is like a religion."

"Will she be cooking then?" he asked, afraid they'd recognize him.

"Yes. They kind of come with the price of the house; but we can go out too. It's up to me if she cooks or not."

"I see," he said, realizing that of course Diane would want to go out, to restaurants, and he was grateful a cook would be coming in.

"She says that a storm they had two days ago knocked down some telephone lines, but it should be fixed tomorrow." They sat back down.

She said, "I'm not so tired anymore; guess it's because I'm excited about the house; the prospect of writing here."

"I hope I'm not any kind of distraction."

"Don't worry. There's plenty of places I can work."

"You use a laptop to write?"

"I do the first draft by hand then input it into the laptop and do the rewriting there. I like the feel of a pen in my hand when I'm getting down the first draft."

"Mind telling me more about the book?"

"Briefly, it involves the feud between the Sicilians and Calabrians. How a very beautiful independent girl from a Calabrian fishing family falls in love with the son of a Sicilian fishing family, renowned for his strength and looks. And against their families' wishes they manage to get together and have a child out of wedlock who, during a fierce storm, is washed into the sea in a bassinet and found by a Roman aristocrat in a war galley—who makes the boy his son and he grows up to be Marc Anthony, Julius Caesar's confidant and friend. And the man who marries Cleopatra after Caesar's murder; the man who killed many of the senators responsible for Caesar's murder. He later committed suicide, as did Cleopatra, when Octavius—sent by the Roman senate—attacked and overcame Alexandria."

"Sounds fascinating; is that true?"

"Actually, yes, based on all historical facts I've gathered. I'm taking literary license with some of the elements, but keeping it as factually accurate as possible," she said. His eyes didn't leave her face, admiring how the moonlight played in her hair, filled her huge eyes. In all his life he had never, he realized, seen a beautiful woman in the light of a full moon.

They sat for a time in contemplative silence staring at the moon, its soothing reflection on the calm sea. Here in Amalfi it was cooler than Rome and there was a pleasant breeze off the water.

She said, "So, Frank, tell me about this memoir you have in mind," as if she somehow knew what he'd been thinking. He sat for a long time staring at the ocean, not sure if he should tell her anything about who he really was. He didn't want to frighten her, turn her away from him, make her think he had a pile of dirty laundry inside his head. But against his will, he began to think of Sacred Heart. She waited, believing he was collecting his thoughts, having no idea that his mind had gone back to the night he murdered the priest at Sacred Heart, seeing it, hearing it—even smelling the blood. He forced himself to come back and in a soft voice he began, surprising himself, to tell Diane about what had happened to him at the home—leaving out the more sordid details: the depth of the abuse, the murder, how he'd been placed in a state hospital. He told her how he'd been adopted by a nice couple; how they nurtured him and got him interested in books; how they helped him get over the things that had been done to him at Sacred Heart.

"I'm sorry," he said, "to be talking about such ugly things in such a beautiful place . . . but you asked me, and I . . . I wanted to tell you the truth, to be honest."

Her mouth slightly agape, Diane told him that he should definitely tell his story; that it was important and socially relevant; that he should expose how he'd been treated by members of the Church—that he should "purge" himself of the experience.

He said, "Truth is, I've been wanting to write about it for the longest time, even when it was happening I used to fantasize about writing a book so others would know the truth—what they were doing; how they acted all holy and pious and righteous when they were really a bunch of freaks, you know."

"It's just amazing how the Church allowed all these people to become priests. I was brought up a Catholic. I believed in the Church and its teachings. I used to go to church every Sunday. When my husband was sick I went to church every day to pray and light candles. But not now. I won't set foot in a church. What they allowed to happen completely turned me off. I still believe in Jesus Christ but definitely not the Catholic Church."

"What I could never figure out," he said, "was why God would allow such things to happen. You'd think . . . you'd think being God and all he'd do something to stop it, expose it."

"Maybe he is. Maybe everything becoming public now is *His* work," she said.

"Yeah, maybe," he said, though doubting it. No God, he was sure, would ever allow what was done to him and the others. *And what about the Crusades*, he thought, *or the Inquisition: Why did God allow the Church to do those terrible things in His name to all those people.*

"Thank you for listening," he said. "I hope you don't think," he added, "I'm some kind of mixed-up basketcase . . . I'm not. I would not have even told you if you didn't ask . . . It happened so long ago—another lifetime, that it doesn't even seem real to me anymore."

"That's good," Diane said. "That also means you are far enough away from it so you can effectively write about it."

"Yeah, I guess," he said. "I'll think about it."

"I'd be happy to help in any way," she said. "If you like I'll even tell my agent about it."

"I don't know . . . I mean I don't know if I could actually do it, sit down and cohesively get it on paper."

"In theory if you can talk you can write. You just have to believe you can and every day get a little of it done. It doesn't matter how long it takes; it doesn't matter if the first draft is as good as you'd like it to be. In truth, writing is about rewriting, going over the early drafts and perfecting it, editing out the repetitious, making sure it's the story you want to tell. The story you feel inside. The story you see in your mind's eye."

"You make it sound so easy."

"Oh, it's not easy. In fact it's very difficult, but I guarantee you if you believe you can do it, you can. You just have to put yourself to it. To set up a writing regimen and stick to it. You'll see after a while it will start writing itself. The key is just to sit down every day, no matter what. You have a natural affinity for books, the written word, and that helps a lot."

"You think?"

"I know."

"I wouldn't even know where to begin," he said, but he knew exactly where he'd begin—the first time he saw Sacred Heart. The first time a priest, a full-grown man, came at him with lust in his eyes.

"Begin at the beginning. The first memories you have of what happened. Just keep it simple and honest and don't hold anything back. Tell it like it was, like it is. Like you saw it. Like you felt it."

"I'll try," he said. "But I don't want you to see any of it until I say it's ready, okay?"

"Yes, of course," she said.

"Thank you, Diane."

"Thank you for sharing all you told me," she said.

If, he thought, he had told her everything she would get up and run.

"How about going for a swim?" she asked, looking at the pool, the cream-colored moonlight quivering on its surface.

"I'd love to," he said, smiling. "But I . . . I don't have a bathing suit."

"You don't need one. Neither do I," she said, slipping out of her robe in one easy movement and, suddenly naked, she walked to the edge of the pool and dived in, barely making a splash. She came up, a big smile on her face.

"Come on in. The water is perfect. It's sea water. Don't be shy."

But he was shy. He stood and slowly slipped out of his clothes and dived in after her, the water salty, cool and so very welcoming.

FORTY-TWO

The first thing Nino Maranzano did was to have the revised sketch put up all over Naples—on poles, in shop and restaurant windows and the main piazzas. He also ordered police cars with loud speakers to drive all over Naples, telling the Neapolitans that the suspect in the priest killings in Rome had come to their city.

Neapolitans, he knew, minded their own business, did not talk with the police—a thing that was deeply engrained into their culture—but Maranzano also knew that the Neapolitans were a religious people and would gladly help find a man who mutilated and murdered Catholic priests. That was something, he knew, they would not tolerate. The killer, he also knew, might very well be handed over to him dead, murdered by the very violent criminal element that was an integral part of Neapolitan society.

It didn't take long for the respective heads of the Camorra crime families to order their people to start looking for the priest killer, with specific orders that when he was found he should be beaten to death and castrated.

As violent, treacherous and brutal as the Camorra was—far more so than the Mafia—they were devoted members of the Catholic Church; were married by the Church, their children baptized in the Church and, more importantly, all the wives and mothers of the crime family heads demanded that their husbands and sons *do something*—make sure *l'assassino del prete* paid dearly for his unspeakable crimes.

Spurred by the public outcry in Italy—the constant news reports—Italian corporations began adding to the reward money, seeing an opportunity for good PR. Wanting to associate themselves with a just and righteous cause, they gladly contributed large amounts of money. Fiat, Bennetton, Armani, Gucci, Ferrari, Versace, all pledged money, and it didn't take long for the amount being offered to exceed one million euros, an astronomical sum for a reward in Italy—the most ever.

With that kind of money at stake, everyone in Naples was looking for the priest killer—the young and the old, in addition to all the various Italian police departments, as well as professional killers with razor-sharp knives, excellent marksmen, who were making it their business to find *l'assassino del prete*.

All this caused the parking attendant Giuseppe Pisano great anxiety, but Maranzano assured him several times over that the reward money would be his.

One million euros, Pisano kept saying to himself, imagining the house he'd buy, as well as his new car and wardrobe. Pisano stayed glued to the television, wanting to keep abreast of the hunt for the man he saw.

Maranzano was sure, if the killer was in Naples, that he would quickly be found. As well as making certain the composite was plastered all over Naples, Maranzano told the Italian press that the killer was traveling with an American woman who spoke Italian and was driving a green BMW. He ordered Italian artists to work with the pizzeria owner and Pisano to create a composite of the woman, and soon this sketch was given to the media and posted around Naples.

Maranzano took over an empty office in Naples Central, on Via Garibaldi, and made it a command center. He would run the hunt for Frank Coogan like a military operation.

He received numerous reports that Camorra soldiers were questioning restaurant and shop owners and the desk people at every hotel in Naples. As much as Maranzano hated the Camorra—indeed they were his sworn enemy—he was pleased that they had become involved, for with them stalking Naples it wouldn't take long for Coogan to be found, to be killed. Maranzano even ran a wire to the underworld saying that he had to have the body intact.

Maranzano knew Tony Flynn and another New York detective were on their way to Rome from New York, and he arranged for them to be met at Leonardo Da Vinci airport and flown on a police helicopter to Naples. He even found them rooms in a four-star hotel with magnificent views of the bay of Naples.

He only hoped that Tony Flynn would not get in the way, try to tell him what to do, make an already difficult situation more difficult. At this point all he could do, he knew, was sit and wait, sure the Neapolitan underworld would find this Frank Coogan. He was so sure he would soon have Coogan's body, he even made arrangements for DNA comparisons to be made with the corpse that would soon be laid at his doorstep.

All through this, Maranzano kept trying to reach his wife Lina, was on the cell phone with the Rome police who were spearheading the search for her, all to no avail.

Near midnight his cell phone buzzed, and it was his wife. His heart rose and lodged in his throat when he heard her voice.

"Where are you? I've been worried sick. How could you just run out on me like this? Lina, I love you more than life itself; I'm sorry, I'm so sorry I had to leave the restaurant like that, but, Lina, a madman from New York is killing our priests and it is in my hands . . . where are you?"

"I'm at my sister's," she said, her voice small and far away.

"I've left five messages on her machine."

"I heard them. I've been watching the news. You are in Napoli now?"

"We received a tip that he came here. Lina, if you like I'll quit the force, I'll do anything to make you happy. I didn't realize you were so upset. Why didn't you tell me? You—"

"Nino you never have time to really listen to what I tell you. I have told you in a hundred different ways how upset I've been.

"But Nino, I know, I realize now how important your work truly is. I'm sorry I left like that; it was foolish—I was acting like a stupid schoolgirl. Will you forgive me?"

"Yes, of course. I love you Lina."

"And I love you, Nino. I can't live without you," she said, and began crying, as did he, walking away from his men, not wanting to be seen in such a state. Men didn't cry into telephones.

FORTY-THREE

For most of that day Carole Cunningham was negotiating with Bishop Arnold's team of attorneys. The bishop was willing to tell all he knew about the aiding and abetting of predator priests within the Catholic Church, about Cardinal Bernard Hound's role in the sexual abuse of thousands of children in the Boston archdiocese, and what roles cardinals and bishops played in archdioceses throughout the country. Specifically, he said, in New Orleans, Florida, Los Angeles and Chicago. It was they—the Church hierarchy—whom Cunningham was most interested in prosecuting.

Arnold said, through his lawyers in offices at 401 Broadway, that Church officials close to the pope knew about everything—including the Secretariat Vatican, the man in charge of all legal matters at the Vatican. He not only did nothing to stop it, but facilitated abuse continued by never reporting any of the predator priests to authorities.

Arnold claimed, and was willing to tell the grand jury, his lawyers said, that the reason so many sexual predators had found their way into the Church was because bishops and cardinals, some of whom themselves were pedophiles, endorsed and encouraged their own kind into seminaries—into the ranks of the priesthood. He had, he said, names and dates and specific instances he was willing to testify about, including photographs; only, however, if he received total immunity, a new identity, and was placed into the witness protection program. After what happened to John Krol, who had been in protective custody, Arnold was deathly afraid of going to prison—any prison—and would do whatever necessary to stay out of jail. He felt no allegiance to his fellow molesters . . . or apparently anyone else.

As much as Cunningham wanted Arnold's testimony, she could not promise all he was asking for and she had to make numerous trips to her boss's office, who in turn had to speak to the mayor and the governor. In the end, they reluctantly agreed to give Arnold everything. Arnold, in turn, finally agreed to testify at Cunningham's grand jury the following day, at 9:00 AM sharp.

Hating Carole Cunningham, sure she was a politically motivated "Catholic Hater," no doubt a Protestant, Arnold, who had made bail because the Church put up the cash and a bond for his release, left his lawyer's office near 8:00 PM and was driven back to a plush home for retired priests, the John Cardinal O'Connor Residence in Riverdale, a nice neighborhood in the Bronx. Even though the Church was having serious financial difficulties because of all the money that had been paid out to keep the abused and their families quiet, the home served sumptuous meals, had a daily cocktail hour, a fifty-seven-inch color television in the common room, a professional pool table, six hundred square foot wall-to-wall carpeted suites, and a large Jacuzzi bath on every floor. A former seminary, the house was situated on fifteen acres of quiet, well-groomed grounds crisscrossed with neat rows of flowers, shaded by huge oak and maple trees, often the only sound that of chirping birds.

Bishop Arnold was a large man with a protruding Adam's apple, a narrow face, dark eyes, thin lips, and a bulbous nose mapped with broken blood vessels from which long hairs protruded like insect tentacles.

Wanting to be prepared to deal with Carole Cunningham, his testifying at the grand jury, wanting to get all this behind him, Arnold made himself some chamomile tea, retired early to his particularly plush, air-conditioned suite.

A man without guilt, Arnold went to sleep quickly. The only remorse he had was that he'd been found out, and that he was being forced from the Church, forced away from the free access he had for over twenty-nine years to trusting children. Looking forward to his new life, he slept like a baby.

Near 3:00 AM, the door to Bishop Arnold's room, which had been locked from the inside, was slowly opened, and a short, burly man carrying a three-foot length of rough hemp with knots at each end, silently walked toward the sleeping form of Bishop Arnold. He also carried, slung over his shoulder, a second piece of hemp, a fifteen-foot length with a noose at the one end. With thick callused hands, he took the shorter piece of rope, moved to the side of the bed and, suddenly, violently, wrapped the hemp around Arnold's neck and pulled it tight with terrific force, as he straddled Arnold to keep him still, whispering Italian in Arnold's ear in a rough Sicilian dialect: "Brucerai nelle fiamme dell'inferno per il tuo tradimento, maiale, figlio di puttana." *You will burn in hell for your treachery, you pig, son of a whore*, he hissed as if a large poisonous snake.

FORTY-FOUR

Holding on to the edge of the pool, Diane watched him swim toward her, admiring how his muscular body seamlessly cut through the salt water pool. He slowed and made his way to where she was and took hold of the pool's terracotta edge, just next to her, a large smile on his face. "Amazing," he said. "Thank you."

"You are a great swimmer."

"It's the only sport I ever really took to. Even as a kid I loved the water—the feeling of freedom I had when I was swimming, you know?"

"Yes, of course, me too. I was brought up right across the street from a beach."

"That must have been nice."

"One of the few good things in my childhood . . .

"I don't . . . Frank I don't want to give you the wrong impression. I mean that I'm some kind of loose woman because I dived in the pool like this."

"I thought it was great. I've never known anyone like you—so comfortable within your own skin, who does in life exactly what she wants to do. Diane, you are an inspiration. I feel very lucky to have met you," he said.

"Thank you. Nice of you to say," she said and they stared at one another. He so wanted to kiss her, but was hesitant. He didn't want to do anything to make her uncomfortable, but as he looked into her eyes, she seemed to be talking to him . . . silently telling him it was okay; that she wanted him to come closer . . . *come closer.* He moved toward her, as she did to him and they kissed there in the pool, the only witness the all-seeing, all-knowing moon.

He got out of the pool first, took her arms by the wrists and effortlessly lifted her.

"You are amazingly strong," she said in little more than a hoarse whisper, her heart racing, looking at his athletic body, how his muscles looked like steel cables alive and moving under his flesh. He brought her closer and kissed her deeply, softly—gently. He had dreamed and fantasized about passionately kissing a beautiful woman all his life and now it was actually happening. He quickly became aroused, keeping his eyes open as he kissed her, wanting to be sure this was real, not something he was imagining. Because of what the priests had done to him he had no idea of his real sexuality, if he liked women, if he liked men, but now all that doubt, confusion and indecision were instantly swept away, and he pushed himself against her.

She, too, was surprised this was happening, but very much, she realized, wanted it to happen. Needed it to happen. Every time she had seen him—on the bus to Rome, in the Vatican, especially in the Colosseum—she wanted to make love to him.

Illuminated by the Italian moon, he picked her up and carried her to a lounge near the end of the veranda and gently laid her down.

"You are the most beautiful woman I've ever seen," he said, taking her, consuming her . . . savoring every inch of her.

FORTY-FIVE

Chief Inspector Maranzano had a police helicopter pick up Lina and take her to Naples. He met her as the helicopter landed, took her in his arms and held her so tight he nearly cracked one of her ribs, over and over again telling her how much he loved her, how much he missed her, needed her, as she did him.

He had taken a suite in the same hotel where Flynn would be staying, The Vesuvius on Via Andria, and he sped to the hotel now, kissing Lina in the elevator as he kissed her when they first met, passionately and recklessly. In the room he very nearly tore her clothes off and he made desperate, passionate love to her, telling her over and over how much he loved her: "Ti amo tesoro mio, ti amo tesoro mio, ti amo tesoro mio" *I love you, my darling,* hot burning words whispered in her ears with the raw intensity of a large cat's growling, as he pushed himself deep inside his beloved Lina.

So intense was his love, his passion, she began to cry and he moved deeper inside her still. "Mi dimettero', Lina. Se lo desideri abbandonero' questo maledetto lavoro," *I'll quit, Lina. If you want I'll walk away from this cursed job,* he said.

FORTY-SIX

Carole Cunningham was angry. She considered herself a seasoned professional, but that night she could not sleep. She tossed and turned, thinking about Bishop Arnold, the questions she'd ask him, the task force she planned to mobilize to arrest all the people he named. She knew now, because of the brutal murder of John Krol, they'd all be much more willing to talk, to point the finger, to cooperate with the law, with her, and she planned to put as many of them in jail as humanly possible. She was surprised that O'Brian and Dreyfus had not also tried to cut deals for themselves.

She knew she needed sleep; she needed to be rested to deal with all this. But sleep stayed elusive and impossible, and finally she climbed out of bed, cursing Arnold, grabbed a yellow legal pad and began adding questions to the ones she'd already written for him, seeing his bitter narrow face as she worked. She made herself a strong espresso and some toast and carefully constructed her questions to get the most from Arnold's testimony. She had already arranged for him to be taken, after he testified, to an apartment on West 96th Street that the District Attorney's office kept for witnesses, a four-story brownstone owned by the city, just off Central Park West. She planned to visit him there after his first day in front of the grand jury to help prepare him for his second day of testimony. Her plan was to keep him in front of the grand jury until she squeezed every drop of information out of him.

Looking at her watch, she thought about Tony Flynn, realized he'd just about be landing if his flight had taken off and arrived on time.

Thinking about Tony, the night they made love, still not quite believing that had happened after all the years she'd known him, but looking forward to seeing him again, she felt a flush of heat on her face. The phone suddenly rang, shattering her reverie.

"Tony?" she asked, sure it was him, pleased that he was calling, warmed by it.

"It's not Tony, I'm sorry," came a strange male's voice. "This is Sergeant Gusman of the 64th Precinct in the Bronx. I got your number from the office. I'm sorry to be calling so early, counselor, but I've got news I understand you will want."

"Yes?" she said, suddenly filled with trepidation, bracing herself for bad news.

"We found a priest, actually I understand he's a bishop, at the home for retired priests here in Riverdale—he hung himself."

"Is he dead?"

"Very."

"I don't believe this! He was going to testify in the morning about abuse in the Church."

"Yeah, I heard. That's why I called right away. I thought you'd want to know."

"Absolutely. Thank you, Sergeant. But I . . . I don't think

he killed himself. We gave him everything he asked for, a new identity, money, a passport. He played hardball with us all day. It doesn't make any sense."

"Counselor, I saw him myself hanging from a beam in the ceiling over a chair which he clearly kicked over."

"Is he still there—I mean like that."

"Yes, fact is, I'm here now, just outside of his room. I'm looking at him."

"Sergeant, please don't let anyone touch him. I want to see him for myself; and I'm going to bring Chief Medical Examiner Richard Russo with me."

"That's fine with me, counselor. I'll make sure no one touches him."

"Thank you," she said, picking up her phone book, finding the number of Dr. Russo and calling him at his home. He was in a sound sleep but, accustomed to being awakened in the middle of the night, he was quickly wide awake and readily agreed to go out to the Bronx with Carole when he heard what happened.

Russo was the finest coroner in the business and if there had been foul play, he'd know, he'd see the truth. Running, Carole got dressed, arranged for a car, picked up Dr. Russo and sped out to the Bronx.

FORTY-SEVEN

With the help of Chief Inspector Maranzano, Flynn and Rocco Genovese were able to get permission to bring their weapons to Italy, but the guns had to be stowed in a locked box and given to them upon their arrival in Rome. At Kennedy Airport, Flynn had seen the video footage of Coogan going through security, but the killer had pulled down the brim of his cap and all that was visible was from his upper lip down, not really much help.

The Alitalia flight took off uneventfully, on time, and both men looked out the window, solemnly staring at lower Manhattan, the place where the World Trade Towers had once stood. Rocco had lost a nephew who worked at Cantor Fitzgerald that day, and both of them had lost good friends in the department.

They each ordered scotch on the rocks, toasted their lost comrades, sat back, and Tony now told Rocco everything that doctors Hartock and Lawson had told him. Rocco asked to read Coogan's file from Creedmore, which Tony had brought and he gave it to him. His hard face appearing as though it had been chiseled out of granite, Rocco put on his reading glasses and read the report, as Tony thought about the case, about Frank Coogan . . . the rotten deck of cards life had dealt him, and the more he thought about the case, about what he'd learned from the doctors, the more he felt for Coogan.

He was, Flynn knew, a cold-blooded killer who had to answer for his crimes, but he was also severely abused as a child, over a long period of time, with no one to turn to for help. It was all so very sad and depressing, he was thinking, and hoped that Coogan would be taken alive and put back in a hospital, where he belonged, for the rest of his natural life. But he also knew that Coogan had clearly exhibited cunning, malicious intent and premeditation. Proving he was legally insane, not responsible for his acts, would be an uphill battle for even the best defense attorney.

Whatever the eventual outcome, Flynn had a job to do and planned to assist Chief Inspector Maranzano any way he could, and when Coogan was caught, to help arrange his extradition back to New York, which, he knew, was a lot easier said than done. The Catholic Church was vehemently opposed to capital punishment and he was sure the Church would exert all the pressure it could to keep Coogan from being extradited, and, by extension, executed.

Finished reading, Rocco put down the report and took a long, disgusted breath.

"So the Church created this monster," he observed in a matter-of-fact tone with his Bronx accent.

"Seems that way, yeah," Flynn said.

"All that kind of abuse happening to a little kid like that has got to bend his head out of shape, no?"

"I'd say so."

"This priest he killed was a sexual sadist. If he had done those things to me I would've probably killed him too."

"I know," Flynn said, smiling at his friend.

" 'Cept I would'nt've cut his head off."

Rocco became quiet, stared out the window, at the endless blue sky unblemished by clouds. This was a very tough, hardcore law-and-order New York City detective brought up on the mean streets of the Bronx, on Arthur Avenue, and even he was touched—disturbed, actually— by what he had read; by what the boy had been through at Sacred Heart.

"You know," he said. "There was this priest at our church, Father Moony. Remember him?"

"Sure."

"I remember how I always felt uncomfortable around him. There was just something off-color in his eyes, the way he walked, the way he looked at you, and I remember one day, right in the church, after a Friday confession, he started asking me questions about sex—if I had a girl-friend, did I masturbate, weird shit like that. Then he asked me if I'd help him move some stuff in the room behind the altar. I said sure, and the next thing I know he's trying to open my zipper, telling me how God wanted him to teach me all about sex. Man, I haven't thought about this in a hundred years, you know. And for a few seconds I just froze. Like a deer in headlights. I didn't know what the hell to do. Then this creep he started going down on me right there behind the altar and I pushed him away, and he gets all red-faced and angry and threatens me with hell, you know; and again he goes down and he's trying to get my dick outta my jeans so I popped him one right in the eye."

"You gave him that shiner?" Flynn asked incredulously. "I remember he had this big black eye."

"Yeah, I gave it to him all right. I should've beaten the living daylights outta him but I was scared *God* would be mad at me because I socked one of his priests and I high-tailed it outta there."

"Bravo," Tony said, shaking Rocco's massive hand, not saying anything about how he'd been sexually accosted by this same priest; how he'd been frightened, coerced into submission and, in the end, refused to enter the church. Any church. Rocco was Tony Flynn's best friend, but still he would not tell Rocco what Moony had done to him because he was still so ashamed of what had occurred. *Hell of a thing*, he thought.

The stewardess came around with the food carts and served dinner. They ate in reflective silence, sharing a bottle of red wine, these two men who had known each other all their lives and were comfortable and at ease with one another's silence. They hit some turbulence. The captain warned everyone to stay seated, buckled in.

FORTY-EIGHT

Finished, spent, they laid next to one another on the green and white lounge chair near the pool of Casa Bella Luna. The moon had passed out of sight by now and the sky was a deep charcoal gray dotted by thousands of brilliant stars.

"I didn't expect that to happen," she said in little more than a whisper.

"Nor did I, but I'm glad it did. You're an *amazing* woman, Diane . . . so very beautiful . . . thank you. Thank you for sharing so much with me."

She hugged him, kissed him.

"Thank you. No one *ever* made love to me like that," she whispered. "My God," feeling a slight burning where he had been.

"I have a confession," he said after a few moments.

"Please."

"Truth is, you are the first woman I ever made love to."

"I don't believe that, no way—"

"Oh, but it's true."

"I thought you had a girlfriend."

"I did but we never, you know, had sex," he said.

"So you were, like, a virgin?" she asked.

"Yes," he said, forcing himself not to think of his experiences with sex, not wanting to go there now . . . ruin this beautiful moment.

"This have to do with what happened to you?" she asked, immediately going to the heart of the thing, as was Diane's way.

"Yes, I guess so," he said.

"It's getting late. Let's go to bed, okay?" she said. She took him by the hand, led him into the house and to her bedroom. She had put on the air conditioner and the room was cool and comfortable, the pure cotton sheets welcoming. He took her in his steel-like arms and held her tight, afraid of what was to come.

"*Buona notte*, goodnight," she said in a small voice.

"Goodnight," he whispered. Not quite believing all this was real, thinking he was surely dreaming, he pinched himself; it hurt. He smiled and sleep soon stole them both away.

FORTY-NINE

"I'm sorry, Nino," Lina Maranzano said. "I don't know what got into me. It's just . . . after you left the restaurant and I was sitting there alone, I just . . . I just lost it, went to the bathroom and began crying hysterically."

"No, Lina, it is I who am sorry. I should not have walked out on you like that . . . please forgive me. It was a brutal thing to do. It will never happen again, I promise. I'm going to quit. I've been thinking about it since I read your note. I've got enough years in to get a full pension. Lina, we'll travel. Go to New York and San Francisco, to Mexico and Brazil. All the places we always talked about visiting. I've had it with this job. I'm sick and tired of seeing bodies, telling people their loved ones are dead, and I'm sick of stupid ministers telling me what to do and how to do it. I don't want to be anyone's puppet anymore. And most of all, I don't want to hurt you."

"But, Nino, you love your work—I know you do. From the first day I met you, I knew what you did and that it would require sacrifice. You are passionate and driven—and, Nino, you really make a difference; that's what I realize now.

"At my sister's, I saw you on the television news, heard what you said—how you said it—and, Nino, you make the world a better place. Men like you, tough men with ideals who really care, are rare. You can't quit because of me, what I did. Promise me you won't. I was wrong. Maybe . . . I don't know, maybe it's because of the change in life. It's coming now to me and it makes a woman crazy, you know . . .

"My love, you do what you do best . . . please. This man, this butcher of our priests, he must be stopped. You must stop him. My God, what terrible crimes. *Never* in my lifetime did I ever think I'd be witness to such an abomination as this. Not even when the Nazis controlled Italia—the worst creatures of the twentieth century, did they kill priests. They, the Church—spiritual faith—it's all that separates us from jungle creatures . . .

"No, my love," she said. "You do your job and you find this monster, and you send him to hell where he belongs. You understand?"

"I understand," he said, taking her in his arms, frightened by how much he loved her.

FIFTY

Bishop Arnold was hanging from the second beam off the south wall of his room at the O'Connor home for retired priests. He was naked, his neck obviously broken, his tongue protruding five inches from his open mouth, a deep purple color. Blood had gathered in his feet, and they were as red as two large chili peppers.

Carole Cunningham had seen many naked men—she had vacationed on the Greek islands last summer and was on nude beaches every day—but seeing Arnold hanging like a side of beef at the meat market made her uncomfortable, and she felt compelled to look away.

Arnold had been discovered by a fellow priest, an eighty-two-year-old man who had trouble sleeping and was pacing the hall, silently saying prayers, when he noticed Arnold's door slightly ajar. He saw him hanging there, swinging back and forth like a slow moving pendulum. When the police first arrived, the uniforms took one look and called it in.

No one, Dr. Russo was assured by the detective who responded, had entered the room. By law a body cannot so much as even be touched until the coroner examines the deceased. All the cops there knew who Dr. Russo was, and they respectfully acknowledged him when he arrived.

Russo, a tall contemplative man with a full head of black hair parted on the left side, had dark, slow-moving eyes that seemed to see everything at once; he had worked over 15,000 murders and had a kind of sixth sense that often proved to be uncannily accurate. Carole stayed at the doorway as he slowly entered, his shoes covered with green cloth boots. He carefully looked at the body, the position of the chair, moving in slow reflective circles. He then scrutinized the bed, the depressed spot on the pillow where Arnold had been sleeping. He asked for a ladder to be brought in and the detectives went and found one in the garage. Russo climbed up the ladder and scrutinized the rope around Arnold's neck.

He said, "It looks like he hung himself. He managed to get the rope over the beam, tied the end there on the radiator riser pipe, put the noose around his neck and kicked the chair away."

"Suicide?" Cunningham asked, still skeptical. Arnold had fought tooth and nail for everything he wanted. Like a man who had plans, who wanted to live life, who was concerned about his future, where he'd live, a passport so he could travel. Certainly not acting like someone on the verge of killing himself, she was thinking, watching Dr. Russo work.

The doctor untied the knot around the pipe and, with the help of two detectives, slowly let Arnold down. He was stiff as a diving board with rigor mortis. The doctor removed the noose from Arnold's neck and put it into a large clear plastic bag. He then carefully examined the rope marks around Arnold's neck, his brows slowly knitting together, forming a kind of question mark, as he moved closer and closer still. He stood and retrieved a large magnifying glass and bright light from his case and, again, examined the rope marks around Arnold's neck with the help of the magnifying glass and light.

"Hmm," he said, standing up.

"This man," he said, "was murdered. There are two, not one, circular hematomas caused by two different ligatures. Though the ropes used are identical, there are clearly two separate marks. The killer very carefully tried to make this look like a suicide, but it's definitely a murder."

"I knew it," Cunningham said.

"You were right."

At that moment Flynn's partner, Frank Salerno arrived, saying he had heard what happened through the grapevine. He, like Carole, didn't believe Arnold had killed himself and wanted to check out the crime scene. Dr. Russo showed Salerno what he found. Carole asked if he could reach Flynn. Salerno checked his watch. "He should just about be landing," he said. "I'll try him." He walked to the window and dialed Flynn on his cell phone. There was no answer.

"He's probably not on the ground yet," Salerno said.

"I know who did this," Carole said.

"Who?" Salerno asked.

"The Church. They found out Arnold was going to talk and *they* sent someone; they tried, and almost succeeded, to make it look like a suicide, but thanks to Dr. Russo they failed. I want everyone in the home questioned, Sergeant . . . I bet my license to practice law the killer is still here," she said.

Russo said, "If you do find him there should be some red marks on his hands left from the ropes. This is course, hard hemp. It takes tremendous force—pressure—to choke a man to death with a thick piece of rope like this. There should also be some rope burns."

"What if he wore gloves?" Cunningham asked.

"There should still be some sign of the tremendous force it would take to do the job with rope this thick, you see," he said, holding up the rope.

"I'm calling the task force and getting our detectives over here," Salerno told the Bronx detectives who had initially responded to the call.

"Shit!" Carole exclaimed. "We *had* them. We had them by the balls . . ."

FIFTY-ONE

The police sketch Chief Inspector Maranzano had done of Diane Pane didn't resemble her. Giuseppe Pisano, the parking attendant, had never really looked at her face because he was too busy looking at her full figure, and the owner of the pizzeria where they had eaten had stopped looking at the faces of his customers a long time ago. In the sketch, which Maranzano released to the press and had posted all over Naples, the lips were too thin, the forehead too high, the face long and narrow, whereas Diane's was full and heart-shaped.

When, that morning, Maranzano went to work, Lina stayed at the hotel. She would, she said, remain in Naples to be near her husband until the case was resolved. "I want to help you," she said. "To support you ... to rub your muscles when you come back to me." To keep herself busy, she said, she would shop, swim in the hotel pool and visit Neapolitan friends she hadn't seen in a while.

Content, very pleased Lina was back, Maranzano went to work with a newfound vigor and intensity, confident the case would be closed soon. Regardless of what Lina had said, Maranzano was planning to quit police work. He just didn't want to do it anymore. He was sick and tired of the morgue, getting calls at all hours, taking orders from appointed politicians who knew nothing about real police work. Now he wanted to enjoy life, travel, spend more time with his son ... maybe even write a book about his career. Rent a house in Tuscany near the famous spas of Saturnia and write. He'd just quit, he resolved, not tell Lina until it was done. The idea of retiring made him smile as he walked into the cramped, dusty office where the command center had been set up.

Tips were pouring in from all over Naples, from people who believed they had seen *l'assassino del prete*, anxious about the reward. Even people who had in reality seen nothing, called in tips, hoping they'd be able to share, in some way, in the reward. As Maranzano looked at his watch, finishing his second cup of espresso, he figured Tony Flynn would just be arriving at the airport, looking forward to meeting him though still concerned that he'd turn out to be a *distrasse*—distraction. He called Rome to make sure people had been dispatched to meet Flynn. He was assured they were. Flynn had been very helpful and he planned to be as accommodating to him as possible.

Sure it would be just a matter of time before someone spotted Coogan or this woman he was traveling with, or one of the Camorra hit teams found him, Maranzano sat at his makeshift desk and waited; the traps were set; everything was in place. All he had to do was be patient, ready to pounce when the moment came.

FIFTY-TWO

Both Tony and Rocco fell asleep after the movie. They were awakened when the Alitalia crew began serving breakfast. The sun, off to the left, was just coming up. A fiery orange ball shyly appearing out of the eastern horizon. They had some coffee and fruit, both went to the lavatory to freshen up, knowing they would hit the ground running. The captain soon announced they were landing, as the plane banked sharply and they flew over a long stretch of golden beach, then once fertile fields, which were now, for the most part, burnt by the fierce summer sun and three months of drought. Instead of being bright green, the land was a giant patch quilt of dull yellows and pale oranges. The plane landed smoothly fifteen minutes early.

"Have you been to Rome?" Flynn asked.

"Never. Me and the wife talked about going to Italy a dozen times, but it never happened, you?"

"No," Flynn said, remembering that he and his wife had plans to visit Italy and Ireland, but then she had become sick, and his world was suddenly turned upside down and traveling became impossible.

When Flynn and Rocco left the plane, the heat slammed into them as they walked down to the tarmac. They were met by two Roman detectives who spoke little English, but Rocco spoke Italian and after talking to them he told Flynn that they would quickly usher them through customs, get them their weapons and put them on a helicopter to Naples, where the investigation had moved, where Chief Inspector Maranzano now awaited them.

"Naples?" Flynn asked.

"Naples."

After they went through customs, as they made their way to the luggage carousels, Flynn learned that Coogan had positively been seen in Naples, traveling with a woman driving a BMW.

"A woman?" he said, shocked. "An accomplice? He has a female accomplice?"

This, he was told, was something they were not sure about, but he was definitely in the company of a woman—an American who spoke Italian. They had pizza together, Rocco translated, and Coogan's prints were found on the table where they ate. Flynn had been sure that Coogan was traveling alone, that he was in this alone, and he was really surprised to hear that he was with a woman. They retrieved their guns and were taken back to the steaming tarmac, where a police helicopter was waiting for them. In minutes they were speeding south. "My family," Rocco said, "on my mother's side is from Naples."

"You have any relatives still there?" Flynn asked.

"Not that I know of. They all left between 1906 and 1910. There was nothing to eat, no work. Fact is, they left on a steam ship from the Bay of Naples," Rocco said, feeling all emotional about going to the place where the seeds of his family had first taken root. Suddenly Naples loomed up ahead, built on a series of giant hills, crowded with life, Mt. Vesuvius in the background.

The city, they could see, was embraced by a giant bay. The sky was clear and the fierce sun reflected off the water and was hard on the eyes. They soon landed and were met by more of Maranzano's detectives, put into a black, air-conditioned SUV and taken directly to the hotel. "Chief Inspector Maranzano arranged rooms for you. He thought you might wish to freshen up and change before we take you to him," one of the detectives told him.

"That would be nice," Flynn said, and he and Rocco went upstairs, showered quickly, changed clothes and were soon speeding through the teeming streets of Naples, stopping in front of the antiquated police station where Maranzano had set up shop. Dusty palm trees surrounded it. Here it was as hot as in New York, but it was not humid and a pleasant breeze off the bay came to them. Maranzano knew they had arrived and he left his desk, the hurly-burly of the war room, went upstairs to meet them, and was standing at the entrance as Tony and Rocco began up the well-worn granite steps.

"Welcome, welcome," Maranzano exclaimed, coming down the stairs and embracing Flynn, who was surprised at how big and strong and youthful Maranzano was. He introduced Rocco and Maranzano embraced him too, two giants of Neapolitan background. They looked much alike, Flynn thought, except that Rocco had a broken nose and scars on his face, where Maranzano's face was unmarred, his nose long and straight.

"Come, come inside where it is cool and I will tell you all," he said, and led them down to the war room, had iced cappuccinos brought for all of them from a café next door. Flynn and Rocco were somewhat surprised at what they saw—there were many sketches of Coogan, with different hairdos, hats, with glasses, with a beard, all over the walls, and still Italian artists were working on more sketches of him with different looks . . . with a beret, a mustache.

Maranzano explained, "We know this man is very clever and there's no telling how he might altar his appearance. So we are preparing posters that will show him with different looks."

"Way to go," Flynn said.

Also on the walls there were black-and-white crime scene photographs of the men Coogan had killed in Rome. When Maranzano saw Tony and Rocco studying them, he said, "These are to remind us all what we are doing here." He introduced Rocco and Tony to the men and women on his task force, seventeen people in all, few of whom spoke English, but all were respectful and polite. Maranzano then ran down everything that had happened, beginning in Rome and working forward to when he received the call from Giuseppe Pisano, the reward-hungry parking attendant.

Maranzano said, "At first I was skeptical, you know, thought it was maybe bullshit, but then we found his prints on the table in the restaurant and on the chair where he sat and so we knew it was him, that he left Roma and came here.

"In Roma we very nearly had him. He ran from the flat he rented—over the Internet—just minutes before we arrived, and with the help of dogs we chased him through Villa Borghese, but he disappeared on the Via Veneto. Then the next thing we know he's here in Napoli and so I moved all our people here."

Their cappuccinos arrived. They were cold and delicious and nothing like the ones you get in New York, Flynn was thinking.

"Here, in Italia," Maranzano continued, "the killing of a

priest is an infamy, and many corporations as well as the Church have added to the reward money, which now is one million euros."

"That should get good results," Flynn observed.

"A little too good. Everyone and their grandmothers are calling, lying to share in the reward in some way—even people who know nothing. And all these calls are a big distraction, consuming the time and energy of my people; and organized crime has gotten involved."

"How's that?" Flynn asked.

"In Sicily there is the Mafia, as you know, but here in Napoli is the Camorra, and they are far more ruthless and brutal than the Mafia ever was, and they too have joined the hunt for Coogan."

"Because of the reward?" Flynn asked.

"That and also because they genuinely want to punish any man who would murder their priests, you see. It's personal. We, here in Italia, have not had the scandals you have in the States and priests and the Church are still held in reverence. Respected.

"We also have two hundred people scouring Napoli, looking in all the hotels, pensions, apartments to rent, restaurants, etc. They were in a green BMW, and we are also looking for the car. We will find him soon. All of Southern Italia has their eyes open for them, you see."

Both Flynn and Rocco were impressed. Maranzano knew what he was doing, it was obvious, and for both of them it was a pleasure to meet a brother in arms who had his act together, knew the intricacies and nuances of real police work, and the ways of the street.

"What happens if the Camorra finds him first?" Flynn asked.

"They will, of course, kill him," Maranzano said in a matter-of-fact tone. "I only hope the body is in one piece by the time they hand him over to us ... but I doubt it.

They will torture him, mutilate him as he did the priests, before they kill him. Are you hungry? Would you maybe like something to eat?" he asked. "I know a great place nearby."

FIFTY-THREE

Diane Pane slowly opened her eyes, surprised at first that someone was in the bed with her, but she quickly remembered all that had happened.

I don't believe it, she thought, turning her head to face him, hoping she hadn't made a mistake to allow him into her life, to have become so intimate with him so quickly. But Diane prided herself on being a progressive, free-thinking, independent woman, and all her instincts told her he was safe, a good man, someone she could trust. It had been so long since she had felt such unbridled passion for a man, and she was not about to shut the door on someone she desired so much. *It's over and done and I'm not going to have any second thoughts or regrets*, she thought. He was sleeping soundly and, not wanting to disturb him, she silently slipped out of the bed, took a shower and went outside.

The day was glorious, the sun shined cheerfully, birds chirped happily. It was good to be alive. In the kitchen she found Antonella, the woman who would cook and clean the house, as her husband Giovanni was tending to the garden, picking blood oranges from one of four orange trees on the grounds. Diane greeted them both with large smiles, speaking perfect Italian, savoring every drop of the bloodred orange juice Antonella made for her from the just picked oranges. As Antonella prepared a basil and potato omelet for Diane, she went for a swim, everything coming back to her. Smiling, she did a dozen laps, then went back to the house to discuss with Antonella what they'd have for lunch. After that, she went to work on one of the terraces on the upper floors with an unobstructed view of the sea majestically spread out before her, the Italian sun seeming to caress the calm water. Diane was planning to begin writing in a week or so, but when she picked up the pen and pad, the story she had in mind, the first sentence she'd been wrestling with, poured out of her and she knew better than trying to stop it.

The Sicilians, she wrote, *are a hardy, fierce people made up of many different cultures, Greek and Scandinavian, North African, French and Spanish and just about everyone in between.*

And like that, her long-planned book began. Diane loved to write in places where when she looked up she saw the ocean, an unobstructed horizon, where sky and sea met.

Boy did I come to the right place, she thought, and went back to work.

Both Giovanni and Antonella had read about *l'assassino del prete*, seen the posters, watched the news reports, but the sketch of Diane released by the *polizia* didn't remotely resemble her—the famous American writer who rented the house—and they didn't connect Diane in any way to the woman the authorities were looking for.

At seventy-eight Giovanni Pasqueli was a hardy man whose skin was lined and the color of cinnamon from the strong southern Italian sun. He didn't much pay attention to the outside world anymore. Like his father, he was a trusted caretaker of homes in the Amalfi region, and he had learned a long time ago that it was best to mind your own business, to keep your nose out of others' affairs; to concern himself with the gardens, grape vines and homes under his care.

However, his wife Antonella was just the opposite. She made it her business to learn as much as she could about the people in the homes she and her husband cared for. A nosey woman by nature, she believed—something she often argued with her husband about—that the more you knew about someone the better prepared you'd be to avoid difficulties. Though, these days at seventy-six, she had severe arthritis in her right foot and knee and she walked with a pronounced limp, and her eyesight was failing her as well. Every year she had to get a new pair of glasses and the ones she wore now were so thick children in the area made fun of her, but never in front of Giovanni, for he was a fierce protector of his wife of sixty years. Everyone in Amalfi knew that Giovanni was a mild-mannered man, but had a fierce temper and had twice sent men to the hospital, one of whom insulted Antonella, and the other he caught robbing chickens from the hen house of one of the properties he oversaw.

Neapolitan by birth, Antonella was a marvelous cook, which was one of the reasons she and her husband were so sought after by home owners in the area.

When Frank woke up that day, he felt rested and happy—a very rare thing for him and, even rarer, was the fact that he'd had no horrific nightmares, something that had plagued him all his life.

He found Antonella in the kitchen making hand-rolled pasta for lunch. As she'd done for Diane, she made him two large glasses of fresh red orange juice, and he marveled at how good it was. Because she could not speak English, Antonella wasn't able to question Frank, ask him what kind of work he did, where he came from, where his parents and grandparents came from, and all the rest. She also prepared an omelet for him, which he happily ate on the terrace just outside the kitchen in the welcome shade of a large cypress tree, the sweet smells of lavender, fresh basil and lilies coming to him. After he ate he went looking for Diane, saw her writing on the terrace upstairs, but didn't disturb her. The last thing he wanted to do was distract her from her work. But she saw him and called to him. They hugged and kissed. She told him how well her work was going.

"I'm so pleased," he said. "I don't want to distract you at all."

"You aren't. Don't worry," she said. He asked her if it would be okay to borrow the car and go get his luggage.

"Of course," she said, and soon went back to her work. He went for a swim in the pool, picked up one of Diane's yellow pads, sat down in a lounge in the garden and, remembering what Diane had said, began writing. To his surprise, actually astonishment, he was able not only to write about the things that had haunted him all his life, but he wrote about them effortlessly. The words, images and memories, the hatred and emotion, poured out of him. He soon forgot where he was and transported himself back in time, back to the Sacred Heart Home for Boys, more like an interested observer watching everything from above than a put upon victim, and before he knew it, he'd been writing, he realized with a start, for nearly two hours.

Pleased, feeling whole and accomplished, he got up to go for another swim. Diane, he saw, was still writing. He noticed a staircase at the far end of the veranda where the pool was located, walked to it and realized for the first time that there were a steep set of steps down to the ocean. He slowly went down these steps and dived into the sea. The water was cold and refreshing and he swam way out, turned and saw the house majestically perched at the top of the cliffs. There were few other homes around. From this perspective he was able to see a series of small caves in the leather-colored cliffs. Gulls and cormorants had set up nests in front of the small openings. He swam back, climbed out of the water and went up the stairs; if he had to make a sudden escape he could use the stairs instead of jumping off the top of the cliffs, he was thinking, pleased.

No matter how comfortable he was, he knew he was being hunted, remembering Nino Maranzano, knowing this man would never give up. He would stay here as long as he could, until things cooled down, then go back to Rome. He thought about the disguise he'd wear to get into Vatican City. Maybe he would dress as a nun.

Regardless of how much he enjoyed Diane, he reminded himself that he had a job to do, a solemn promise to keep—a mission. But still, the thought of leaving Diane, this place, unsettled him, left him cold and empty. All his life he had hoped and pined for a woman like Diane, passionate, sincere and affectionate and he could lose it all, he knew, any moment. This angered him greatly; it was all so unfair. Life was unfair.

When he got back to the house, Diane was nowhere to be seen. He returned to the pages he'd written, sure now that he could put his story down on paper the way it had really happened, if they—the police—would just leave him alone, which he didn't think would happen. Thinking about the pope, the devastating effect his murder would have on the Church, he stared out at the ocean, at the distant line where the sky and water became one . . .

He put on sunglasses and a baseball cap, jumped in the car, drove to town, bought a suitcase, some clothes and toiletries, and came back to the house, thinking about the pope . . . going back to Rome.

FIFTY-FOUR

Altogether there were thirty-seven clergymen staying at the O'Connor Home for Retired Priests. Early that morning all of them were brought down to the day room and questioned by Sergeant Salerno and other task force detectives who had driven up to the Bronx. Cunningham carefully scrutinized every one of them. Few of the priests, she and Dr. Russo agreed, would have the necessary physical strength to choke a man to death with a thick piece of rope, and they focused on the ones who seemed fit and strong enough to do such a task. They all readily agreed to let Dr. Russo examine their hands and none of them seemed unduly concerned, nor did any of them have any kind of telltale marks on their hands.

The killer had, they began to think, come into the house, committed the murder and left. In that there was no sign of forced entry, someone either let the killer in, or he had been given keys.

The last one to be examined and questioned was Monsignor Johnson, who ran the place. He, unlike the others, was defensive and put off by the fact that he and his charges were under suspicion. A heavyset, bug-eyed man, Johnson insisted that no one there was capable of murder; that surely Bishop Arnold had committed suicide, he said, making the sign of the cross. "All this is a waste of time and manpower," he said. "You should devote yourselves to catching criminals, not harassing us."

Sergeant Salerno said, "Sir, we apologize for any inconvenience, but we have good reason to believe that this is a murder. And that someone tried to make it *look* like a suicide. We'd like a list of the people who have keys to the premises, and we'd like to fingerprint all the residents here."

"But why?" Johnson asked, his jaw setting into a defiant line.

"Because we are investigating a murder, sir, that's why," Salerno said, having little patience, at this juncture, with pompous priests acting like they were above the law.

"We've been very cooperative in every way, but I refuse to let *you people* fingerprint us as though we are common criminals. Every man here has worked all his life for the good of others, sacrificed their own lives for the benefit of others, and I'm not going to let you people make a mockery of them, of us, of the Catholic faith. I'm calling my attorney," he said, and began to storm off.

"Fine," Carole Cunningham said, her face flushing with anger, stepping forward. "I'm having a warrant drawn up to get the fingerprints of everyone who was in this building when Arnold was murdered." She whipped out her phone and called her office and told a law clerk what she wanted.

Monsignor Johnson went to phone his lawyer, but Salerno insisted on going with him.

"Why?" Johnson demanded.

"Because we are conducting a murder investigation and you are a suspect—that's why; and if you aren't careful I'm going to cuff you, read you your rights and book you for obstruction and accessory and you'll be on the first bus out to Rikers Island after your arraignment." That sobered Johnson right up, like a bucket of cold water over his head.

"Forgive me," he said. "Perhaps I'm being overly protective."

"Yeah, perhaps," Salerno agreed. "Now are you going to let us fingerprint everyone here or not?"

"Well, I guess it's all right. If I say no, I'm sure District Attorney Cunningham could get warrants to do it."

"Take that to the bank," she said.

"Fine, okay," he said. "I don't mean to be difficult." Within minutes all the retired priests there were being printed.

"Is everyone who was here last night here now?" Salerno asked.

"Yes," Johnson said.

"Except Father Pastore," one of the oldest priests piped up.

"Who's that?" Salerno asked, curious.

"He was here on a visit from Rome on behalf of the Vatican, the Opus Dei," said the elderly priest. "The Opus Dei is a body of senior church officials who, from inside the Vatican, run the Catholic Church."

"Really," said Salerno, suddenly interested. "And where is he now?"

"I believe he left for Italy last night," the elderly priest said, all eyes curiously moving to Monsignor Johnson.

"Yes, he left last night," Johnson confirmed, but Salerno sensed something in the wind, out of sync. *Not kosher*, as he would later tell Tony Flynn.

"Really, when?" he asked. "What flight? Who took him to the airport?"

"I took him," Johnson said, "to Kennedy Airport."

"Did you see him get on a plane?"

"No . . . I just dropped him off at the terminal."

"Did he have keys to the place?"

"Yes, yes he did. He was here for several days checking on the homes for retired priests on the East Coast."

"What flight was he catching?" Salerno asked, moving closer to Johnson, staring at him intently.

"I'm not sure, but it was an Alitalia flight," Johnson said.

"What's his full name?" Salerno asked.

"Alberto Pastore."

Salerno wrote down the name and pulled two of the task force detectives to the side and told them to hustle out to Kennedy and see if this priest, Alberto Pastore, was on the Alitalia flight.

"Will do, Sarge," one said and they were out the door and soon speeding toward Kennedy Airport.

Alitalia, however, refused to give them access to their passenger lists, and Carole Cunningham was forced to seek a court order forcing the airline to divulge the names of their passengers. She was sure the airline was being so uncooperative because they wanted information on a Catholic priest and Alitalia didn't want to do anything to offend the Vatican.

FIFTY-FIVE

Flynn had to leave the police station in Naples to use his cell phone. Standing outside, he tried to reach Carole Cunningham but her answering machine picked up. He left a message saying he had arrived, that he was in Naples, that Coogan had fled there—was with a woman—and that the Italian police were doing an excellent job in trying to find him. He then called Salerno, who ran down to him what had happened—told him about Arnold's murder, how it was made to look like a suicide, that a priest from Rome was a prime suspect; how Alitalia wasn't cooperating. Flynn wrote down Alberto Pastore's name, the flight he was supposed to be on, went back inside and told Maranzano and ·Rocco about the murder of Bishop Arnold, how Alitalia was being difficult.

Maranzano said he'd find out if the priest was on the flight and he called a friend of his at Alitalia—a vice president he had recently done a favor for—and within minutes he was told that Alberto Pastore was definitely not on that flight. Flynn immediately called back Salerno and told him Pastore wasn't on the plane, and asked where Cunningham was.

"She's on her way to the office, left here about twenty minutes ago."

"I'll try on her cell number. If I can't reach her, I'll call you back. I want to talk with her. Meanwhile find this Alberto Pastore. If what the monsignor said is true, maybe he just missed the flight . . . but something tells me he's the man."

"Yeah, me too."

"Put out an all points on him, and see if he checked into a hotel near the airport. And also check with the emergency medical people at the airport, maybe he had a heart attack, something like that."

"Will do," Salerno said. They hung up and Flynn tried Carole on her cell phone, reaching her as she was heading south on FDR Drive.

"I'm so glad you called," she said. "You hear what happened?"

"I did, and we managed from here to find out that Pastore was not on that flight. Inspector Maranzano has a friend at Alitalia and they told him right off the bat—"

"The dirty dogs gave us a hard time. I was just going to my office to sign a warrant application demanding the passenger list. Tony we had them. Arnold was going to tell us everything. They somehow found out about it and sent an assassin to make his murder look like a suicide," she said and quickly ran down to him how Dr. Russo discovered the two rope marks on Arnold's neck; that he'd been hung from the ceiling after he was already dead.

"Tony, these dirtbags murdered him to protect their asses," she began, but was suddenly cut off. He tried her again and again but kept getting a busy circuit and couldn't reach her.

Perplexed, Flynn walked about the piazza where the police station was located, thinking this out, wondering if the Church would really resort to murder to protect themselves. They had, he knew, done far worse things in years past. They had an incredibly bloody history. But still, he was hard-pressed to believe a priest would actually commit murder. Then again, he knew the Church hierarchy would do whatever necessary to protect themselves.

Maybe this Alberto Pastore wasn't a priest at all, he thought, but someone who had been recruited—hired— by a Church official to kill Arnold. He decided to run all this past Maranzano and see what he thought.

Again, he tried Carole but still couldn't get through. He called her office and left a message for her to phone him and went back downstairs and ran down for Maranzano and Rocco what had happened.

Maranzano said, "I could not imagine the Opus Dei contracting the killing of a bishop in New York. But I could certainly see an *individual* in the Church ordering such a thing if it would protect the Church—its cardinals and bishops. It would seem more likely that someone in New York, fearing arrest, took a contract out."

"That's what I was thinking," Flynn said.

"Let me make some calls and see if in fact a priest by this name was sent by the Vatican to New York."

"You can do that?"

"I believe so," Maranzano said and placed a call to the Vatican and asked a cardinal he knew well if they had sent a priest named Alberto Pastore to New York for the purpose of reviewing a home for retired priests. The cardinal told him he would find out and get right back to him.

"You ever hear about the Church having someone bumped off?" Flynn asked.

"No," Maranzano said. "Not since I've been on the force, but in the past, yes."

"Recently?"

"Not so recently."

One of the detectives Maranzano had assigned to find out if an American woman had rented a green BMW excused himself and said that he had found a woman who lived in San Francisco who had rented a green BMW 525 from an Avis car rental company in Rome. Her name, he said, was Diane Pane. The last Italian address the car company had was the Pantheon Hotel on Via Veneto, he said. When Maranzano heard that his face lit up. "Did you call the hotel?"

"I did, sir. She checked out just yesterday. They have no idea where she went." A slight smile on his face, Maranzano turned to Flynn.

"The Pantheon Hotel," he said, "is where we lost Coogan. Remember, I told you he disappeared near the Via Veneto? Well, the tracking dogs stopped right in front of this hotel."

"Spell her last name," Flynn said, writing it down, picking up the phone and calling New York.

FIFTY-SIX

Diane's day had gone well. She had written the first chapter of her book and was pleased, for it had come out better than she'd hoped. She stood and stretched and went looking for Frank, delicious aromas coming from the kitchen greeting her as she walked. She found him in the garden reading a book about the Vatican. They kissed hello. "I came down earlier," she said, "but saw you were writing and didn't want to bother you. How'd it go?"

"Very well. I did what you said and it worked. I'm surprised. I didn't think I could do it. But apparently I can."

"Lovely. Did you get your luggage okay?"

"I did."

"Just stick to it, and try to get something done every day, no matter what."

"I plan to. How'd your work go?"

"Well, I wasn't going to start writing until next week, but it started coming and I wasn't about to stop it."

"Great. I was worried my being here would distract you. Please, Diane, you do your thing; don't think you have to entertain me in any way, okay?"

"Okay. Thanks for saying that. I did feel . . . slightly guilty."

"No, please don't. I have a lot to keep me busy. You know there are these stairs cut into the cliffs that lead right down to the ocean."

"I know . . . want to go for a swim, then have lunch?"

"Super idea. I've been smelling her cooking. What is she making?"

"Fresh black pasta with grilled shrimp in a pesto sauce, chicken marsala and an arugula salad."

"Can't wait."

"Do we need bathing suits? Are there people down there, boats around?"

"I didn't see anyone, no."

"We better wear them just in case," she said, laughing. "I'll meet you on the terrace in five," she said, then went off and checked with Antonella, who was busy cooking. The smells in the kitchen made Diane's mouth water. She put on her bathing suit, grabbed a towel, met Frank outside and together they went down the steep set of steps, reaching a flat boulder at the bottom. Diane looked about.

"It's *really* beautiful here. I've got to contact my friends and thank them for telling me about this place. There's no one here," she said, slipping out of the bathing suit and diving in the sea in two easy movements. He did the same.

Together, smiling, they swam out to a yellow buoy about 500 feet from the cliffs. Laughing, she held him. They kissed. "I'm *really* glad you called," she said.

"So am I," he said. "My cup runneth over because of you."

"Funny how unpredictable life can be, you know?"

"I would say you were heaven sent, but I don't believe in heaven," he said, both of them laughing. That was the first time in his life he made light of how he'd been so radically polarized from the Church, its teachings, heaven and hell and all the rest.

"I'll race you back," she said and took off. She too was an excellent swimmer and he was hard-pressed to catch her, but he did and managed to pass her just as they reached the rocks. As she climbed out of the water he marveled at her figure . . . how beautiful she was. They laid in the Mediterranean sun for a while, not talking, just enjoying the glorious, sensuous feel of the sun, the sound of waves breaking on the rocks. He kissed her and, lulled by the murmur of the waves, the heat of the sun, they both dozed off.

The sound of a passing helicopter woke them. Arm-in-arm, they went back up the stairs, showered and had a magnificent three-course lunch on a table Giovanni had set up in the shade of a large fig tree filled with figs in different stages of growth, some ripe and ready to eat, others just blooming. They also had an excellent bottle of ice-cold white wine Giovanni had made from chardonnay grapes that grew on the grounds. Antonella was pleased that they liked her cooking and watched to make sure they ate everything on their plates. Antonella's mission in life, she believed, was to feed people until they could eat no more and walked away from the table *molto contento*.

After they had dessert, fresh fig tarts and rose-colored marsala wine, also made by Giovanni, Diane suggested they go for a walk in town. The phone lines were still down and she wanted to check her e-mail and send some mail.

Going to town and walking around was something he feared, but he agreed to go. He didn't want to do anything to make her suspicious. And he believed the police still thought he was in far away Rome. He put on his Yankees baseball cap and sunglasses and instead of driving they walked to town, Frank believing no one would recognize him here in Amalfi.

"You enjoy the food?" she asked.

"Best I ever had," he said, and they held hands and walked on, a strong breeze off the sea cooling them as they went. There were many Italians out promenading after their lunch.

Because it was July, the town was filled with tourists, all the shops busy, all the restaurants packed. Like he thought, no one paid particular attention to him, but the Italian men paid attention to Diane. Frank was proud to be with her and have her on his arm. Walking about with a beautiful woman was an experience he'd never known.

Diane bought some toiletries she needed and they window shopped, marveling at all the incredible displays of food. They then visited the beautiful Duomo of Amalfi off the main piazza, with its Moorish design and incredible tile work.

For Frank it was a strange, unsettling experience, being inside a church, its smells, the candles, the stained glass, Christ on the cross. He was very uncomfortable. Diane sensed it and understood and headed for the door.

"I'm sorry," he said. "It's just difficult—"

"I understand. You don't have to explain. It was inconsiderate of me. I'm sorry—"

"No need to apologize. It's me. I still get all uncomfortable around churches."

She put her arms around him and kissed him right there in front of the church, surrounded by people.

"I feel better," he said, smiling.

"Good. I'd like to send an e-mail to my friends who recommended the house. I'd call them on my cell, but we are nine hours ahead of the West Coast. Let's see if there's an Internet café in town."

"Okay," he said, and they went looking for an Internet café, found one on Via St. Augustino, but the owner told them that his phone lines were also down. "Should be up and running in a couple of hours, sorry," he said.

From there they made their way to a small outdoor café on the outskirts of town and had zabalone gelato and espresso and watched the world go by. Relaxed, at ease, he was sure no one was paying attention to him. The Italians, it was obvious, minded their own business and were too busy living life to notice or care what the people around them were doing. Diane began talking about ancient Rome, one of his favorite subjects—and she was amazed at how much he knew, dates and names and who did what to whom and when they did it.

FIFTY-SEVEN

It didn't take long for Tony Flynn to find out who Diane Pane was and that she lived in San Francisco. He was able to get her phone number from the San Francisco Police Department and left a message on her answering machine at her house on Edith Street, but he knew she was in Italy and unless she checked her messages, she'd not know he called.

Luckily, one of the female detectives on the task force in New York knew who Diane Pane was and explained to Tony she was a best-selling author. While Tony was on hold, she checked the Internet and quickly found a site for Diane that her publisher had set up. From the site they got the name and number of Diane's San Francisco agent, Loretta Brown. Tony called Ms. Brown, got her on the line and told her who he was, that he was working on a "very important case," but didn't tell her what, or even tell her he was phoning from Italy.

"It's imperative that I talk to Diane," he said. "Can you please tell me how I can reach her?"

"She's in Italy working on a new book right now," Brown said.

"Do you know where?"

"She rented a house somewhere in Amalfi, but, no, I don't know where," she said hesitantly, obviously not pleased about giving information on one of her star clients to a New York detective calling out of the clear blue.

"Does she have a cell phone number?"

"She does, but I'm sorry I can't give it out. She's working, you see. Can you tell me what this is about, why a New York police captain is calling about Diane?"

Flynn did not want to say anything about Coogan. He wanted to be the one to tell Diane who she was traveling with, make sure she was safe and out of harm's way and able to get away from Coogan. He didn't want to put her in any danger, create a hostage situation—compromise her, get her hurt. And, too, he had no idea what Coogan's relationship with Diane was, if she knew what he'd done, about the demons in his head, but he did know that

Coogan was a very dangerous man and would surely kill Diane if he was cornered.

"I'm not," he said, "at liberty to tell you why I need to talk to her right now, but please understand this is a very important police matter—"

"Is she in danger?" Loretta asked.

"She very well could be in danger, yes."

There was a long pause. "Like I said, I don't know where the house in Amalfi is, but I guess I can give you her cell number," she said.

"Thank you . . . thank you very much," he said.

"Please, can you tell me what this is about?" she pressed.

"Not now, but I promise I will," he said. "I can tell you," he lied, knowing he had to tell this woman something, "that it's a very sensitive matter about national security—"

"National security?" she repeated.

"Yes, and please don't call Diane or say anything about me to her. That's imperative, okay?"

". . . Okay," she said.

Flynn soon hung up and told Maranzano and all the other detectives—as Maranzano translated—who Diane Pane was and that he'd gotten her cell phone number from her agent in San Francisco.

When Maranzano heard that Diane had rented a house in Amalfi, he arranged for a police helicopter to take them to Amalfi, which was, he told Flynn, ten minutes away by helicopter.

Not knowing whether Diane knew who Coogan was, if she was protecting him, Flynn was hesitant about calling and alerting her; she could very well tell Coogan, giving him a chance to escape. He decided, after discussing it with Rocco and Maranzano, he would hold off on contacting her.

The first order of business, they knew, was to set up a command post in Amalfi, and find the house Diane had rented. Just as they were about to leave, the phone rang. It was the cardinal Maranzano knew at the Vatican. He said no priest by the name of Alberto Pastore had been sent by the Vatican to New York; that, indeed, they didn't have a priest with that name assigned to the Vatican. They were checking, he said, to see if a priest by that name had ever been ordained. Maranzano thanked him and told him it was very important for them to find this man, and nothing more.

They hurried now from the police station, filled two SUVs and sped out to the police heliport at the Naples airport and were soon speeding south to Amalfi in a police helicopter.

Maranzano said they would use the element of surprise, that they would not plaster Amalfi with posters of Coogan and Diane for that might very well cause Coogan to flee and get away again.

Intent upon finding the address of the house, Flynn called Loretta Brown back and she, again, told him she had no idea where the house was, or even how Diane had found it. She did say, however, that her lawyer Susan Hasse may know, and she gave him Hasse's phone number. Flynn called her but was told she was in court. He left an urgent message for her to phone him back. Her assistant said she'd return shortly.

Maranzano then called a friend of his, Alfredo Serra, the head of the Amalfi *polizia*, a man he knew could be trusted. He found Serra at his home and briefly explained that he was coming to Amalfi to work on an important case, that he needed to discreetly set up a small task force in Amalfi. Alfredo said he'd meet them at the heliport outside of town and bring them to headquarters on Via

Leonardo and would arrange for whatever Maranzano needed. When Serra asked what the case was about, Maranzano said he'd explain in person. Maranzano knew the Camorra had ears and eyes everywhere, and he didn't want them to know that Coogan was in Amalfi because Camorra hit teams would soon be stalking the small seaside town like hungry jungle cats.

Maranzano said, "If this American writer rented a place in Amalfi, she more than likely did it through a real estate agency in town. One of the first things we'll do is contact all the agencies that do such work and see if they know her."

"Good, good idea," Flynn said, admiring how Maranzano thought on his feet. Any cop worth his salt, he knew, must have that ability—to quickly react to leads, situations and circumstances that suddenly present themselves in the field, while working a case, hot on the trail of a dedicated killer.

Thinking of Lina, Maranzano didn't like leaving her in Napoli by herself; they had made plans to have dinner. But he felt she'd understand and, he knew, she had many friends in Napoli. He remembered the first time he'd seen Lina, talking with a professor in the hall of a university where he'd gone to lecture a group of students interested in police work, how her dark-eyed gaze slowly came to rest on him, how the sunshine streaming through a nearby window seemed to put a fiery halo about her head—

"We'll be landing in two minutes," the pilot called out, bringing Maranzano back to the moment. The sooner Coogan was caught—or killed—the sooner he could be with Lina, make up for all the times he had to leave her because of his work.

They were met at the small heliport just outside of town by Capitano Serra. Introductions were quickly made. Alfredo Serra was a tall, broad-shouldered man with a serious face, salt-and-pepper hair, blue eyes that seemed at perpetual half-staff. He and Nino Maranzano were personal friends, had worked as partners in Naples for two years when they first graduated from the academy in Friuli, Italy. On the ride to the small police station on Via Leonardo, Maranzano, speaking Italian, told Serra why they had come to Amalfi, whom they were hunting, how important it was that their mission stay between them. Serra spoke no English.

"I had a feeling this was what it was about," he said. "If he is in Amalfi we'll find him."

"What's important," Maranzano said, "is that he doesn't know we are here; this a very cunning individual. He got away from us once before. And I'm concerned about the Camorra. As you know, there is a one million euro reward for him and we don't want them getting in our way, you understand?"

"Of course. We will involve only people I know well and trust implicitly."

"Excellent . . . it's good to see you, my brother."

"Good to see you, Nino. How's Lina?"

"Very well. She's in Napoli now."

"Please give her my best. Maybe when this is done you can come to the house for dinner. Tina would love to see her."

"That would be nice."

"As you know, Nino, there are only two ways out of Amalfi—the drive going north back to Positano and south, to Salerno. I suggest the first thing we do is set up road blocks on both the roads. It might be best if we use your people for this."

"Yes, of course," Maranzano said, turning to Flynn. "There are only two ways in and out of Amalfi. We are first going to set up road blocks— using my people so this stays between us—to make sure he cannot get away."

"Beautiful," Flynn said.

They arrived at the Amalfi police station. It was in a small two-story terracotta structure at the end of a street lined with shops. The air was filled with the smell of fresh-baked bread. Before they went inside, Maranzano took Flynn to the side and said: "I should tell you now that I have been given very strict orders to make sure Coogan is finished when we find him."

"Really, from who?"

"From the people who run Italy."

"I see. I was hoping we could bring him back to New York, expose him and all the elements of this case, his childhood, to the public."

"Is that's what you want to do—I mean personally—or would you rather have him dead?"

"If possible, I'd like to bring him back alive, put everything on the table."

"I see. I understand. The public should know the truth. If possible, I will make sure he's taken alive. But you understand if you plan to seek the death penalty, Italy—the church—will never allow him to be taken back to the States."

"We'll give you a written waiver guaranteeing we won't look to fry him."

"I'll do my best."

"Thank you, I appreciate it," Flynn said, they shook hands, went inside and up to the second landing and began putting together exactly what steps they'd take, who would do what, Maranzano translating for Flynn.

The first thing Maranzano ordered were teams of his people from Rome to set up twenty-four hour road blocks on the north and south ends of town. The second thing they did was compile a list of real estate agents that arranged the renting of villas in Amalfi.

Flynn's cell phone buzzed. He walked to the corner of the room, answered it, "Hello," he said, hopeful.

"I represent Diane Pane," she said. "I understand you called my office."

"Susan Hasse?"

"Yes."

"Thank you for getting back to me so quickly."

"What's this about?" she asked, not too friendly.

"Do you know where Diane is in Amalfi?"

"I do, why?"

After making her promise what he was about to tell her must remain between them, that it was a matter of life and death, he briefly outlined the situation.

"And you believe," she said, incredulous, "Diane is with this man?"

"We are sure of it. They left Rome together and were seen in Naples as they were on their way south to Amalfi."

"I'm shocked. How would she know him?"

"We have no idea. All we know is that they are together and she could be in *grave* danger—"

"I'm sure she has no idea who he is, Captain."

"Of course. Fact remains we must find her, and if he's with her make sure he's taken without hurting her. We have to keep the element of surprise ours. That is vital."

"Yes, I see," she said. "Are you in Italy now?"

"I am."

"In Amalfi?"

"Yes. You know the address where she's staying, this place she rented?"

"I do. I recommended it to her. I honeymooned there last year. Hold on a moment, I'll get you the address."

"Great, thank you," he said. She put down the phone. He called to the others that he had the address of the house. All eyes moved to him, everyone suddenly smiling.

She came back. "Number 7 Via Roreto," she said. "Please make sure nothing happens to Diane. I'm sure she has no idea who he is. You get that, right?"

"I get it. Nothing will happen to Diane, I promise," he said.

FIFTY-EIGHT

"Green pizza? I never saw green pizza in my life," Frank said, as they arrived back at Casa Bella Luna and entered the kitchen, Antonella smiling.

"Antonella made it with pesto sauce," Diane explained. "She knows I like pizza and made it in case we wanted something to eat."

"Eat, after that meal . . . I'm not hungry, you?"

"Not now, but maybe later," she said, laughing. Antonella asked if they needed anything else. Diane told her they didn't, she said *buona notte* and left. Giovanni was waiting for her outside. Because of her bad eyesight, she had much difficulty seeing at night. By now the fierce Mediterranean sun was disappearing into the western horizon, seeming to light the sky on fire.

Holding Antonella's arm, Giovanni opened the front gate and they slowly started up the narrow one-way road toward their house a quarter of a mile away. They hadn't gone fifteen feet when Nino Maranzano suddenly approached them, showed them his identification and began asking questions. He was soon joined by Capitano Serra, who Giovanni knew since he was a child.

"Why all the questions? What's this about?" Giovanni demanded.

"We are interested in the man staying here. Is this him?" Maranzano asked, showing Giovanni and Antonella the sketch of Coogan without hair.

"... *Si*," Giovanni said. "That is him," knowing he wanted nothing to do with any of this, wanting to walk away, get his wife home safe and sound.

"Does it look," Maranzano asked, "like the woman is being held against her will?"

"Not at all," Antonella said. "They sleep in the same bed."

"I see. Do you have a key?" Maranzano asked.

"*Si*," Giovanni said, and reluctantly handed him a master key he had that could open both the front gate and all the doors of the villa.

"Thank you," Maranzano said, used his walkie-talkie and a car appeared out of nowhere.

"This car will take you home. Please make certain you tell no one you spoke with us, understand?" Maranzano told them.

"*Si, si*," Giovanni said, helping Antonella into the unmarked police car. Maranzano told the detective driving the car to stay with the couple until "this thing is done."

FIFTY-NINE

"The sunset is beautiful," Diane said. "Let's sit outside and watch it."

"I'd like that," he said and followed her to the green and white striped lounges at the end of the large veranda. They lay down facing the gorgeous sunset. There were sailboats moving in a northern direction and their white

Philip Carlo

sails were alive with the hot colors of the dying sun, bold reds and shy pinks, searing oranges and brilliant yellows.

"I had no idea Italy was so beautiful," he said. "Thanks to you I'm seeing an Italy I never knew existed."

"I love it here. This winter I'm buying a house in the Tuscany region. Have you ever been there?"

"No, but I hear it's really nice."

"It is. It's also a great place to write, very quiet and magnificently beautiful, and eating there is a religious experience. It all has a very dreamlike quality. I'm buying an old villa that I'm going to refurbish."

"You already found one?"

"Not yet, but I have some Italian friends looking for me."

"Why didn't you rent a place there now?"

"I wanted to be near the sea. I heard about this place, saw photos of it and took it."

"You must be rich."

"I'm comfortable. The great thing about what I do—I mean writing—is that you can pretty much do it anywhere, and it's always been a fantasy of mine to have a house there, since I first saw the Tuscany region when I went on a school trip in my second year of college. It was like I'd been there before . . . kind of like I lived there in another life. You know what I mean?"

"I do. That's exactly how I feel about Rome."

"Yes, I remember you telling me," she said and they each became quiet and contemplative and watched the sun melt into the horizon, filling the sky with magnificent colors.

"It's good to be alive," he said, a thing he never thought would come out of his mouth. Though, still, he knew, he was being relentlessly hunted. But all that—what he'd done—was far away now.

"The Italians call it *la dolce vita*," she said. "Here in Italy the people enjoy life. It's not only about money, making

276

money and screwing everyone else. The Italians know how to live and they enjoy the short time we have on this crazy planet. That's one of the reasons, actually the main reason, I enjoy Italy so much—the pace of life. Here people stop to smell the roses, as it were, you know."

"Yes, I can see that."

"I'll be right back," she said. "Have to use the loo."

"I'll be here," he said. She got up and walked into the house via the sliding doors off the kitchen. Her eyes immediately came to rest on the pesto pizza Antonella had left on the yellow-tiled counter. Diane was thinking she had to have a taste, just a taste, found a knife and cut herself a small piece. She didn't notice the hulking form of Rocco Genovese as he quietly came up behind her. As she brought the pizza to her lips, his huge hand was suddenly clamped, like an iron vise, across her mouth, his other arm locking around her waist like a piece of steel. Fear exploded inside her. She squirmed and kicked desperately. One of her kicks knocked the pizza tray off the counter.

Tony Flynn was suddenly in front of her. "Diane, we are the police," he said. "Calm down. No one's going to hurt you," showing her his gold badge, his identification, as Nino and Serra and the rest of them appeared, seemingly out of thin air, all of them with guns in their hands.

Why, her mind raced, *would New York cops be here?*

"Please, don't scream. Don't make any noise. We are here because of him. We want him. Diane, he's the man who's been killing priests in New York and Rome."

My God, no! she thought, it all suddenly making sense, the incomprehensible crystal clear. She nodded that she understood. Tony told Rocco to remove his hand, but he didn't let go of her. "Is he armed?" Flynn whispered into her ear.

"No, not that I know of," she whispered. "My God."

"Okay. We are going to take you outside. We don't want you in any danger," Flynn told her and she nodded okay and was quickly taken away, out to the street. Still in shock, she didn't know what to think, what to do, just stood there, numb.

When the pizza tray hit the tiled floor, Coogan heard the sound, went to see what made the noise and saw Rocco holding Diane, saw Flynn, then saw Nino Maranzano. He turned and ran toward the stairs that led down to the water.

Just as he reached the stairs all of them came running out of the house after him, and suddenly there were two helicopters roaring overhead. He made it halfway down the steps before Flynn screamed for him to stop, to freeze, but he kept moving down the stairs. Repeatedly Flynn screamed for him to stop. He kept going. Nino Maranzano had given him the opportunity to give up but it was obvious Coogan was not about to let them take him and Maranzano gave the order to shoot to kill. A chorus of guns spoke at once and bullets struck the steps all around Coogan, zipped past his head. He suddenly dived off the steps and just made it to the water's edge, and disappeared.

Flynn leading the way, they ran down the stairs. Flynn dove right in after him, but Coogan was nowhere to be seen in the dark water. Five of Maranzano's men joined Flynn in the water, but none of them could locate Coogan. The helicopters turned on their flood lights, came down low—but Coogan seemed to have vanished. More police were called in, more helicopters. Police boats were summoned.

When Coogan hit the water, bullets coming very close to him, he went deep, then left and staying under water he made it as far as he could, quickly came up for air, went back down again and continued along the rocks, knowing if he didn't stay under water the helicopters would see him and he'd be shot dead.

When he couldn't hold his breath any longer, he came up a good 150 feet south of the steps, saw that no one could see him and he quickly hoisted himself out of the water and hid in thick foliage, then moved serpentlike up the steep cliffs, crawling and climbing, very nearly falling twice, intent upon getting away. His plan was to hide in one of the small caves he'd seen from the water until the police left, then make his way south to Salerno where he would stow away on a cargo ship. *I knew it was too good to be true; I knew it was too good to be true*, he kept saying to himself.

Halfway up the rocky cliffs, he found a small opening covered by a gull's nest with two eggs in it. He pushed the nest to the side, backed into the opening and waited, hearing the helicopters and men shouting in Italian, shots still being fired. There was a floating piece of driftwood. They thought it was him, and blew it to pieces.

SIXTY

As the search for Coogan continued, as still more men and dogs, boats and helicopters were called in, back inside the house Diane Pane sat quietly at the dining table—the pesto pizza still on the floor—while Tony Flynn ran it all down for her. He told her the truth about Coogan's childhood, the priest he murdered, the psychiatric hospital where he spent twenty-one years of his life, how he began killing priests two years after he was let out of the hospital.

She, in turn, told him how she had first met him on the bus to Rome, ran into him several times, how he called her and they came south together and ended up becoming "involved."

"I'm shocked," she said. "He had me completely, totally fooled. Seemed like he couldn't hurt a fly, I swear. My God, I can't believe this. He did tell me about the home, but said he was adopted by a nice couple and that they helped him get over what had happened to him."

"He told you he'd been abused?"

"Some, yes, but it didn't sound, you know, that bad . . . anything like what you're telling me now."

"It was very bad. I read his medical file from the hospital—he was severely abused over a five-year period, from when he was eight to twelve, and he killed one of his abusers, beheaded him and stuck his head on a post at the front gate of the home—"

"No?"

"Yes."

"Oh my God," she said, bringing her long, tapered fingers to her lips. "Can I . . . can I read the file?" she asked.

"I guess so—I don't see why not," Flynn said.

Tears filled her eyes and slowly rolled down her high-cheekboned face.

"Just unbelievable," she said, wiping at the tears, hurt and angry, feeling like she'd been duped . . . used, mad at herself for trusting someone she'd just met. "He used me," she said.

Flynn said, "I'm sorry we scared you in the kitchen like that, but we didn't want to give him the opportunity to harm you, make you a hostage."

"Yes, I understand, no problem. I came to Italy to write a book, to get away, for peace and quiet, and now this. How did you find me? How did you know he was here?"

"You stopped in Naples for pizza. There was a parking attendant—"

"Yes, I remember him."

"Well, he recognized Coogan."

"So it's all because we had pizza together?"

"Yeah, seems that way," Tony said, looking at the pizza that had fallen on the floor. "Never saw green pizza before," he said.

SIXTY-ONE

Frank managed to move a large kidney-shaped stone in front of the small opening to the cave. He left just enough room for air to get in. With luck they would not be able to find him. He knew the cliffs were far too steep for the dogs to navigate. He dozed off. Harsh black-and-white images of what had happened to him at the Sacred Heart Home for Boys exploded inside his head, as violent and as sudden as lightning bolts. When he woke up he was covered in sweat. He moved the rock and looked to the right. There were boats and helicopters and *carabinieri* and *polizia* with powerful search lights looking in the water. He moved a little deeper into the opening and pulled the stone back in place, closed his eyes and saw Diane, remembered when he first met her on the bus—saw her at the Sistine Chapel, at the Colosseum, suddenly standing there. How she saved him by getting him out of Rome.

It all seemed preordained in some way, he thought, and he resolved to travel to the ends of the earth if need be so he could tell Diane the truth; how sorry he was; how much he cared for her; what really happened to him and why he'd done what he did.

Thinking those thoughts, he again dozed off and dreamed now about the Colosseum. He was a famous gladiator being cheered by the crowds as he entered the arena. Or was he dreaming? He wasn't sure. Often, in his mind, dreams and reality mixed, became one—the way the sky and sea sometimes blurred, became one . . . became indistinguishable.

All that night the Italian police, under the careful direction of Chief Inspector Maranzano and Captain Serra of Amalfi, searched for Frank. Special alpine *polizia* were brought in and they carefully searched the cliffs to the right and left of Casa Bella Luna, using ropes to lower themselves down, but they didn't find the small opening Coogan had secreted himself in.

By dawn they began to think that he drowned; that one of the bullets had hit him and he died in the water; or, perhaps, he struck a rock with his head when he dove and was knocked unconscious and drowned. Maranzano ordered special gaffing hooks attached to long poles, which were pulled in a vertical position through the water at different depths, to see if they could hook Frank's body. Divers with scuba tanks also looked for him, all to no avail.

With the coming of dawn, the weather suddenly changed. Dark storm clouds hurried in from the sea and a strong wind built up. Waves violently crashed against the cliffs. Tony Flynn had this nagging sensation that Coogan hadn't been killed, that he was hiding somewhere, and he and Rocco paced the top of the cliffs looking for him.

Diane didn't want anything to do with Casa Bella Luna any longer and packed all her things and checked into a hotel in town, the Marco Polo. Truth was, she wanted nothing more to do with Italy. From the hotel Diane called Alitalia to arrange a flight back to San Francisco the following day.

When she had packed her things at the villa she also took with her what Frank had written; she didn't think he police should have it. They already had all the evidence they needed, and she was very curious to see what he'd written. She knew, too, that the only reason he'd written anything was because of her.

Diane's room at the hotel had a terrace with comfortable lounge chairs and she went outside, sat down and opened a copy of the medical report from Creedmore State Hospital that Tony Flynn had given her. Sitting there, the wind howling, Diane slowly read Frank Coogan's medical file, how he'd been found battered and bruised with severe head trauma in a basket on the steps of a church in Spanish Harlem; how he attacked children in the foster homes where he had been placed; how foster parents kept returning him; how he killed one of his abusers.

And as she read, her heart rolled over in her chest and she began to cry, shocked and distressed that any child would suffer the abuse Frank had endured. When Diane finished the report, she felt empty and beaten up, incensed and outraged.

She stood and paced back and forth, her anger mirroring the stormy Mediterranean weather. She then read what Frank had written, his very first memories of foster homes, being brought to Sacred Heart, what had been done to him the day he arrived, and that's where he stopped. It was well written, she thought, filled with emotion, simple and honest, and it made her even angrier. She stared out at the turbulent sea. A giant lightning bolt ripped open a foreboding, swiftly moving dark gray sky.

Depressed, Diane left the hotel and slowly made her way back to Casa Bella Luna, wanting to talk with Tony Flynn, to thank him for giving her the report; thinking about it, her life, her new book, which suddenly didn't mean anything anymore, seemed trite and unimportant compared to everything that had happened. As she walked she called her lawyer, Susan Hasse, and briefly told her what had occurred, that she was all right and thanked her for telling the police where the house was. She then called her agent to let her know she was okay, that she had an idea for a new book.

Diane found Tony Flynn near the pool. He was talking on his cell phone, telling Carole Cunningham what had happened; that it looked like Frank Coogan was dead. When he hung up, Diane approached him. "I wanted to thank you for allowing me to read the report."

"You're welcome."

"It's so disturbing. It's almost logical that he'd want to kill priests after what he's been through, you know?"

"I know," he said.

"I'd like to . . . I'm thinking about writing a book about him—about everything that happened. Would you help me? Will you tell me what you saw and learned in New York, Captain?"

"I'd be happy to," he said, pleased to hear this. "The world should know the truth about Frank Coogan," he said. "I'll help you every way I can."

"I was going to go back home to San Francisco, but now I think I'm going to New York."

"Because of this?"

"Yes. I want to find out as much as I can . . . maybe speak to some of the foster parents he had, the doctors who treated him. Perhaps even some of the priests who abused him, if that's possible, and of course you."

"I'll do all I can to assist you," he promised.

"Thank you. Thank you very much," she said, hugged him and kissed him on the cheek.

"You think he's dead?" she asked.

"Apparently. They thoroughly searched the cliffs and the water, no sign of him."

"It's all so very sad," she said, taking a long deep breath.

"Yes, yes it is," he agreed.

Behind Tony a giant lightning bolt suddenly tore open the dark sky. It began to rain hard. Tony, Diane and Rocco went inside the house.

"When do you think you are going back to New York?" she asked.

"Soon as we know for sure what happened to him," he said, thunder exploding like a giant cannon had been discharged, rolling and echoing across the turbulent Tyrrhenian Sea.

SIXTY-TWO

A thunderclap woke him up. Stiff from lying on the hard ground, Frank listened carefully, heard nothing. He pushed the stone and saw that the sea had grown rough; that all the police boats and helicopters had gone. He moved the stone out of the way, pushing it a little too hard and it tumbled down the cliff, crashing into the rough water. He waited, nothing; cautiously, he crawled out of the small space. No one was about. He stayed still and listened—all was quiet. Thinking about Diane, that maybe the police had gone and he could talk to her, get away from Amalfi, he slowly began to climb up the cliff.

Tony Flynn wasn't able to properly use his cell phone inside the house. Carrying an umbrella, he went outside to talk with Sergeant Frank Salerno, who had called Tony to tell him that Alitalia had contacted them and said that the "priest" suspected of killing Bishop Arnold, Alberto Pastore, had boarded Alitalia flight 611 to Rome and was scheduled to land at 10:00 AM. Standing at the edge of the cliffs, Tony said he'd make certain the Italian authorities grabbed him when he left the plane. As Tony turned to go tell Maranzano this news, he heard the stone Frank had accidentally let fall tumble down and crash into the water.

Curious, looking down, Tony moved along the cliffs, to where he heard the noise, and he stood there wondering how a big rock suddenly rolled down the cliff, when he discerned movement, someone climbing up. Immediately he knew who it was, closed the umbrella, drew his weapon, hid behind some foliage and waited.

Winded from the steep climb, Coogan reached the top of the cliff, got down low and stayed still, making sure the coast was clear. Looking for Diane, he stood and moved closer to the house, crouched low. He saw that the lights were on in the house, men moving about. Realizing the police were still there, he backed up and made for the road, planning to go south to Salerno. He hadn't gone five feet when Tony Flynn stood up and was suddenly blocking Frank's path, his Berretta pointed at his chest.

"I'm Captain Tony Flynn. I came from New York to find you. It's over. Lie down with your arms and legs spread wide," Flynn said, very aware that Frank had studied martial arts, that he probably had the knife he had killed the priests with on him.

Coogan didn't move; they stared at one another. Tony cocked his weapon.

"Frank, I don't want to kill you, but I will. Lie down!"

Wanting to pick the moment he made his move, Coogan slowly got down on the ground. He was not going to give up. He'd die first. Tony came closer.

Tony had, over the many years he'd been a New York cop, subdued and handcuffed thousands of bad guys, but with Frank Coogan he took extra care, paid careful attention. When Frank was flat on the ground, Tony made him spread his arms and legs, which he reluctantly did. Tony then walked around to where Coogan's legs were, moved them still wider with his feet, pulled out his handcuffs, bent down and put the barrel of his gun to the back of Coogan's head and let him feel the cold, hard steel.

"Frank, I'm going to cuff you now, don't move—you understand?"

No answer.

"Understand!" Tony demanded, pushing the barrel of the gun harder into the back of Coogan's head.

"Yeah, I understand," Coogan said.

"Raise your left wrist," Tony ordered. Coogan complied. As Tony put one link of the cuffs on his wrist, Coogan suddenly moved his head, Tony fired, missed, and Coogan attacked him, kicking the gun from Tony's hands. They grappled. Coogan brought Tony down. Coogan was incredibly strong—the strongest man Tony had ever fought with and they rolled and furiously punched at one another. Fighting with Coogan was like fighting with a very strong piece of steel cable, and Coogan managed to get on top of Tony, pull out his knife and bring it to Tony's throat. Tony grabbed his wrist with both hands, but Coogan's strength was almost supernatural and Tony's resistance was merely a slight annoyance. Just when he was about to slit Tony's throat, an incredibly powerful hand grabbed Frank Coogan, pulled him off Tony and threw him into a tree with terrific force.

"You want to fight with someone, sonny, fight with me," Rocco Genovese said.

Coogan got up and ran toward Rocco, raising the knife. Rocco hauled off and hit Coogan in the chest so hard he felt like he'd been struck by a truck. Coogan went down. Realizing he could not overcome Rocco, seeing Maranzano and more police running from the house, Coogan got up and now ran for the cliffs, intent upon diving into the water again, getting away. But Tony chased him and, just as Coogan reached the cliffs, Tony dove and tackled him. Outraged, Coogan turned and was about to stab Tony, but Rocco hit him and knocked him out cold. Tony handcuffed both his wrists and ankles.

"We got him," he said, standing up, out of breath.

"We got him," Rocco agreed, and they high-fived each other. "Strong son of a bitch."

"Tell me about it," Tony said, winded, breathing hard, as though he'd run a hundred-yard dash. "I'm getting too old for this," he said.

Maranzano shook Tony and Rocco's hand. *"Bravo,"* he said. *"Molto bravo!"*

SIXTY-THREE

In Rome the following morning, when Alberto Pastore walked off the flight from New York, he was promptly arrested by four of Maranzano's men. He was a short, bull-like man wearing a clerical collar, and he refused to say anything to the police, even after they roughed him up. They took his fingerprints, and he turned out to be a career criminal with a long history of assorted arrests. He worked for the Bonafanti crime family out of Castle del Mare, Sicily, and was believed to be a professional hit man. His real name was Salvatore Calese and he had been arrested three times on suspicion of murder but never convicted. When Maranzano heard this, he personally went to talk with Calese, but he refused to give him any information, and soon one of the finest criminal attorneys in Rome showed up at the jail and made sure no one spoke to Calese, and that was that.

* * *

When Diane heard that Coogan hadn't been killed, that he was taken alive, she was relieved.

Even though she had grown to despise him for duping her, using her, she couldn't help feeling sympathy for him after she learned all that he'd been through . . . *out of no fault of his own making*, as she had come to think of it. She also found out that when Rocco Genovese punched Coogan in the face, he broke his cheekbone. There were no medical facilities in Amalfi where Coogan could be properly treated and kept in a secure place, so Chief Inspector Maranzano ordered him brought to Rome by helicopter where his face was operated on at the Mother Cabrini Hospital on Via Da Vinci—where the pope had been taken.

Coogan was then brought to the prisoner ward of the hospital on the fourth floor where he was put under tight surveillance, handcuffed to a special steel-framed bed bolted to the floor. Tony and Rocco went to talk with him at the hospital, but he refused to see them.

Working with Chief Inspector Maranzano, Tony began the process of extraditing Frank Coogan back to New York. Italy wanted nothing more to do with him, but before the Italian authorities would allow him to be extradited, they—and the Church—demanded a waiver guaranteeing that the State of New York would not seek to execute him. Carole Cunningham drew up the waiver, the governor signed it and Carole e-mailed it to Flynn in Rome that same day, care of the American embassy.

When the press got wind of what had happened in Amalfi, how the priest killer had been caught, they were all over Tony Flynn and Rocco Genovese, but the two men wanted nothing to do with sensation-seeking media.

However, the New York police commissioner, the mayor and governor, all wanted as much media coverage as possible about the very successful outcome of the hunt for Coogan, and Tony Flynn and Rocco were made to attend a news conference at the American embassy on the Via Veneto, just down the block from the bookstore where Diane had been when Coogan first phoned her.

The press conference was held in a wood-paneled auditorium on the first floor and was packed with news outlets from all over the globe, cameras and microphones and pushy reporters. Tony Flynn told how the capture had taken place, thanking Chief Inspector Maranzano many times over as he spoke.

"The real hero of this case," Flynn told the assembled press, "is Chief Inspector Nino Maranzano. Without his expert guidance, experience and know-how, Frank Coogan would still be free." Everyone there gave Maranzano a rousing ovation. Maranzano's wife, Lina, also attended and she felt so proud of her husband, tears came to her eyes and she had a big lump in her throat.

Diane Pane also attended the press conference. She was intent upon writing a book about the case and she took photographs of the podium where Rocco Genovese, Tony Flynn and much of the Italian police hierarchy stood proudly with smiling faces, shaking one another's hands.

Diane had entertained the idea of visiting Coogan in the hospital, but she felt it was important for her to distance herself from him if she was going to be able to effectively write about the case, his story. There would be, she knew, time enough to talk with him after she interviewed the main players in this real life drama in which she suddenly found herself smack in the middle.

Already, several New York publishers showed interest in the story and had contacted Diane's San Francisco agent offering large sums of money for the world rights to the planned book.

For Diane, though, this book was not about money, and she decided any proceeds from the book would be devoted to helping those who had been victims of predator priests. Never in her life did Diane feel so strongly about a book. This story, she believed, was vitally important because it was an exacting case study of how the Church allowed itself to become populated by so many molesters and the lasting damage they caused. Diane viewed the abuse of children by people representing a powerful holy order as a true sin, and she was intent on exposing it all—and, hopefully, make the Church accountable for its part in this human tragedy. The more she learned, researched Coogan's story and the Church, spoke with attorneys in Boston who represented victims, the more incensed Diane became, and with Tony Flynn's help she began contacting the people she needed to interview while she was still in Rome.

Diane found a serious ally in Carole Cunningham, who promised to make sure Diane had immediate access to police reports and grand jury testimony. Carole was so supportive of what Diane wanted to do, she put her in touch with a downtown real estate agent, who helped Diane sublet an apartment where she could stay during her time in New York, a large loft on Greenwich Street with an outdoor deck facing the Hudson River.

Carole had, in fact, read Diane's book that played out during the great San Francisco earthquake of 1906, enjoyed it very much, and the two became friends even before Diane left Rome.

With the help of Chief Inspector Maranzano, Diane visited the apartment where Coogan had stayed in Rome, and she also went to the Rome morgue where the priests and bishop he killed were still housed. She had never been to a morgue and found the experience very unsettling, but she wanted to see and know exactly what Coogan had done and there was no better way of truly understanding his anger—his raging psychosis—than to see what he did to those he felt were responsible for what had been done to him. She was absolutely appalled at the sight of the murdered priests, how he had mutilated them. She shuddered and felt all cold inside when she thought about how intimate she had been with him. When she left the morgue, Diane was a changed person. She only hoped the horrific images she'd seen would not plague her sleep, cause her nightmares. Diane also interviewed friends and family members of the priests Coogan murdered in Rome and came to know that they were good men who had devoted their lives to helping others.

SIXTY-FOUR

When the pope learned the truth about what had been done to Frank Coogan at the hands of Catholic priests running a home for orphaned children, he was livid with anger. Against all his advisors' wishes—and there were many—he insisted on seeing and talking to Coogan. His doctor also advised him against the trip, but the pope was adamant. The Vatican contacted Chief Inspector Maranzano and he said he would, if possible, arrange it.

By now Maranzano had also read Frank Coogan's medical file, and he had come to think of Coogan as a man made mentally ill because of what had been done to him as a young boy. Maranzano had a son and when he thought about what had happened to Coogan in a Catholic home for orphaned children, his blood ran cold. He knew too that he might very well have committed violence against a man, dressed as a priest, who lusted after his son, Stephano.

When Maranzano arrived at the hospital, Coogan—his head swaddled in bandages, his right eye black and blue—was staring at the ceiling. He wanted nothing to do with Maranzano. He refused to even talk with him until Maranzano said: "I came here today to tell you two things. The first is that I read your file from the hospital in America and I want to say how sorry I am for what happened to you. It was truly a sin."

Coogan's dark eyes slowly moved down and came to rest on Maranzano's strong, hard face. They stared at one another.

"I have a son," Maranzano continued. "And if such things had been done to him when he was a boy, I would have been hurt and angry beyond words. Gone crazy myself.

"The other thing I want to tell you is that the pope would like to come and talk to you."

"The pope. Really?" Coogan said, suddenly interested, sitting up, wincing with pain, for Rocco had also broken three of his ribs when he hit him in the chest. "One of the reasons I came to Rome was to see the pope . . . to kill him," he said.

"Yes, I was thinking that."

"How did you find me?"

"People saw you—a man dressed as a priest on a bike near two of the murders—and we began talking to workers in the bike shops and realized you were near the east side of the Villa Borghese and began doing a house-by-house search . . . and we got lucky."

In disgust, Coogan shook his head back and forth.

"The bike?" he said.

"The bike."

"I should have known. And how did you track me to

Amalfi?" Coogan asked, his brow creasing slightly with curiosity.

"When you stopped in Napoli for the pizza, the parking attendant recognized you," Maranzano said. "Do you remember him?"

"Ah, him. Yeah, I remember him. . . . Is he going to get the reward?"

"He is."

"Where's Diane?"

"Here in Rome. She is a very nice lady."

"Yes . . . very nice. I'm sorry I got her involved in all this. She didn't deserve it. Please tell her to come see me. Please."

"I will tell her."

"Yes. I'd like to see the pope. Talk to him," Coogan said, thinking this would be an opportunity to hurt the pope, to shock the Church.

"I will let the Vatican know."

"When will he come?"

"This I don't know. He is very sick now. It is an extraordinary thing that he wants to see you."

"It's an extraordinary thing that he allowed the Church to fill up with predators. Most of this happened on his watch."

For this, Maranzano had no answer.

Sixty-five

When the media learned—via a leak from the Vatican—that the pope was going to visit Frank Coogan, a virtual army of press gathered at the Mother Cabrini Hospital, and the police had to be summoned to move the press so traffic and pedestrians could use the streets and side-walks.

By way of Chief Inspector Maranzano's office, the Vatican also received a copy of Coogan's medical file, and was soon clandestinely telling reporters—without the pope's knowledge or consent—that Coogan's mental instability and criminal behavior had nothing to do with what had occurred at Sacred Heart, but was a direct result of what happened to him even before he was found by a kindly priest on the steps of Our Lady of Lourdes Church in Spanish Harlem. That he had "severe brain damage," which caused his murderous rage directed at "innocent Catholic priests." And soon this version of the facts found its way to the media, and reporters on all the Italian news shows told how *l'assassino del prete* had been a battered child the Church had taken in and helped.

When Diane heard how the Vatican was perverting the facts, she held her own press conference and told—this being the first time she had spoken to reporters—the assembled media the truth about Coogan's childhood. How he had been abused and by whom, which the Vatican quickly condemned, saying that Diane Pane was looking to sell a book on the case and was, "making up these sordid tales to increase sales." That she was "Catholic-bashing."

And with that Diane—after getting permission from Carole Cunningham in New York and Frank Coogan by way of Inspector Maranzano—gave copies of the medical report to the media. It soon appeared verbatim in papers all over Europe, on the front page of every Italian newspaper.

Diane received threats of violence at her hotel and Maranzano assigned heavily armed detectives to protect her, guard her hotel, stay with her as she moved about Rome. Diane was again staying at the Pantheon, but was planning to leave for New York soon.

SIXTY-SIX

To avoid a press circus, the pope decided to see Coogan in the middle of the night. These days he didn't sleep much and was suffering from cancer of the stomach, a recent stroke and severe arthritis, but, still, he made it his business to come to Mother Cabrini Hospital in an unmarked black van with tinted, bulletproof windows. The van pulled directly into the underground garage of the hospital and none of the reporters even knew the pope had arrived.

From the garage, the pope was taken by the service elevator to the fourth floor. Hospital personnel didn't know of the pope's visit and were shocked to see him, surrounded by steely-eyed bodyguards, moving down the hall in a wheelchair being pushed by Cardinal Marino, one of the pope's closest confidants.

When they arrived at Coogan's room, the *polizia* guarding him nearly fell down they were so stunned to see the pope at the hospital wanting to visit a man who had killed so many of his priests. Coogan was wide awake when the pope arrived, and he silently watched the pope being wheeled into his room, his face an angry granite mask. Only Coogan's feet were handcuffed. The *polizia* and the pope's bodyguards wanted to handcuff his hands to the bed, but the pope, speaking slowly though firmly, spittle falling from his thin lips, told them that wasn't necessary.

Everything about the pope seemed old and infirm except his eyes. They were filled with wisdom, compassion and deep intellectual curiosity. The pope raised his bowed head and looked directly into Coogan's fierce dark eyes.

"Leave us," the pope ordered, and without question the pope's aides and bodyguards backed out of the room, their eyes nervously regarding Coogan.

"Close the door," the pope demanded, and the door was promptly shut. The pope managed to wheel himself closer to Coogan's bed. Coogan prepared to wrap his hands around the pope's neck and squeeze the life out of his frail body, but something in the pope's eyes stopped him cold.

"We understand the hatred in your heart, my son," the pope said. "But you must rid yourself of this anger, or you will only suffer more. I know what was done to you by members of the Church and I am so very sorry for this. My heart pains for you and all those abused by priests. We know the names of the priests who served at the home where you were and we will make sure they are defrocked and excommunicated."

He went on: "This *thing* is a terrible crime against all humanity and must be driven from the Church. Here, in Roma, we did not know the extent to which this cancer had grown in the Church, but now we will make certain it is cut away." Coogan was about to speak, but the pope raised his trembling right hand and, without hesitation or fear he came closer still and placed his hand on Coogan's head, closed his eyes and, in Latin, began to fervently pray. The pope's hand stopped shaking, became still and strong.

The strangest sensation now came over Coogan. "A peaceful warmth," he would later relate, and he closed his eyes and the pink insides of his eyelids became a gleaming golden white and he felt serenity and tranquility wash over him, as though he were under a warm waterfall, a feeling he had never known before. As the pope prayed on, Frank Coogan felt himself lift up and out of the bed and he was suddenly looking down at himself in the bed, curiously watching what the pope was doing, clearly seeing the top of the pope's bald head. The pope took his hand off Coogan's head, said, "Give me your hands, my son," which Coogan obediently did and the pope took Coogan's two hands in his own frail hands, both of which were steady now.

"Welcome Christ into your heart, my son. All your pain will leave you now. Let Jesus Christ heal you, my son. Let the demons that were forced upon you go. Love, don't hate, my son, and you will find peace here on earth and in the afterlife. This I promise you."

The pope now removed a gold crucifix on a gold chain from around his neck.

He said, "This has been mine since I was a boy. My mother gave it to me, and I want you to have it. Bless you . . . bless you, my son. Bless you," he said.

Coogan took the cross from the pope's outstretched hand and, without hesitation he put it around his neck. The cross was still warm with the heat of the pope's tortured body.

"Thank you, Papa," Coogan said, so touched by this gesture that tears filled his dark eyes, ran down his face.

"You will suffer no more, my son," the pope said.

Coogan reached over and hugged the pope, kissed his hands.

"We'll meet again in a better place," the pope said, smiled weakly, then called to his aides. The door quickly opened. The pope said some words in Latin, his voice strong and true. He made the sign of the cross, indicated with a wave of his hand it was time to go, and Cardinal Marino deftly turned his wheelchair around. The pope was suddenly gone, though his presence stayed in the room. Frank cried into his cupped hands, feeling understood for the first time in his entire life.

III

STATUTE OF LIMITATION

SIXTY-SEVEN

It didn't take long for the media to learn that the pope had visited Frank and now that story—how magnanimous and forgiving the pope was, a paragon of true Christianity—was being talked and written about.

Diane Pane tried to have an audience with the pontiff, but she was told he was too sick to see anyone.

True to his word, Chief Inspector Maranzano went to see Diane at the hotel and told her how Coogan had asked her to visit him. But Diane didn't want to see him just yet. She wasn't ready for that.

That night, Tony Flynn, Rocco, Chief Inspector Maranzano, his wife Lina and Diane had dinner in a small out-of-the-way restaurant in a building that was two thousand years old. They had a wonderful four-course meal, at the beginning of which Nino Maranzano announced that he would soon be retiring from police work, that he and Lina planned to travel, to see the world, first beginning in New York. Tony said they would be the city's guests, and he'd arrange for them to meet the mayor and the governor. Lina said, "We'd very much like to see the Statue of Liberty and Ellis Island. Would that be possible?"

"Most definitely," Tony said. "I'll take you personally. Be my pleasure."

Lina was sitting next to Diane, and she told Diane that she heard she was planning to write a book about the case, what she had been through.

"That is," Lina Maranzano said, "a very brave thing to do. You should be commended. This is a story the world must know. Would you please send us a copy? I should very much like to read it."

"I will," Diane promised, and she began talking to Lina about her husband, how they had met, when and where they fell in love, what it was like to be married to a crime-fighting superstar, all of which Diane would use in the book.

That night Diane also spoke to Nino and he briefly told her why he'd first been drawn to police work, how he hated organized crime, which had a strangle hold on Napoli, his hometown. How the Camorra had murdered his uncle Filippo, his father's youngest brother. And he told her how, at his uncle's funeral, he had vowed to devote his life to fighting crime.

Fascinated by him, Diane asked if she could come talk to him at his office the following day. He readily agreed and they had "one of the best meals in my life," as Maranzano would later put it.

Diane told Tony she'd very much like to interview him when she arrived in New York and he said he'd be happy to meet with her; tell her everything she needed to know. "When are you planning to come?" he asked.

"Within a couple of days."

"I'll see you then," he said, pleased that a writer of Diane's caliber was going to tell this story.

SIXTY-EIGHT

Two days later, on July 13, Frank Coogan was brought back to New York in a special medical plane that had been provided by the US Air Force. When he arrived at Rome's Leonardo Da Vinci airport a phalanx of reporters were there to document his leaving Italy. Tony Flynn and Rocco were on the flight, and Tony could see that there was clearly something different about Coogan; the frowning, bitter hatred that he had seen on his face was gone.

Both Tony and Rocco were exhausted. Rocco slept pretty much all the way back to New York, but Tony couldn't sleep. He kept thinking about Coogan. The priests he killed. Whether he'd be tried in a criminal court or be put back in a hospital, where, he knew, Coogan could be released again if doctors at the hospital diagnosed him as cured. He also thought about how close he came to losing his own life. If Rocco hadn't been there, Coogan would have surely cut his throat and the thought of that, dying on a wind-blown cliff in Amalfi, Italy, left him cold and unsettled.

Maybe, he began thinking, he too should retire. But what would he do? He loved police work, being in the field, running investigations, putting bad guys away. Tony had come to know the world as a very dangerous place and people like him, experienced in crime fighting, who knew what to do, how to do it and when to do it, were sorely needed. He also thought about Carole Cunningham; how much he enjoyed talking to her, being with her, making love to her, and thinking these thoughts, they arrived at Kennedy Airport. The plane landed at 3:00 in the afternoon. A police ambulance was used to take Coogan back to Creedmore Hospital, where he'd stay in a medical ward on the third floor until he recovered from the operation to repair his face. Because Coogan had been released on leave from the hospital when he committed the murders, he had to be brought back to Creedmore, where he was technically still a patient. The police commissioner wanted him to be housed at Riker's Island, but the law mandated that he be taken back to Creedmore. When the ambulance arrived at the hospital gate, a wall of press had to be pushed back so the ambulance could get onto the hospital grounds.

During the twenty-one years Coogan had spent at the hospital, he had, for the most part, been an ideal patient and he had made many friends. Nurses and doctors and people on the staff all came to visit him, to say hello, to wish him well. No one spoke about what he'd done while he was free, but everyone who came away from Coogan said that he had *changed* . . . that he seemed *at peace.*

Frank's old friend Dr. Hartock also came to visit him and, for the first time, Frank told someone why he had to do what he did. He said: "I felt like they all got away with what happened and every time I read or heard about another child being abused—in Boston, right here in Rockville Center, all over the country—it just outraged me, and I had to do something to let them know . . . the priests, the Church, the Vatican, that they had to answer for what was happening; for what they *allowed* to happen, you see," he said.

"How did you feel after you killed the first priest?" Hartock asked in a matter-of-fact tone, without judgment.

"Wonderful. He was one of the priests at Sacred Heart. I felt whole and complete and alive when I killed him. Just before he died—just before I cut his throat—I told him

304

who I was and he remembered me and knew why he was being killed. When I saw the recognition in his eyes, I cut him and I watched him slowly die, the way I slowly died a little every time I was raped. I watched his life spill all over the church floor."

"I see," Dr. Hartock said.

Knowing Frank's sanity would be a serious legal issue, the doctor asked Frank if he heard voices, commands, telling him to kill.

"Not voices as such, but I often see a train in my head. At first it is far away, but it comes closer and closer and in the train I see myself as a child and I see what they did to me and I did what I had to do."

"So you are hallucinating?"

"Yes."

"How often?"

"Several times a day; but mostly at night when I'm alone in bed with the lights out."

"This train, did you see it when the murders occurred?"

"A few times but not always."

"I see. Do you have any remorse, Frank?"

". . . I do now, yes," he said after a long time. "The pope came to see me in Rome and something . . . I know this sounds nuts, maybe like bullshit, but something he did . . . it kind of changed me, and he promised me all the molesters would be forced from the Church; and that's all I ever wanted really, you know."

"You heard about the $85 million settlement Archbishop O'Malley made in Boston?"

"I did, yes. But that's not really justice being served, because most all the predator priests who were and are responsible are going to walk because of the statute of limitations. That's what needs to be changed. There should be no statute of limitation for sex crimes, for rape—especially against children—like there is for mur-

Philip Carlo

der. It's a crime unto itself that these people, these pedophile priests, can walk away from what they've done just because some time went by. That's wrong."

"Maybe you, your case being made public, could help effect change in that regard."

"I'd do anything I could to make that happen."

"This writer you met in Rome, Diane Pane, she called me. She sounds quite nice."

"Oh, she is. Nicest person I ever met. I'm so sorry I got her involved in all this . . . this mess. And God, she is beautiful."

"You know she's planning to write a book?"

"I heard."

"How do you feel about that?"

"I don't know. On the one hand I'm pleased, but there's so much I'd like to say, to be part of this book, and I don't know how she'd feel about that. But I can tell you this: I'm not really sure what love is, you know, but I think I love her. There's just something—an intelligence, a passion . . . a sensitivity about her that's very special."

"Would you like to see her?"

"Yes, very much!"

"I'll arrange it if she asks me, okay?" he said.

"Yes, please."

"Did you make love?"

"We did. That was the first time I'd been with a woman, and it was . . . well, wonderful. Changed me. Just to kiss her, to hold her, was like some kind of beautiful dream. And now I know who I am—I mean sexually. I'd never been aroused like *that*."

"I'm pleased to hear that."

"I'm pleased to say it."

They both laughed.

"Did you like Rome?" the doctor asked. "Was it all you thought it would be?"

"Yes, very much—an amazing place. I'm sure I lived there in another life. Please, Dr. Hartock, talk to Diane about coming to see me. I must talk to her."

"I'll do what I can," the doctor said.

SIXTY-NINE

Diane arrived in New York the following day and hit the ground running. She was pleased with the loft she had leased with Carole Cunningham's help. It was large and spacious, furnished tastefully, on the seventh floor with an unobstructed view of the Hudson River, and there was an outdoor deck.

As Diane was unpacking, setting herself up for the extensive research she was planning, the doorbell rang and it was Carole. Pleased to finally meet her, Diane gave her a big hug, and the two of them hit it off well. The same age and both graduates of Berkeley, they each felt as though they'd known one another a long time.

They went for lunch at the nearby Tribeca Grill and Diane told Carole everything—how she'd first met Frank on the bus to Rome and all the rest. Diane felt so totally comfortable with Carole that she even told her that she and Frank had become intimate.

"Really . . . what was that like?" Carole asked.

"Intense—actually quite amazing."

"He wasn't, you know, *weird* at all?"

"Nothing like that, but very intense; and he was always a perfect gentleman. Fact is, the first two times I ran into him he was standoffish, wanted nothing to do with me."

"Hmm."

"I had no idea about who he really was."

"Of course—I know."

"And he is, well, he is very good looking."

"Yes, he is—I saw him on the news when he was put on the plane in Rome."

"I hope you don't think I hop into bed with every guy I meet. I just kept running into him, and there was something about him that . . . well, that drew me in, you know."

"I understand, Diane. You don't have to explain. It's happened to me. Pretty recently, too," she said, thinking of her liaison with Tony Flynn.

Carole, now, in turn, told Diane all about what she had seen and learned while working on the case. How priests who lived in rectories where there had been murders were in possession of extreme child pornography. "This," Carole said, "is something I plan to prosecute to the fullest extent of the law. We had a bishop who was willing to talk, but he was murdered, did you hear?"

"I did, yes. Captain Flynn told me."

"Seems the guy we think did it is a hit man for a Sicilian crime family."

"I know. I tried to talk with him at the jail in Rome, but he refused to even see me."

"Diane, do you think Coogan's playing with a full deck? Because I'm pretty sure that's going to be his defense here."

She took a deep breath. "Truth is, I'm really not qualified to say, but if you look at what was done to him in his formative years, it almost stands to reason that he'd come away from it as seriously damaged goods. I'm going to see if I can find out who his parents really are—and what happened to him even before he got to Sacred Heart. The medical report says he had serious brain damage from being battered."

"I know. I cried . . . I swear I cried like a baby when I read it. It's just so unfair, you know—a child being treated like that, then being placed in that home filled with molesters. It's unconscionable."

"Are you, your office, planning to prosecute him criminally?" Diane asked.

"At this juncture we are still discussing it. My boss wants to see what the court-appointed doctors who interview him have to say. I can tell you this—there was a lot of premeditation and planning in what he did, which flies in the face of an insanity defense."

"But I mean how do you feel, Carole—do you think he should be tried?"

"I have mixed feelings."

"How so?"

"Diane, he murdered eight people, and most of the priests he killed were good men who never abused anyone. Killing the people who abused him is one thing, but murdering innocents is another thing entirely."

"Frank doesn't belong in prison, Carole. He needs to be in a hospital setting," Diane said. "None of what happened to him was his fault."

"I agree," Carole said. Their food arrived and they had lunch, not talking anymore about the case for now. Diane insisted upon paying for the lunch. Carole promised her she'd give her access to all the information in her files on the case and, as friends, they parted, Diane going back to the loft and Carole on to work. When Carole arrived at her desk, there was a message from Tony Flynn. She hadn't seen him since he'd returned and called him right back. He explained that he was still exhausted from the trip, had to meet with his boss, the mayor, governor and Cardinal Edam; that he wanted to get some sleep and meet her for a late dinner.

"That'd be very nice," she said. "I've been looking forward to seeing you—hearing everything."

"And I've been looking forward to seeing you," he said and they soon hung up.

Back at the loft, Diane began calling people she wanted to interview. She spent the whole rest of that day contacting individuals she wanted to talk to. For the most part she did well, made appointments with Dr. Hartock and Dr. Lawson, who ran Creedmore, and Dr. Russo, the physician who had done the autopsies on the New York priests Coogan murdered. And she made appointments to meet with some of the attorneys who represented victims of sexual abuse in the Boston area. She also made an appointment to talk with Cardinal Edam. She then went outside, paced back and forth on the deck, left the apartment and took a cab up to Spanish Harlem. She wanted to see the church where Frank Coogan had been left thirty-four years ago, take photographs of it, perhaps find out more details—who found the child and under what circumstances. In Diane's mind the story really began there.

As the cab neared 110th Street, Diane's cell phone sounded. It was Cardinal Edam's assistant calling to cancel Diane's appointment, which didn't surprise her at all. She knew the Church viewed her as an adversary and that was fine with her. Diane had come to think of the Church as a large, powerful, multi-faceted criminal enterprise that coddled and protected molesters. She knew that the Church did many good things, but all the good they did was, she believed, cancelled out by allowing so many abusers into their ranks.

She believed, and was intent upon proving, that sexual predators had also made their way into the Church's hierarchy; that they had become bishops and cardinals and had even infiltrated, in a large way, the Vatican itself. In her mind that was the only way this blight could have gone on for so long. Become so widespread.

Our Lady of Lourdes was on 126th Street and 3rd Avenue. It was an old church constructed of brownstone with a tall, pointed steeple topped by a cross. Above the entrance there was a large, round stained glass mural depicting Jesus in the manger. Everything about the church looked old and worn. Pigeon droppings dotted the flaking facade. There had just been a wedding earlier in the day and rice covered the five worn stone steps that led to the entrance. For the longest time Diane just stared at these steps, imagining a small child left at the front door, wondering if he had been in a basket, was it winter, who found it, was he crying? She finally entered the church and there was a young priest talking with an elderly man off to the left of the altar. As Diane approached this priest, the elderly man shook his hand, kissed it and turned to leave, as did the priest.

"Please, Father, may I have a word with you?" Diane asked.

"Certainly," said the priest, a tall, thin man with a long pointed nose that veered off to the right—as though it had been broken and never reset. Diane introduced herself as a journalist researching a story about a child who was supposed to have been found on the church steps.

"And when was this?" he asked.

"A long time ago, more or less thirty-four years ago."

"I would have no knowledge of such a thing. I've only been here four years."

"Are there any elderly priests here that might have been assigned to the church then?"

"No, I'm sorry. All the priests assigned to this parish are relatively new," he said, looking at his watch.

"Would there perhaps be a record somewhere in the parish files?"

"Not that far back. I'm sorry, but I have a funeral I must attend. I'm already late," he said, then turned and hurried off. There was, Diane was thinking, something off-key about him. She sat down in one of the pews and stared at the altar, at Christ up on the cross—shadows caused by candles skulking along the walls like malicious spirits—wondering how He could allow the Catholic Church to become a big private club for sexual predators. *Real wolves in sheep's clothing,* she thought, slowly got up and left the church. Outside, she walked to the middle of the street and took a few photographs of the front of the church, the steps. Just as she was about to leave, the elderly man she'd seen talking to the priest came from around the back of the church carrying a wide broom and dust pan. He began to sweep up the rice on the steps.

Curious, Diane approached him, introduced herself and explained that she was interested in finding out about a child that was supposed to have been left on the church steps thirty-four years ago and if he knew anything about such a thing. He gave her a long hard look out of eyes that were stained with cataracts, his bushy eyebrows coming together.

"Why are you so interested?" he asked.

"I'm going to write a story that involves this child."

"How . . . involves him how?" he asked.

Diane never said that the child was a male.

She said, "It's a long, involved story. How long have you been working here? My name is Diane. How do you do?" She reached out and shook his hand.

"I'm Gino. Forty-one years," he said.

"So you were here then?"

"Yes, I was."

"Do you remember what I'm talking about?"

". . . I do. Father John found the baby," he said.

Wow, she thought. "Where is Father John?" she asked.

"He retired some years back. I think he lives in a home for retired priests in the Bronx."

"Really? Can you tell me the name of it?"

"Sure, the Cardinal John O'Connor Home, right here in the Bronx," he said, pointing uptown.

"Do you remember the baby?"

"Yes, I do; I saw him. He was in very bad shape . . . he had a swollen head big like a melon; it's something I'd like to forget . . . but I never will."

"Do you know where he came from?"

"Have no idea. Father John found him on the steps. It was a bitter cold night, I remember that. I was doing work in the rectory and Father John just walked in carrying the baby—poor little guy. I'll never forget that he didn't cry. All beat up like that and didn't make a peep, you know. It depresses me . . . even now, it depresses me."

"Of course, understandably."

"You gonna go see Father John?"

"Yes . . . I am."

"Please don't say how you found this out from me, okay? They don't like us saying anything about church business around here, since, you know, all the scandals."

"No, of course, I won't. Father John, is John his last name?"

"No, De Mazio is his last name. We just called him Father John. Hell of a nice guy, loved baseball, a big Yankee fan. He had a ball signed by the great Joe Di Maggio himself, and God he just loved that ball. Used to carry it around with him all the time."

"Thank you so much," Diane said, hugging the old man. She took out her wallet, grabbed a hundred dollar bill. "Please take this—"

"No, I couldn't—"

"Please," Diane said, forcing it on him. "Buy yourself a nice dinner and bottle of wine on me," and she pushed it into his shirt pocket.

"Thank you," he said. "That's very nice of you, Diane."

"You're welcome, my pleasure," she said, thanked him several more times and started toward 3rd Avenue, taking out her cell phone as she went. She called information and got the number of the O'Connor Home for Retired Priests. She was going to phone the home right away to see if Father John De Mazio was still there but she hesitated. She wanted to first think it out—the best way of going about this. Maybe, she was thinking, it would be better to just show up and ask for him. She hailed a cab and had it take her back down to the loft, deciding she would go to the home and knock on the door and ask to see John De Mazio. She didn't want anyone to have time to think about what she wanted, and why she wanted to see him. The Church, Diane knew, would not be helpful in any way.

She got online, went to the archives of the *New York Times* and looked for stories they'd written about pedophile priests. There were hundreds of them. She went back to the first one and began printing them all out, knowing if she was going to be able to write about this case effectively she had to understand and know as much about predator priests as possible. When she printed out all the *Times* articles, she then went to the Boston newspapers and found many more stories and printed them out too. For most all that night Diane Pane read about predator priests in the Catholic Church, and was more and more amazed at how many molesters there were, and the great lengths that the Church had gone through to cover it up. She found numerous photographs of ex-Cardinal Bernard Hound, a heavy jowled man with the face of a bulldog. There was, she thought, something outright evil about him, an obvious condescending arrogance. She learned that he had lived like a king in a palatial mansion in one of Boston's best neighborhoods, from which he did nothing but cover up for pedophile priests and gave the thousands of victims of these priests a very hard time, had teams of belligerent lawyers play hardball with them. *The prick!* she thought.

Angry beyond words, Diane changed into shorts, put on her running shoes, went outside, stretched and began to jog uptown, along the Hudson River, thinking out all that she had learned, read about, hoping that Father John De Mazio was still alive, willing to talk with her.

There was, she sensed, something more to the story of an abandoned baby being found on the church steps of Our Lady of Lourdes. Something she'd seen in the caretaker's eyes, his facial expression—the set of his mouth. She ran up to West 72nd Street, turned around and made her way back downtown, marveling at the beauty and grandeur of the Hudson River. Diane hadn't been able to jog much in Italy because of the heat but now the temperature was a comfortable 78 degrees and there was a strong breeze off the river, many people out jogging. The running cleared Diane's head and loosened her muscles. As she ran, she couldn't help remembering the first time she'd seen Frank Coogan, on the bus to Rome, and she remembered when they made love out in the open in the magical light of the full moon. *Bella luna*, she said to herself, knowing she would not forget that night as long as she lived.

She wasn't, she realized, mad at Frank anymore. She knew now that what he had done, calling her, using her to get out of Rome, was, for him, a matter of life and death—survival. She was angrier with herself for allowing him to get so close to her so quickly; though she knew if she had to do it over again, she'd do the same thing and, in reality, she had no regrets.

When love comes knocking on your door, you open the door, she mused as she reached Greenwich Street, stopped running and walked to the building where she was staying, feeling much better, renewed and healthy. She was looking forward to finding out the truth, unraveling and understanding all the elements involved in this incredible story she suddenly found herself in the middle of, looking forward to, she realized with some surprise, seeing him again.

Back inside, she made herself an omelet and read more of the newspaper stories, making notes, finding many more people she would contact, particularly a group who called themselves Voice of the Faithful, which was, she learned, made up of faithful Catholics—and victims of priests—who were appalled at the Church's handling of predator priests.

Governor Frank Keating, she read, who was in charge of a panel looking into the Church's conduct, had publicly said that they—the Church hierarchy—were acting like a "Mafia family out to skirt the law." She would contact the governor and see what he had to say.

SEVENTY

Certain Carole Cunningham was the most beautiful woman he'd ever seen, Tony Flynn took her in his arms when she opened the door to her apartment and kissed her deeply. He hadn't realized how much he'd missed her, longed for her, until he saw her. Without one word he picked her up and carried her to the bedroom.

Afterwards, lying next to one another, breathing hard, Carole told Tony how much she missed him; that she thought of him often; that she wondered why they hadn't become lovers sooner, because she'd always been attracted to him.

"I can't believe," he said, "a woman like you, such a serious fox, would want an old coot like me."

"Old coot my foot. You are a gorgeous man. All the women in my office are always talking about you. You've got this Sean Connery-Clint Eastwood kind of thing going on."

"So you say."

"I swear, and, Tony, you are a real man, a caring, wonderful guy . . . and a great kisser," she said, slowly moving toward him and kissing him deeply, slowly, and they made love again.

Later, as they were leaving Carole's place to go get a bite to eat, Tony told Carole about his trip—being flown to Naples by helicopter, meeting Maranzano; how the car Diane Pane rented had led them to Diane's lawyer, who told them where Diane was staying in Amalfi; how Coogan had first gotten away; how he came across him coming up the cliffs. How they fought and Coogan very nearly killed him . . .

"If," he said, "Rocco hadn't been there, he would have killed me for sure. I felt . . . I felt the blade of his knife against my throat."

"My God," she said, stopping and staring at him.

"Thank that same God that I had Rocco with me. He actually pulled Coogan off me and threw him ten feet into a tree."

The thought of Tony being killed unsettled Carole, and she could feel anger spreading inside her.

"What do you think of Diane Pane?" she asked.

"I think she's good people. Just in the wrong place at the wrong time."

"How do you feel about her writing a book on the case?"

"I think it's a great idea. This is a story that should be told, and I'm glad it's a real writer—I mean someone not just looking to do a quickie book, you know."

"Actually, she's a very good writer. Does a lot of research. I read a book of hers that takes place during the great quake in San Francisco in 1906—amazing details. We graduated Berkeley a year apart."

"Did you know her?"

"No. But I like her. I like her a lot, and I'm very pleased she's doing the book."

"It's a hell of a story. I remember the day we found the first priest he killed at Saint Mary's like it was yesterday."

"Father Joseph. You know he was one of the priests that abused Coogan?"

"Yeah, I've heard," he said, slowly shaking his head.

"You think he should go to prison or a hospital, Tony?"

"I don't think it matters one way or the other, but he should never be free again, that's for damn sure."

"Yes, yes, I agree," she said, and entered the restaurant, Argo's on Hudson Street. It was late and the place was nearly empty. After they ordered, Carole said, "Tony, the issue of his sanity is going to come up; what do you think—is he playing with a full deck?"

"Everything he did was carefully planned and premeditated; but when you look at what was done to him even before he arrived at Sacred Heart—the brain damage—it's pretty clear that he could very well have serious mental instability. I mean, I don't know if he hears voices and all the rest, but he had to come away from everything he's been through with loose screws and bolts. He told me, when we landed at Kennedy, that he was sorry for trying to kill me."

"We have two court-appointed physicians going out to the hospital to talk with him; to determine whether he's legally sane. If you ask me, he's crazy all right, crazy like a fox. I feel terrible about what happened to him as a child, you know, but he killed all these priests with malice and forethought—just look at how he rented that apartment in Rome over the internet; how he first flew to Milan, then took a domestic flight to Rome—that certainly looks like someone who is sane; and, also, the way he presented himself to Diane Pane. She didn't have the slightest inkling that anything was wrong with him."

"True. I'm very curious to know what these two shrinks have to say. Keep me posted."

"I will," she said. Their food arrived. They quietly enjoyed their meal and a bottle of cold white wine, finished eating, walked back to Carole's place, went upstairs and quickly fell asleep in one another's arms.

SEVENTY-ONE

In the morning, Diane took a cab up to the Bronx. She had it wait while she rang the bell at the O'Connor Home for Retired Priests. She noted that there was crime scene tape up on the side of the house, how well cared for the grounds were. The day was clear and dry and the sun shone. Bees happily went from flower to flower collecting pollen. Birds chirped. An elderly priest opened the door. Diane had a feeling if she said she was a journalist she wouldn't get past the front door.

"Good morning," she said in her cheeriest voice. "I'm looking for Father John De Mazio."

"Yes, please come in. He's upstairs just now. Who shall I say is calling?"

"My name is Diane. We were friends a while back and I wanted to say hi, see if maybe he needed anything."

"Isn't that considerate," he said, smiling pleasantly. "I'll get him," and he began up a shiny wooden staircase. Diane looked at the portraits of distinguished priests that had resided at the home, most of whom had Irish names.

Father John De Mazio soon came down the steps. He looked to be a hundred years old, moved slowly, had a hunchback and his left hand shook. Without recognition, he regarded Diane, obviously wondering who she was.

"Hello, Father," she said respectfully. "Thank you so much for seeing me. I have a problem, Father, I need to discuss with you."

"Why me, my child, have we met?" he asked.

"Well, no, not exactly, but only *you*, Father, can help me," she said.

He gave her a long careful look. "Is this about the murder of Bishop Arnold?"

"No, Father, nothing like that," and she suddenly realized why the crime scene tape was strung up on the side of the house, kind of freaked out that the bishop had been murdered here.

"Please," he said, "come this way," and led her into a comfortable sitting room in the back that faced a well-tended garden, with neat rows of flowers—roses and tulips and chrysanthemums.

"Would you like something to drink, perhaps a nice iced tea?"

"No, thank you."

"How can I help you?" he asked, his aged face filled with curiosity.

"Father, I came to see you about a child you once helped."

"I've helped many children."

"Yes, I'm sure you have. But this was a little boy, Father. He was left on the steps of Our Lady of Lourdes a long time ago."

With that his eyes widened, and he sat back as though the air had been sucked out of his fragile body.

"A little boy," she added, "who had been badly battered."

"Yes. I remember . . . just tragic," he said.

"Do you have any idea—"

"Why are you interested in him, my child?" he interrupted.

Sensing that he was a good, caring man, Diane told the priest what she had learned about Frank Coogan's childhood, though not saying a word about what Frank had done. She had no idea how the priest would react to that.

"So he ended up at Sacred Heart?" he said, not pleased, as if he knew well what had happened at Sacred Heart.

"Yes."

"And was he abused there?"

"Yes, yes, he was."

"My Lord, how tragic," he said and sadly shook his head from side to side. "The Church," he said, "will *never* recover from this. Every day I pray that the predators are purged from the Church, that the Holy Father has the wisdom and strength to deal with this unspeakable curse that has plagued us. They should have never let it go on and on the way they did. They protected them instead of having them promptly arrested. This, I believe, is one of the darkest hours in the Church's history."

"Father, can you please tell me about the day you found him?"

"What is your relationship with him?"

"Friends . . . good friends."

"Has he . . . has he hurt someone?"

"Yes . . . he has."

"I see. Is he in trouble with the law?"

"He is. Do you have any idea who he is, where he came from?"

He took a long, pained breath, his mind going back to that time. He said, "I'm going to be ninety-one this Friday. My mind isn't as sharp as it was. But I'll never forget him, the night I found him. It was snowing heavily; just a few days before Christmas. I was returning from having dinner with some parishioners and as I was making my way to the rectory, I noticed some blankets, a bundle of cloth, on the church steps off to the left as you faced the church. Thinking perhaps someone left clothes for the needy, I went and picked it up. To my utter astonishment it moved when I touched it, and after the initial shock, I opened the blankets and there he was.

"It was dark just in front of the church and at first I didn't see . . . I didn't see the injuries, how terribly beaten he'd been, until I walked down the church steps and under a street lamp there, and I looked. His face was all black and blue, his eyes nearly swollen shut. Broke my heart. Seeing this little child beaten up like that just tore me in two. I hurried back to the rectory and there we uncovered him. His whole body was covered in black and blue, and cigarette burns, too, and his arm, I believe it was his right arm, was obviously broken. The strangest thing was that he didn't cry—nothing. Just stared through those swollen black eyes up at the ceiling. I immediately called 911 and an ambulance came and we took him to the hospital."

The priest became quiet, withdrew into himself. Diane remained still, waiting for him to come back.

"Tortured, that poor little guy had been tortured," he said. "To hear that he's in trouble for hurting someone doesn't surprise me. Never in my life have I ever seen a human being, let alone a child, beaten like that . . . ."

"Father, do you have any idea where he came from, who put him there, who did that to him?"

"I didn't then, no. But several years later, I did find out. The police were, of course, summoned to the hospital and they filed a report. I stayed with him all that night. In the morning I left him there. Everyone at the hospital was very upset by his condition and he received the very best care. I went back to see him a few times a day for several weeks, maybe a month, and little by little he healed—was a tough little guy, but the strangest thing was that he never cried. No one at the hospital ever heard him cry.

"There were stories about him in the papers, some reward money even offered for any information regarding him, but no one came forward and eventually he was taken out of the hospital and placed in the New York foster care system and I lost track of him. . . .

"So, anyway, what . . . about five years later, a teenage girl, a very beautiful girl, she came to see me at the rectory one evening and she told me that the boy was her brother. That their mother was an alcoholic and she had a boyfriend, a very mean individual who drank a lot and did drugs. He was beating on her brother all the time and her mother wouldn't do anything to stop it, and so she took him and brought him to the church and left him there, hoping, praying, she said, someone nice would find him. She said that the boyfriend had recently been killed in a knife fight and that's why she came to see me. I mean to say that she was obviously deathly afraid of this man, this sadistic creature. She said her mother had been arrested just that day for prostitution and that she had to come to see me and thank me for helping her baby brother."

"That's so sad," Diane said, thinking about what Father De Mazio just told her, feeling tears coming to her eyes. "Did she say what his name was?"

"Yes. She called him Carlos."

"Carlos?"

"Yes. I never did anything more because there was nothing more I could do. The abuser was dead, his mother locked up and I understood Carlos was adopted and I wasn't able to contact him."

"He was returned by whoever adopted him. He was violent. Assaulted foster siblings, and tried to stab one of his foster mothers," she explained.

"My Lord, how tragic . . . how very tragic."

"And then he was sent to Sacred Heart, where he was abused some more," she said.

He shook his head in dismay, closed his eyes and began praying, his lips silently moving. Diane waited. A white pigeon with pink eyes landed on the windowsill and strutted back and forth. The priest opened his eyes.

"Do you know how I can contact his sister? What her name is?" Diane asked.

"Gabriella. We became close after she first came to see me. She came to church every Sunday, regularly came for communion. A good girl—a very good girl. Then she just stopped coming. I know she became a nurse at Harlem Hospital, but we've been out of contact for quite a few years now."

"I see. Do you know her last name, Father?"

"Yes, Hernandez. She's a tall, dark-haired woman, very beautiful; all the boys were always ogling her. But she was shy, quiet, withdrawn . . . no doubt this sadistic boyfriend had abused her, too. Can you tell me what kind of trouble Carlos is in?"

Diane thought about this long and hard, not sure if she should tell the priest what happened, but decided that he should know; that he had a right to know. That he might very well be helpful in proving the extent to which Frank—or Carlos, she thought—had been abused.

"This might come as a bit of a shock, okay?" she said.

". . . Okay."

"Father, we are talking here about Frank Coogan—the man who killed all the priests here in New York and in Rome."

". . . No," he said, his eyes opening wide, his mouth falling open.

"Yes."

And in the next instant Father John De Mazio was crying hysterically into his cupped hands. Surprised he was taking this news so hard, Diane stood and put her hands on his thin shoulders. She knew he'd be upset but didn't expect anything like this. After some minutes, he calmed himself, took out a plaid handkerchief and blew his nose.

She said, "I'm sorry—I had no idea you would take it so hard, I—"

"You don't understand," he sobbed. "The priest he killed at Our Lady of Miracles in Manhattan, Paul De Mazio, that was my younger brother."

"No, I'm so sorry, I had no idea!" she said, feeling terrible that she had told him; he seemed to age further and shrink right before her eyes.

"It's extraordinary that the little tortured child I helped ended up killing my own brother—my baby brother. You know I always had a feeling Carlos would be a problem. That all the abuse he suffered would have a bad effect. A very bad effect . . . Where is he now?" he asked.

"Back at Creedmore Hospital. You see, when he was a boy he murdered a priest—one of the priests who sexually abused him at Sacred Heart and he was sent to Creedmore State Hospital for twenty-one years. He was let out on a contingency basis about two years ago, and he, as you know, killed five priests here and three in Rome."

"My God," he said. "My God." Closing his eyes, again he began to pray.

SEVENTY-TWO

Blown away by what she learned, Father John's grief, Diane left the home and headed straight to the Harlem Hospital, intent upon finding Gabriella Hernandez. She first went to the administration office and learned that Gabriella had left the hospital in 2000, moved to Florida and secured a job at Palm Beach General. Back outside, Diane called Palm Beach General, found out that Gabriella Hernandez still worked there, that she was a supervisor in the orthopedic ward.

Diane hailed a cab and returned to the loft, digesting and thinking about everything she had learned, realizing that the more she found out, the more extraordinary the story became. She called Carole Cunningham from the cab and told her what happened. Carole was equally blown away by these revelations—that the priest who found the boy on the steps so long ago lived where Arnold had just been murdered; that Coogan had a sister, who was the one who had left him on the church steps; that Coogan murdered the brother of the priest who had rescued him. Diane explained that she planned to go to Florida to interview the sister, hear what she had to say, to let her know what happened and where her brother was. Carole thanked her for the call, hung up and contacted Tony Flynn to tell him what Diane had learned.

"I knew she'd get to the bottom of this," he said.

At the loft, Diane paced back and forth and decided to go to Florida right away to talk with Gabriella. If, she reasoned, she called Gabriella, she might want nothing to do with her, with her brother, refuse to see her, to even talk with her. It was best, she decided, to just show up, look her in the eyes—not do this on a phone—and tell her what happened. Diane called her travel agent and managed to get a flight directly to Palm Beach out of La Guardia at 3:00 PM that same day.

One of the things Diane enjoyed most about her work was the research, finding out the truth, the facts and details that no one knew. She wondered how Frank would take all this . . . if he'd want to meet his sister or Father John De Mazio, the priest who had brought him in out of the cold.

As Diane prepared an overnight bag, she shook her head at the extraordinary coincidence of Father John living where Bishop Arnold had been killed, and that his brother had been murdered by Frank. *Just mind boggling,* she thought. She'd always believed Frank was Latin, and she wondered where his family came from.

Diane took a cab out to La Guardia, boarded the plane and made notes about her conversation with Father John. She then read more of the Boston newspapers' accounts of predator priests, how the Boston archdiocese hid and protected them. She was amazed to learn that one priest, John Shane, was openly a member of N.A.M.B.L.A., the group that publicly advocated sex with young boys, and that he had even had the temerity to talk about "the virtues of the group," as she read, at Sunday masses he presided over. *Mamma mia,* she thought, shaking her head in disbelief. Diane was beginning to realize just how truly insidious the child molestation within the Catholic Church had become, and wondered why the hell all the people who hid and protected the molesters weren't in jail, especially Cardinal Bernard Hound and his many assistants, who were now, she read, in charge of parishes all over the country, in Los Angeles, Miami, Brooklyn, Rockville Center and New Orleans.

Disgusted, Diane put down the stories and just stared out the window, numb, thinking about the depressing injustice of it all. Doing that she dozed off and dreamed about the day she first met Frank on the bus to Rome.

SEVENTY-THREE

At Creedmore Hospital Frank managed to secure a few legal pads from Dr. Hartock and he continued to write his story about his childhood, what happened at Sacred Heart, intent upon getting it all out of him, down on paper. He was determined to tell his story. He had, he knew, all the time in the world now, realizing he'd probably never be free again; not, at least, without some kind of miracle.

As he wrote, he often thought about Diane and looked forward to when she came into the story, to when she came to visit him. Though he didn't think she really would. He had come to believe that she was angry at him and wanted nothing more to do with him. *Who could blame her?* he thought, remembering what she had told him about writing a book, setting a goal every day and sticking to it, *no matter what*, as she put it.

Because of the pope's visit, the transformation he went through—as he thought about it—the burning hatred Frank felt was for the most part, he realized, diminished. His anger was now more directed at the policies and the politics of the Church—how they encouraged, fed, clothed and provided aggressive legal counsel to abusers. That was something he could never forgive, he knew.

That day, one of the court-appointed doctors came to interview Frank. His name was Herbert Goldberg. He had a beard, wore thick glasses, seemed like he'd much rather be somewhere else. He asked Frank all the usual questions, about his planning, why he'd gone to Rome, why he rented a bike, which Frank answered honestly. Then Dr. Goldberg asked, "Did you feel any kind of sexual arousal when you killed any of the priests?"

"No, never. I just felt like I was getting even for what had been done to me," Frank said.

"I see. Did you ever hear voices, commands to kill?"

This, Frank knew, was the million-dollar question because it would, in strict legal terms, define his sanity.

Frank said, "I heard, still hear actually, a whole chorus of voices. I often see a gleaming silver train coming toward me from far away, getting closer and closer and then speeding by me, making a lot of noise. Like thunder. I see people in the train. Some are priests and they are abusing children.

"And I have this . . . this recurring fantasy that I am in ancient Rome, in the Colosseum. That I'm a gladiator and the crowds cheer me wildly as I kill predator priests. I see it so clearly, I smell it . . . I mean the blood, and I hear the screaming of people as they are killed by animals—all kinds of big cats, huge bears and bulls," he said.

"I see," Dr. Goldberg said and soon left Frank there, chained to his bed, thinking he was definitely mentally ill—"a schizophrenic psychopath with sadistic tendencies, who clearly has hallucinations," as he would later tell Dr. Hartock, and write in his report.

Frank went back to his book, reread the twelve pages he'd written that day. He wasn't pleased. It was missing something. He put the pad down in disgust, wondering where Diane was, if she thought about him, how angry she was at him. He spoke to her in his head—asked her to please come and see him.

SEVENTY-FOUR

Diane took a cab from the airport to Palm Beach General, a five-story white brick structure surrounded by tall palm trees. She went straight to the orthopedic ward on the third floor, found the front desk and asked for Gabriella Hernandez.

Nurse Hernandez was, Diane was told, making her rounds. Diane took a seat and waited. A few minutes went by. Doctors were paged over the intercom system. Off to the left a woman was complaining loudly about pain in her leg. As Diane rehearsed what she'd say, she heard soft footsteps off to her right, looked in that direction and a tall, particularly attractive woman in a nurse uniform, carrying a red clipboard, came walking down the hall, a stethoscope hanging around her neck. Diane immediately knew she was Frank's sister; the similarity between them was striking. She, like him, had thick black hair, high cheekbones and big doe eyes, which now slowly came to rest on Diane.

"Excuse me," Diane said, standing and approaching her. "Gabriella Hernandez?"

". . . Yes?"

"Gabriella, my name is Diane Pane. I was wondering if we could talk for a few minutes."

"About a patient?"

"No, Gabriella, about your brother." When Diane said that it looked like she had slapped Gabriella.

"My brother, what are you talking about?" she demanded.

"You know Father John De Mazio?"

"Yes, of course," she said, the color suddenly draining from her beautiful face, her long-lashed eyes rapidly blinking. "Come, we can talk in the conference room. I have a break now," she said.

Diane followed her back down the hall, into a spacious room with a long table, comfortable chairs and couches. Bright Florida sunshine streamed into the room through oversized windows. They sat in two easy chairs facing one another. There was the smell of fresh coffee in the air.

"How did you find me?" Gabriella asked, and Diane took a long deep breath and slowly explained everything— right up to her meeting Father De Mazio that very morning.

Stunned and speechless, Gabriella sat there, large, glistening tears falling from her huge eyes.

"What's he like, I mean you spent time with him in Italy, right?" she asked.

"Yes. He's very sweet. Loves to read, loves books. One of the best-looking men I've ever seen. I only found out about him, what he'd done, when the police were suddenly there—in the kitchen of the house in Amalfi."

"In Italy?"

"Yes."

"I tried to find him, for years I tried to locate him, but they wouldn't tell me anything. I even hired a lawyer, but we couldn't find out who adopted him or where he was— nada. But I thought about him; not a day went by when I didn't think of my brother." She now began to cry in earnest. "This is just," she gasped, "unbelievable. I have to see him. I want to see him!"

"I'm sure that could be arranged," Diane said.

That very night Gabriella Hernandez and Diane Pane left Palm Beach and flew to New York. Gabriella told Diane how her mother had become strung out on alcohol and drugs and hooked up with a Dominican man named Ricardo Ramos; that he drank and used cocaine and speed. "He was mean like a rattlesnake. My mother gave birth to my brother, but he was not Ricardo's child. He was my father's son—my father had been killed in jail. And Ricardo just hated my brother. I'm not sure why exactly, but he did. Was beating on him all the time. My mother was very frightened of Ricardo and she didn't do anything to stop it, or to stop what he was doing to me, you know. And she knew . . . he used to force me into bed with her right there. So I just couldn't take it anymore and ran away with my brother, and I left him at the church. I figured someone nice, one of the nuns or priests would find him and take good care of him," she said, crying nonstop as she talked.

"How old were you when you ran away?" Diane asked.

"Eleven, maybe still ten."

"Where are your people from?"

"Cuba. That's why I moved to Florida, to be near some relatives, and to get away from New York, the cold, the violence . . . the memories of my childhood, what happened to my brother. My God, I can't believe I'm going to finally see him."

"I'm sure he'll be very pleased."

"You think?"

"I'm certain."

"Are they going to execute him?"

"No. The Italian authorities wouldn't allow him to be extradited unless New York agreed not to seek the death penalty. Have you been married?"

"Divorced, that's another reason I left New York, to get away from my ex."

Diane thought about showing Gabriella her brother's medical report from Creedmore—she had it with her—but decided against it. It would, she knew, only freak Gabriella out and depress her, and there was plenty of time for her to learn all the sordid facts.

Diane had called Dr. Hartock from Florida and he was very pleased to learn that she had located Frank's sister and said he was sure she could visit, but for her to bring picture ID. They discussed whether he should ask Frank if it was okay, but decided against it.

"He will, I'm sure, be very happy to see her," Dr. Hartock said. "He talked to me many times about finding his real family. It was kind of an obsession with him."

That night Diane insisted Gabriella stay at the loft with her. Gabriella didn't want to put Diane out, inconvenience her, but Diane was adamant and Gabriella, in the end, agreed to stay with her.

They didn't sleep much, however, because there was so much to talk about. Gabriella explained that she had been a devout Catholic but, like many, drifted away from the Church because of all the sexual abuse of children by the clergy. She still, she said, prayed and believed in Jesus Christ, but wanted nothing more to do with the Church or the people, "tyrants" she said, who ran it.

When Diane told her some of the details of how her brother had been sexually abused at Sacred Heart by numerous priests, Gabriella turned red with anger, and the tears that had been falling from her eyes disappeared. Her eyes became hard and cold, black like onyx.

She said, "To think that my brother ended up there, after what he'd been through, in the hands of those degenerate scumbags, makes me sick. Man, this can be a cruel world. The Church was supposed to be a place of refuge, solace, spirituality, but it's become a big candy store for pedophiles. Talk about sin."

Diane suggested Gabriella should see a lawyer about bringing a lawsuit against the Church, and Gabriella thought that an excellent idea. "It happened too long ago to bring criminal charges against any of them, but you can go after them civilly," Diane said.

"And he killed one of his abusers?" Gabriella asked.

"Yes, he did."

"Hope that priest is burning in hell," she said.

"I'm sure he is," Diane said.

In the morning Diane called a car service to take them out to Creedmore. The ride took nearly an hour. The sky had clouded over and a light rain fell. The hospital was six stories high, made of red brick, hidden behind tall maple and elm trees, like it held terrible secrets about the dark side of human nature and didn't want to be seen. All the windows had thick bars. It was a sad, ominous structure—the home of New York's criminally insane; people who were so violent and psychotic some of them had to be kept in straightjackets, in rooms with padded walls and floors.

The two women met Dr. Hartock in the lobby. He wanted to meet Gabriella and take her upstairs. Diane, for now, wasn't going to go up. She wanted, as Dr. Hartock did, for Frank and Gabriella to have time alone. However, he said, after thinking about it, that he thought it best if he first went into Frank's room to let him know his sister was here. "He's going to be very surprised, and I want to make sure he can handle it, okay?" he said.

"Of course, I agree," Gabriella said, and she and Dr. Hartock boarded the elevator and went upstairs. Diane wanted to see Frank's reaction, experience the emotion, but she knew this should be a private moment between Gabriella and Frank and didn't want to come between them in any way.

Nervous, hoping all went well, Diane paced back and forth.

SEVENTY-FIVE

Frank was in room number 310. When Dr. Hartock knocked on the door, Frank was struggling with his book. Pleased to see the doctor, the man he believed was his only true friend in the world, Frank smiled and put down his writing pad. The dressing on his face had been removed and he only had on an oversized bandage where his cheekbone had been mended. Already his thick black hair was beginning to grow back.

"How's your book coming?" the doctor asked.

"Not so good. It's a lot harder than I thought it would be."

"I have a surprise for you, Frank."

"Really? What's that?"

"As you know, Diane Pane has been researching your story—"

"Is she here? I've been so wanting to see her—"

"Frank," the doctor stopped him, "in the course of her research, Diane found out who discovered you on the steps of Our Lady of Lourdes all those years ago—"

"Really?"

"And Frank, she found your sister—"

"My sister . . . what sister?" he asked, stunned.

"Your sister Gabriella, Frank. And she's here, right outside the door."

"My parents too?" he asked hopefully, sitting up, his eyes wide and excited at the thought. *He looks like a child on Christmas morning*, the doctor thought.

"No. They both passed on, but your sister Gabriella is here. Would you like to meet her?"

"Would I? My God, yes, please," he said, a huge smile on his face, the first time Dr. Hartock ever saw him truly smile.

"Okay, I'll get her," he said, returned to the door and waved for Gabriella, who was waiting a little way down the hall to come in. A slight smile was on the doctor's face.

Gabriella walked to the door, cautiously looked in and when she saw her brother, she began crying. She slowly moved toward him and, sobbing, took him in her arms and held him tightly. They hugged and cried, wetting one another with hot tears that sprang from each of their hearts. Dr. Hartock silently closed the door, so happy tears of joy came to his eyes.

"I'm so sorry, I'm so sorry," she said, gently taking his face into her hands. "I tried to find you; I tried so hard to find you, but they wouldn't let me. My God, I missed you so much it hurt. Every day I thought of you; prayed for you. My God, you are gorgeous! You look just like Mama. Brother, I missed you *so* much!"

Frank was speechless. All he could do was stare at his lovely sister and cry. She was, he thought, so very pretty and he knew he looked just like her. She hugged him, kissed him, couldn't let go of him. He made her sit down in a chair near the bed and she told him all that had happened—how their father was killed in jail, how their mother took up with Ramos, how he abused him—and how she stole him away one winter night and brought him to the church.

"Brother," she said, "I couldn't take seeing him beat you anymore and so I took you. I had no idea you'd end up in that terrible place—I'm so sorry—"

"Don't apologize. There's no need. None of it's your fault. How old was I—how old were you, when you took me to the church?"

"You were two, I just turned eleven. Diane told me what happened to you at Sacred Heart—I'm so so sorry! Please forgive me, please," she said, again crying hysterically, kissing his hands.

"Please don't say that—there's nothing to forgive. None of what happened to me is your fault. I'm so happy to see you, hear your voice. I always knew—I could feel it inside somewhere, that I had people out there who loved me. Who cared. Who would stop what was happening, but I had no way of finding them, finding you.

"I used to all the time sneak into the records office, trying to find out who I was, where my family was, but they'd bust me and punish me," he said, his teary eyes suddenly hardening, his jaw muscle swelling.

"All the time," he continued. "I used to think of escaping, getting away from them, finding my family, but it was impossible; they'd always catch me and beat me. And instead of thinking about escaping, I began thinking of revenge, getting back at them for what they did to me, for what they made me do, made me become, and so as soon as I was old enough, strong enough, I killed one of them. But by then I'd become . . . I'd become so filled with venom that it was like I wasn't human anymore. I not only killed him but I . . . I cut his head off and left it on the front gate," he said.

"Diane told me," she said in a small voice, appalled at the thought.

"And they decided I was crazy and put me here. If it wasn't for Dr. Hartock I would have probably lost it completely. He was kind and understanding, never made any judgments, and he gave me books. Lots of books and they helped me get out of myself, out of this place, away from what happened, but I was always filled with this . . . this venomous hatred and all I thought about was getting back at them—the Church, the priests . . . even the pope; the main reason I went to Italy, to Rome, was to kill the pope.

"Every day there were stories in the papers and on television of how priests were abusing kids all over the country, and every time I read another one or saw a news report I became more incensed and I made up my mind to get back at the Church. That's all I thought about. It was like this burning fever I had inside—in my soul. And when they let me out, I started planning and putting it all together—killing priests; going to Rome and killing the pope. In my mind what I was doing was about justice, retribution, letting them know they had to answer for what they let happen—by covering it up they were encouraging the abuse, caused more and more abusers to join the Church . . . to seek its protection; to cloak themselves in the guise of priests, you understand?"

"Of course, yes."

"When I got caught and was in the hospital in Rome, the pope actually came to see me, which shocked me to no end, and the strangest thing happened to me. It's so hard to put into words, but I suddenly realized that I had to let go of the anger, the hatred, what happened—or I'd always be tormented, never find any kind of peace, still be a victim, and so I did.

"And now you, I finally found family. I always knew you were out there somewhere—I swear I felt it in my heart . . . I just knew." She stood and took him in her arms.

"And you'll always have me, Brother," she said.

"What is my real name?"

"Carlos Hernandez," she said.

"I like that. It's got a nice ring to it. The people in the foster program named me Frank Coogan—a name I was never comfortable with. So my name is Carlos."

"Yes. Carlos, after our grandfather."

"Is he still alive?"

"No, Grandfather was killed in a plane crash ten years ago," she said, and went on to tell him about their family and her life, explained that their parents had escaped from Cuba in a raft their father made. She was only two years old at the time. They had come to New York because they had cousins there. Their father, she said, got a job as a superintendent in a building on East 111th Street and for a while everything was good, but their parents started arguing, their father drinking and he hurt someone in a bar fight and went to prison and was killed.

"He was," she said, "murdered in jail. Mom had you a few months later, got involved with a real bad guy named Ramos, he got her into drugs and from there everything went downhill fast. It was Ramos who hurt you. He was the reason I got you out of the house."

She told him that Ramos had died when she was a teenager, and how she went to see Father John De Mazio and told him that she had brought her brother to the church and wanted to find him. She said Father De Mazio had tried to locate him, but the foster program wouldn't tell him anything. She also told him how she later even hired an attorney to help her find him, but that proved to be a big waste of time.

She said, "You never left my mind. Every night when I went to sleep, I thought about you, prayed that I would find you. And then Diane just showed up at the hospital yesterday and said she wanted to talk to me about my brother. I swear I nearly hit the floor.

"I'm going to move back to New York and get a job here so I can be near you. We'll get you the best lawyers we can find to help you get out of this mess. Diane said we should sue the Church, make sure they pay for what they did to you."

"Good idea. I have no problem with that. They should pay. I've been trying to write a book about what happened. At first it seemed easy, just poured out of me, but now I'm kind of stumped."

"Diane wants to write a book."

"I heard."

"How do you feel about that?"

"I'm honored, she's a great writer . . . is she here?"

"She's downstairs."

"She is? I'd love to see her."

"I'll go get her, if you like."

"Yes, please. Thank you," he said. Gabriella walked out the door and found Dr. Hartock talking on a cell phone. He hung up and the two of them went downstairs to get Diane. Gabriella was never so happy in her life, but she was worried about her brother's future, knowing he could very well spend his life in a state prison, one of the most dangerous places in the world, the place her father had been killed—at Ossining Prison, better known as Sing Sing.

They found Diane sitting on a wooden bench outside the front entrance. All smiles, Gabriella told her how pleased she was to finally find her brother.

"He'd really like to see you," she said.

Diane hadn't wanted to see him until after she finished her research, but finding Gabriella changed all that and she agreed to go upstairs, and, suddenly nervous, her stomach tightening, butterflies fluttering, she went back upstairs with Dr. Hartock and Gabriella, who said maybe it would be better if Diane and her brother had some time alone. Dr. Hartock agreed.

Her hands sweating, Diane hesitantly walked down the checkered linoleum floor to the door and stood there, kind of frozen. From his bed he could see her. Their eyes locked. He looked, she thought, like he'd lost weight, was pale. In a flood of unexpected emotions, memories, sights and sounds and intimate feelings, everything returned to her in a rush; was suddenly right there in front of her.

"Please, Diane, come in," he offered, smiling, his teeth large and white.

She slowly walked toward him, stopping at the foot of the bed, on the one hand happy to see him but on the other angry and depressed because of the violent, dreadful world he had dragged her into.

"Words," he said, "cannot express how sorry I am for getting you involved in this mess, my troubles."

"You used me," she said.

"I did, I know, I'm sorry. Will you forgive me—can you ever forgive me?"

She didn't answer him. Her stare was so intense he could feel her eyes boring into him like two drills.

"Diane, you know all about me now. My mind, my soul, was poisoned. All I could think about was revenge, getting back at the Church, hurting it, making it bleed. Hurting it the way it hurt so many. And then you came into my life, and it all changed. Diane, you were like golden sunshine in a brutal black-and-white world. Everything that happened in Amalfi was real, was heartfelt, was beautiful—I wasn't using you. When we kissed, when I felt your warmth, your passion, affection, it was like I was reborn, I swear. I know that sounds a bit kooky, but it's true—I swear it's true! Please . . . forgive me, Diane."

She didn't answer him, just stared at him for the longest time. Pages for doctors resonated in the halls. Somewhere off to the right a woman screamed. Diane finally said, "I forgive you and I do understand," and before she knew it she went to him and they hugged. She slowly drew back, stared at him, into his huge liquid-black eyes. He moved toward her, wanting to kiss her. She quickly pulled back. A nurse came in and said he had to take medication, a yellow pill she put in his mouth. He took a swallow of water. The nurse smiled and left, pleased that Diane was there. The nurse had seen Diane on news reports and knew exactly who she was.

He said, "Diane, I've been thinking about us—our meeting, how we met, was some kind of preordained destiny."

"Really, how's that?" she said.

"The way we first met sitting right next to one another on the bus to Rome, at the Sistine Chapel and then at the Colosseum. That was more than coincidence. It was like some kind of fate—the hand of some higher power kept pushing us together. And then—when I realized I'd been identified—I knew you were the answer; that you would make everything right, and you did. Diane you gave me the two things that I wanted most all my life, that I wanted as long as I can remember: You gave me kindness and genuine affection, and you gave me my sister, my family . . . a history. For the first time I know who I am. My real name is Carlos Hernandez. My family was from Cuba, don't you see? I am somebody. My sister tried to find me but couldn't. I always believed I had family out there, people who loved me, who thought about me, who worried for me, and because of you I found them. For the first time I can breathe, I can see colors . . . I have feelings other than hatred and anger and malice. Diane, you made me whole . . . you made me human," he said.

"Frank," she said, and stopped. "What do you want me to call you?"

"Carlos. The priests who abused me named me Frank Coogan—I don't want that name anymore. I'm going to legally have it changed."

"Good idea. I had this neat perfect life I created for myself. Then you came along and everything got turned upside down. But, Carlos, I want you to know that I have no regrets about anything that happened. In fact I'm glad I met you . . . it's all the baggage you have that's the problem. I know now that none of that is your fault; your sister told me everything, and I'm going to do what I can to help you."

"Thank you."

"Dr. Hartock tells me you've been working on your memoirs."

"I've been trying to, but it hasn't been coming out that good. I hear you are planning to write a book," Carlos said.

"Thinking about it . . . if it's okay with you."

"Of course it is, I'm honored, are you kidding? It's just that, well, there's so much that only I know, which I would really like to be included—"

"I'll interview you until I have it all, and everything I write you can review and I'll respect any changes you want, any input you have. In fact I welcome it, okay?"

"That's great, that's perfect."

"There will be, I'm sure, a substantial advance. I don't want any money for this—"

"But you must take the money!"

"No. I never have to worry about money again. I want to do this from my heart," she said. "To expose what was done to you, how the Church aided and abetted thousands of abusers. I believe in this more than anything I've ever written. All my life I've been looking for a story like this—one that matters, one that must be told, one that will open the eyes of people all over the world. If it's all right with you, I'd like to donate half of the advance to victims of predator priests and the rest to you, for your defense, to get you the best legal counsel, the best doctors."

"You are just unbelievable. Of course it's all right with me. So you're going to live here in New York?" he asked hopefully.

"Yes. I've already sublet a loft downtown."

"No, really?"

"Yes."

"Diane, you truly are heaven sent. Maybe . . . maybe there is a God after all, you know?" he said.

"Yeah . . . maybe," she said. "I heard the pope came to see you; what was that like?"

"Actually, quite amazing. He was very nice; kind of blew my mind. He gave me this," he said, and showed her the gold crucifix around his neck. "I never thought I'd wear one of these. I grew to hate it, the repression and the cruel symbolism it represented. You know the word *cross* comes from the Latin word *cruciare*, which means torture—but I really enjoy having it on. Makes me feel good. He said his mother gave it to him when he was a boy."

"Really?" she said, amazed that the pope would part with something so personal, to a man, no less, who had killed priests right at the doorstep of the Vatican—the heart of the Catholic Church.

He said, "I'm not exactly sure what he did, but whatever it was it had a profound effect on me."

"How so?" she asked, very curious, sensing that perhaps something very unusual had happened here.

"Well, first off it was the way he looked at me—with such compassion, and he told me how truly sorry he was for what had been done to me; then he talked about my letting go of the anger and hatred—said that as long as my heart is filled with hatred I'll continue to suffer, be a victim, and he's right, I realize now. Then he began praying and he put his right hand on my head—he had absolutely no fear of me—and something happened to me. I felt as if I were covered with this pleasant warmth, and I kind of lifted out of myself and was able to look down at him and me in the bed, there in the room. It was the strangest thing—and when he finished I was another person. I never believed in any of this miracle bull, you know, but something . . . something very unusual happened to me. Then he blessed me, made the sign of the cross and was suddenly gone. And I was a different person. I am a different person. I forgive the priests who abused me. Even the sadistic creeps at Sacred Heart."

Diane looked at him long and hard, her blue-green writer's eyes studying him, reading him, boring into him, wondering if maybe he was making this all up, but what she saw, she knew, was heartfelt sincerity.

"I'm very pleased to hear this," she said. "If you were to gain your freedom again, Carlos, would you—"

"Want to hurt priests?" he finished for her.

"Yes."

"No. That is over and done. What matters now is the future, not the past. What happened to me is history, as ancient as the Colosseum."

"I'm very pleased to hear that."

"I'm very pleased to say it," he said. "Please, Diane, will you kiss me?" he said.

"No," she said. "I can't. I don't want to go back there."

SEVENTY-SIX

The second doctor to interview Carlos Hernandez was a close friend of Dr. Hartock's. His name was Sam Spaldin. He was the chief resident at Bellevue Psychiatric Hospital, highly respected in the field, and often evaluated people for the Bronx and Manhattan District Attorney's offices. A short pensive man with a high-pitched voice, he gave Hernandez a much more thorough examination and came away thinking that the brain damage he had suffered as a child made it hard for him to differentiate between right and wrong; that he suffered from hallucinations, was a "delusional paranoid schizophrenic," as he told Carole Cunningham.

And based on Dr. Spaldin's and Dr. Herbert Goldberg's evaluations, with the help of the excellent legal team Diane and Gabriella had found for Carlos, Supreme Court Judge Lewis Starke ruled that Carlos Hernandez would be recommitted to the Creedmore State Hospital.

This was what Gabriella was hoping and praying for, because it essentially meant that her brother would not be charged with the killing of the priests—which caused a huge uproar in the Catholic community and Catholic Church—and that he would never go to prison, and, most importantly, he might actually be set free one day, though considering what he'd done that seemed like a real long shot, his attorneys advised.

Gabriella managed to secure an excellent supervisory position at Sloan Memorial Hospital on 5th Avenue and found a studio apartment that had a small garden—with Dr. Hartock's help—only a few blocks away. Nearly every day Gabriella went to visit her brother, brought him books and things he liked to eat, intent upon making up for all the years they'd been apart.

Though she knew what had happened to him at Sacred Heart was not her fault, Gabriella deep down still blamed herself for everything because she had brought him to Our Lady of Lourdes; she had, unknowingly, put him in the hands of the *monsters*, as she thought of them.

She began seeing Dr. Hartock to discuss her feelings of guilt and he assured her that none of what occurred was her fault. The doctor was very touched and moved by Gabriella, and as a particularly pleasant fall turned to a brutal winter with strong winds and much snow, they became close and soon began dating. Not sure how Carlos would take this, Gabriella was reluctant about telling her brother, but Dr. Hartock felt he had a right to know and, in fact, he was delighted—"very pleased," as he said.

Carlos didn't want his sister to be alone in a world he knew could be cold and dangerous, and he encouraged and advocated their relationship.

As it happened, in December of that year, on Christmas Day, Dr. Hartock asked Gabriella to marry him, and she said yes.

Overjoyed by this news, Carlos couldn't stop smiling, and they had the ceremony in his room at Creedmore Hospital—attended by a few close friends, one of whom was Diane Pane—so Carlos could give his sister away.

During those cold winter months, Diane interviewed many people connected directly and indirectly with Carlos's story. She read tall stacks of police and autopsy reports; she spent many hours at the hospital interviewing Carlos. She spent eight days in Boston interviewing lawyers who represented victims of predator priests and numerous victims, both men and women, who had been molested, more and more amazed and outraged at how blatant and aggressive the abuse had truly been, and that no one in law enforcement or the Church did anything to put an end to it.

"It was," one of the victims told her, "the dirty secret everyone wanted to hide, including me, I was so ashamed of what was happening."

Another said: "All a pedophile had to do was attend a seminary, put on a clerical collar and they were in heaven, had access to all the trusting children they could hope for. The first of six priests who abused me told me 'if you want to get close to God, get close to this,' as he exposed himself."

In Boston, Diane learned that many of the victims of abuse by clergy suffered from a gamut of maladies: were alcoholics, drug addicts, had marital problems, dysfunctional sex lives, and suicidal tendencies. In mid-February a report about abusive priests, prepared by the John Jay School of Criminal Justice, was released, and it stated that 4,500 Catholic priests had been accused of assaulting minors.

However, lawyers for victims told Diane the number was in truth far greater—that the report was based on information provided by the Church and definitely could not be trusted. "They have a vested interest in not divulging the whole truth. That's like a farmer asking a wolf how many of the farmer's sheep he ate," Boston attorney Bob Shine told her.

Come the spring, Diane, inflamed by all she had learned, was ready to begin writing, but she couldn't decide on how to tell the story—the voice of the book. Whether it should be in the first person, with the main players telling what they knew, saw and felt, or only from Carlos's point of view, or perhaps in third person narration. She discussed it with Carlos and her agent and writer friends back in San Francisco and decided in the end to tell the story in the third person. She began writing in mid April. She'd run in the morning along the Hudson River, then sit on the deck—weather permitting—and write. All the research, reading and interviews she had done paid off, for the words, facts, feelings, the emotions and unspeakable brutality, poured out of her in a torrent of simple, honest prose. It was going so well, she had to force herself to stop each day. Diane had learned from experience that it was always better to stop writing when the work was going well, rather than working until she was exhausted. This, she found, enabled her to pick up strong the next day.

Deep inside Diane felt that fate, some *higher power*, as

she explained to Carole Cunningham, had put this story into her lap; brought her and Carlos together, and she was intent upon making it as good and real and true as it could possibly be. At the end of each day, Diane carefully reviewed what she'd written, correcting and editing, and she was pleased. In the evening, she often had dinner with Carole Cunningham.

Every Friday Diane went to visit Carlos at Creedmore and she told him about what she'd written, but didn't want him to see any of it just yet. Over the months when Diane had been researching the story and doing interviews, she and Carlos became close, and he often tried to rekindle a romantic involvement with her, but she didn't want to go back there. She had deep feelings for him, perhaps in her own way she even loved him, but she would never forget what he had done; the sight of the priests he had killed in Rome.

Oddly enough, women from all over the country began writing Carlos, sent him romantic cards, letters and gifts. He became quite the celebrity, had tall piles of mail all over his cell from admiring women. Though he was not, he told Diane, interested in anyone but her, and on April 18 of that year, he actually asked Diane to marry him, which stunned her and completely caught her off guard. There was no way she would marry him; however, she didn't want to hurt his feelings, cause him any more pain than he had already suffered, lead him on in any way, and she had to say no. He seemed to take it pretty well but he did withdraw into himself; became quiet and introspective and rarely smiled, if at all. But Diane believed he would get over her; that one of the many women writing him, even coming to visit him at the hospital now, would inevitably take her place.

Diane's only concern was the book . . . telling the world this story.

SEVENTY-SEVEN

All that winter Captain Tony Flynn and Carole Cunningham dated, fell deeply in love with one another, and on New Year's Day Tony asked her to marry him and she said yes. They were wed at Saint John the Divine on Amsterdam Avenue. Tony's best friend, Rocco Genovese, was his best man. All Tony's daughters were there, very pleased that their dad had found happiness with a good woman, they knew, who loved him dearly.

Because of the success Tony Flynn had in capturing Hernandez, he was promoted—against his wishes—to a chief, an administrative position he hated. He ended up retiring from the force and quickly secured a lucrative position in the security department of the American Express Company.

Though he missed the action of running investigations, being in the field, putting bad guys in jail, Tony enjoyed his new job, chasing down people who committed frauds, stole credit cards, and he was making twice the money he earned at the NYPD; plus, he had full pension from the city because he injured his right hand on the job during the last week of his employment for the NYPD. He had a huge retirement party at The Tavern on the Green restaurant in Central Park, attended by a hundred seventy-five people, including the mayor, police commissioner, Dr. Hartock, Gabriella Hernandez and Diane Pane.

Nino Maranzano also retired from his position with the Italian *polizia* and as they planned, he and his wife Lina went on an extended three-month trip around the world.

The first place they visited was New York City and were there when Tony had his retirement party, at which they had *un bellissimo pomeriggio, a very beautiful evening*, as Lina would later say.

SEVENTY-EIGHT

His name was Austin Johnson. He was a hulking African American, 6'11" in his stocking feet with broad shoulders, giant hands, huge biceps and enormous feet—size 21. A handsome man with an ingratiating smile, Johnson was a registered sex offender. He had been convicted of a series of abductions and rapes spanning an eight-year period and was sentenced to forty years. He was doing his time at Elmira State Prison when the United Stated Supreme Court ruled that sex offenders could not be charged and tried for crimes committed more than six years earlier—a ruling that allowed eight hundred sex offenders to get out of prison—one of whom was Austin Johnson.

If Johnson had learned anything while he was locked up, it was never to let a victim live. Four of the women he had raped in the mid-90s came to court when he was finally apprehended, pointed their fingers at him and identified him in open court. He would never, he vowed the day he left prison, allow that to happen again. His enormous size and particularly dark skin made it easy for detectives to find him once they heard his description, he knew.

Unable to control his burning desire to rape, to dominate, to hurt women, Johnson had attacked three women since his release from prison and killed each of them after he was done with them so they could not tell the police what he looked like, or come to court and identify him. One woman he raped and murdered at the north end of Central Park in June. She had been jogging early in the morning and he grabbed her as she passed a tree he hid behind, dragged her into the woods, raped and killed her and left her naked battered body in a stream parallel to west 109th Street. This was the same woman Tony Flynn had seen the morning after the three priests had been killed in the rectory of Saint Joseph of the Holy Family in lower Manhattan. The second woman he raped and murdered on a roof at 136 west 117th Street, an eighteen-year-old girl, an honor sstudent who had been sent to the store by her grandmother to buy milk and bread. The police found the milk and bread next to the girl's unclothed body up on the roof of the building where she lived with her sick grandparents. This was the girl the repairman had found the day Flynn and Genovese had left for Rome. His third victim had been a housewife he came upon in the laundry room of the building where she lived at 107th Street and Amsterdam Avenue.

Johnson knew that it would be best if he didn't keep striking in the same area—upper Manhattan—and on this day he purposely went downtown looking for his fourth victim.

As it happened, he was walking along Hudson Street in the Tribeca area when he spotted Diane Pane as she was leaving her building to go for a run. Through unblinking dark eyes shaded by heavy brows, Johnson watched her warm up, stared intensely at her shapely legs, her well-formed body, bending and stretching and purposefully teasing and taunting him, he was sure, though Diane didn't even know he existed. She began to run. Knowing she would soon be coming back, Johnson sat on a nearby bench and waited patiently for her to return, brutal images in living color of what he would do to her and how he would do it running through the foul sewer that was his mind.

Thinking about the book, her work, her experience with Carlos, Diane had a good run up to the 79th Street boat basin and back, and did not notice the large man walking behind her when she entered the building, thinking about what she would write.

Preoccupied, Diane opened the front door before she even knew anyone was there. When she did realize a man was behind her, she looked up to be greeted by Austin Johnson's smiling face, his large ivory white teeth. Normally a trusting woman, Diane's first reaction to Johnson was surprise and alarm at his huge size. But his pleasant smile relaxed her and he immediately began talking in a friendly way, telling her how he, his wife and twin daughters had just moved into the building, had taken an apartment on the top floor. As they waited for the elevator, he even took out a brown wallet and showed Diane photographs of his family, his wife and children, which completely disarmed and relaxed Diane, and as she was looking at the photographs, the elevator came and together they entered it. She pressed 7, he pressed 8, and the elevator began up, and when Diane reached her floor, the pleasant smile about Johnson's face suddenly vanished and before Diane knew it he had his huge hand around her mouth, picked her up and carried her into her rented loft.

With all her strength Diane fought Johnson, kicked and bit and scratched him. She was by far the strongest woman he ever attacked.

As valiantly as Diane fought Johnson, however, it was like a child fighting an adult and he overcame her, gagged her and tied her up with rope he had brought and had his way with her, brutalized her body, then went to the kitchen, found a sharp knife and stabbed her to death.

In the beginning Johnson killed so as not to leave any witnesses, but he had taken a liking to the killing and became aroused by it.

SEVENTY-NINE

Diane was to have had dinner with Carole Cunningham that evening. The two had become very good friends and often dined together. The plan was for them to meet at a Tribeca Indian restaurant. Tony was at a security convention in Miami. When Diane didn't show up, Carole called her a dozen times and finally walked over to the loft, ringing the bell to no avail.

Carole knew Diane to be very responsible and she began thinking something happened. She went and found the super of the building, showed him her identification and told him how Diane didn't show up at a planned meeting, wasn't answering her phone, and asked if he would let her look in the apartment. Any reservations he had about doing such a thing were quickly dispelled when he saw Carole was a district attorney. He found the key and together Carole and the super, whose name was Felix, went up in the elevator. He opened the door with a passkey and they walked into the dark apartment. "Man, what's that smell," he said.

Carole froze. She knew exactly what the smell was. She would never forget the smell of the bodies at the Church of Saint Joseph. Felix turned on the lights and there was Diane, the way Johnson had left her, tied in an obscene position.

"My God," Felix said and stood there turning white. He began to back out of the apartment. "Man I don't want to see this, I don't want to see this."

Shocked, stunned, unbelieving, Carole stared at her through wide, tear-filled eyes, wondering if this in some way had to do with Carlos, Diane's planned book . . . the Church. Carole used her cell phone and called 911; then she phoned Tony in Florida. She managed to get him on the phone, told him what happened. He said he'd be back on the first available plane, that he would start making phone calls.

Stunned by this news, the first person Tony called was Rocco Genovese, who was still on the force. He too had been promoted and was now a captain. Tony asked him to get over to the crime scene and make sure nothing was moved until he got there. Rocco said he was on the way. Rocco had taken a liking to Diane and was saddened and angered by her murder, and when he saw what had been done to her, how her killer had left her, he silently vowed to find who did this and make them pay.

EIGHTY

Tony landed at La Guardia airport at 9:32 the next morning. He was met by Frank Salerno and they sped to Tribeca in downtown Manhattan. Technically, Flynn was still on the force and would remain so until mid-May. He was using up vacation days he was due and increasing his pension payments.

By now the press had learned about Diane's murder and the two men had to push their way through an unruly mob of reporters and news people with a lot of questions. The murder of Diane Pane, the woman involved with the notorious priest killer, Carlos Hernandez, was big news. Felix the superintendent was blatantly selling interviews to news producers in the lobby.

When Tony got upstairs he found Captain Rocco Genovese talking with detectives just inside the apartment. They hugged hello. Tony slowly walked in and saw Diane just the way the killer had left her, in the all-telling light of day streaming in through the living room's oversized windows. Her body was still stiff with rigor mortis, so battered and beaten she didn't remotely resemble the vivacious, intelligent, beautiful woman he had known. She didn't even resemble a human being, she had been so severely beaten. Large clumps of her hair, which lay on the floor near her body, had been torn from her head. He remembered the murdered woman in Central Park. Her legs had been tied open just like Diane's were now, and she, too, had large clumps of her hair ripped from her head.

As Tony moved closer to her, his eyes reading and evaluating the murder, what exactly had been done to her, red-hot anger spread throughout his body. His face flushed. He had grown very fond of Diane, thought the world of her, and to see her like this left him cold and empty and very angry. Standing there, he remembered when he first saw Diane in the kitchen of the house in Amalfi when she went to take a bite of the pesto pizza; he remembered the shock on her face when he told her who Hernandez really was; he remembered, too, the beautiful dinner they had all had in Rome, her intelligent eyes, the pointed, probing questions she asked. Tears filled his eyes and rolled down his face. Neither Rocco or Frank Salerno ever saw Tony Flynn cry at a murder scene. This was a first.

"You think this has anything to do with her relationship with Hernandez?" Rocco asked.

"Hard to say. Guess it's possible. Some religious wacko saw her on the news, read about her in the paper, came and did this. Who can tell what goes on inside the head of a man capable of something like this . . .

"The woman we found in Central Park, the jogger, remember she had been tied like this, and her hair had been torn out just like this. Anyone see or hear anything suspicious?"

"No one's come forward yet. Got a dozen of our best guys knocking on doors and stopping people in the neighborhood," Rocco said.

"Any sign of forced entry?"

"None."

"Hell of a thing. This was a really nice lady. . . . Hell of a thing," he repeated, shaking his head in disgust, moving still closer to her, bending down and studying her. The sight of her there like that stole his breath away, paled his face and narrowed his lips.

"You find the knife?" he asked.

"Was on the floor in the kitchen. The company she sublet the apartment from said it was theirs."

"Who lived here before Diane?"

"A square stockbroker, clean as a whistle; doesn't appear like he has anything to do with this," Rocco said. "Coroner says the knife wounds probably killed her."

"Techs find anything?"

"Just a partial footprint," Rocco said. "Barbara Green lifted it." His walkie-talkie came to life: "Captain, we may have something; a woman who owns a bar across the street might have seen him."

"Where is she now?" Rocco asked.

"She's here with me in front of the building."

"We're on our way," Rocco said and without speaking, Tony, Rocco and Salerno headed downstairs.

Word of the murder had spread through the neighborhood like wildfire and now there was a huge crowd of curious onlookers with worried faces surrounding the building. Reporters tried to talk with Flynn, but he had nothing to say to any of them.

The bar owner was a tall woman with fine blond hair, a full pleasant face. Her name was Isabella Waters. So they could talk with her out of the glare of media attention they made their way into her bar, which was just across from the building, on the northeast corner. It was called Isabella's. Rocco, Flynn, Frank Salerno and Isabella sat in a large booth in the back. She offered them coffee; they declined. A small walnut-colored Mexican man was mopping the floor. The smell of disinfectant hung in the air.

"I heard what happened on the radio, on 1010 WINS," she said. "I was in my office downstairs and had no idea what was going on across the street until I heard it on the radio, came up and saw all the police cars and people. They are saying in the street that she was brutalized and raped . . . beaten to death; that true?" she asked Flynn. He seemed in charge.

"That's true," he told her.

"It's the writer, right? That's what people are saying."

"Yes. Did you know her?" Flynn asked.

"She used to come in here every so often. Once with a blond woman just last week." Tony knew she meant his wife, Carole, that she and Diane had met for a drink last week.

"I recognized her because she'd been on the news. I saw her do an interview on CNN talking about predator priests, so I knew who she was. Never spoke much to her, only hello. I was very curious to talk to her about what happened; I had my own problems with a priest when I was a kid, but I didn't want to seem pushy . . . nosey, you know.

"The thing of it is, I saw her yesterday. I was at the window talking on my cell about a broken piece of stained glass over the front door when I saw her cross the street."

"What time was this?"

"In the morning . . . about eleven. And there was a man behind her, a very large African American guy, and he kind of followed her in the building. I didn't think much about it at the time. I mean he didn't grab her or anything like that. He was just walking behind her."

"She seem alarmed?"

"No."

"Close behind her?"

"Yes, quite close. That's what I mean."

Flynn looked at Salerno and Rocco and they all knew this woman probably saw Diane's killer and said so to one another with their eyes.

"Can you describe him?" Flynn asked.

"Big, very big, like I told you. Short hair. He kind of looked like a football player; was real strong looking. Like I said I wasn't paying so much attention—I was on the phone."

Flynn asked Rocco to stand up. Rocco was 6'5".

"Bigger than him?" Flynn asked.

". . . Bigger than him, yes."

"Dark skin, light skin?"

"Very dark," she said. "Short hair, nearly bald. And muscular."

"What was he wearing?"

"Jeans and a dark-colored T-shirt, I think dark blue, but I'm not sure. Slim, fit—no belly, very, you know, athletic."

Just then criminalist Barbara Green walked in the front door. She had worked the murder of the three priests at the Saint Joseph Church on Mulberry Street. When she saw Tony she waved him over. By her facial expression he knew she had something important that he'd want to hear. He excused himself and walked over to Barbara. They kissed hello.

"Good to see you," she said.

"Good to see you, Barb. What's up . . . I know you've got something for me."

"I do. We found a portion of his foot print on the parquet floor just next to where the area rug stops. A small portion, really just a segment near the ball of the foot. But it was enough for us to scan it into the computers and get a profile of his foot; and it's big, really big."

"How big, what size?" he asked, his brow knitting together, the image of a man he had arrested years earlier for rape coming to him, as if a face drifting out of a fog in a horror movie . . . a man who had been released from prison because of the Supreme Court ruling reinstating the statute of limitation for sex crimes.

"Size 21, Captain," she said, and with that alarm bells sounded inside Tony's head.

"That's very helpful, thank you, Barbara. You are the best. I think I know who it is."

There were, Barbara knew, very few men who had a size 21 shoe, and even fewer men who were out-of-control sexual predators with a foot that big. Tony quickly went back to the booth. He said, "Barbara did a profile on the portion of the footprint she found. It's a size 21. Huge black guy with a size 21 foot—sound familiar?"

"Austin Johnson," Salerno said, his eyes widening.

"Exactly. Let's go talk to Austin," he said and they were up and out of there in seconds, speeding uptown on the West Side Highway, siren blaring, just Rocco, Tony and Salerno.

EIGHTY-ONE

Carlos Hernandez had a radio in his room, an inexpensive Panasonic that Gabriella had bought him. That morning he heard about Diane's murder on a news program, and he went berserk, banged on the cell walls and doors screaming that he had to be let out, screaming about what a terrible world this was, screaming Diane's name over and over again. Dr. Hartock had to be summoned and he tried to calm Carlos, but it was impossible—he was inconsolable. The doctor was forced to have him put in a straightjacket and inject him with Valium to calm him down.

EIGHTY-TWO

Austin Johnson lived on the top floor of a beat-up tenement on Manhattan Avenue and West 113th. Just across the street there was a small park, on the far side of which, on top of a tall outgrowth of solid bedrock, was Saint John the Divine Church—the place where Tony Flynn and Carole Cunningham had been married several months earlier. From Johnson's window he had an unobstructed view of the back of Saint John, a ten-foot-tall statue of the angel Gabriel perched upon the church's giant medieval dome. The dome was 150 feet across and surrounded by crosses every twenty feet.

Having no idea he had been linked so quickly to Diane's murder, Austin Johnson was up on the roof of the building. He was the superintendent of the property and the owner allowed him to keep a small flock of pigeons in an eight-by-eight foot, three-tier mesh cage he had built on the roof. Johnson loved each of his twenty-two birds as if they were his children. He was known in the neighborhood as "The Pigeon Man." He cooed and talked to his birds and cried like a baby if one of them was sick or hurt. Two months earlier he had seen a falcon grab one of his beloved pigeons in midair and he cried on and off for two days straight. He could readily cry for his birds; but never people.

Today Johnson was on the roof feeding his birds a special formula he had developed. He didn't see Flynn, Rocco and Salerno as they stoically entered the building. They found Johnson's name on the mailbox. He lived in apartment 4 on the second floor. Knowing now that Johnson lived a half mile as the crow flies from where the jogger had been murdered in Central Park, they went upstairs and rang the bell, knocked on the door. No answer.

Johnson needed pliers to repair a piece of the cage and he went downstairs to get a pair and through the stairwell saw the three detectives standing in front of his door, guns in hand. He knew Flynn and Salerno and he knew why they were there. He quickly turned and hurried up the stairs on the balls of his huge feet. Knowing if they caught him he would surely be put away for life, maybe get the death sentence, he decided he'd rather die than go to jail . . . be taken away from his birds, his free access to any woman he wanted.

Rocco heard him moving up the stairs and they caught a brief glimpse of him as he disappeared onto the roof. Rocco and Flynn went after him, and Salerno went back down to the street to be there if Johnson doubled back down. On the way uptown Flynn had asked that they take Johnson without anyone else being there and Rocco and Salerno readily agreed, both knowing, but not saying a word about it, that Flynn wanted to kill Johnson; that he wasn't about to give Johnson another chance at walking because of some technicality, a glitch in the system. Flynn was going to make sure Austin Johnson never hurt another woman.

Thinking that there were more detectives than the three he'd seen, Johnson ran from roof to roof until he reached the last building, at 112th Street. There he looked down and was surprised not to see a line of double-parked police cars. He realized now that it was just the three bulls he'd seen and he hurried downstairs, went to the basement and out the back of the building. He saw a police car that just happened to be there, on the next corner, turned west and made for Manhattan Avenue. Using the cover of an oil truck making a left onto Manhattan Avenue from 112th Street, Johnson made it across the street without Sergeant Salerno seeing him. Johnson quickly made his way south, intent upon getting up to Saint John's. He knew the church would be open and he would hide there until nightfall, then get out of town.

When Rocco and Tony reached the roof, Johnson was gone. They quickly searched all the adjoining roofs and couldn't find him. Baffled, wondering where the hell he'd gone, Tony looked down and saw him hurrying away on Manhattan Avenue. He called to Salerno, pointing to Johnson. Salerno began to run after him. When he was close enough to Johnson to get a clean shot, he called for Johnson to stop. Johnson, however, took off with disarming speed and Frank gave chase. Johnson entered the park and was running towards the bedrock Saint John the Divine was built upon. Both Rocco and Tony now took careful aim and began firing at Johnson. They had an unobstructed line of vision and one of their shots hit John-son in the leg. He went down but got up and continued to run, disappearing into a thick cluster of pine trees. They hurried downstairs.

Running, Salerno didn't see Johnson hiding behind a wide oak tree. He grabbed Salerno, broke his neck with his hands, took his gun and ran on, reached a black metal fence that cordoned off the church grounds, climbed over the fence and made his way up the stone cliff, but the climb was steep and with his injured leg, it was difficult. When Flynn and Rocco entered the park and saw where Johnson was heading, Tony cut left, around and up so he could be at the top of the bedrock when Johnson got there. Rocco began after Johnson and he found Frank Salerno.

Running full out, Flynn made it to the top of the cliff just as Johnson reached it, and was standing there with his gun pointed at Johnson. Rocco shouted that he killed Salerno. Tony moved closer and took aim at his head and began to squeeze the trigger, but he heard the sound of children, looked left and there was a group of kids with a soccer ball looking at him. There was no way he could kill Johnson in front of these children.

"You gonna shoot me, go ahead, Captain," Johnson said, "there's no way I'm going peacefully," and he began to stand, a slight smile about his face. His leg was bleed-ing profusely now and his blood was running down the stone face of the cliff. When Johnson put his left foot on the blood-soaked stone, it abruptly slipped and he fell backwards. He violently tumbled down the cliff, landing square on the black picket fence, impaling himself. The sharp points of the fence went right through the upper portion of both his legs and he screamed and tried furi-ously to free himself, but that proved to be impossible. Rocco reached him and he was about to shoot him, but neighborhood people had heard all the gunshots and commotion and were watching him from Manhattan Avenue. A patrol car pulled up. If Rocco shot him now, he knew, he could very well be arrested. He holstered his weapon, looked up at Tony. "What a shame," Rocco called to him.

"Terrible thing," Tony said and began back down. Rocco called the incident in, asked for an ambulance, told the dispatcher there was no hurry, as an impaled Austin Johnson still tried to free himself. "Help me," Johnson demanded.

"The only help you are getting from me is to help put you six feet under," Rocco told him.

Several of Johnson's pigeons perched on the fence near Johnson and looked at him curiously, and above them, along the roof edge of Saint John the Divine, a half dozen crows silently stared, with their marble-black eyes, down at Johnson impaled on the fence.

EIGHTY-THREE

Because of the brutal, sadistic nature of Diane Pane's murder, Austin Johnson was ordered by the courts to undergo psychiatric tests to determine if he was fit to stand trial. Eleven days after he was arrested, Johnson was taken from the medical wing at Harlem Hospital to Creedmore State Hospital for the psychological evaluation. Carole Cunningham's office would be prosecuting him, and Carole was intent upon making absolutely certain Johnson never knew freedom again.

Carlos Hernandez knew days before Austin Johnson reached Creedmore that he was on the way, and Carlos carefully planned for his arrival. Carlos had a job in the library and several times a week he took a large aluminum cart filled with books to different wards for distribution among the patients. Carlos kept thinking that someone at the hospital would make the connection between him and Diane and Johnson, and he would be forbidden to go down to the third floor where Johnson was housed. But no one apparently did. Carlos thought long and hard about what he'd do, stayed up all night thinking of diabolical ways to make Johnson suffer. He didn't want to kill him right off; what he wanted to do was make him feel and know intense pain. He stole two bottles of rubbing alcohol from the infirmary and he managed to steal a nurse's book of matches from a preparation station.

Johnson was housed in an open ward with four beds. Both his legs had been operated on and pins had been used to set and mend the smashed femur of his left leg. All things considered, the doctors told him, he was very lucky. Each of his legs was now covered with thick bandages. He was in the room by himself because the other patient in the room had died just the day before. Because he had multiple felony convictions against him and was thought to be a "flight risk," Johnson was handcuffed to the bed and the bed was bolted to the floor. The two windows in the room were crisscrossed with thick steel bars.

At 11:15 that morning Carlos calmly wheeled the book cart into Johnson's room.

"Like something to read?" Carlos pleasantly asked, his dark, predatory eyes boring into Johnson's face.

"Not in the mood to read right now," Johnson said dismissively.

"I've got something you might like," Carlos said.

"Yeah, what's that?"

"This," Carlos said, taking out a widemouth plastic jar. In front of Johnson he slowly poured the two bottles of alcohol into the container.

"What the hell is that?" Johnson demanded, sitting up.

"I want you to know," Carlos said, moving closer to Johnson, "that Diane Pane was a good friend of mine. She was the first person in my life who had been kind to me."

By now Johnson knew all about who Diane was.

"You're the priest killer?" Johnson said, his eyes swelling out of his face, as he recognized Carlos.

Carlos smiled and poured the highly flammable alcohol all over Johnson's body. Johnson tried to get up out of the bed, but he was handcuffed and the cuffs held. He screamed for help. Carlos suddenly had the matches in his hand and he lit one and threw it on Johnson. Immediately the alcohol caught fire.

Screaming, Johnson tried to put out the flames, but only made it worse. Carlos closed the door and jammed it shut with a thick wooden chair so it could not be opened. There was a water sprinkler in the ceiling of room, but Carlos had shut the main valve for the sprinkler system on the third floor.

By the time hospital security broke open the door, Johnson's body was actually on fire. Guards used two fire extinguishers to put out the flames. Johnson was still alive, but was covered with extremely severe third-degree burns, in excruciating pain, his eyes so burnt he was blind.

EIGHTY-FOUR

Later that same day, as night fell, Carlos Hernandez was brought back to his cell in handcuffs. He had done what he set out to do and didn't care about what happened to him one way or the other. Indeed, if it weren't for Gabriella he would have surely killed himself there and then. He had come to view the world as a brutal, dangerous place filled with evil and he wanted nothing more to do with it. He had secreted a piece of razor in a book binder and he could have slit his wrists with it in seconds and ended it all, but because of Gabriella he did not use the razor—he would not kill himself.

Carlos woodenly walked to the small barred window in his cell and stared at the darkening sky . . . at animal-shaped clouds that hurried toward the setting sun. As day turned to night and dusk settled over Creedmore State Hospital, Carlos slowly got down on his knees, closed his eyes tightly, took hold of the crucifix the pope had given him, and prayed for the first time in thirty-seven years:

I don't know if there is really a God or not, but if there is, can you please make sure that Diane is in Heaven. She was a kind, giving, wonderful person and didn't deserve to die like that . . . didn't deserve to die at all . . .

Diane, if you can hear me, I want to tell you that I will never forget you. I will never forget your kindness, your love, your smiling face. I will never stop loving you, Diane. I don't know where you are now, but I know wherever it is, it's a better place than this.

Rest in peace, Diane . . . Rest in peace. . . .

EPILOGUE

*Austin Johnson died from his injuries thirteen days after Carlos Hernandez set him on fire.

*Diane Pane's body was returned to San Francisco and she was buried next to her husband at the Catholic Memorial Cemetery in Marin County.

*The parking attendant, Giuseppe Pisano, received the reward money for helping in the capture of Carlos Hernandez, and he promptly bought himself a house in Sorrento, Italy, a Fiat 525, a giant television, and a new wardrobe. He also married a woman twenty-five years his junior.

*Ramon the ice-cone maker received the reward money in New York for his assistance in creating the composite drawing, which, ultimately, broke the case. Tony Flynn also made sure he secured a green card.

*Salvatore Calese, aka Alfred Pastore, the man suspected of killing Bishop Arnold, was shot in the head and killed four days after he was released from jail on bail.

*With Dr. Hartock's help, and the assistance of a Boston attorney, Carlos Hernandez sued the Church. They ended up settling the suit out of court for $1.2 million. The last thing the Church wanted was a trial about this case, a public airing of what Hernandez had been through at the Sacred Heart Home for Boys.

*Carlos Hernandez is presently working on a book about abused children who turned to crime as adults and are spending the rest of their lives behind bars, or have been condemned to death. As of this writing there are still criminal charges pending against Hernandez for the killing of Austin Johnson. Carlos has become a born-again Christian and presides over prayer meetings at the hospital three times a week.

*In the spring of the following year, Gabriella Hernandez Hartock gave birth to a healthy seven-pound baby girl, and they named her Diane.

*Each of the New York priests in possession of child pornography—as well as Monsignors O'Brian and Dreyfus—pleaded guilty and, because of Carole Cunningham, received the maximum penalty under the law, five to seven years. Both O'Brian and Dreyfus refused to assist the police or the District Attorney's office in any way, and are serving their time in the protective custody unit—better known as "Punk City"—at Elmira State Prison.

*As of this writing, the Catholic Church has paid over $857 million because of the damage done by predator priests. The Boston archdiocese alone paid out $85 million, and more recently the Orange County diocese of Los Angeles paid $100 million to victims of sexual abuse at the hands of clergy.

If you know of an exploited or abused child—or if you recognize a missing child—you can help immediately by telephoning or writing to the National Center for Missing and Exploited Children at 1-800-843-5678 or 202-634-9821. The address of the Center is Suite 700, 1835 K Street NW, Washington, D.C. 20006.

You may also visit the following Web sites for information regarding victims of abuse at the hands of priests: www.snapnetwork.org, www.thelinkup.org, www.votf.org.

If you wish to get more information regarding sexual abuse by predator priests, please contact Voice of the Faithful at www.voiceofthefaithful.org or survivorsnetworkofthoseabusedbypriests.org.

If you want to let the Catholic Church know your feelings on the issue of sexual abuse by the Catholic clergy, please write:

Congregation for the Doctrine of the Faith
c/o Vatican City
Rome, Italy

VICKI STIEFEL

THE DEAD STONE

It starts with a mysterious phone call, summoning homicide counselor Tally Whyte back to the hometown she thought she'd left far behind her. Almost as soon as she arrives, Tally hears that a young woman she knew as a child has been found ritualistically murdered and mutilated.

The deeper Tally probes into the bizarre murder, the more chilling it becomes. Each glimpse into the killer's dark mind only unnerves Tally more. Despite frustrating secrets and silences, Tally suspects she's getting close to the truth, but perhaps she's getting too close for her own good. As each new body is found, Tally has to wonder…will she be next?
